Blood Of The Earth

Susan —
I hope you enjoy this
little jungle adventure.
My best —
Clay

Copyright © 2003 Craig Goheen
All rights reserved.
ISBN: 1-59109-879-3
Published by BookSurge, LLC
North Charleston, South Carolina
Library of Congress Control Number: 2004109039

Blood Of The Earth

A NOVEL

Craig Goheen

2003

Blood Of The Earth

CONTENTS

Prologue		xi
One	HONEYMOON IN MEXICO	1
Two	A KIDNAPPING	23
Three	*NA-BOLOM*	37
Four	THE RAIN FOREST	49
Five	RESCUE AND ESCAPE	69
Six	E-MAIL	79
Seven	DEMONS IN THE NIGHT	97
Eight	INTO THE JUNGLE	113
Nine	THE PHONE CALL	125
Ten	OBSTACLE COURSE	137
Eleven	TARGET PRACTICE	155
Twelve	UNEXPECTED DIRECTIONS	165
Thirteen	THE ZAPATISTAS	185
Fourteen	THROUGH THE SWAMP	205
Fifteen	SEPARATION	227
Sixteen	*LA BRUJA*	233
Seventeen	DREAMS	253
Eighteen	THE *BALCHE* CEREMONY	293
Nineteen	CHOICES	319
Twenty	THE CAMP	335
Twenty-one	A LINK HOME	339
Twenty-two	*XIBALBA*'S CAVE	367
Twenty-three	THE THREAT	387
Twenty-four	THE SACRIFICE	397
Twenty-five	CONFRONTATION	403
Twenty-six	*XU'TAN*	407
Twenty-seven	THE FIFTH WORLD	421
Epilogue		427

*To The Women Who Helped Make This Happen:
Sarah, Karen, And Louise*

PROLOGUE

El Palacio Nacional
Ciudad de México, D.F., México
Thursday night, early June

> Before the first step is taken,
> the goal is reached.
> Before the tongue is moved,
> the speech is finished.
> More than brilliant intuition is needed
> to find the origin of the right road.
>
> Ekai, Zen master
> 1183—1260

The foot traffic in the main *zócalo* of Mexico's capital was light at this late hour. The street lamps bristled yellow in the quiet, humid night air. A *campesino*, dressed in a faded, old wool *serape* and holding a brown paper bag by the bottle top it covered, leaned against one of the lampposts. He was watching a young police officer, smart and neat in his black uniform and sidearm, walk his rounds. The eighteen-year-old *judicial* strolled past the *Palacio Nacional*, stopped at each entrance, and checked each door handle.

As the uniformed young man approached, the *campesino*, an unlit cigarette dangling from the corner of his mouth, staggered up to him.

"Match, *señor?*" he asked, leaning into the officer.

His breath smelled so strongly of tequila the *judicial* stepped back. The drunk lost his balance and caught himself on the officer's arm.

"*Perdóneme.*"

"No, *señor*, no matches," he replied, smiling at the drunken *campesino*. The police officer led him over to the building and propped him against the corner.

"Hornito's?" asked the man, holding up the brown bag.

"No thank you, *señor.*"

"What time is it?" he asked, slurring his 'es'.

The officer looked at his wrist watch.

"Almost one a.m.," he said.

The *campesino* snorted in response, pushed himself from the wall, and reeled around the corner, disappearing into the dark alley. Smiling, the *judicial* turned back to the *zócalo* and walked away, again checking each door and glancing into the darkened office buildings along the block.

In the shadows of the alley, the *campesino* spit his cigarette out, put the tequila down, and faded deeper into the darkness. He stopped in a recessed doorway hidden by the night, pulled a pair of thin, dark gloves from his back pocket, and slid them on. He turned his back to the large door and twisted his head side to side, peering into the looming night. The moist, warm evening, blind and deaf to his passage, ignored him.

The door's grip handle didn't turn, but the door came open when he pulled. Lodged against the jamb, a small rock had kept the door from locking shut. He flipped the stone away with the tip of his worn sneakers and slipped inside.

After a few minutes, his eyes adjusted to the dim, red light of the exit sign. He was in one of the smaller stairwells reserved for the use of high level officials. He crept up three flights, ignoring the painted, dead eyes that stared from the dark, somber portraits at each level, and exited through the heavy wooden door into an unlit hallway.

He stood for a moment, spidery and quiet in the corner, his fingertips pressed against the wall. The odor of cleaning solvent hung in the still air. Ghosts from the street lights danced around the edges of his vision. The muffled blast of a car horn echoed in a distant alley, and an ambulance siren faded in waves to nothing blocks away.

He padded down the wide, carpeted hall until he came to the first corner office. Inside, the lights from the street reflected off the white ceiling tiles, catching the rich oiled surface of a large, mahogany, roll top desk. He took a breath and looked over his shoulder into the empty hall. The silence magnified the arterial pulse in his chest and ears. He rotated his head back and, predatorily rigid, he scanned the room. Then, in three long, quick steps, he was at the massive desk.

With one hand on the camber roll to keep it quiet, he lifted the roll-top. Inside sat a modern computer station, tower, printer, twin monitors, and keyboards. He took a 3.5 inch diskette from under his *serape* and inserted it in the A: drive. He pressed the power button. Nothing happened. Flicking it back, he looked for another source and found the power strip and surge protector under the desk. The strip's orange light winked on when he flipped the switch. The tower wound up, and the left monitor blinked on. After the boot finished, he tapped the left keyboard a few strokes and hit 'enter'.

He stepped back to the doorway and twisted his head into the hall. Still nothing. Waiting for the download to finish in the government's main frame, the bitter memory of his captivity at the hands of the Zapatista terrorists returned, tasting like bile. He gritted his teeth at the recollection of his kidnapping in front of a church in San Cristóbal de las Casas, that distant mountain town of *indios* and terrorists. That was over nine years ago. And he could still feel the blindfold and handcuffs. The Zapatista terrorists had feigned such gentlemanly manners, so polite and non-threatening, but those self-righteous, unwashed rebels had treated him as little more than a common criminal. In a filthy camp somewhere in the depths of the uncharted rain forest, he had spent his nights on the ground and his days fighting hunger and diarrhea. His daily meal was *frijoles* and rice because, as he was reminded every time they served him his small portion, "the *indígena* rarely get more".

Even hidden in their jungle, he'd been so sure a well-armed rescue was planned. But for forty days he waited, thinking each day his government would find him and finally destroy these rebels. Then on the fortieth day, he was again blindfolded and moved by truck. After many hours bouncing over rough dirt roads, he was simply dumped on his backside outside the mountain town of Altimirano for the local police to find. The memory never left him, not for a day or an hour. The humiliation burned into his mind. No more, he told himself. Finally, no more.

Two minutes later, he removed the floppy. His breath came short. If this virus he'd just implanted could avoid prying eyes for a few days, his path to revenge, and wealth, would remain secret. He pocketed the diskette, pulled the desk closed, and turned off the power strip with his toe.

Out of the office, he slipped through the silence to the end of the hall. He opened the door a crack, held his breath, and stepped into the stairwell. On the balls of his feet, he skittered down the steps, one hand extended to the wall, fingers nervously flitting across the smooth, wooden wainscot. At the exit door, he paused and listened. Nothing but the quiet night.

He cracked the door. Up the alley, walking toward him

from the street and looking around with some focus, came the same young *judicial* he'd talked to before. Backlit by the street light, the *judicial* stopped at the tequila bottle and tapped it with the toe of his boot. The officer hadn't seen him, so he eased the door shut, removed his gloves, and waited in the darkened stairwell.

With his ear pressed against the cool metal, a sharp clank from several flights above startled him. A narrow beam of light jerked into the stairwell above. His heart raced. He had no time to think.

He opened the exit door enough to squeeze his hips through and stepped into the warm shadows outside. He held the handle, and it clicked quietly shut. Without looking up, he put his right hand into his pants pocket and leaned forward, holding himself against the doorway with his left forearm as if he were vomiting.

"¿*Señor?*" The *judicial*'s voice was close and young and too naïve.

The *campesino* pushed himself upright, turned to the officer, and smiled. Wiping his mouth with his shirt sleeve, he stumbled toward the young man in his neat, black uniform.

As the *judicial* reached out, bracing to catch the momentum, the *campesino* grabbed him and spun him around. Before the officer could react, the *campesino* knocked his knees to the ground, covered his mouth, and yanked his head sideways with a crack. The metallic click of his blade filled the silent night. He thrust the knife so swiftly it pierced the carotid artery and struck the first cervical vertebra, knocking the *judicial* back into him. Warm, thick spurts of blood ran across his hand and down the young man's neck.

"*Qué tristeza, amigo,*" whispered the *campesino* incongruously.

The *judicial*'s legs twitched as the life ebbed from his young body. Still holding his victim, the *campesino* put his ear to the door. Hearing nothing from inside, he dragged the body into the deepest shadows of the alley and dropped it along the wall. He cleaned his stiletto on the black uniform and took the *judicial*'s sidearm, an old .38 S&W.

He stood over the dead youth and sighed. Crossing himself, he pulled a scrap of red and black cloth from his back pocket and stuffed it into the slack-jawed mouth.

Heading back out the alley, he stooped to retrieve his bottle of Hornito's. He leaned against the wall and took a long pull of the tequila. It burned his esophagus, and he coughed once as it gripped his stomach in a scorching knot.

Shuddering, he staggered out into the yellow light of the *zócalo*.

CHAPTER ONE
HONEYMOON IN MEXICO

Ciudad de Mexico
D.F., México
Friday night

> I have seen flowers in stony places
> and kind things done by men with ugly faces...
> So I trust, too.
>
> *An Epilogue*
> John Masefield
> 1878—1967

For Griffith Grant, the first night of his honeymoon was distinctly different than he had expected. He and his new wife, Karen, had just finished an elegant dinner of *pescado en tikin xik* and *chiles rellenos en nogada* in the privacy of their ninth floor suite in *el Gran Hotel*. The large window by their dining table overlooked the main *zócalo* in the heart of Mexico City, *el Centro*. They were alone, finally, and the anxiety of his first trip out of the United States melted in the sated warmth of this shared moment.

What made it different, however, was his apprehension and uncertainty about their ultimate destination. A honeymoon devoted to exploration and camping among some of the poorest, most primitive natives of the Mexican rain forest struck him as more challenging than romantic. He'd never left the States—he had hardly been outside of Virginia—having spent his entire academic and young professional career in a university setting.

Orphaned just before he finished high school, Griffith had coped with the chaos of his loss in the stability of books. The steadiness of science had always attracted him, and he had done little but study throughout his undergraduate and graduate years, all at the University of Virginia. After receiving his Ph.D. in particle physics, he even remained to become the youngest, tenure-track professor at Thomas Jefferson's University, secure in the foothills of the ancient Blue Ridge Mountains.

Now, in this beautiful, old hotel with its gilded balustrades and quaint, wrought iron elevator cages, this was just the first stop of their honeymoon. He shook his head in wonder. This certainly wasn't the rain forest, but they'd be there tomorrow on their *luna de miel en la Selva Lacandona*, their honeymoon in the remote, barely populated jungles of Chiapas, Mexico's southernmost state.

He smiled and looked at his wife as she studied the bustle of people and vendors below in the yellow light of the *zócalo*.

"Karen," he said, "this has been so remarkable. I really expected to stumble through all this. But here I am, in a foreign country I know nothing about, and I'm happy. I love you so much, Karen. I can hardly tell you how much you've brought to my life."

"Oh, Griffith," she replied, "I knew you'd love all this. You just needed to get out of your laboratory. And I'm so happy we're here together. This trip means so much to me. I've always wanted to see the rain forest and learn how the indigenous people live, and now, with you... oh, this is going to be a wonderful adventure."

"Yes, an adventure. You know, Karen, weekends with you on the Appalachian Trail hardly qualify me for camping in the jungle. I mean, I know nothing about the dangers of the rain forest, the snakes and hungry jungle cats and poisonous plants and spiders and..."

"Relax, Grif. I know what I'm doing in the woods. I've camped all my life. You know that."

"Yes, I do," he admitted. "But just how safe is this jungle? Wasn't there a revolution in southern Mexico a while ago?"

"Years ago. But it's a very large jungle, and the last I read, the fighting is over. They've even built real roads into some parts of the rain forest. Look at it this way—we may be the only tourists there."

"That's supposed to be encouraging?" he asked.

"We'll be alone a lot. And aren't new experiences always an aphrodisiac? What could be more exciting than this? Two young lovers sharing every new sight and scent, riding horses through the jungle, camping under a tropical moon in remote Indian villages."

"Karen, I've never even been on a horse. No, that's not exactly true. I was once, for about half a minute. I think the horse knew he was a lot bigger."

"Grif, it'll be all right."

"Of course it will. I'm just apprehensive because I know so little about Mexico, that's all. And I doubt I'd have ever come here without you. But we're here, and..."

He smiled and reached for her hand.

"Oh, Griffith, I love you. I'm so happy," she said, lowering her eyes and gently squeezing his hand. "Do you want to... explore the notion that love making is better after marriage?"

"Ah, yes," he replied softly. "Love in a Latin land."

And they found their love that first night was unhurried and gentle. Their attention lingered on touch and smell, every caress held for an extra moment, each kiss savored. Enamored with themselves, the sounds of the busy city with its horns and sirens, its rhythmic ebb and flow of voices, and the music of the streets, soon faded out their window into the sultry night. Alone in their room, above the center of the world's largest city, they made slow love.

***

Flying into the small, whitewashed airport on the outskirts of Chiapas' capital early Saturday morning, Griffith and Karen tightened their seat belts. Their Aerocaribe flight from Mexico City to Tuxtla Gutiérrez was nearly over. The newlyweds were headed for the rain forest of Mexico's most southern state to camp among the nearly extinct Lacandon Indians, the last direct descendents of the great Maya lords.

Tuxtla's Teran Airport was surrounded by military personnel carriers, black jeeps, a half dozen tanks, and two 7.62 mm machine gun mounted bunkers. Soldiers unloaded several dozen wooden crates from the jet before the baggage handlers were allowed near the plane. The crates were removed to a fenced enclosure; then the passengers' bags were brought to the tiny, cinder block terminal.

Griffith shouldered their large backpack, and Karen carried the two smaller daypacks as they worked their way through the throng of passengers, families, and soldiers.

"Karen," asked Griffith, "did you notice the bunkers protecting this airport? I thought you said the terrorist uprising was over?"

"For the most part, I guess," she said absently. "I never heard of the Zapatistas targeting airports. Probably just a precaution." She was smiling, obviously more excited about being in Chiapas than worried about a squad of young soldiers. "Come on, let's find a taxi and get to the bus station. I'll bet we can make it to San Cristóbal by noon."

Outside, in the bright morning light, Griffith stopped at the curb. Already the heat was suffocating. Travelers jostled out of the terminal around him, and the dusty parking lot vibrated with the engines of dozens of taxis and old buses left idling in dancing vapors. Within the din of vendors and vehicles, children hawked Chiclets and individual cigarettes in tiny voices.

In brilliant sunlight, taxi drivers cruised the crowd, offering to carry bags to their Toyota, VW, or Nissan taxis. A young man, dressed in a plain white shirt and beige slacks approached Griffith and Karen. Griffith nodded a somewhat confused assent, and the young man took the small daypacks from Karen. In Spanish, she told the driver they needed to get to the bus terminal, and he led them through the lot, past every taxi, and out into the street.

Just as Griffith was beginning to wonder if they were going to walk to the terminal, the young man stopped by a white Nissan, opened the trunk, and deposited the daypacks. He motioned for Griffith to put the heavy backpack in and then unlocked the doors for them. Karen got in front to practice her college Spanish with their driver, and Griffith settled back to adjust to the new, overwhelming stimuli of this foreign land.

The trip through Tuxtla was quick, but the Mexican style of driving was too impatient for Griffith. Here, their driver tapped his horn several times a block as he sped along the narrow streets. The locals heeded the car horns, looking both ways before stepping into the street. Griffith suspected only an actual collision would get their driver to slow down.

Within half an hour they boarded a *Primera Clase* Mercedes bus headed to San Cristóbal de las Casas, high in the rain forest mountains to the south. The bus, luxurious with its wide, first class seats and abundant leg room, had individual televisions, privacy curtains, and a coffee and soda bar in the back. Even at ninety *pesos* a ticket, the bus had numerous empty seats.

"Karen, this is amazing. This is more comfortable than any bus I've ever been on. Hell, than any plane, for that matter."

"Well, most Mexicans can't afford to travel this well, and once we're into the rain forest, we won't be able to. So don't get too spoiled, Griffith."

"Too expensive, huh? These tickets were how much? Nine bucks apiece."

"Different economy."

"No kidding."

As they left the brown and beige architecture of Tuxtla Gutiérrez, PanAm Highway 190 was congested. The two lane highway rose into the foothills, and the traffic thinned to trucks, a few cars, and the *colectivos*, the ubiquitous VW vans that served as the least expensive form of public transport. Griffith curled up against the window and watched the country pass from the dusty valley of Tuxtla to the green mountains of southern Chiapas.

"Look how quickly the topography has changed," mentioned Griffith as the bus began its slow ascent into the *Sierra los Altos de Chiapas*.

"God, I wish we could stop this bus so we could explore those hills," said Karen excitedly. "Oh, Grif, look at that tiny village way back in that valley. This is so fascinating."

"If we stopped every time you wanted to dart off and explore something interesting," Griffith replied with a smile, "we'd never get anywhere."

"Yeah, you're right, Grif. But think of the adventures we'd have."

"I think just visiting the jungle will be exciting enough for me. Look how beautiful this country is."

June was the beginning of the rainy season. Intense green hillsides grew dark and thick, and tropical foliage crept to the edge of the road. Up and down the steep, winding roadsides, dark-skinned women dressed in embroidered *huipiles* and the bright pink skirts of the Zinacantán Indians carried oversized bundles of firewood across their stooped shoulders. Small road crews cut back the emerging growth with machetes and loaded their rusty dump trucks by hand. Bony cattle, pale-skinned Brahman with their distinctive dewlap and long droopy ears, grazed the shoulders of the highway, indifferent to the chickens, sheep, dogs, burros, and traffic on the asphalt beside them.

The steep, winding, two lane blacktop was unmarked except for the more dangerous hairpin curves. Their severity was indicated by the number of small, decorated crosses planted along narrow shoulders commemorating those who had failed to negotiate the turn. Thick rain clouds enshrouded the peak of each ten thousand foot mountain they crested, and the bus lumbered noisily from sunny valley through mountain downpours and back down again into sunshine.

During one shower, their bus driver decided to pass an old dump truck belching exhaust and struggling up the mountain. As he downshifted and pulled into the other lane, the truck driver waved him on. Slowly they picked up speed. Abreast of the groaning dump truck, Griffith looked over at the truck driver whose deeply lined eyes suddenly grew wide.

Ahead of them, from around a blind turn, an approaching *colectivo* slammed on its brakes and swerved onto the narrow shoulder. The bus's engine wound its diesel voice high, and passengers shouted encouragement. Straddling the center of the road, the bus rounded the turn with inches to spare on each side.

Griffith decided not to watch anymore and opened his travel guide to the Maya Route to read.

Within the hour they descended into an enclosed mountain valley and arrived in San Cristóbal de las Casas, founded in 1528. The city was named after Fray Bartóleme de las Casas, the original defender of the *indígena* against their initial exploitation and enslavement by Spanish colonizers.

Griffith and Karen's first destination, near the edge of San Cristóbal, was *Hacienda Na-Bolom*. *Na-Bolom*, made famous by Gertrude Blom, photographer, journalist, amateur anthropologist, and heir to Fray Bartóleme's struggle to save the *indígena*, was a combination small hotel, museum, library, and cultural center for the Lacandon Indians. The old, two-story mansion, built at the turn of the century in a European/tropical style, stood solidly with its wide, overhanging eaves, large verandah, and expanses of dark wood. Trees and dense foliage crowded the house, shading it during the sunshine and sloughing away the water during the rainy season.

The inside was dark and cool. The smooth, brown wooden walls were covered with a variety of faded weavings, a few carved masks, and a great many paintings with flower, bird, and jaguar motifs. Behind ancient wave-streaked glass hung some old photographs of *indígenas* with long, dark hair and pale, white tunics.

They set their packs down, and a housekeeper introduced herself as Esmeralda. She was short and thick-waisted, and her skin was dark as mahogany. Her long, lustrous black hair was tied back with a bright, multi-colored band. Dressed in a white cotton skirt and a colorfully embroidered *huipil*, Esmeralda spoke softly and confidently. Griffith and Karen introduced themselves and followed her through the house.

"The library here," said Esmeralda turning in the first large room off the hallway, "contains the most complete collection of archeological, linguistic, ethnological, and ecological volumes on the Lacandon rain forest and the Lacandon Indians."

Griffith stood for a moment and breathed in the scent of ancient paper, leather, and wood. Overstuffed reading chairs sat under the heavy curtains of the windows. The warmth of the books, old paneling, and thick carpeting embraced him in its solid comfort.

"This is a good room," he declared. "Very friendly."

"Since *Señora* Blom's death, this room is not used so much as it should be."

Griffith recalled his parents' death over a decade ago when he was in high school. Libraries had become his sanctuary then. Books had given him the security he'd lost, and he'd grown to love the cloistered atmosphere of university life which had become his home. And until Karen came into his life, he'd known little else.

At their first meeting that frosty autumn morning almost two years ago, Karen had brought her fourth graders on a field trip to the University's science labs. Griffith Grant, young Ph.D., dressed in his white lab coat and sneakers, had been working among the numerous instruments, computers, and expensive electronics. He was barely taller than she—she was five-seven—and they were both slim. Other than these similarities, they were night and day. His complexion was ruddy, his eyes dark brown behind wire-rim bifocals, and his hair and beard both thick and dark. She was fair and blonde. And she was much more athletic than he, but her trim, muscular physique, very attractive to him, was not what caught his attention. He'd never seen such focused energy. She seemed completely absorbed by her students, matching their enthusiasm with her own.

Karen's students had been well-behaved, but they had completely upset Griffith's lab routine, firing non-stop questions about this screen or that dial, how to input data, what computer games he liked, and whether they could write him at his e-mail address. He had patiently shown them the lab's home page on the network where they linked with universities and research centers around the world. The children's fascination with communicating globally had tied up an extra hour of lab time on the network.

But despite the turmoil, he'd watched how Karen handled herself, her eyes and ears moving from child to child. Her confidence around so many curious children had drawn him like a magnet. Her outgoing presence had sparked the quiet life he'd made for himself.

Although he tended to reflection and she to action, the attraction was mutual. His obvious intelligence and dark, handsome features were appealing to Karen, but his calm, deliberate responses to the children had grabbed Karen's eye, as well. When she offered to repay his kindness with a dinner, she intuitively knew this shy man standing in a clutch of inquisitive, eager children would accept.

Now, nearly two years later, standing in a library in the mountains of southern Mexico, Griffith shook his head in wonder. No longer living alone, no longer just an academic who rarely left his lab, much less traveled beyond the Charlottesville city limits, he was in another country for the first time because he'd fallen in love with his opposite nature.

"Karen," he said, "when we return from the rain forest, I'd like to spend some time in here. I love this library."

"You are going to *la selva?*" exclaimed Esmeralda. "I am

Lacandon. My village is near the Guatemalan border, deep in the rain forest. I have not been home for many months. Oh, the jungle is *muy bonita, hermosa.*"

"*Sí,*" replied Karen. "We're on our honeymoon, *luna de miel, sí.*"

"*Ah, recien casados! Excelente.* Let me show you your cottage."

They followed her through the large, airy kitchen with its old fashioned stone hearth and slightly more modern gas stove. A long, heavy wooden table was gouged, nicked, and rubbed smooth from generations of use. She led them out a back entrance, past the small museum, and along the gardens.

Roses, gladiolas, and hibiscus bloomed in neatly-kept plots. Beyond the flowers, cilantro, sage, basil, and flowering garlic grew in separate, small gardens. Several of the sunnier gardens were devoted to different varieties of *chiles*, and marigolds and chives bloomed as borders to many of the patches.

"The herb and flower gardens," explained Esmeralda, "provide dyes for the local *indígena* weavers. They grind and soak the flowers, leaves, fruits, or roots with lime juice, ash, or limestone to produce their dyes. Yellow comes from the chives and marigolds, greens from the salvia sage, pinks from the scarlet sage, burgundies from thyme, and browns from moss."

The gardens were joined by trails lacing back and forth toward a small tree nursery. Banana, papaya, and lime trees were setting fruit despite the altitude. Beyond the fruit trees, stands of young pines and cedars spread up the hillside and disappeared into the mountains.

Tucked among the trees were several white-washed, cinder block cottages. Esmeralda led them to the nearest one. Inside, their cottage was dark and warm. Paneled in old, dry pine, with woven throw rugs covering the wooden floor, the tiny cottage was sparsely decorated. A photograph of a Lacandon paddling a dugout canoe on a small, jungle lake and a crudely framed painting in pastels of the same lake hung to either side of the single window. A small dresser, with a chipped, ceramic wash basin and towels, and an old, wood-framed bed covered with a wool blanket stood against the opposite wall. On the adjacent wall, a small well-used fireplace, with a poker and kindling beside it, had been cleaned of its ashes.

"The nights are cold in the mountains. There is firewood outside."

"This is lovely," said Karen. "I'm sure we'll be comfortable."

"This is great," agreed Griffith. "What can I do to help?"

"Please, be comfortable here," answered Esmeralda.

"Thank you. *Gracias.*"

"*De nada*, Griffith."

"Please, call me Grif."

***

That afternoon, Griffith and Karen walked the nine blocks to the crafts market. The local vendors, including *indígena* from the villages in the surrounding highlands, had spread their blankets in the shady courtyard of the pink, stuccoed Santo Domingo church. Each blanket was stacked high with regional handicrafts and textiles, and the vendors, mostly women, sat behind their goods, weaving, cooking, or tending to their young children. The smell of charcoal and blackened corn hung in the warm air.

Rain threatened, and brightly colored plastic tarps stretched like lean-tos over the profusion of shirts, woven *serapes*, *huipiles*, shawls, jackets, hats, dresses, belts, shoes, *huaraches*, purses, blankets, trinkets, tiny ceramic animals, jade and amber jewelry, and miniature dolls. The dolls, from an inch to a foot tall, were wrapped in a variety of native dress, but the most common were Zapatista dolls in black ski masks, their tiny wooden guns held across their chests and their woolen bags slung over their backs.

The newlyweds strolled by the numerous vendors, managing to resist the polite but persistent offers when they stopped to admire some work. Although the bright synthetic dyes were most prevalent, Karen particularly liked the naturally-dyed, embroidered skirts and *huipiles*. When she found a traditionally dyed skirt, a dark green and blue print with a full embroidered waistline in a bird motif, she held it up for Griffith to admire.

"Who do I ask the price?" Griffith asked.

Karen nodded toward the woman at the back of the blanket. She was breast-feeding an infant, and, unsure of the etiquette involved, he hesitated. To her left, an older woman—the grandmother, he supposed—was cooking shucked ears of corn on a small grille, and beside her, two small girls were making more Zapatista dolls to add to the dozen at their feet. On the opposite side, a young boy, oblivious to his surroundings, was reading an *X-Men* comic book.

As Griffith turned away, looking for someone to ask about buying the skirt for Karen, one of the young girls, still holding the doll she was making, stepped in front of him. Pointing to the skirt Karen was still holding, she looked straight up at Griffith with her soft brown eyes and said, *"Muy bonita, señor."*

"Uh, yes," he replied absently. He turned again.

Slightly louder, she repeated herself, *"Muy bonita, señor."*

Griffith's Spanish was little more than *'por favor'* and *'gracias'*, so he tapped Karen's shoulder and nodded toward the girl.

Karen smiled, held up the skirt, and asked *"¿Cuánto cuesta?"*

Without looking at her mother, the girl promptly replied, *"Cien pesos."*

"A hundred?" asked Griffith.

"*Cien pesos*, Grif, yes, a hundred."

"A little under ten dollars."

"Too much. I'll start at fifty *pesos*."

"Huh?" he asked incredulously. "But that's what she... oh, I see. We're bargaining, right."

"With no fixed prices, it's the only way. They start high, and we haggle until we agree on a fair price."

"Even if we can afford the extra dollar?"

"It's expected, and we don't want to look like foolish *gringos*. Nobody would bother bargaining with us then."

The little girl gently touched Karen's sleeve and asked again, "*¿Cien pesos, señora? Muy bonita, ¿no?*"

"*Sí, muy bonita, pero no gracias, niña. Es muy caro.*"

"*¿Noventa y cinco pesos?*"

"*Cincuenta pesos,*" countered Karen.

"*Noventa y cinco pesos,*" the girl repeated.

"*Imposible. Uh, sesenta pesos.*"

"*Noventa.*"

"*Setenta pesos.* Seventy," she said to Griffith.

For the first time, the girl looked to her mother who said nothing.

"*Noventa pesos,*" she repeated.

"Time to walk away, I think," suggested Karen.

"Couldn't we just pay the, what is it, *novento*, ninety pesos?"

"*Noventa,*" corrected Karen. "Let's look at some others." To the girl, she said, "*No gracias. Tal véz más tarde.* Maybe later."

Karen took Griffith's arm and walked with him to the next vendor a few feet away. Griffith glanced over his shoulder and saw the mother talking quietly with the daughter for a few moments before she smiled and returned her attention to her infant.

A young boy in frayed denims, a torn, faded cotton shirt,

and tiny, worn cowboy boots, had been watching this exchange from the next row of vendors. He was barely four feet tall, and he was carrying a shoe shine box larger than his chest. Attached to the side of the shine box was a card holding a few small amber, jade, and bead earrings. When he caught Griffith's eye, he immediately walked up to him, pointed to Griffith's new, white sneakers, and held out the shine box.

"Shoe shine, *señor*?" he asked with a grin.

"No, *gracias*," replied Griffith, gently laughing at the thought. "*Tall bez mas tardy*," he said in rough imitation of Karen's Spanish.

"I clean them very good, *señor*." His grin grew into a smile. "Like new."

"They are new, actually," said Griffith, smiling back.

The boy motioned for Griffith to bend down, away from Karen who continued browsing through the different vendor's goods.

"*¿Señor*," he whispered in Griffith's ear as he nodded toward the dress Karen had picked out, "*te gusta la falda*, the skirt, *para la señora?*"

"*Muy bonita*," he replied even though he was unsure what the boy was asking, "but it's too expensive."

"*Muy caro, sí. Comprendo.* I can buy the dress for you."

"I don't understand. *No comprendo.*" He smiled at the boy's hustle.

"How much did *la madre* want for the skirt?" he asked.

"Uh, ninety... what's that? *Noventa pesos.*"

"*¡Noventa!* Too much, *señor*. No, *señor*, for you, I can buy the dress and a beautiful *huipil* for your *señora por... cien pesos*. One hundred *pesos, señor.*"

"What's a *weepill*?" asked Griffith.

The boy, unsure of the English equivalent, tugged on his shirt.

"Oh, a blouse," said Griffith. "But how? Do you know that family?"

"No, *señor*, but I am very good. Watch me. I save you money, and I make a little, *¿no?* My name is Alejandro. Just call me Al."

Amused at the idea that for a hundred pesos he would get to watch little Al work his entrepreneurial skills and get something for Karen, as well, Griffith smiled his agreement.

"Which *weepill?*" he asked the boy.

"Watch me, *señor*. It will be pretty."

"A hundred *pesos*, for both?"

"*Sí, señor.*"

"Okay. This is probably dumb, but what the hell. It's only a few bucks."

"Trust me. It will be a beautiful *huipil y falda.*"

"I will, Al. I'll be right here."

He took a hundred *peso* bill from his inside billfold and handed it to Al.

Al discreetly pocketed the money and casually turned a full circle before he walked past the blanket with the skirt. He paused at another blanket to look at the offerings and then turned up the next row of vendors. He stopped and knelt down. Griffith watched him as he picked up a *serape*, expressing some admiration to the vendor. He set the *serape* down and moved to the next vendor, a young mother selling dolls, toys, and amber jewelry. He turned and smiled at Griffith across the rows of blankets.

Griffith smiled back and wondered where Al was headed. This was seeing less like a generous thing to do and more like a lesson in Mexican economics. He turned, looking for Karen.

She was still nearby, but in those few moments it took to turn around, Al was out of sight.

"Perfect," he mumbled. "This is great. Now what? Karen," he called over to her, "I'm going to look around some, okay?"

"Have fun," she answered back.

Griffith headed off in the direction Al had taken, but when he got to the aisle where the woman was selling amber jewelry, he stopped. Unable to help himself, he laughed out loud.

The woman looked up and asked, *"¿Ambar, señor?"*

"What? Oh, sorry. I was just laughing at myself."

"¿Ambar, señor?" she repeated.

Griffith looked at her, laughed again, and then knelt down to survey her collection. Mostly, they were small polished drops, each containing some piece of insect. He found one larger, crudely carved drop with a complete, tiny wasp trapped inside.

"How much for this one? Er, what's the Spanish?" he stammered to himself.

"Diez pesos," she said.

"Diez? Ten. Is that all? Okay, *diez pesos."*

She held out her hand.

Griffith hesitated, and then realized what he had done.

"Uh, *señora…"* he started, repeating to himself the first seven numbers in Spanish. *"Siete pesos."*

She shook her head. *"Diez pesos."*

Griffith smiled and said, *"Ocho."*

She didn't shake her head this time. She just held out her hand and said again, *"Diez pesos."*

It didn't seem like much bargaining was happening, and Griffith thought she probably knew he was willing to pay the ten *pesos*.

"Okay, *diez pesos, señora."*

She flashed a smile so warm Griffith wanted to believe he

had gotten the better of the deal. He smiled back and handed her a ten *peso* coin. He held the amber pendant up, letting the light glisten off the insect frozen in time eons ago, and then put it in his shirt pocket. He was sure he'd lost the hundred *pesos* he'd given to Al, so this small present for Karen just became a hundred and ten *peso* piece of amber.

He continued around the courtyard of the church. Taking his time, hoping to catch a glimpse of Al, he passed dozens of vendors whose goods ranged from tacky, cheap plastic trinkets to items that seemed authentic, at least to his untrained eyes.

Toward the back stone wall, farthest from the street traffic, he found the artisans: jade carvers, leather workers, and hippie ex-patriates selling their hand-strung necklaces and carved hash pipes. Their hair was long and wild, and most of them, both men and women, were dressed in tie-dyed blouses, faded jeans, and sandals, and then decorated with numerous, brightly woven, Guatemalan bracelets. It looked to Griffith as if he'd stumbled onto a tribe of Deadheads who'd gotten lost after some concert and missed the bus.

Picking up a small, carved jade piece, dark green and veined with streaks of pale green and rose, he noticed Karen's blonde hair across several aisles in a lower section of the courtyard. Her back was to him, and as he started toward her, she held up the skirt they had looked at earlier—a similar one, anyway.

"*Muy bonita, señora,*" said a young voice from the other side of the skirt.

"*Sí, pero no comprendo,*" responded Karen.

"Karen," Griffith called as he came up behind her.

"Oh, Grif, look," she said turning around still holding up the skirt.

As she completed her turn, Griffith saw Al standing behind her, smiling broadly.

"You were not here when I returned," he said proudly, "but your *esposa* is."

Griffith laughed and said, "That's very good, Al."

"You watched me, *¿no?* And you trusted me, Grif." Through Al's accent, Grif's name became 'grief'.

"I guess I did, Al. Thanks. *Gracias*. Is that the *weepill?*"

"*Sí, la huipil para* Karen." He held the blouse out for Griffith to give to Karen.

Griffith motioned for Al to give the *huipil* to Karen and said, "No, you do it. And Karen, I'd like to introduce you to Al. Al, my wife Karen."

She reached out and shook Al's hand.

"Very nice to meet you," she said grinning broadly. "Have you known Grif long?" she joked.

"Oh, no, Karen," he replied earnestly. "We meet here, today, but I help to buy Grif this beautiful clothes for you."

He held up the soft, forest green cotton blouse, showing off the black, geometric corn motif embroidered around the low collar and short sleeves. The *huipil* complemented the darker greens in the skirt and accented the light ochre and sienna tones in the birds of the wide waistband.

"And it is lovely, too, Al," replied Karen. "That was sweet of both of you. *Muchas gracias*, Al. And thank you, Grif. It's beautiful."

Griffith thought about asking Al where he'd been. Instead, he smiled.

"That was a very good choice, Al. You did well. Now," he said, "while I was looking around, here's what I found for Karen."

He pulled out the insect and amber pendant and handed it to his wife.

"Oh, Griffith," beamed Karen, "it's amber. Oh, and look inside. There's a wasp. That's fascinating. Thank you, Grif."

Al pulled on Griffith's sleeve and motioned for him to bend down.

"I know, Al, I could have gotten one from you. I saw the earrings on your shine box. But you had left, and I was, you know, waiting around, and I found this on my own. Sorry."

"*Señor*," Al whispered to him, "you no understand."

Griffith humored him and bent down to listen.

"That is not amber," revealed Al.

Griffith stood up and laughed. "Not amber? How do you know?"

"Grif, trust me."

Karen held out the pendant and said, "How would we know? It looks like amber, but I don't really know much about it, how it smells or feels."

"No, you're right, of course," agreed Griffith. "Our ignorance is exceeded only by our trust, isn't it, Al."

Al knelt on the paving stones and opened his shine box. Inside, he picked through the shoe brushes, old stained toothbrushes, sponges, spring water bottles, an open pack of Marlboros, tins of shoe polish, and a number of small, plain grey boxes. Finding what he wanted, he pulled out one of two dozen Bic lighters from its grey carton. He lifted one of the amber earrings from its backing.

"*Ambar*," he said with his best tourist smile. "*Diez pesos.*"

He lit the lighter and held it under the earring. The yellow flame wrapped around the amber, and at that moment, Griffith understood what this young street hawker was showing them. He laughed again at his own ignorance. After a few seconds, Al took the lighter away, leaving a tiny flame still burning. The amber began to melt, and a thin column of dark, black smoke curled into the air. Griffith caught the unmistakable odor of burning plastic and jerked his nose away from the acrid petroleum vapors.

"*Falso,*" announced Al. "*Ambar es muy caro,* very expensive."

"Amazing, Griffith," said Karen. "Fooled me, too. Do you make these, Al?"

"*Yo, no,* Karen. *Mi amigo* gets the plastic in Villahermosa at a Pemex *refinería*. He puts in the *insectos* and sells them to all my friends."

"But you know they're fake?" asked Griffith.

"*Sí, claro,* but only for the *turistas.*"

"But we're *turistas,*" he protested.

"*Sí,* but I never cheat you. You trusted me."

"Then how can we know who's going to cheat us?"

"You can't," Al replied. "You can only trust. But I can find real amber *por tu.*"

"*No, gracias,* Al," said Karen. "We really don't have the time, I'm afraid. *La falda y la huipil son muy bonitas. Muchas gracias.*"

"*De nada.* For my friends, who trusted me."

"Thank you, Al," said Griffith. "*Muchas gracias.* We haven't had dinner, yet."

"*Sí, comprendo.* You must go to your dinner. *Vayan con Dios, mis amigos.*"

"*Vaya con Dios,* Al," said Karen. "May God be with you."

Al picked up his shine box and turned down the nearest aisle. Before he disappeared behind a row of hanging green tarps, he waved.

"I wonder how much he makes?" mused Karen. "I bet everyone in his family has to work. God, it's so tough being a kid here."

"Maybe we should have given him some extra money," suggested Griffith.

"Maybe," replied Karen, "but he'd probably have refused it. Even in this economy, a sale is a sale. But this skirt and *huipil* are so lovely. Thank you, Grif. God, I love this country—the people, Al, Esmeralda, just everything, this market, *Na-Bolom*, the mountains."

She hugged his arm as they headed out of the market. With the evening sun warming their backs, they walked along Avenida Comitán back to *Hacienda Na-Bolom*.

CHAPTER TWO
A KIDNAPPING

Tuxtla Gutiérrez
Chiapas, México
Saturday afternoon

> Where force is necessary, one should make use of it boldly, resolutely, and right to the end.
> *Was Nun?*
> Leon Trotsky
> 1879—1940

In Tuxtla Gutiérrez the main *zócalo* was open and hot. At one end of the square, the beige, Spanish colonial cathedral reflected the sun, bleaching everything pale and dry. Too far south and too much in the open plains, the state capital of Chiapas was oppressive in June.

Decorated this Saturday afternoon for the visit of the President of Mexico, the open plaza was filled with banners, posters, and bunting of the National Action Party. The *PAN* was *la República*'s newest ruling party. Following their gain of senatorial control, as well as winning the mayoral race in Mexico, *Presidente* Rodolfo Urbano Patrillo Sonador had decided it would be expedient to schedule speaking and networking opportunities wherever the former ruling party, the Party of the Institutionalized Revolution, still controlled the elections, specifically in the southern mountains and jungles of Chiapas. This was not because television and the print media weren't effective—his government controlled most of the content anyway—but because after nearly seventy years of uninterrupted rule by the *PRI*, the *PAN* had yet to make connections with many of the people, especially here in Chiapas, *la República*'s poorest state.

In reality, he wouldn't travel throughout the entire state, since there were literally hundreds of tiny villages scattered all over the mountains and lower rain forest. The great majority of the people, however, either lived in or made regular journeys to the only three commercial centers in this region: Comitán near the Guatemalan border, San Cristóbal de las Casas, the colonial capital high in the mountains, or here to Tuxtla Gutiérrez, the city closest geographically and emotionally to the mainstream of Mexican economic and social life.

Patrillo knew the importance of being seen where the people made their living. He also knew too much public exposure was tempting to the long-standing guerrilla movement among the peasants. In the states farther north, especially closer to the U.S. border, candidates could be, and were assassinated at times, and Chiapas had seen its own Zapatista uprising result in the deaths of both peasants and soldiers. Although Patrillo firmly believed his government was correcting the abuses of the past within the only effective structure, he feared those who wanted more radical solutions.

So here he was, comfortably cool in the cathedral's quiet sacristy with his wife and the two oldest of his five children, waiting out the introductory speakers. Patrillo shook his head as he looked out the small window to the side street. The crowd continued to press toward the *zócalo*, and the cheers from the square echoed between the buildings. The security had been a nightmare. During the week prior to traveling here, he had repeatedly questioned Juan Bicho, *Comandante de la Policía Judicial Federal de México*, about the specifics of his security plans.

Bicho was Mexico's most powerful police official, even considering the large number of agencies and authorities which shared Mexico's law enforcement responsibilities. The *judiciales* of *Comandante* Bicho's *PJF* were the largest and most effective police force although they competed with *la Policía Federal de Caminos* who patrolled the highways, the Federal narco-police, *la Policía Municipal* in the cities, and *la Policía Judicial de los Estados* of each state, as well as the various agricultural, commerce, border, and local defense forces. Even *la Secretaria de Defensa* had authority over internal conflicts, and there were any number of secret police units whose authorities were, naturally, kept secret. And in eastern Chiapas, the *latifundistas* who ranched the valuable rain forest valleys had their own powerful *guardias blancas*—the private paramilitary units who protected their investments and insured political correctness during elections. *Comandante* Bicho had assured the President that the dozens of alleys and open streets entering the *zócalo* would be secured. Unless someone wanted to attack by air, the chance of trouble was insignificant.

If anyone knew the Zapatistas' tactics, Patrillo reasoned, it was Bicho. After all, Bicho had actually been a hostage of the rebel army at one time. Whether he had escaped from his captivity, as he claimed, or was released into the jungle was no longer even discussed. *Comandante* Bicho knew their habits. He had told Patrillo more than once the Zapatista insurgents lacked the resources to strike this close to the heart of the government.

"But if this rebel leader," the President had insisted, "if this *Subcomandante* Marcos decides the government isn't moving fast enough, he could resort to any number of ways to threaten us."

"*Señor Presidente*, relax. My intelligence has found no activity among their rebel army. Marcos' army of toy guns, women, and children remains hidden in the jungle, teaching arithmetic to the *indios*, or something naïve like that."

"*Indígena*," the President had corrected. "You must use the correct terminology."

"Yes, I know that, but weren't we all born here? What's wrong with '*indios*,' anyway? That's what they are, aren't they?"

"*Comandante*, we've got to please everyone these days, don't we? It used to be the people listened to money and power. Now we must convince them we know what's best for them."

"Nevertheless, *Señor Presidente*, you may rest assured our security will be sufficient."

Patrillo hoped Bicho's final words were right. He crossed himself and turned to the notes of his standard speech to *la Gente*. His wife and children sat quietly on the large, leather couch watching him pace the stone floor. His wife, *Señora* Elena de Juvenal Patricio, was dressed conservatively in a dark suit, her thick auburn hair tied back. Since the children's private school had just had ended its spring semester, fourteen-year-old Sara and eleven-year-old Tito were with them.

Throughout their short lives, Sara and Tito had enjoyed the privilege and endured the strain of a wealthy family dedicated to public service. Well-behaved when necessary, they were both head-strong and intelligent. Sara took after her mother, physically and mentally. Although still gangling and growing fast, the initial aches and embarrassments of puberty were past her. She chose her own interests and her own wardrobe. Today, she had selected a simple off-white dress, saying it expressed her lack of involvement in the political process. Tito was not yet old enough to wear long pants at public functions—his father's bow to tradition—so he usually appeared in his private school uniform, dark blue, stiff, and uncomfortable. Like his father, he could be arrogant, and the siblings often argued.

The four of them were alone in the quiet room. Patrillo's security team was waiting outside the heavy door, and Archbishop García, the spiritual leader of the Chiapas See, had excused himself some time ago, returning to work in his adjoining office. Patrillo paced, waiting for the opening speeches to end.

He tossed his notes onto an end table and left the sacristy. Pulling the heavy door closed behind him, he heard the muffled cheers of the crowds outside the cathedral. He walked through the nave toward the bright light pouring in the vestibule doors, his four bodyguards falling in place around him.

As he strode between the pews, the shadows of the soldiers guarding the cathedral's entrance stretched back into the vestibule. For a moment the silhouetted figures, their rifle barrels pointed upward, looked like dark apparitions of the Zapatistas he had seen on the steps of the *Catedral de Santo Domingo* in San Cristóbal following the New Year's uprising in 1994. He remembered the motley uniforms, the red and black bandannas, the ski-masks, and the weapons raised against the rule of law.

Here, in this harsh light and shadows, his own soldiers were indistinguishable from the Zapatista rebels. He knew there was no way the Zapatistas could have seized this church, or even be in Tuxtla, so far from the mountains and jungles, but he couldn't suppress the chilly shudder which crawled up his spine.

He shook his head clear and focused on the cheers as the speaker stirred the crowd with high emotion and energy. He appreciated the old-fashioned oratorical style even though it was not what he intended to give them. *La República* was no longer a third world country. She was a player on the world stage, and Mexicans were proud. He knew what the people wanted—jobs and a stable economy—and he knew they feared any collapse, economic or governmental, which could destroy what they had spent years building. He would give them a stable, secure government. And more. He understood that a strong family on stage with him encouraged all the families of his country. And he was confident the newspapers would carry just such a powerful picture.

At any rate, it was time to get the family. Walking back toward the sacristy, he listened to the rhythm of the audience's responses. His guards watched the vestibule and studied the cool, deep shadows obscuring the far corners of the nave. Patrillo reached the door of the sacristy and looked around once. Nothing hiding in the shadows, he joked to himself. When he reached for the doorknob, he noticed a faint odor of... something different, something he couldn't place. Damp earth, perhaps.

Pushing the door in, the base hit something, like a foot in the way. Before he could utter "Excuse me," the door slammed back into his face. The sound of his nose breaking and the rush of air from his lungs were very distinct as he collapsed to the stone floor.

Dazed, blood flowed through his mustache into his mouth. He spat and blinked his eyes back into focus. Shouts erupted from within the sacristy.

His children were shrieking.

"Oh, God!" he screamed. "Tito. Sara. Something's wrong. Elena!"

Patrillo swallowed his surging panic, tasting blood as he refilled his empty lungs. Fighting the pain in the center of his face, he struggled to his feet. He grabbed the doorknob and shouldered his way into the room. Behind him, his security was sprinting across the stone floor of the nave.

He flew into the middle of the sacristy, stumbling into chaos. Sara and Tito kicked and yelled at their two ski-masked attackers who were dragging them out the rear door. A third intruder, dressed in rumpled turquoise slacks, a fatigue shirt under a bandoleer filled with shells, and a dark ski-mask, waved a shotgun in the air.

"Get them out of here!" he shouted at his accomplices. "Now!"

Elena was struggling to get off her knees. Hands bound, she crawled across the carpet, trying to get between the open door to the Archbishop's office and her children. The intruder lifted his rifle above his head and was about to strike her with the butt end when Patrillo launched himself across the room.

He knocked his wife down and spun toward her attacker just in time to see the rifle butt hit the center of his forehead. As he collapsed, a gunshot, so close it hurt his ears, exploded, echoing into the unconscious distance before he hit the floor.

**

Fear was all he knew.

Until he tried to move. Then the first twitching muscle snapped all the pain of a broken nose and a severely gashed forehead back into his now wide-awake brain. Wads of gauze stuffed his nostrils, forcing him to breathe through his dry mouth. He touched the bandages around his head, and then the leather couch and its sticky, drying blood.

When he opened his eyes, he saw he was surrounded by medics crowding the sacristy with their equipment. An I-V roller stood by the couch, dripping saline and antibiotics into his arm.

"He's awake," said one of the medics.

The medic next to him repeated it, and the announcement was passed around the room and out both doors.

"My wife. The children?" he whispered, unable to breath properly with his nose full of blood and cotton.

"Do you know your name?" asked the medic kneeling beside him.

"What? My name?"

Patrillo was awake, but he couldn't understand why they were asking him if he knew his own name. He was the President.

"Are the children all right?" he repeated.

"Do you know where you are?" the medic insisted gently.

Patrillo tried to sit up, but the sharp reminders of his injury prevented that. Lying back, he reached out and took hold of the medic's arm.

"Listen to me," he said. "Are my children and wife safe? Tell me right now."

Before the medic could answer, Elena appeared and knelt next to the couch. The Archbishop, wringing his hands, followed and stood behind her. *Comandante* Bicho was directing people out the back door.

"Are you all right, Rodolfo?" Elena asked, her voice filled with emotion.

"What about the children? Are they safe, too?"

He saw in her eyes they were not. She fought back the glistening of tears and set her jaw.

"Rodolfo. They have kidnapped our children."

"Who? Why? I don't understand. What happened?"

Patrillo was having some trouble absorbing the information. Archbishop García made an effort to compose himself and tried to explain.

"They came in through my private entrance. Broke the lock. I was gagged and tied before I realized what was happening.

From their dress, I think they must have been Zapatistas. But I'm confused."

"Of course they were those damn terrorists," snapped *Comandante* Bicho from across the room. "How high and noble are they now, those sons-of-bitches? Kidnapping children."

Smartly dressed in the black uniform of his *judiciales*, *Comandante* Bicho was a short man with wide hips and disproportionately long, thin legs. His arms were thin, as well, and his long, pointed face and prominent, straight nose gave him an air of insect efficiency. When he focused on something, he would stretch his neck forward, turning his head either way with an almost segmented quality, as if looking at a problem from more than one angle would give him a better understanding.

"Believe me, *Señor Presidente*, we will find these terrorists and return your children."

"I feel it was my fault somehow," interrupted the Archbishop. "Perhaps I could have done more. I am absolutely..."

"You were tied up!" exclaimed Bicho. "What could you have done? I can't believe they brought rifles into the church, into the sacristy. They are damned for this."

"*Comandante*, we are all very upset by this, but we cannot presume to know God's justice."

"Bishop," spat Bicho, "don't tell me my business where these terrorists are concerned. They kidnapped children from a church, for Christ's sake. From your Church! I will tend to justice for these cowards. Then when I am finished with them, God can have what's left."

The Archbishop recoiled, unsure how to respond to his vehemence.

"Rodolfo," said Elena to her husband, "you must help us."

"Of course I will."

If they really were in the hands of the Zapatista National

Liberation Army, the EZLN, he had no idea how to rescue their children. The Zapatistas would take them to the most remote hideouts in the rain forest. No one knew how to find them in the inaccessible depths of the jungle except the Zapatistas and their *indígena* friends.

He was having trouble breathing; he needed to sit up. Gingerly, he rolled sideways on the couch, each tiny movement of his head intensifying the pain. He pushed himself up with his left arm into a sitting position. A wave of nausea rolled up from his stomach. He gagged, hacking up a clot of blood into his mouth.

Before he could gesture for help, Elena picked up an old, brass silent butler from the end table. Without the least sign of revulsion, she flipped the lid up with her thumb and held the open tray out for him. He looked into the old cigar butts and ashes and promptly threw up. Vomit and clotted blood filled the silent butler and poured onto the carpeting.

The only sounds for the next few seconds were the intake of astonishment from the Archbishop and the dripping of vomit as Elena moved the tray into the ornamental fireplace. She produced a handkerchief for her husband. He wiped his mouth and mumbled a weak apology. Elena spoke through the awkwardness.

"Excellency," she said to the Archbishop, "let's move to your office. *Señor,*" to one of the security guards, "please get someone to clean this. Rodolfo, let me help you."

In the office, Patrillo eased himself onto the couch. Elena steadied the I-V roller and sat next to him while Bicho paced, making impatient little clicks with his tongue. The Archbishop moved behind his desk and lifted his large armchair from its side. Papers and books were scattered on the floor, and the wood around the bolt to his outside entrance was splintered. The corpulent priest sat down and sighed.

"As you can see," he explained, "they surprised me. They gagged me and tied me to this chair, then pushed me over. I was obviously frightened for myself until they entered the sacristy. It is most egregious and upsetting for them to use such measures."

"Excellency," asked Patrillo, "you said you believed they were Zapatistas?"

"Yes. Didn't you see them as well?"

"Yes, I did, momentarily. *Comandante* Bicho, how did these rebels manage to find their way here from the jungle?"

"*Señor Presidente*, I will find the answer, and I swear on my father's grave, I will punish these terrorist insurgents. I will find them, and I will end this threat. I knew we should have pursued them into the jungle and hunted them down years ago."

"*Comandante*," the Archbishop asked, "why would the EZLN risk all the political good will they've already established with the media and the public?"

"They're rebels," answered Bicho. "Calling them the EZLN or any other euphemism just dignifies criminal behavior. They intend to overthrow the government."

"Did they leave any demands?" asked Patrillo.

"Not yet, but they will."

"Before you broke in and rescued me," said Elena, her voice thick, "he pointed his rifle at me and said they would be back. And we had better not follow them."

"That is correct," the Bishop confirmed.

"Then your guards came in and killed the one who hit you. They ran out the back into the alley, but the kidnappers were already gone. Rodolfo, why would anyone do this?"

"Why!" interrupted Bicho. "They're Zapatistas. Terrorists! He saw them. You saw them. That's not the question here."

"I think, for now, *Comandante* Bicho is right, Elena," agreed Patrillo. "We have to assume, at least until we hear from them, they're Zapatistas."

"So," declared Bicho, "we must use all the might of the *judiciales* and the military to rescue your children and destroy this threat."

Through his throbbing, bone-numbing pain, Patrillo realized this had the potential to become much more than a kidnapping, even more than a political kidnapping. Although the goals of the Zapatistas—medical clinics and schools for the jungle and highland villages, and greater involvement in the electoral process for the *indígena*—were generally recognized as legitimate, many in Mexico's burgeoning middle class justifiably feared economic chaos. The most recent *peso* devaluation had been difficult enough for the politicians to deal with, but not nearly so difficult as for the middle class. They wanted stability and order.

Since the poor, especially in Chiapas, have always struggled, their smoldering anger could be used to deepen the schism between them and the middle class. If the Zapatistas were again ready to rise up and confront the government violently, then inappropriate reactions to this abduction could compound the problem of the children's rescue. This kidnapping could explode in any number of directions, including the unthinkable—two dead children and a very hot civil war.

An ambulance pulled up to the office's entrance. Patrillo wondered if he could slip into the ambulance without being seen. He dreaded facing the press without any answers. Blood and fear, especially his own, were too much fodder for the media. Missing his speech would certainly have gotten their attention.

"*Comandante*," he asked, "would you make sure the media are away from the alley when I get in the ambulance?"

"It's already done, sir. And I've arranged to have you and the *Señora* flown back to the capital with a medical team. One of my men will accompany your security, with your permission, sir."

"Yes, thank you, *Comandante*," he said, appreciative of his efficiency. Patrillo looked at each of them. Elena's eyes were red, and her lips quivered. Bicho's narrow jaw was clenched, and the Archbishop kept wringing his hands over his large abdomen.

"Let's get out of here," Patrillo decided. "We've got work to do. *Comandante*, do your job and bring me some idea for our response. Tomorrow, if possible. Certainly by Monday. My office at the *Palacio Nacional*. Bishop García, please use whatever spiritual influence you might have. We're going to need some outside help, I'm afraid."

CHAPTER THREE
NA-BOLOM

San Cristóbal de las Casas
Chiapas, México
Sunday

> They all disappear, and soon the souls of the Lacandones will also disappear… their souls will wither and die as their magnificent forest is destroyed, and all of us will share the blame.
>
> *The Last Lords of Palenque*
> Perera and Bruce

Griffith and Karen spent Sunday afternoon strolling the quiet streets of San Cristóbal. Families, lovers, and friends, all dressed in their Sunday finery, gathered in the *zócalo*, chatting or courting, and listening to the small string bands playing in the large gazebo. The slow pace and sunny day warmed them.

Hungry after their long leisurely day, the newlyweds were back at *Na-Bolom* before dark. They sat at the large kitchen table as Esmeralda set out plates, bowls, and utensils. Following large bowls of *sopa de ajo*, garlic soup with cheese in a chicken broth, Esmeralda served them *pollo Mexicana*, a baked chicken breast in a tomato and *chile* sauce, with side dishes of black beans and a *guacamole*. She then sat with them, nibbling a *tortilla* while they ate.

"You are so fortunate," Esmeralda said with some nostalgia in her voice, "to see the jungle. To me, the forest is the most beautiful with its mountains and valleys and rivers. We have much wealth in the forest?"

"Wealth?" repeated Karen.

"*Sí*. And the pressure to sell our wealth will destroy us. What can someone with no education say to a pocketful of *pesos*? Maybe three hundred Lacandones still live. Like most of *la República*'s ten million *indígena*, only a few of us speak Spanish. We must build roads into the jungle for clinics and schools, and to teach everyone to speak Spanish."

This was an issue on which Griffith was much too ignorant to pass any judgment. The conflict between traditional culture and the inexorable flood of today's technology confused him. Was culture an historical model or an evolving concept? He suspected the imposition of a western educational system, with its concepts of ownership and commerce, and even its idea of what constitutes basic comfort and need, might destroy the remnants of these cultures anyway.

"Esmeralda," he asked, "do you think the culture, the arts and languages, and the skills of the *indígena* can survive the modern world? Is it possible to find some way to adapt and still maintain what they value from their heritage?"

"Perhaps," she said, "but *en la Selva Lacandona*, we live in thatch and board houses, with dirt floors and no plumbing. In many villages the people defecate beside the streams where they drink. We have no future, and our past is lost. Only one man, old Chan K'in of Na'ha still keeps the old ways. The rest of us have forgotten everything, even how to make the god-pots to burn the incense. We are uneducated and unhealthy, and the government has ignored us.

"But the loggers and ranchers have not. They buy the

mahogany and clear the forest for the big ranches of the *latifundistas*. Now the only law in the jungle is theirs."

She was referring to the *guardias blancas*. Working as an association of privately-hired soldiers and weapons experts for the *latifundista* ranchers who controlled the cleared valleys of the rain forest, the *guardias blancas* operated in virtual autonomy. These mercenaries were ostensibly utilized by the wealthy landowners to protect their large ranches from Zapatista seizures and terrorism. To the disenfranchised and ignorant, however, to those scratching a subsistence living from the hillsides of a fragile jungle ecology, the *guardias blancas* were the boot heel of oppression.

"So with the *guardias blancas* to keep everyone 'safe', the *evangelistas* arrive," she said, and her sarcasm was clear to Griffith, even through her thick accent. "And the Protestants, the Seventh Day Adventists, the Baptists, even the Unification Church preaches at us. If our men quit smoking their cigars, quit drinking their *balche*, and marry only one woman who must bring her babies to their Savior, they offer us a better life *after* we die."

"So far," said Griffith, "this doesn't sound much different than the treatment the Native Americans have gotten in the United States, or even the Inuit of northern Canada."

"My people," she said, "call ourselves *hach winik*, 'true people', not Lacandon, which meant 'savage' to the colonial powers. We hid from these *conquistadores* and their *sacerdotes Catolicos* for over four hundred years. Until today. Even though we are the only direct descendant of the last Maya lords of Palenque, our men can no longer take more than one wife. There are not enough women.

"After they logged my valley, the only trees standing were a few ceiba. They paid for each stump, of course, but the rest of the forest was destroyed to remove the mahogany. The game left, and so my father, who was a very good hunter, had to drive his new truck to buy Spam and gas with his new *pesos*. Like many other men in our village, my father died in his *milpa*, his garden, from the bite of *nauyaca*."

Commonly called *la barba amarilla*, since its only distinguishing feature is the yellow mouth and throat one sees as it strikes, the *nauyaca* is known to science as *bothrops atrox*, the fer-de-lance. In the cleared forest of a logging operation, *la barba amarilla* hunts the rats that come with the logging camps and their garbage.

"A woman died," said Esmeralda sincerely, "cleaning her husband's wound when the venom got into a open cut on her hand. All this is true."

When the fer-de-lance strikes a *campesino* in the fields, the venom, a hemolytic, enzymatic protein, literally dissolves the blood cells. The intercellular walls break down, and internal bleeding from the stomach, lungs, eyes, and mucous linings of the mouth and nasal passages all occur before coronary thrombosis mercifully ends his life.

"I can see," said Griffith, a little unnerved by the effect her story was having on his imagination, "I've still got a great deal to learn about the rain forest."

Given what he didn't know about the cultural, social, economic, and ecological conflicts throughout the rain forest, Griffith felt a little guilty about his ignorance of the country he was set to explore. He caught Karen's eye, and they got up to leave.

"The dinner was excellent, Esmeralda. *Muchas gracias*," said Karen.

"It was not much, but I am pleased to serve you. Few of our visitors spend any time at the *hacienda*. I am grateful to practice my English. I hope I was not so boring to you."

"No," replied Griffith. "It was enlightening. I had no idea how little I actually knew."

Esmeralda escorted them outside onto the flagstones under the back roof. It was raining steadily, slapping the leaves and splashing into puddles under the eaves. The drops glistened and danced in the yellow light from the kitchen.

"I remember a story," she said, "my mother used to tell me about the differences among people. She heard it from her mother. Whenever the fighting men from Guatemala would cross the river, my father would hide in the jungle. My mother would hold me and sing in the dark of how the Creator Hachakyum, the Plumed Serpent, tried three times to create a perfect man."

She spoke softly, in gliding rhythms and tones, more song than story. With a backdrop of rain, Griffith and Karen closed their eyes and held hands while she told the mythic history of her people.

> *Listen to the silence*
> *before the Plumed Serpent made the world.*
> *All was empty,*
> *and his long tail feathers trailed rainbows in the silent, blue sky.*
> *Humming, Hachakyum called forth the great trees of the forest*
> *to hold the world together*
> *and cried the tears to water their roots.*
> *He sang life into the birds,*
> *into the orchids which scent the air,*
> *and into the jaguar who protects the night.*
> *Throughout the great forest covering the world,*
> *the gods then brought their food and drink,*
> *their songs and dances,*
> *to play and make love in the forests of Hachakyum.*

To honor the gods and enjoy the beauty,
the Creator made His first man, a creature of mud.
But the men of mud could not remember the songs of thanksgiving,
and they could not learn to make love.
With His cries of sorrow and pain, Hachakyum brought the rains
which melted these dark and lonesome creatures
washing them to the sea of salt His tears had formed.

The great Plumed Serpent then looked to His forest
and created a new race of men from its wood.
Tall and strong they were,
these pale men who could hunt and build.
These wooden men soon learned to farm and reproduce,
but they were dry and stiff
and could not bend their heads.
Their voices were hard and splintered,
and they forgot how to make the incense.
The Creator could see they were soulless,
these men who multiplied over the earth.

Again, He cried to rid the forest of these men.
He brought the jagged fire from the sky
and told the jaguars to tear out the eyes of his creation.
The dogs turned on their masters who had beaten them
and they ripped off their limbs.
Even the grinding stones which had worked so hard for man
crushed their faces.
The remains of the wooden men were burned,
and their ashes filled the sky.
The few who survived left the forest.
Or perhaps they are the monkeys in the trees.

BLOOD OF THE EARTH

The Plumed Serpent then asked the jaguar, the dog, and the quetzal
to find the perfect material to create a perfect man.
The jaguar looked for strength, the dog for loyalty,
and the quetzal sought beauty.
They covered the world, and each returned
carrying white and yellow maize for this perfect man.
So Hachakyum brewed the blood from the yellow maize
and shaped the teeth from the kernels of white maize.
This true man, a man of corn, was intelligent and wise
and could see into the future and into the heavens
where he watched the gods at play and love.
He sang the songs and burned the incense
and all true men praised the gods.

The Creator had made the perfect man,
but in his perfection there was a flaw.
That flaw was his perfection.
Afraid of the godlike powers of His creation,
He changed one small part of his perfect man.
Into man's perfect, crystal clear eyes
He blew a mist, filling them white
so man could see only what was close to him.
Because of this,
the heavens and the future are forever unclear to us.

Now when the gods are remembered in your ceremonies,
be aware of what you cannot see;
that men of mud, and men of wood,
and even the true men of corn are not perfect.

Rain filled the silence. Karen and Griffith were both smiling, unaware they were soaked to the knees from the splashing drops.

"Esmeralda, that was beautiful," exclaimed Karen. *"Muchas gracias."*

"Yes," agreed Griffith. "Thank you very much. Creation stories are so fascinating, and your mother's is wonderful. Does she live around here?"

"No, I'm sorry. My mother died from the cholera several years ago."

"Oh, God," gasped Griffith, embarrassed and apologetic. "I'm sorry."

"De nada. You are kind," she smiled, "but I must continue to work and study if I am going to be accepted to the University. And then I will teach anyone who wants to learn."

"I'm sure you'll do well," said Karen.

"But now, you must find your cottage in the rain. It is still your honeymoon, no? Before you go, *un momento, por favor."*

Esmeralda stepped back into the kitchen and retrieved a large woolen bag. She lifted out a long, blue and green woven purse. From the purse, she took a plain, dark green feather. The quill had been tied with bright threads and strung with a few beads. On this nondescript feather, a small, red-breasted, green bird with two very long tail feathers, twice the body length, had been painted.

"For the bride," she said. "A quetzal feather. The quetzal, sacred to the Maya, is called Lord of Light. He lives in the Light World but can see into the Invisible World. If you follow him, the demons of the jungle will not harm you."

Griffith was aware of the great number of species whose habitat was threatened throughout the Americas. He wondered if the quetzal were among them.

"Esmeralda," he asked, "is the quetzal endangered?"

"Sí, Griffith. We get the feathers from *la Reserva Ecológica,* and one of our Lacandon artists paints them to sell in the *mercado.*

For your bride." She held the feather up to Karen's blonde hair. "May I?"

"*Sí*, of course," she answered.

Esmeralda braided the loose threads into a lock of her hair.

"*Muy bonita con tu pelo*," she said stroking Karen's blonde hair.

"Thank you," said Karen, "*muchas gracias*, Esmeralda."

"*De nada*. A small present for visiting *Na-Bolom*. You will return after your stay *en la selva*?"

"*Sí*, we're scheduled for another two nights next week. But we do have to leave early tomorrow."

"I will have breakfast and a taxi waiting for you. *Buenas noches*."

Karen and Griffith stepped carefully onto the wet trail. Rain spotted Griffith's glasses, and he put his hands on Karen's back, urging her to hurry through the shower. Trotting into the darkness, a large elephant fern poured cold rainwater down the back of Karen's blouse, forcing a chilled giggle out of her. Griffith was still moving forward, wondering why Karen was laughing when his face stopped the large, rebounding leaf. Slapping the branch out of the way and spitting out imagined insects and dirt, Griffith stumbled past Karen.

"Don't get lost," she called.

In the shadows, Griffith realized he had no idea which way their bungalow was, so he slowed as the trail entered the tree nursery. Turning to see how close Karen was, his sneaker caught a root growing on the surface. His momentum sent him sprawling onto his back, down onto the leaves, needles, and mud of the trail.

Before he could warn her, Karen appeared out of the shadows, saw him on the ground, and tried to dance over him. Instinctively, he lifted his knees to protect his groin. His calf hit her foot, tripping her forward onto his chest. His arms caught the brunt of her fall, and she dropped to her elbows, still on top of him. She relaxed her weight between his raised knees, forcing him to lower them to the wet ground.

Lying in the rain and cold ground water, Griffith saw the excitement in Karen's eyes. She smothered his breath with a long, deep kiss. In the warmth of her mouth, he tasted rainwater, earthy and sensuous. As it ran across her cheeks and into his mouth, it cooled his tongue and heated his desire. On his chest, her small breasts warmed him. She pressed her pubic bone against the bulge in his pants, sending a tingle heightened by the rain dripping from the leaves above. They broke their kiss, and Karen nuzzled her face into the side of his neck. The quetzal feather brushed his cheek.

"Let's go in, love," she whispered.

***

Later, standing under the front eave of their cottage, Karen and Griffith listened to the night, the chirps and clicks, the buzzes and splashes filling the forest after the rain. They had slipped on long tee-shirts to step out into the cool air before returning to their very soft, warm bed.

Water still dripped through the jungle foliage, and small rivulets gurgled under the peeps and chirrups surrounding them. The lights of the *Na-Bolom*'s kitchen cast a distant, pale yellow glow through the leaves. Neither of them said anything. Griffith leaned against the rough wood column and held Karen against him.

Through the crystal night, a faint rhythmic beat started. To their left, some thirty yards off in the woods, another cottage winked its solitary light. Somebody's boom box was playing just loudly enough for the music to reach them. Griffith heard an organ, its reggae bass line syncopated with a highhat cymbal and timbales. Two measures, then a voice, an inarticulate wail from this distance, hovered over the back beat.

"The Clash," said Karen.

Griffith was amazed.

"How do you know this?" he asked.

"The Clash? Oh, they were popular in the late seventies. Probably some Euros staying at that other cottage."

He heard the singer's voice, but the lyrics were too soft to distinguish. Then a loud rim shot, and driven by the guitar, bass, and organ, the Clash's distinctive London style of Caribbean rhythms rolled into the night. What London's Caribbean immigrants called Zanzibar, a Jamaican-African-European hybrid, the city's white rock and rollers had pushed into the music of confrontation.

"Combat rock," she said. "Listen."

Vertical bells on the upbeat through three more measures of rhythm before Joe Strummer's emphatic voice, clearly enunciated over the heavy ska beat, sang its challenge.

A lot of people won't get no supper tonight.
A lot of people won't get no justice tonight.

The battle is getting harder
In this i-racial Armagideon time.

The rhythm and bass guitars pushed the Jamaican beat for four more measures before his voice joined again.

A lot of people running and hiding tonight.
A lot of people won't get no justice tonight.

Remember to kick it over.

No one will guide you—Armagideon time.

Thinking of the odd juxtaposition at hearing the Clash in the jungles of Chiapas, Griffith shivered. Coincidence, he knew, and his chill was because the night was cool; that was all.

"Let's go in, Karen. I'm cold."

"Good idea. It has gotten chilly."

They turned to enter the cottage, and the rain abruptly started again. As he followed Karen in, the groans of resigned pain in Strummer's voice moaned through the increasing downpour. Griffith pulled the door snugly, shutting out the night.

Back under the blanket, lulled by the hiss of the low pine fire in the fireplace, the shushing of the rain, and their own breathing, sleep soon wrapped them in its silent, blind security.

CHAPTER FOUR
THE RAIN FOREST

Lagunas de Montebello,
Near the Guatemalan border
Monday

> *Todas las gentes siempre tienen miedo.*
>
> Traci Gutiérrez,
> independent taxi owner

For the majority of Mexicans, long taxi rides were as infrequent as trips on *Primera Clase* busses. Griffith and Karen, on the first Monday of their marriage, were already packed when another white Nissan taxi picked them up at *Na-Bolom* to drive them southeast sixty miles to Comitán, the last city before the Guatemalan border, and then along unmarked, two-lane blacktop for another forty miles into *la Parque Nacional de las Lagunas de Montebello.*

Traci, their driver, was in his mid-twenties, had thick, dark hair, and was casually dressed in a print shirt and beige slacks. A photograph sealed in plastic hung from the rear view mirror. When Karen noticed it swinging wildly from the mirror, Traci announced with a smile, "*Mi esposa* and *mi hermosa* Julietita."

They sped across the narrow, cobblestone streets, past walls covered with political graffiti, and out of San Cristóbal. On the highway south of the city, they zipped past a well-maintained park. Several new frame and block buildings were scattered around the mown meadows and open pine forests. A newly-paved road led from the entrance past the buildings and disappeared through a gated fence into the woods.

"That's nice," said Karen, nodding toward the park as they sped by. "Is this a new park, Traci?"

"Not so new, *señora*," he replied. "Not so old."

"*No comprendo.*"

"The park is old," he began. "Before the Zapatistas awoke, the park was trees, wild, nothing there, you understand? Just a park."

As they passed the entrance, the large, newly-painted sign announced the park was maintained by *la Secretaria de Defensa*.

"*Sí*," replied Karen. "So they fixed the park up after the...?" She paused, unsure of Traci's attitude toward the EZLN.

"The rebellion, *sí, en enero*, '94," he finished for her.

"Why?"

"The Zapatistas were moving weapons from San Cristóbal through the park to the villages."

"And the new buildings, then?" asked Griffith.

"*Sí*. For the soldiers, *y sus familias*."

"Barracks," said Griffith quietly.

"Interesting," added Karen. "Does anyone visit the park now?"

"*Sí*, the families of the soldiers." And then he laughed. "And some *campesinos* have moved in and started farming. It is much safer now."

South of San Cristóbal, the highway dropped out of the highest, perpetually-clouded mountains. The small subsistence farms crouching in the narrow valleys gave way to tracts of soybean, cacao, and potatoes. As the valley spread its shoulders wide, large tobacco farms with their huge, open drying barns, and sugar cane, coffee, and sorghum fields filled the vista. At the edges of each of these huge farms, little communities of a dozen or so small, rough homes gardened for themselves and supplied the workers for the large farms.

Leaving Comitán, construction sprawled eastward from the city. New *barrios* of unfinished cinder block houses and dusty roads were crowded with families. Hundreds of teenagers, reluctant for the school day to begin, congregated outside a recently-completed public high school. Beyond the school stood a massive factory, its concrete walls and fences giving it a somber, austere appearance. To Griffith it appeared the school and factory had the same architect.

"What do they manufacture there?" asked Griffith as they drove past the factory. A large number of identical dark, Ford sedans were parked in a distant fenced-in lot.

"*Hombres, señor,*" and Traci laughed again.

"But the sign on the highway said '*Fábrica de*' something or other."

"*Verdad, señor.* But it is a prison for bad men."

"Zapatistas?" ventured Karen.

"Perhaps. Some ranches were stolen here in Chiapas. Some people were killed."

"Why did the Zapatistas steal ranches?" asked Karen.

"There are many lazy people, I think." he suggested.

Lazy was one attribute Griffith had yet to notice. He'd seen people selling their crafts while tending and teaching their children, and school age children working the streets and markets. Men built roads and loaded dump trucks in the hot, tropical sun with no more than shovel and pick, and women, bent under the weight of firewood strapped to their foreheads, climbed steep mountain roads. He hadn't seen lazy.

"It is *muy difícil* to support a family today," continued Traci.

"The economy is not certain. My wife works. I don't like that. Our daughter must stay with her *abuela*, her grandmother. It is okay, but she should be with her mother. This cab is very expensive. The interest is now one hundred percent, and I must work even longer. I would like to have a big ranch, too. But I don't, so my wife and I must work."

Ahead of them, just before the turnoff to the *Lagunas* at *la Trinitaria*, all the traffic stopped in both directions. Men in black uniforms, each with a bright yellow *PJF* stenciled on his back, and each armed with an automatic rifle, sidearm, and Kevlar vest, strode down the middle of the road looking in every vehicle.

Approaching Traci's taxi, two of the soldiers walked around to the front passenger's door. They stopped and smiled at Karen. One of them glanced at Griffith in the back seat, checked the floor, and nodded. They smiled again at Karen, and after a moment, continued on to the next car.

"Looking for narcotics, I think," explained Traci, and he pointed east. "From Guatemala."

When they reached the checkpoint, they were told to pull into a large parking area at an abandoned Pemex relay station and wait in line. Small groups of *judiciales* surrounded several of the vehicles in front of them. A diesel fuel tanker truck passed through after a perfunctory check of the driver's papers. A *colectivo* was parked, and eight or nine *campesinos*, eyes to the ground, were standing by their open van, waiting to be inspected. Karen and Griffith were the only tourists.

Four *PJF judiciales* approached the cab and motioned, as politely as possible with rifles in their hands, for them to get out. Two of them pointed to the trunk, and Traci removed the backpacks. The others, standing by the front end, checked Karen's and Griffith's passports.

The oldest officer looked up from Karen's passport and asked in very thickly accented English, "New Jersey?"

"No," she replied, smiling. "I live in Virginia."

"Have you been to New Jersey?" he repeated with a frown.

"Yes, *sí*, sorry, *sí*, I was born in New Jersey. See?" She reached over and pointed to 'Cherry Hill, NJ' next to her photograph.

"Atlantic City?"

"No, Cherry Hill. *Lugar de nacimiento*. Where I was born."

"*Sí*. I have been to Atlantic City."

When Karen and Griffith both smiled in dumb reaction, the officer beamed.

"You have been to Atlantic City?" he asked.

"No, not actually," confessed Karen. "I left New Jersey when I was very young."

"*Con sus padres?*" he asked sincerely.

"Uh, *sí*, with my parents, yes."

"Too bad." He sounded a little sorry. "Atlantic City is very nice. *Turistas?*"

"Uh, *sí*," she replied hesitatingly. "*Recien casados*," she added.

She's good at this, admired Griffith. He, however, was having real difficulty following the man's transitions, so he just smiled in agreement.

The *judicial* peered at Karen's passport once again, held her photo next to her face, and gave it back to her. He glanced at Griffith's for a brief moment, and then snapped the passport smartly closed. Handing it to Griffith, he nodded at both of them.

"*Gracias. Felicitaciónes*. You may go."

He snapped his fingers, his squad fell in, and they proceeded to the next vehicle.

When Griffith walked back to help Traci put the packs in the trunk, he saw both packs lying open. Really open. Everything was unpacked and spread on the ground. The tent had been loosened from the pack, the foam bed rolls were flopped open, and the mess kit was in the dirt.

"Great," he muttered. "And felicitations to you, too, assholes."

"Shhh," Traci hissed under his breath. "*Por favor, señor.* Better to wait quietly."

"Yeah, right. Christ, I don't believe this. Next time, I'll keep an eye on them."

"Sometimes they will do this, *señor*, and sometimes no."

"Must be a slow day," joked Griffith feebly. "Karen, come here. Look at this."

Griffith knelt to start repacking. Karen put her passport in her fanny pack and walked back to join him.

"Oh, Griffith, what happened?" she exclaimed.

"Shh, Karen. Traci thinks we should not protest too loudly."

"Probably right. Not wise to upset armed men, is it?"

"Fear therapy, huh?"

And Griffith did feel threatened. The *judiciales* didn't have any logical reason for the style or extent of their search. Probably just his *gringo* expectations, he told himself, fueling his disquiet with images of uniformed thugs and their weapons.

"Why should I be afraid?" he asked aloud. "We didn't do a thing. They didn't really do anything either, other than treat us like shit, but this is bad public relations. No wonder the tourists don't come here."

"I doubt they'll do anything worse than delay us," replied Karen.

"*Señora*, it is wise to be fearful, sometimes," advised Traci. "These days, it is difficult when people are angry. Some say this, some say that, but everyone wants it to be different. *Y todas las gentes siempre tienen miedo.*"

"Everybody is always afraid?" repeated Karen.

"*Sí, señora. Siempre.*"

They finished their packing in silence and loaded up the trunk.

Back on the road to *las Lagunas de Montebello,* Traci was soon smiling again. He asked them if they were going to camp at the *Lagunas.* He said they would drive by the prettiest lakes first, and he offered to find horses and a place to camp. Griffith was uncertain about the horses, but both Traci and Karen assured him they would be quite manageable.

So Traci took them on a driving tour of the Park. Over twenty-three square miles, and at an elevation of 5,000 feet, the forest was predominately pine and live oak. Underground rivers, caves, and stream beds connected the Park's sixty-eight small lakes. Some of the lakes stretched northwest across a wide valley, while others appeared around hairpin turns on dusty roads or were tucked away in tiny ravines. A dozen or more of them were brightly colored by the heavy calcite and metallic ores leeched from the thick, ancient limestone beds of the crumpled southern mountains.

At one of the larger, more remote lakes, *Laguna Tziscao,* straddling the Guatemalan border, they stopped. Griffith and Karen got out and stumbled down a rough, water-eroded trail to the shore. The sparkling, bright green lake was surrounded by the darker viridian of evergreens and mountain laurel. The air was cool with the scent of pine and cedar.

For the first time, they were alone, and the contrast was vivid. At the edge of the lake, they stood quietly by the clear water watching the colorful fish swim among the dead trees scattered along the rocky shoreline. Griffith traced the underwater path of a barred cichlid near the rocky shore. Around them, the cicadas, loud and continuous, were joined by other insect clicks and buzzes. The faint songs of birds, distant at first, drifted on the breeze toward them. Griffith nodded at each new song. Spying three vultures circling above the treetops, he was captivated by how easily his senses were filled with the gentle stimuli of nature. He stood in silence, absorbed and awed by this primeval scene.

A child-like urge to play filled him. He bent to pick up a rock, planning to skip it across the water. An old, rusty Coke can lay among the rocks, and the blue, plastic cap from a milk jug floated at the water's edge. He looked up into the woods. These pines, cedars, and live oaks clustered at this end of the lake were all second growth, or worse.

Apparently, empty of people did not necessarily mean empty of their effects, he thought cynically.

Traci honked the car horn and waved, so they climbed back to the road. Backtracking a few miles, they stopped at *Restaurante Bosque Azul* with its new, wood-frame dining room and large rose garden overlooking its namesake *laguna*. While Karen and Griffith sipped *refrescas*, Traci talked with the owner, *doña* María del Carmen al Borís, who told him they could rent horses near *Cinco Lagunas*, a dozen miles of narrow road from *Bosque Azul*.

The only other patrons were a few Mexicans—local workers, guessed Griffith. At that moment, he realized he actually enjoyed the possibility the two of them were the only visitors in all of Chiapas. Not likely, of course, but the thought generated a more romantic, more authentic experience for him. And to his honeymoon. Even the idea of riding and camping began to assume an exotic mystique.

"Karen, I have to admit this is very exciting," he confessed. "Everything's so new and stimulating. I feel like a giant sponge. We're really going to be alone in the rain forest, aren't we?"

He remembered his first camping experience with her along

the Appalachian Trail, and it had rained all weekend. But Karen had shown him how to make a comfortable site, and the two of them discovered each other during many hours together in their tent. Karen's spontaneity had so altered his life that, instead of his books and computer, his weekends had become devoted to whatever adventure caught her interest.

"I knew you'd love it, Grif, and the deeper into the jungle we get, the more you'll find to excite you. This is just beginning for us."

"Well, you're right so far. And I don't want to miss any of this."

On their way again, they drove past the tiny village of Emiliano Zapata, one of perhaps a hundred with that name throughout *la República*. The road worsened, and Traci swerved and dodged most of the ruts and rocks to maintain his speed. After winding through thick evergreen and oak forests, and passing several large cuts of downed timber, the dusty road finally left the forest.

They arrived at a small collection of plank houses clustered in the middle of a dry valley whose timber had been harvested years ago. This was San Antonio Buenavista, although the few *campesinos* who had not moved onto the big ranches to the north referred to it simply as Buenavista.

Buenavista was quiet. The dozen tin-roofed houses were small—only one appeared larger than a couple of rooms—without floors or glass in the windows. None had running water or electricity. Chickens and roosters milled about in front of the houses, listlessly picking through the weeds and dirt. A couple of scrawny dogs lay in the shade of one house. Several young children, dressed only in cotton blouses or tee-shirts, stopped playing as the taxi drove by. Karen waved, and the children ran into the road waving back.

When Traci pulled up at the last house, it was nearly noon. A small barn stood to the side, and several acres of meadow were crudely fenced around it. A young man, perhaps eighteen-years-old, came out of the barn carrying a rope bridle. Traci discussed the rental—Karen had said two nights—while she and Griffith unloaded their backpacks.

"It is all arranged for you," Traci told them. "Jesús says one hundred *pesos*, and the horses will carry enough corn in their saddle bags for three days, each. He says you may camp anywhere in the hills, in the forest. Do not cross any fences, and be careful when it rains. If you get lost, follow the road."

"*No problema*," said Karen. "*Muchas gracias*. This will be fun."

Jesús returned, leading two large, brown and white horses, one following the other, his reins tied to the tail of the leader. Nothing special, they seemed to Griffith. Just big. He petted the nearest horse lightly on the neck and noticed these horses were not in the best shape. The larger horse had an open sore in the right corner of his mouth, and shook his head in irritation whenever his bit was pulled that way. The other had a fist-sized sore on its hip with some green ointment rubbed in it.

Karen, talking gently to each animal, helped Jesús saddle the horses. When the horses were cinched, packed, and ready, Griffith paid the hundred *pesos*. Jesús stood silently staring at him, holding out the *pesos*, until Traci noticed the awkwardness.

"Ah, *cien pesos cada persona*, uh, each one."

Griffith smiled, and took out another hundred *pesos*. He gave the money to Jesús, and turned to pay Traci.

"*Ciento y veinte*, one hundred twenty *pesos*, Grif."

Griffith smiled at the pronunciation of his name, and asked, "*¿Cada persona?*"

They laughed, and Griffith tipped him an extra thirty pesos. Traci tried to refuse the tip, but Griffith insisted.

"*Muchas gracias, recien casados.* I will return *miercoles,* Wednesday, this time. *Vayan con Dios, amigos,*" he called as he turned his taxi around and drove back toward the *Lagunas.* They waved goodbye.

In the paddock, Jesús led the larger horse by the reins to Griffith and held the bit so Griffith could mount. Griffith chuckled to himself, thinking that Jesús must see how little experience Griffith has had with horses. Keeping an eye on everything Karen did, Griffith pleased himself by successfully mounting the beast on his first attempt. Once in the saddle, his horse, Robledo, continued to chew the grass at his hooves. Jesús told Karen to keep them tethered because they would probably return if left to graze freely. They thanked him, and Karen led them on her horse, Bellota, out of the paddock at a walk.

They turned north, along the dirt road beyond the village. They wore their backpacks, but had their tent and bedrolls tied over the saddlebags. The light blue, tropical sky was clear with only small, white puffs of cumulous cloud hugging the eastern horizon. Ahead of them a few miles, the valley narrowed as forested hills squeezed toward their trail from either side. Pastures were overgrown with second generation scrub pines, brush, ferns, and vines. Although the road was rough, with long ruts and potholes large enough to break a leg, the wide grassy shoulders provided room for the horses to walk single file.

The sun baked the short grasses and dusty road, and Griffith's shirt was soon soaked with perspiration. He was fully aware he was six feet off the ground on an animal weighing over half a ton. The slow, twisting rise and fall of the horse's motion brought back the visceral memory of his single encounter with the species many years ago at an earnestly forgotten Boy Scout camp. The weight of the pack and the width of the horse's back put added pressure on Griffith's tailbone and cramped his inner thighs. Reaching back, he grabbed the saddle to lift himself and readjust the pack. He put his hand on wood. The saddle was wooden! With only a thin cushion covering it. No, not a cushion at all, just a horsehide cover.

"Karen," he said, "these saddles are made of wood."

"I know. Doesn't that tell you something?"

"Yeah," he joked, "my butt is splintered. They actually use these things every day?"

"You'll get used to it, Grif. I can't imagine these poor folks ever being able to afford the luxury of a leather saddle."

"I'd think bareback might be better."

"Can't work a horse bareback very well."

Griffith settled into his saddle as comfortably as possible. After an hour or so of slow riding, they entered a young forest. Before long, a narrow stream joined them from the east. Heading upstream, they continued toward a small clearing surrounded by pines.

"Let's check out this spot," suggested Karen. "If we set our camp early, we'll have time to do some exploring this afternoon."

Griffith had no objections. He was certainly ready to get something to eat and drink and to give his backside a rest. The constant threat of falling off his horse was enervating and had begun to wear on his romantic sensitivities.

A small trail cut through the trees to the grassy clearing. It had a few exposed rocks, some scrub bushes, lots of fiddlehead ferns, and a couple of live oaks giving a little extra shade. Several flat spots looked like potential tent and cooking areas, so they tied their horses to graze at the edge of the clearing. Karen asked Griffith to pick a campsite and carry the gear while she got the horses some water and gave them a quick rubdown.

After walking across the entire site, Griffith finally chose a level spot across the clearing under some large pines. He found Karen's well-used portable ditching shovel among her other gear. Checking the hillside above them, the thickness of the grass cover, and the path of the sun, he began to dig.

When Karen finished with the horses, she nodded with approval—her tenderfoot had chosen the highest flat spot in the clearing. Since Griffith was into his engineering project, she went ahead and set the ground tarp, tent, and rain fly, and laid out their bedding and gear. She cleared a spot for a fire, organized food prep and cooking areas, and gathered some dry firewood. When she was done, she got the reverse osmosis water purifier out of the tent and filled their canteens with clear running, stream water.

With the water in, the tent and tarps secured, and firewood stacked, she surveyed Griffith's project as he finished connecting the left and right channels around the camp site. Above the tent, he had ditched to the right so any rain water would carry down the side of the hill. He sloped the ditch around the other side into the field and brought in a couple of side channels from the fire and the front of the camp site.

He stood and took off his glasses. Wiping the sweat from the lenses and out of his eyes, he walked over to her.

"An excellent camp, don't you think, love?" he asked. "I'm impressed, again, with how efficiently we work together. Look at that. Everything's set up. Actually, I'm impressed with you, Karen. You've got this camping routine down."

"Thank you, Grif. And your ditching project will definitely keep away anything short of the Flood."

"And even then. Notice that our gear would all get caught right down there in that laurel thicket. Everything else might find its way to the Gulf of Mexico, but if the laurel stand stands, we're okay."

"So we're set for a couple of days."

"Absolutely. This is great. Let's play. What do you want to do?"

"Well, let's get something to eat. I've got some fruit and trail mix here. Then we can take the horses and explore for a few hours before dark."

They ate a little and then added the trail food to the horses' saddlebags. Karen wore her fanny pouch with their money, the *pesos* and travelers' checks, and her passport. She clipped the canteen and purifier to her belt.

Griffith carried the other canteen and the small, detachable pack with toilet paper, flashlight, knife, lighter, a traveler's first aid kit, passport, and his travel guide. Lugging around a book was habitual for him, and after Esmeralda's lesson at last night's dinner, he wanted to read more about the history and culture of *la República*.

Karen checked her compass as they left the woods. Heading northeast, the dirt road wound beside the edge of the forest. A small stream tagged along the road, at times a few feet across, running and splashing over rocks, at other times, wider and lazier with just inches of clear, dark brown water. Mimosas, with their round pink flowers already in bloom, grew abundantly along the roadside. To the east, rolling hills and open fields of scrubby grasses and yucca stretched toward a range of small mountains a few miles distant.

Since leaving Buenavista they'd seen no one. Numerous lizards skittered across the road, and butterflies hovered in groups around the flowering hibiscus. Along the roadside was some trash, not a lot, but colored plastic bottles and crushed soda cans here and there poked through the grasses in the ditch. Occasionally small rodents, rabbits probably, or rats, would dart away into the fields when they approached. Only once did they hear a lone dog barking in the distance.

"Let's head that way, Grif," Karen said, pointing to a trail running across the open countryside.

They rode slowly through the scrubby fields in the rising afternoon heat for another hour. Near the eastern edge of the valley, a ceiba with its distinctive, umbrella-shaped foliage high in the tree, stood alone. Sacred to the Maya, it was the only live tree standing in the large, open field. Along a seasonal stream bed, a small stand of sycamore gave some little shade to a few birds. Swarms of mosquitoes hovered over large clusters of arrowhead ferns filling the moist depressions. Several egrets stood motionless some distance from them, and a half dozen vultures drifted on the thermals from the surrounding mountains. Perched on a high limb of an exposed dead tree, a red-tailed hawk surveyed his territory patiently.

At the edge of the valley, they rode into forest again and followed the trail as it gently climbed the mountain. More silk-cotton ceibas grew through the canopy. An occasional liana vine draped motionless above them. Growing through the shrub layer were numerous bull's horn acacias with their two large thorns at the base housing huge armies of protective ants. An insect hum filled the still air of the intensely green forest.

Griffith was enjoying the change under the canopy, especially how much cooler it had gotten out of the sun. He didn't notice the thunderhead clouds building as the afternoon sun baked the moisture off the large, timbered cuts of exposed earth. The rising heat sucked the moisture from the surrounding jungle, and by the time Griffith and Karen reached the top of the ridge, a strong wind was pushing a heavy line of squalls toward them.

They crossed the ridge and in front of them a swath of stumps was cut all the way across a valley. Rutted, dirt roads crisscrossed the barren ground. A few rusting tractors sat half-buried among abandoned stacks of weathered logs. On the scarred earth, vines and brush grew through the refuse and garbage that lay strewn around several rough, wooden shacks.

The rain line pounded across the small valley, obscuring the far side.

"Let's ride to one of those shacks," said Karen, "and wait this out."

"Do you think that would be all right? Suppose someone's there?"

"Then I'm sure they'll invite us in. This can't last long. We won't stay for dinner if you don't want, Griffith."

"That's funny, Karen, but why can't we just stay under the trees. I don't hear any thunder. Just the rain we're about to get soaked in."

The rain and wind gusted into his face with large, cold drops. For a moment the wind dropped to a whisper just before curtains of intense, heavy rain poured over them, one after another. The trail flooded, and rivulets quickly grew to small gushing streams. Griffith was dismayed at the fierceness of the fickle weather, the amount of instant mud, and the lack of visibility.

"We're going to get wet either way, Griffith. At least we'll be able to dry out under a roof. Come on, I don't see anyone down there anyway. Follow me."

"I can't see *anything* down there, Karen. This is some rain. Hey, Karen. Karen, wait!"

When Robledo saw Bellota gallop down the muddy trail into the rain, he decided not to be left behind. With Griffith gripping the reins and squeezing his thighs tightly, Robledo cantered through the downpour. At this gait, Griffith couldn't find the rhythm to keep his rear end from slamming into the wooden saddle with every other step.

Worried that Robledo might trip in the mud and break both their necks, he wanted the horse to slow down. He adjusted himself in the saddle to rein the animal in, but the momentary slackening of the reins meant something different to Robledo. Lowering his haunches, the horse leapt forward into a gallop.

Caught by the sudden change in gait, Griffith fell backward. Squeezing desperately with his thighs to hold on, his feet dangled loosely in the stirrups. He struggled to lift himself over the front of the saddle and regain some control. Just as he pulled himself upright, ready to lean forward into the bouncing saddle, a muscle over his left ribs grabbed back in resistance. For a moment he feared the muscle would give, and he'd fall back again, this time off Robledo. The horse's next step, however, slapped the saddle into Griffith, lifted him up, and planted him firmly upright. His feet were under him, but the injured muscle burned, cramping his left side.

To ease the pounding, Griffith leaned forward over his legs, crouching in the stirrups. And accidentally discovered the rhythm of Robledo's gallop. The pounding eased as he let the horse run under him. His head stopped bobbing, and muscles he didn't realize were tense, relaxed.

Amazed, he chanced to look up. His glasses had fogged up, and the rain blowing across his lenses turned his vision kaleidoscopic. He swallowed back the panic of blindness and looked down at Robledo's neck. Trusting his horse only because he had no choice, he let go of the fear.

Their speed was frightening enough, but if he kept his legs in synch with Robledo, the ride remained stable. And unquestionably exhilarating. Flying in rhythm with this powerful animal beneath him, they splashed across a wide, shallow stream surging with rainwater and raced through the downpour. Even with the pain in his side, and even in the rain, he was grinning.

Through the downpour they sped until the afternoon light abruptly darkened in front of them. Robledo stopped short, skidding to a halt in the mud. Griffith was thrown forward. His face slammed into Robledo's neck, his temple smacked the side of Robledo's jaw, and, with an iron grip on the reins, he flew out of the saddle.

Landing in the mud on both feet and jarring the aching muscle in his side, he stayed erect for only an instant. The mud offered no grip for his wet sneakers. He slid backward until he was face down in front of his horse, still holding the reins with one hand.

Karen stood beside Bellota in front of a rough shack and applauded.

Favoring his left side, he stood, careful not to slip back into the mud. He took off his glasses and held them out in the rain to wash them off. Letting go of the reins with a deliberate motion, he looked at Karen. With as much nonchalance as he could muster, he wiped the mud from his face and eyes. Karen, soaking wet, her eyes sparkling with glee and rainwater, restrained her laughter.

Griffith, on his honeymoon, thrown from a horse in the middle of a driving tropical rainstorm, and covered in mud, burst out laughing. He put his glasses back on to find one arm so bent the frames sat crookedly on his nose. Karen's laugh escaped to join his.

"Come on, let's get out of this," Karen panted. "Get your reins for me, would you?"

She tied Bellota's reins to a rough corner beam of the shack and took Robledo's from Griffith. She tied them to Bellota's tail as she'd seen Jesús do, and both horses moved against the building out of the wind.

The building's age was indeterminate. The rough-hewn

planking was gray and weather stained, and the nail heads had streaked the wood a deep, burnt red. Only four or five yards wide, it had no windows, at least on this side. Around the front corner, under the short eave, was the door with an old, wooden fruit crate for a step. On the other side of this shack, obscured by the heavy rain, were several other work sheds and a larger, decrepit bunkhouse. Karen and Griffith huddled under the eave next to the crate. The rain was driving in their faces.

"Well designed, don't you think?" asked Griffith sarcastically. "Front door facing the weather. So, what'll we do?"

"This is probably just a tool shed," answered Karen, her voice raised over the rain and wind. "Look, no windows, trash and rusting machinery everywhere. Let's go in."

"Karen, why don't you knock first? Just in case. I mean, this rain's not real comfortable, but I'd rather not just go in, you know, uninvited, in a foreign country."

She stepped onto the crate.

"Karen?"

"Yes, sure," she replied, knocking on the splintery door frame.

They waited a few seconds.

"Maybe a little louder," suggested Griffith.

Karen looked around, and then she pounded three times with her fist on the plank door. It swung open a few inches.

"Go ahead, look in," said Griffith. "I don't see anyone around. Why would there be? It's raining like hell. Everyone except us is inside."

The door was heavy, and the rusty hinges shrieked as Karen used both hands to push it open. She looked inside.

"*¿Hola?*" she said into the darkness.

"See anyone? Anything? Can we go in?"

"Yeah, let's go in."

Karen stepped up over the threshold onto a plank floor. The one window on the far side was boarded over, and the room was dark. The meager gray light from the doorway got lost in the bare room.

As Griffith stepped onto the crate, he heard Karen gasp.

"Oh, my God," she whispered. "Griffith, come here. Oh, God!"

Grabbing the door frame, he winced at the pain in his side and carefully pulled himself into the room. Standing in the faint light reflecting off the puddle at her feet, Karen was staring into a shadowy corner of the single room. Griffith stepped past her and followed her line of vision.

In the darkest corner, two small children sat motionless on the floor, back to back. Karen pushed the door the rest of the way open. Weak, gray light flowed across the room onto the tiny figures. They blinked at the light and averted their eyes. Blue bandannas were stuffed in their mouths and tied with several loops of hemp twine. The heavy baling line was also wrapped and knotted around their chests and legs.

"Oh, Christ," Griffith muttered. "This is not possible."

CHAPTER FIVE
RESCUE AND ESCAPE

The Rain Forest
West of the *Lagunas*
Monday afternoon

> I wake to sleep, and take my waking slow.
> I feel my fate in what I cannot fear.
> I learn by going where I have to go.
>   *The Waking*
>   Theodore Roethke
>   1908—1963

Griffith turned from the sight of the bound children and looked at Karen. She stood still, one hand holding the door, the other reaching toward the children. He put his hand on her outstretched arm.

"We have to go, Karen." His voice was soft, but shaking. Bile churned in his stomach. "Right now. Don't even think about it. We're in Mexico, Karen, not Charlottesville."

"Griffith, you know we can't leave them." Her voice was matter of fact.

"Yes, I know that. But we also cannot get involved in something like this. Whatever this might be. I can't imagine a single, positive outcome here."

"Griffith. Watch the door."

Karen approached the children.

"Karen! What are you doing?"

"I'm going to untie them. At least we can find out what happened."

She looked at him and nodded toward the door.

"Yes, of course, you're right. We can do that." He turned to the doorway, muttering to himself. "I'm sure it's really nothing. Nothing for us to worry about."

But Griffith *was* worried. The very idea of anyone restraining children like this scared him. And he knew it outraged Karen.

He looked at the rain spattering the floor inside the doorway. Leaning against the plank wall next to the door, he saw it. A rifle. An old, Russian-made, AK47 automatic rifle with its distinctive, curved banana clip.

The weight of his small daypack pressed his wet shirt into the raised flesh on his back. Despite his denial that this just wasn't possible, he had the keenest sense his and Karen's lives had just been significantly altered.

He glanced furtively outside the door. The rain still obscured everything. Behind him, first one voice, a young male voice, than an older girl's voice spoke rapidly until Karen interrupted them.

"*Por favor,*" Karen whispered, "*más despacio, niños.*"

"*¿Habla español, señora?*" asked the boy.

"*En inglés,* Tito," corrected the girl.

"*¿Habla inglés, señora?*" he asked sneering at the girl.

"Yes, *sí, hablo inglés,*" answered Karen as she untied the rough hemp line. "Better than Spanish."

"Please, *señora,* we must leave quickly," insisted the girl.

"You have a car?" asked Tito.

"No, we don't. Horses. We're camping. Why are you tied up like this? Who did this to you?"

"We've been kidnapped by Zapatista terrorists," Tito burst out. "They want to kill us, so we have to leave now."

"Kidnapped!" Karen exclaimed.

"Oh, Christ, Karen," pleaded Griffith across the room, "we've got to get out of here."

"Zapatistas?" asked Karen, incredulously. "Kidnapped the two of you? Why?"

"They were not Zapatistas, *señora*," responded the girl, mostly to Tito. "My brother hates the Zapatistas and believes everything our captors tell him."

"I do not," snapped Tito.

"Karen," interrupted Griffith, "we have to leave. Right now."

Karen looked at him in the doorway. He nodded toward the rifle.

"God, yes," she whispered. "Quiet, *niños*. We'd better go."

"*Señora*, I do not think you should tell me to be quiet," replied Tito bluntly. He finished untying the knot at his feet and stood up. Wearing his dirty, blue school shorts and jacket, he stood no more than four feet tall.

"Tito, be polite," insisted his sister.

When she stood, she unfolded catlike to a lean, fourteen-year-old, wiry and tall. Even though her white, cotton dress was torn and streaked brown with mud, she almost succeeded in looking detached from the unseemly elements of her predicament.

Griffith knew they had little time to act and no time to consider the consequences. And that was extremely difficult for him. Karen had no trouble reacting spontaneously, but his whole life involved questioning and relying on an academic approach to problems. Danger was not an academic pursuit. Now, without the luxury of time to think, he was caught by the obvious fact they were in a great deal of danger. And since the children were in greater jeopardy, he knew Karen would not leave them.

Reluctantly, he stepped out in the rain and untied Bellota's reins from the building. The young girl followed and while Griffith held the reins, she hurried back to loosen Robledo's reins from Bellota's tail. When Robledo jerked his head sideways and tugged against her lead, she grabbed his bit firmly and led him out into the slackening rain.

"I will not," came Tito's voice from behind Griffith, "and you cannot make me."

"Tito," he heard Karen say, "you can't take that with you."

Tito stood in the doorway holding the automatic rifle across his chest.

"It's too dangerous," she insisted. *"Muy peligroso."*

"I understand English, *señora*, and I will not put it down. They cannot shoot us without their guns."

"Christ Almighty," muttered Griffith. "Tito, put the rifle down. We have to leave now."

"You can leave the horses with us if you would like, and we will escape without you," said Tito in obvious reference to Griffith's reluctance.

Griffith was undone by Tito's unexpected truculence in the midst of his rescue. Standing in the rain, he just looked at Karen.

"Tito," said Karen, giving in, "keep the rifle until we get away. That way your kidnappers can't use it."

"The Zapatistas."

"Yes, whatever. You understand you must keep your hand away from the trigger. Now, get on the horse so we can get away."

"Of course, *señora*."

Without the least bit of hesitation, he took Robledo's reins from Griffith. When he tried lifting himself with the large rifle, the stirrup proved too high for him.

Griffith held out his hand.

"Give it right back to me," Tito demanded.

"Of course. Just get in the damn saddle, and let's go, okay?"

With a glare, Tito handed Griffith the rifle and climbed into the saddle. Griffith turned the rifle over, looking for the safety. He found a small lever above the trigger guard and clicked it down through two settings. Having no idea which was on or off, he flipped the metal bar back up, parallel to the barrel. Tito reached down for the rifle, and Griffith gave it to him.

When Griffith lifted his foot to the stirrup, Tito's was still in it. Griffith took the stirrup off and reached across Robledo's back. Grabbing the far side of the saddle, his right arm nudged Tito forward in the saddle as he lifted himself. As gently as he could, he swung his leg over, and landed behind Tito, bumping him farther forward in the saddle. The tip of his spine smacked the wood of the saddle.

"I apologize for my brother, *señora*," said the girl while lifting herself onto Bellota in front of Karen. "My name is Sara."

"I'm Karen, and that's Griffith. We're not from around here," she said with a small laugh.

"Shall I take the reins, Karen?"

"No, thanks. Let me for now."

She looked over her shoulder. Tito held his rifle firmly in front, and Griffith's arms were around him holding the reins. Griffith smiled grimly and nodded. Karen kicked Bellota gently forward. With Sara holding onto the mane, they leaned into Bellota's muddy canter away from the shack and back up the trail toward the forest.

As Griffith got Robledo turned around through the rain, he saw a door swing open at nearest shack, fifty feet away. Griffith kicked Robledo, and forgetting about the horse's mouth sore, snapped the reins. Robledo just stood still, shaking his head.

A man dressed in khaki strolled out under the cracked green plastic awning. He was looking down, buttoning his fly. Behind him, a young woman followed, buttoning the front of her faded, print dress. She glanced up through the rain and looked directly at Griffith and Tito. She flicked her eyes back to the man, then shook her head at Griffith. Turning around, she stepped back inside. The man continued to struggle with his fly.

Slack-reined, Griffith kicked Robledo's flanks hard. This time he was prepared when Robledo jumped to a gallop. Up the trail they went, rain in their faces, mud flying from hooves. With two of them riding, his side ached every time he hit the saddle.

The first time he slid forward to ease the pounding on his coccyx, Tito came down hard in his crotch, squeezing his testicles. The pain gagged him with nausea. Struggling to keep from throwing up, Griffith felt his panic quickening. He knew he wasn't going to vomit—he never did—but frightened by their cramped flight from imminent danger, Griffith wondered, in an odd flicker of lucidity, what form his panic might take: screaming fits, misdirected rage, or more probably, he thought, catatonia.

Then in that tiny instant of objectivity, the panic began to recede. *Just keep riding*, he heard in his head. *That's all.* Through the pain and into the mist and rain, they had to keep riding. A part of him was aware they could be shot in the back—would be shot if they were caught—but he also knew as they rode closer to the tree line and deeper into the rain, immediate discovery was becoming less of a possibility.

In the deluge of probable consequences ahead of them,

no acceptable outcome jumped to mind. The sum of negative choices gave way to a gripping fear. His life had had its sad and scary moments, the loss of his parents, the broken hearts common to everyone, but never had such dark possibilities dominated his vision. He shook his head in disbelief. It was his honeymoon, and his immediate future terrified him.

They just kept riding, back across the rushing stream, then uphill the way they had come. He looked up to see if Karen and Sara were in sight. His glasses were streaked brown with rain and spatterings of mud. Tito had his head down, over the rifle. Small clods of wet earth flew by, hitting Griffith's face and shoulders.

The rain eased dramatically, and the light dimmed. Griffith, still looking up, was smacked in the forehead with a needled branch. He mumbled a curse as Robledo slowed to a walk under the pines. Rubbing his forehead, he turned to look back down the hill. The rain had nearly ended. All seemed quiet around the logging outpost.

"We did it," whispered Tito, unnecessarily low.

"Do you think they know we're gone?" asked Sara.

"If not now, then soon," replied Griffith. "As we rode away, I saw someone come out of the next building. I guess he didn't see us in the rain."

"The next step, then," said Karen, "is to get you two somewhere safe. Where's your home?"

"*Señora*," asked Tito surprised, "do you not know who we are?"

"I'm afraid not, Tito."

"I am the son of *Presidente* Rodolfo Patrillo. Sara is my sister."

"*Presidente*?" repeated Griffith. "Like president. Your father is the President. Not of Mexico, I hope?"

"*Sí, de la República*. A very important man," replied Tito proudly.

"Oh, Christ in heaven. A political kidnapping."

"Grif, nothing's changed. We've still got to get them to safety."

"Then let's find the nearest police station."

"*Señor*," interrupted Sara. She was staring down at the camp

The others turned and looked down the trail. In a steady drizzle, two men, armed and in fatigues with bandoleers across their chests, were following another unarmed man. He was leading them to the shack where Tito and Sara had been restrained.

"They're about to find out," said Griffith, hoping his nervousness didn't show too much. "What's our plan now?"

"Keep riding," suggested Tito.

"Tito, look," said his sister pointing to the camp.

The men came out of the shack and slogged through the mud to the other shed where Griffith had seen the man and his camp girl. The first one unholstered a pistol, opened the door, and motioned inside. Three young, peasant women came out and huddled together under the faded, green awning. The unarmed man pointed to the middle woman.

Obviously upset, the *pistolero* spoke to the other armed man who then ran toward the largest of the buildings. Waving his handgun in the air, the *pistolero* struck the unarmed man with the back of his hand, then brandished the pistol toward the young camp girl. In the midst of his animated display of anger, he motioned for the woman to step forward. With deliberate menace, he pointed his pistol at her head.

From their wooded hillside, the four of them stared through the drizzle without a word. Before the gunshot's report reached them, they saw the puff of smoke and watched the woman's head jerk backward before she fell to the ground. The other two women scrambled, terrified and screaming, around the shack and disappeared into the brush.

"Oh my God," Karen whispered.

"He shot her," said Griffith incredulously.

Three more men ran from the largest building pulling on ammo vests. The *pistolero* gestured, and they scattered, one of them searching the site, looking in the mud, along the trail, and into the brush, while the others grabbed saddles from the camp girls' shack.

The leader shouted something to the unarmed man and turned away. Without looking back, he struck the man solidly across the face with his pistol, knocking him to his knees. The *pistolero* then strode off, heading to a pickup truck while the other man knelt in the mud, bloody hands covering his face.

The drizzle turned to rain again as dusk settled on the valley. Griffith crouched between his wife and the children, shivering as cold rainwater ran down his neck. The shot still echoed in his ears. He shook his head trying to erase the image of the young woman blown to the ground.

CHAPTER SIX
E-MAIL

El Palacio Nacional
Ciudad de México, D.F., México
Monday afternoon

> He knew human folly like the back of his hand,
> And was greatly interested in armies and fleets;
> When he laughed, respectable senators
> burst with laughter,
> And when he cried, the little children
> died in the streets.
>
> *Epitaph on a Tyrant*
> W. H. Auden
> 1907—1973

"Yes, within three days," said *Comandante* Bicho. "Friday, by the latest."

"But we haven't even received a ransom note," protested Patrillo. His voice was thick through the swollen sinuses of his broken nose. A dark yellow and purple bruise spread like a mask over his face.

"Your children will be in your arms this week, *Señor Presidente*. My men have discovered quite a bit since Saturday afternoon."

Although news of the kidnapping had been picked up by the international media, Patrillo still hadn't met with the press.

A statement had been released concerning the abduction and his family's plea to the kidnappers not to harm the children, but nothing had been said by his office regarding any role by the Zapatistas. From the questions they were getting, however, it was apparent the rumor was afoot.

"In fact," continued Bicho, "we have already traced the kidnappers escape route out of the city."

"That is very fast, *Comandante*."

"It was not difficult, *Señor Presidente*. The people who occupy the nearby shops were... cooperative."

"*Comandante*," asked Patrillo, "how does that help us? We need information. Who are they? Where are they hiding?"

"From the descriptions we've obtained," replied Bicho, "it's obvious this was a Zapatista operation. Their dress and the outdated shotgun leave little doubt. In addition, a witness said she recognized the accent of one of them—from the highlands near her home in Altimirano."

"How soon will you know their whereabouts?"

"Perhaps sooner than you think. I have been able to utilize satellite technology to track your children."

"Excellent," said Patrillo. "You're tracking my children with a satellite?"

"A few contacts have proved useful. But I needed to verify where your children were being taken, so I had some artillery and several squads seen on the roads around Altimirano. At the same time, we had rumors circulated we knew the location of the kidnapper's camp. I figured that might get them to move the children to a new location. With that assumption, I obtained access to some satellite imagery."

Bicho pulled three large, dark photographs from his briefcase. He slid them across to the President and pointed at the top one.

"Right there."

Patrillo loved the advantages technology gave them. He eagerly spread the photos out before him. On all three, splotches of dark, irregular shadows were interspersed with fuzzy dots, blurs, and streaks of light gray.

"Can you explain this?" asked Patrillo.

"Yes, of course."

Stretching his head forward, he took out a pen and pointed the nib at a meandering, dark line.

"That squiggly line is the *Río Tzaconeja*, and those bright spots, that's Altimirano."

He indicated a tiny grouping of lights near the center of the top photograph. He pointed to a similar cluster of lights closer to the edge of the second photograph.

"And there."

He repeated that with the third photograph, where the lights were even closer to the edge.

"Now, look at these very small dots of gray to the east in this first photo."

He pointed to the right of the lights of Altimirano.

"In each of these successive photos, that group moved east into the lowland jungle. In fact, in the last picture, an hour before dawn, you can see they are headed toward the narrow valley of the *Río Colorado*."

"Those are men?" Patrillo asked.

"Probably fifty men, yes."

"I'm amazed," said Patrillo. "Are my children with them?"

"Perhaps."

"So what do you propose, *Comandante*?"

"As soon as we establish the location of their camp, we will secretly move our men into position, efficiently remove your children, and secure the camp and the perpetrators by force.

Very fast and very effective. Sir, my heart is out to you and your family. Tell your wife we will soon have her children home."

Patrillo appreciated the sentiment, but he didn't doubt Bicho's one-pointed perspective as *Comandante de la Policía Judicial Federal*. Given that Bicho had once been the Zapatistas' hostage, Patrillo understood the *Comandante*'s intense desire to repay those who had humiliated him, the top police officer in the country. After all, he'd spent over a month in the jungle because negotiations for his release had gone nowhere.

"Thank you, *Comandante*. I will pass that on to her. I have another question. Are we not going to negotiate with the kidnappers? At least before we use force? Perhaps we can avoid bloodshed."

"The sooner we can secure your children, the less danger, don't you agree?"

"Yes. There is, however, a thin line between urgency and haste."

Bicho responded with a small smile.

"Certainly. And if these terrorists want to negotiate a political or monetary settlement, that will be for you to decide. But while you negotiate, allowing them time to generate public sentiment for their cause, we'll backdoor them and secure the children within a few days."

"Yes, you said that."

"Good, then it's settled," decided the *Comandante*. "We cannot wait to hear from them before we act."

Patrillo heard the professional resolve in Bicho's voice. The man could be ruthless, and it showed in the set of his long jaw and the intensity of his dark eyes.

"*Señor Presidente*," Bicho continued, "the children are the first concern, as you've said, but with the Zapatistas involved, you must understand there are other issues."

"Obviously."

"I have considered them, as well, in our plan, *Señor Presidente*. Since the Zapatistas rely on the international media for their exposure, they will try to manipulate the press themselves. It's necessary for us to generate public sympathy for the children and minimize any political demands you might receive from the terrorists. We must determine the content of the news going out."

Patrillo nodded. That would simply be a matter of reminding the television and radio station owners and senior newspaper editors of the comfortable relation they've had with Patrillo's office. They all tacitly understood the government controlled their licenses.

"I think," added Bicho, "we have already won the first battle for the press. This morning's lead story centered on the injuries you and your wife sustained trying to protect your children."

"But my wife…"

Bicho held up his hand.

"They have a photo of you being assisted to the ambulance. To continue, if I may? The political consequences cannot be overstated. If we get your children back safely, we reap many benefits beyond their lives. You can control the political process much more effectively if the terrorist element is discredited, or even eliminated.

"They are the ones who have chosen this criminal path we warned you and your predecessor about. And now you and your family are victims of their crimes, just like the numerous Chiapañecos who have suffered their thievery, kidnappings, and brainwashing for years. Now we must be part of the solution, or this criminal element will destroy the stability you have given *la República*. They threaten more than just your children."

"A good speech, *Comandante*, but I'll be the judge of what

we might gain," replied the President. "And what we gain is less important than my children's lives."

"Of course, *Señor Presidente*. Forgive me. Besides the capture of the kidnappers, the return of your children is my primary intention."

"Yes, yes. Now then, once you locate my children, what's your plan?"

"*Señor Presidente*, great detail is required in planning such an operation. Unfortunately, I don't have maps of the region with me. I can only approximate our plans for you."

"One moment, *Comandante*. I believe I can get your maps."

Patrillo pressed a button on the desk intercom, and an aide entered from a side door. Patrillo told him what they needed, and the young man crossed to the large roll top desk dominating one wall. He opened the desk with a swoosh of wooden slats. A bright red screen saver peered out. The aide hit a few keys and clicked his mouse. A second monitor blinked on.

Presidente Patrillo, known in the press as the First Technocrat, believed that if *la República* were to advance as a First World country, growth technologies were vital. To assure his office and staff would be able to compete in the twenty-first century, he'd had the entire building wired as a Net server, getting TeleMex to install T3 data phone lines. This particular station, with its Pentium IV processor, 128 megs of RAM, 13.3 gigs of storage, high-speed DSL modem and fax with a dedicated ISDN hookup, and twin, flat 19 inch monitors, was limited to himself, this aide, and at their insistence, his two oldest children, Sara and Tito.

"Topo, *Señor Comandante*?" asked the aide.

"Yes, what is it?"

"Your topographical map. What region, *señor*?"

Bicho hesitated and then turned to Patrillo. He nodded toward the aide.

"Is he cleared?"

"*Comandante*," replied the President, "meet *Señor* Manuel Ramirez. With Manuel's knowledge of our systems, if he weren't secure, he could bring down the government."

"An exaggeration, I trust."

"The region, *Comandante*," said Patrillo.

"Yes. Then I need eastern Chiapas, east of San Cristóbal to the border, north to Palenque, south to Comitán."

"Villages, too?" Ramirez clicked his mouse a few times.

"Yes, of course."

"And roads, trails, airfields, a few schools, the forested and cleared areas, seasonal stream beds, drilling sites…," he continued to use the mouse clicker. "A large area, *Comandante*. This will require several pages."

The printer heads shifted. Four pale green topographical maps of the mountains and valleys slowly scrolled out. Tight elevation lines indicated the steepness of the mountain sides. Dotted lines traced the seasonal roads connecting most of the villages. To the west and north, the roads and villages were larger and more frequent. Large white areas revealed the cleared valleys of the *latifundista* ranches. Fifty miles east of San Cristóbal, the tiny town of Altimirano sat atop the jungle highlands, over six thousand feet above the vast rain forest extending deep into Guatemala. To the south and east, *Laguna Miramar*, a small circular lake, was the single, notable geological feature. Except for the lake, the easternmost region was little more than empty green valleys, a few mountains, and an occasional village name.

"Here you are, sir," he said, handing the maps to the *Comandante*. "Your topos."

Bicho took the maps and scanned them quickly.

"Ah, yes, look here," he said, pointing to the river valleys flowing east from Altimirano along either side of the *Sierra*

Corralchen. "It's most likely they will move their forces, and the children, down one of these valleys, either the *Río Jatate* or the *Río Tzaconeja* to the south. Note the lack of roads. But my agents will locate the children and the rebel concentrations.

"Now, if you care to follow the tactics we've tentatively prepared, let's use one of their rebel leader's favorite metaphors. *Subcomandante* Marcos enjoys chess, I understand. So, assume they have our king and queen pawns—your children—in one of the villages above the *Río Jatate*. The exact village will be targeted precisely before we move. We'll create some engagement from the other side of the *Sierra Corralchen* along the *Tzaconeja*, a feint with one of our rooks to attract their attention. They will move their captured pawns away from the perceived threat directly toward our waiting knights along the only escape route. We will have both the children and their kidnappers. Checkmate. Any questions, *Señor Presidente*?"

"This will require accurate reconnaissance and very rapid response in the jungle, won't it?"

"Why is it, do you suppose, *Señor Presidente*, so many believe the police to be incompetent, thuggish buffoons incapable of subtlety or sophistication? Our enemies, all those who would destroy your government and our country, may believe we're uneducated Third World thinkers, but we'll be using computers and satellites in their jungle to defeat them. As long as everyone continues to underestimate me..."

"Excuse me, *Señor Presidente*?" interrupted Ramirez, still at the keyboard.

"Yes, Manuel."

"I believe we have a message from the kidnappers."

"What?" shouted the President. "Where is it?"

"E-mail, sir. We have an electronic mail message from *white@comunique.com* called 'Our move'."

"Read it!" he urged.

"Sir. If I may..." hesitated Manuel.

"May what?" he asked. "What's the problem?"

"I think I should tag this message before we download it. I'm not comfortable with this."

"Why? It's not a bomb, is it?" asked the President.

"No, sir. Not that kind, anyway. But it could be more than a simple message."

As Ramirez spoke, he worked the keyboard, looking for links to establish some source, some indication whether the message was authentic and whether it was bugged.

"What more could be there?" asked Patrillo. "I don't understand. Is there a message or not? Is it from the kidnappers?"

"It's possible, *Señor Presidente*," explained Ramirez, "to include tag-along viruses or worms in electronic messages which could be added to our system without our knowledge. Even with our virus scans and firewalls, a new bug could affect our programs, permanently alter any of our drives, or even destroy our processors. Just being cautious."

"Smart of you, Ramirez," added Bicho. "Even police files are targets these days. Inspired by the example of our First Technocrat, I had our computer experts overwrite encryption codes into our systems. I've even dabbled in some cryptography myself."

"Periodic algorithms, *señor*?" asked Ramirez as he typed.

Shaking his head ambiguously, Bicho didn't answer.

"Anyway," said Ramirez, "I think I can bring the mail up safely. I'll need some more time to trace the source, but I can find it. I'll send their message to 'number two' while I work at this monitor."

The screen saver on the right monitor blinked out, and

the first communication from the kidnappers scrolled onto the screen. The President, his eyes wide and anxious, leaned over his aide.

```
    MAIL>
    From: subcomandante insurgente
    <white@comunique.com>
    To: Presidente Rodolfo Patrillo Sonador
    <www.ejec1.eumfed.gob.mx>
    Subject: our move
    MessageIO:<Pine.fed/.4.91.966278094357.933
38D
    100000@ comunique.com.net>
    MIME—Version: 1.0
    Context-type: TEXT/PLAIN; charset = EUM—
ASCII

    The game is afoot. Excellent first move re
the press.
    Our move.
    We have two demands.
    One for each child.
    e[
    Number one: announce the following—You,
Presidente Patrillo, will actively work
toward the immediate implementation of ALL
the points of the First, Second, Third, and
Fourth Declarations of the Lacandon Jungle.
    You will seek nullification of NAFTA.

    You will announce the suspension of all
elections in the state of Chiapas until all
Chiapañecos, independently counted, have
voted in autonomous village elections for new
leaders for all offices.
    [;2h
    Completion of the above will guarantee
the safety of the child of your choice.
Verification will be through publication of
the above in La Jornada.

        Press RETURN for more>
```

BLOOD OF THE EARTH

"More!" cried the President. "This is unbelievable. What about my other child?"

"There!" announced *Comandante* Bicho. "Any questions about the identity of the kidnappers now? We were obviously on the right trail from the beginning."

"What about my daughter?" demanded Patrillo.

Ramirez hit 'enter'.

```
MAIL>
One caveat.
]f
Any hint your actions have been coerced
through such heinous acts as kidnapping,
blackmail, extortion, or any other felonious
action will ENDANGER the relationship that
your children and I have established.

If you do not believe we are serious, I
will send you your daughter's underwear?
It smells of fear.

To ensure you understand the lives of
your children, and all the children of la
República, are at stake, a second demand must
also be met.
[;k
Number two: US$250 million will be
deposited in an account of our choice, in the
country of our choice, at a time we choose.
You must have the money available for
electronic transfer within five days.

You have until Friday, 9:00 AM to save the
life of your other child.
;e]3
You may release this second demand to the
press at your discretion.
However, should any judicial, military,
or paramilitary retaliation be directed at
anyone in our movement, your children will
```

```
not understand the sacrifice of two small
pieces for the greater good of the game.

    %[:
    Your move, Black.

    White
    3132976132535611113672532472324136122557913
7127157137313
    7[7m Exit [m8

    no carrier
```

"Unbelievable!" exclaimed the President.

"Common criminals," reiterated Bicho.

Ramirez tapped a few keys and slid a floppy into his A: drive.

"What are you doing?" asked the *Comandante*.

"Nothing," he said absently. "Just a back-up. Look here, this is interesting. The format of this e-mail is really archaic. A couple of generations, at least."

"What does that mean?" asked Patrillo.

"I'm not sure, sir, but it doesn't look like anything I've used for years. Maybe I can trace it that way."

His fingers pattered over the keys.

"Okay then," said *Comandante* Bicho, pacing in short, rapid strides, first three steps one way, then pivoting back for three more. "Let's focus on priorities here. You must now decide whether we're acting for the purpose of a negotiated release or for release and capture."

"We cannot settle for anything less," stated the President, "than the release of my children and the capture of these terrorists. Go ahead with your plan to entrap the kidnappers, *Comandante* Bicho. But if you're not ready by Friday, we'll have to arrange to transfer the money in exchange for my children."

"Excuse me," said Bicho, "but I do not believe these terrorists will be very willing to negotiate. I know their kind."

"They're just going to have to, Bicho."

"Can you afford to lose your children and your money? To ensure you don't lose either, we'll have to strike before the actual exchange."

"If you're ready," decided Patrillo, "then we'll do that, *Comandante*. But you must be absolutely sure before you strike. I would rather lose all my money than my children."

"*Señor Presidente*," said Bicho. His tone changed, more concerned than officious. "I think I can help you with the second demand."

"*Señor*," replied the President, "don't tell me your police salary has made you rich. I wouldn't want to hear that."

"Certainly not," answered Bicho indignantly, "but I have made some initial inquiries. A number of powerful men are sensitive to your situation *and* to the political realities of dealing with these Zapatista criminals. I believe these men would raise sufficient monetary guarantees to cover the ransom demands."

"The entire amount? Really?" Patrillo was obviously pleased with this idea. "That would solve one of our problems. Who are these wealthy patrons?"

"Some of the Chiapañeco *latifundistas* are willing to contribute to the return of your children."

"The *latifundistas*?" he asked. "They would risk their wealth for two children? What do they expect in return for their support?"

"Capture of the terrorists and the return of their money. Other than those two things, a return to normalcy is all they seek. They have been threatened by these terrorists for years. Some of them have been driven off their ranches, others lost their livelihood, their homes, everything. They would see justice done. Nothing more."

"Fine," Patrillo answered.

"I beg your pardon?" said a surprised Bicho.

"I said that's fine. I'll set up an escrow account. Arrange for these men to transfer whatever they can to that account. Then continue your search for my children. And keep me informed."

"Of course, *Señor Presidente*," said Bicho, obviously pleased. "I'll take care of it personally."

"Excuse me," interrupted Ramirez,r terminal. "I have something here."

"Another message?" asked Patrillo, surprised.

"I think so," Ramirez hesitated. "A new icon just appeared."

He clicked the icon. The screen glowed in bright magenta. Blinking in the center were the words:

✻✻✻

YOUR MOVE.

✻✻✻

"It's a trap." muttered Ramirez.

"A trap, Manuel?" asked the President.

"I believe so. And now I've already downloaded it. Damn!"

"How are you going to find out without accessing it?" asked Bicho, his fingers lightly tapping the edge of the desk. "What are you waiting for?"

"*Comandante*," Manuel said softly, "just a minute, all right. Let me think this through."

Bicho cocked his head sideways. "*Señor* Ramirez, your hesitation may mean many things, but most assuredly, it is giving our mutual enemy an opportunity to erase his tracks. I strongly suggest you open that file now."

"*Comandante* Bicho," interrupted the President, "let the man do his work. He is very good at it, and I trust his judgment."

"No, please," replied Ramirez artificially, "it's all right, really. I'll open it for *Comandante* Bicho." Then, to Bicho, he said, "Let's find out how good their hacker is."

Ramirez ejected the A: drive disk, stuck it in his shirt pocket, and took a deep breath. He hit a few keys, paused, and then pressed "enter".

***

OOPS!
WRONG MOVE.

***

"Shit," he cursed under his breath.

The screen flashed blindingly white. From a pinpoint in the center, a rainbow of pulsating arcs spiraled outward. Ramirez typed frantically, ignoring the spinning wheels flooding the screen with pixils of iridescent prominences.

"What's going on, Manuel?" asked the President.

"Chernobyl," he said quietly and kept typing.

"What?"

As the psychedelic display intensified, the voice of dead rock and roller Jim Morrison intoned, "This... is... the... end,... my friend."

Ramirez lifted his fingers from the keyboard. He slumped back in his chair and watched the dizzying display.

"Why did you stop?" asked the *Comandante*.

Ramirez looked at him as if he were a child.

The fiery brilliance finally burned itself out, leaving a dead, flat grayness. Morrison's voice wound down like an old, crank phonograph. When the last faint overtone echoed away, only the whirring of the tower's drives spun on. After an instant of gray silence, a mish-mash of Greek and Roman letters jumbled with mathematical and keyboard symbols—the vocabulary of the microchip trying to save itself—began scrolling down the screen, white on black. Slowly at first, then faster and faster until they became a blur. Finally, with an audible thump from the tower, everything went blank and silent. Nothing more happened.

After a few moments, both the President and the *Comandante* began to move again. They looked at each other, then at Ramirez who continued to stare at his screen.

"How bad is it?" asked Patrillo.

"Nothing to ask about," replied a subdued Ramirez. "We've been nuked. The whole damn system. Nothing but a useless copy of the ransom note." He tossed the disk on the desk. "I can't believe it."

"*Señor* Ramirez," asked the *Comandante*, "why are you upset with yourself?"

"Because," he replied with some antagonism in his voice, "now I can't possibly trace the source of the sabotage. Damn, I thought I had fail-safe protections against this sort of invasion. How the hell did they get in?"

"*Señor Presidente*," said Bicho twisting his head toward Patrillo, "this threat is far greater than even I anticipated."

"Greater than my children's lives and the stability of the government? Explain yourself, *Comandante*."

"The sophistication of this attack makes it apparent the Zapatistas will not only keep the ransom and your children, but international resources must be abetting this crime. They intend to force you, or your government, that is, to send the military into the jungle after them. Remember it has always been their ultimate goal to get us to break our word and attack them. I believe they want *you* to start a civil war."

"Quite an intuitive leap, *Comandante*. And since you spent some time as their unwanted guest yourself several years ago, I assume you have some ideas on how to avoid that and still rescue my children?"

"Oh, *Señor Presidente*, do not doubt what I learned as their hostage. I have not forgotten. Nor have the *latifundistas* who, in addition to the ransom money, have offered the services of their *guardias blancas*. With their knowledge of the terrain and our satellites and computers, we will outflank the terrorists, then surround and isolate them. We'll be able to remove the children under threat of annihilation of this rag-tag Zapatista army of wooden guns and school teachers."

"This is a very aggressive plan," said Patrillo.

"*Señor Presidente*, it's your call. Naturally, armed engagement will be minimized since they will not allow themselves to be eliminated. Terrorist groups never do. They'll want to avoid annihilation, so they'll accept surrender in exchange for any guarantee of inclusion in the political process, which in turn will secure the release of your children."

"But, *Comandante*," insisted the President, "they don't want to be part of the political process. They've retained their arms, they say, until the *indígena* become part of the political process."

"It would be presumptuous of me to lecture *el Presidente* on history, but neo-revolutionary movements always use similar tactics to gain support. Until they achieve real political power, that is. At any rate, we need to be prepared to counter any tactic they devise. With the *guardias blancas* already organized in the lowlands, they'll inform us of any undue activity. I'll use the *PJF* to investigate, infiltrate, and eliminate the threat to the children and the nation. Once their leaders are behind bars, this kind of terrorism will stop."

"Enough," said the President. "It's agreed. Set up your plan, and find my children. If the children aren't released, force their hand."

"I will also pray for your children, *Señor Presidente*."

"Yes, do that. I'm sure it will help."

CHAPTER SEVEN
DEMONS IN THE NIGHT

En la Selva
near the Guatemalan border
Monday night

> When your Daemon is in charge, do not try to think consciously. Drift, wait, and obey.
> *Something of Myself for My Friends Known and Unknown*
> Rudyard Kipling
> 1865—1936

In the growing dusk, they watched the kidnappers mount their horses and ride toward the dirt road out of the north end of the valley. An old, beat-up, white pickup truck sped from behind one of the shacks, bounced past the horsemen, and rattled into the distant forest.

"Now what?" Griffith asked.

"They'll be after us soon," said Sara.

"Of course they will, Sara," replied Tito. "They already are."

"Let's get mounted again," said Karen, "and head to our camp. We'll get our gear and ride back toward the *Lagunas*."

"*Lagunas*? What *lagunas*?" asked Sara.

"*Montebello*," answered Karen. "Let's go."

"See," said Sara to her brother, "I told you not to believe everything they told you. We're not even close to Altimirano."

"That doesn't mean they're not Zapatistas," countered Tito.

"Tito, Marcos would never let the Zapatistas kidnap us."

"Marcos wouldn't," taunted Tito. "You're in love with him, that's all. Just like all the women."

"Tito, that's not true. You know I'm not interested in politics."

"Children," interrupted Karen, "let's get out of here first."

Griffith had already mounted and was holding his hand out for Tito. Tito handed him the AK47 and hauled himself into the saddle by dragging his muddy shoe across Griffith's lap. Once seated, he took the automatic rifle back and hugged it to his chest.

Through the darkening forest, the horses began the climb to the crest. At the top, Griffith looked back and saw nothing but the deep shadows of the trees and brush.

"Karen," said Griffith, "it's still several hours to our camp. Do you think we can find it once it gets dark."

"I think so. The moon's up already, and I've got my compass. But let's follow the trail out of the woods and stop to eat a little. We'll talk then."

They let the horses walk down the hillside. When they reached the bottom and the woods opened up, they halted. Karen asked Sara and Tito to feed the horses. The children began hand-feeding them some of the corn from the saddle bags while she and Griffith walked along the path into the open.

"Karen," said Griffith when they were out of earshot of the children, "we're in a lot of trouble. Whether their kidnappers were Zapatistas or not, I'm sure they won't hesitate to kill us to get the children back."

"I know, Griffith. But what choice did we have? We couldn't leave them!"

"That was a choice, yes, Karen. Unfortunately, not the one we took."

"Griffith?"

"No, you're right. I don't know if we could have done anything else, but we did have a choice. As if that will give us any comfort when things fall apart here."

"Well, they won't. I'm sure of it. We did the right thing. You'll see. And you did great, too. You handled Robledo like a jockey."

"The other way around, I think."

With his hands on his hips, he bent over, stretching the tense, abused muscles over his left rib cage. When the back of his trousers pulled free from the raw skin at the base of his spine, he wished he'd worn underwear. Sighing, he shook his head and smiled grimly.

"So, what do you think our options are from here?" he asked.

"Our options? Well, head back to camp and Jesús's village, I suppose, although I'm not so sure how much good that'll do us. No phones, remember."

"Right," replied Griffith. "I wonder if we could get a car or truck. Do you remember seeing anything there?"

"No, but that doesn't mean there isn't one. Could have been off to work. I'm sure there must be at least one. Then, we'll head back to the *Lagunas*."

"The restaurant. They'll probably have a phone."

"All right," agreed Karen. "That's an option. Certainly people would have heard about this kidnapping. President's kids and all."

"I'll bet that's the reason we were stopped on the highway," concluded Griffith. "I wonder why Traci didn't mention the kidnapping."

"Probably didn't want to scare away paying customers."

"Karen, what if the kidnappers cover the roads out of here?"

"Would they do that?"

"Think about it," he said. "Why wouldn't they? They seemed pretty desperate."

"I know. I can't believe he shot that girl."

"Karen?"

"And the children saw him do it."

"Karen, we can't think that way. I know we were right to grab the children and run, but we've got to give some thought to everything we do from now on."

"Right. Right. So what if the roads *are* watched?"

"I don't know," he admitted. "Keep the horses, I guess."

"Let's ride cross country until we find another village and a phone or a vehicle. Head off in some unexpected direction."

"An unexpected direction. Does that mean you're as scared as I am?"

"Yes, Griffith, I am afraid. But we can't let that stop us."

"Okay, so we go another way," he conceded. "That's fine. When we get to a village, who do we call? What do we do?"

"Find the police?"

"You mean like the *PJF* we met this morning?"

"Isn't that what you wanted?" she asked.

"Suppose they choose not to believe us right away?" he asked. "They might assume we're the kidnappers."

"*Gringo* prejudices, Grif?"

"Perhaps. How about we get the kids to phone their father? He is the President."

"That's a good idea." agreed Karen. "Go straight to the top. Okay, I like it. That's our plan, then."

"Which way?"

"Well, Grif, if we're going to be paranoid, let's not go toward our camp or Jesús' place. East is the rain forest. That might be safe."

"Back past the logging camp?" asked Griffith.

"Why not? It's dark now. So what's in your pack? Can we make it a few days?"

"Not much food, I'm afraid. Some trail mix, a couple of small boxes of raisins. Some of those brown bananas. I tossed in your mag light, toilet paper, a pocketknife, my book, uh, let's see, I don't know, a lighter maybe. And our tiny first aid kit."

"That's excellent. With the water purifier and compass, we'll get along fine."

From the edge of the forest, the horses shook their heads in annoyance. A deep, bass vibration, faint but gathering strength, passed through Griffith's bones. As the volume increased, the sound took on a rhythmic thumping quality. From over the mountains to the west, the distinct rotary chop of a helicopter rose. The bright, white eye of a single spotlight broke into the jungle night at the western edge of the valley.

Griffith stood still, watching the aircraft fly low over the valley toward them. Sara grabbed both reins and led the horses into the forest. By the time she got the horses under the trees, Karen was there to help tether them.

"Where's Tito?" asked Karen.

Sara pointed to him standing in the field, clumsily aiming the rifle at the incoming helicopter. Karen ran over to him. Just before she grabbed the boy, she stopped short.

"Tito," she said calmly, "let's not give our position away. Come with me and hide in the woods."

The weight of the rifle was too much for Tito, and he lowered it. He turned to Karen, then back to the helicopter.

The heavy wump-wump echoed across the valley, the decibels increasing rapidly as it approached.

"Good idea," he said at last. *"A la selva. Vámanos."*

The four of them sat in the grasses under the trees as the helicopter powered toward them. Its spotlight cut a narrow path across the floor of the valley, and the roar of the engines pounded on their eardrums. The horses stamped their hooves and shook their heads in mutual irritation. When the helicopter got within a hundred yards, it angled to their right and roared by them. It disappeared over the mountain toward the logging camp.

"Helicopters?" questioned Karen. "This fast?"

"The kidnappers are using helicopters?" repeated Griffith, mostly to himself. "Karen, should we... I mean, wouldn't it be better if we kept moving?"

"Sí," agreed Tito, "it would be best to move at night."

"¿Por qué, Tito?" asked his sister.

"Because they can't see us. Aren't you supposed to speak English for the *gringos*?"

"Tito!"

"Sara," interjected Karen, "it's all right. Tito and Griffith may be right. That helicopter means they've got lots more resources than we saw in the camp. So I think you're right, Grif—we'd better not try to return to Buenavista. But we should go ahead and eat some of the trail food. We might have to keep moving for a while."

"Where's Buenavista?" asked Sara.

"Yes, let's eat something," agreed Tito. *"Tengo hambre."*

"That's where we got the horses," said Karen answering Sara, "but there's no electricity or phones. And Grif and I don't like our chances of being spotted along the road. Yes, Tito, I'm hungry, too."

Griffith admired Karen's ability to keep focused, calmly

answering both children. And even with her tendency to act spontaneously, he trusted her instincts. And so, it seemed, did the children.

He took a deep breath and tried to relax the knot in his stomach. Stretching the aching muscle pull on his left side, he discovered his tailbone really hurt. The saddle sores.

He settled himself on his right hip, and together, the four of them shared the trail mix and the soft, brown plantains. The plantain's taste surprised Griffith; it was not like banana. In fact, it was rather tasteless, leaving a bitter film on his palate. When he mentioned it, Sara pointed out that plantains are normally cooked first.

He watched Karen as she rested quietly, her back against a tree, eating a handful of trail mix. He remembered her stories of climbing Mount Washington—in the winter, no less—and of hiking several hundred miles of the Appalachian Trail. She'd lifeguarded at Virginia Beach and even sailed through gale force winds on the Chesapeake Bay. Since childhood, her parents had made sure she'd been exposed to enough opportunities, both academically and athletically, to develop plenty of self-confidence.

Despite the variety of outdoor experiences she'd had, the frightened knot in his intestines reminded him they'd gotten caught up in something far more than an "outdoor experience". He cringed at the thought of all the unfamiliar demons lurking under the dark blanket of the jungle night.

"Are we ready?" Karen asked, her voice steady.

"Which way?" asked Sara as she checked Bellota's cinch.

Tito answered, "I think we should go to that village."

"I'm afraid, Tito," replied Griffith, "your kidnappers will probably be watching the road. I think we're the only *norteamericanos* around here, so they probably know about us, as well."

"Here's a thought," added Karen. "What if the helicopter *was* looking for you two? I mean, not to re-capture, but to rescue."

"*Sí*," added Tito, "it looked military. I'm sure my father would have the military out looking for us."

"That's possible, I suppose," said Griffith, "but how likely is it we rescued you two just before the government arrived? And if the helicopter does land at the camp, how would we know whose side they're on, anyway?"

"Let's go that way, after the helicopter," said Tito excitedly.

"Back to the camp, Tito?" Sara was incredulous.

"Tito, weren't you about to shoot the chopper down?" asked Griffith.

"Only if they attacked us."

"Good thinking."

"Actually," said Karen, "if we're quiet, we could easily get close enough to find out if the helicopter is friendly. Maybe get out of this tonight. And if not, we could just slip on past the camp in the dark, ride up the next mountain, and find a road heading south."

"Sounds like a plan to me," said Griffith.

"Karen," Sara asked as she mounted Bellota, "why south?"

"I don't think your kidnappers would expect us to head in that direction."

Karen finished checking Robledo's tack and helped Tito, still holding his rifle, into the saddle.

"Let's go, then," announced Tito. "I'm ready,"

"Shh, Tito," admonished his sister. "*Sí*, Karen, I trust you. Let's go," she whispered.

Once Griffith was in his saddle behind Tito, Karen mounted Bellota with Sara, and they rode back up the trail. Uncertain and anxious, Griffith willed himself to learn something of this environment newly-filled with terrors. Nocturnal sounds filled the thick, moist air around them. The cicadas were loud and continuous, but as the riders passed by, the other clicks and buzzes quieted. The night hung warm and fragrant under the canopy.

They reached the summit more quickly than Griffith expected. Starting down the trail, he reined in the horse enough to keep from stumbling in the dark, and they soon emerged from the edge of the trees. The horses picked their way around the shadowed stumps, dark scrub vegetation, and raw earth trails of the clear-cut valley. The quarter moon rose over the eastern mountains, and long shadows stole across the open valley. In the center, beyond the camp, sat the helicopter, its cockpit illuminated. The knot in Griffith's gut tightened.

Nearing the camp, Karen reined Bellota to a halt where they were still hidden in shadow and held up her hand. She pointed toward the helicopter. Several armed men climbed aboard and shut the side hatch as the pilot strapped himself into his seat. The helicopter rotors began turning and the giant blades, glinting in the moonlight, slowly lifted the awkward beast from the ground. The low thump vibrated through the muggy night air as the helicopter rose, yawed slightly, and gained altitude. It climbed above the tree line and spun slowly. The spotlight came on, blinking its Cyclopean beam toward the camp.

The horses paced nervously in place. Robledo shuffled sideways, pressing against Bellota's side and pinning everyone's legs between the horses' flanks.

"What's happening?" asked Tito.

"I don't know," Griffith whispered through the increasing noise.

They watched the helicopter tilt forward. Its light cut an

arc across the ground to the largest building. Two small fireballs flashed on either side of the spotlight. Sparkling trails of white fire streaked toward the building and exploded, blasting brilliant flame and shards of wood skyward. The concussion and heat swept over their skin and compressed the air in their ears. Griffith felt rather than heard Tito yell.

Karen pulled Bellota aside when she tried to rear, and Sara grabbed her mane. Robledo began to jump, but as Karen turned Bellota away, he shied back instead of rearing and followed the other horse. Griffith held onto the reins, squeezing Tito between his arms as the horses bolted away.

Two more rockets streaked toward the buildings. One exploded into the roof of a shed, blasting it flat. The other passed over the remaining structure and exploded into the ground a hundred feet below them. Small rocks and clumps of earth flew outward from the fireball.

Carrying Karen and Sara, Bellota led their escape from the cacophony and heat. Robledo lurched after his mate, bounding up the far trail with Griffith and Tito struggling to hold on. Along the rough trail between stacks of old logs, they fled toward the far side of the valley, east, toward the rising moon and deeper into the rain forest.

From the sound of its engine, Griffith knew the helicopter had risen and turned away, heading west, behind them. *Without seeing us*, he sighed, realizing they'd just had their second close call.

They passed the last decaying stack of logs at the edge of the clear cut and turned to look back into the valley. The remains of the buildings were still burning. Small fires flickered in the brush surrounding the decimated camp. The vibration of the helicopter's engine quickly faded over the mountain toward Buenavista.

"That was unexpected," said Griffith to no one in particular.

"Our side or theirs?" asked Karen.

"Our side," decided Tito. "I think we should head back that way."

Sara turned toward Tito. "Tito, how do you know? Use your head. Did you see any prisoners? I didn't."

"Oh, Sara," he called back. "They blew up the camp."

"Maybe to destroy the evidence. Or kill any witnesses. You remember where they kept us."

"They can't be on their side," protested Tito.

"Tito, don't be stupid."

"Don't call me stupid, Sara. That's not right."

"Well, don't be, and I won't."

"Sara!"

"Children," said Karen in her teacher's voice, "it's okay. We don't know for sure, so either of you could be right. Right, Griffith?"

Griffith had turned deaf to the young voices. Watching the fires, thinking of their chances of escape—*hell, of survival,* he told himself—he had no idea how to confront such pointless ruthlessness. He wasn't sure he cared which side they were on.

In his gut the fear curled tighter. He wondered if he could keep it hidden. From Karen, and especially from the children. Masculine pride and self-esteem based on somatotype had never been of particular concern to Griffith. He was an intellectual, a researcher, and Karen, as athletic as she was, knew that. But now that he'd begun to confront his own demons, he realized he did not want to let Karen down.

"Right, Griffith?' she asked again.

"Yes, right. Let's do it."

Behind Tito, he stretched his left arm upward, trying to

loosen the ache in his side. He lifted himself with his right hand off the back of Robledo, hoping to ease the sting of his saddle sores. It didn't help. He reached up to rub some of the tension out of the back of his neck, and once again his pants pulled free from his sticky saddle sores. Not a lot of pain, but maybe a little first aid would help.

"Before we leave," he said. "I need to... uh, relieve myself."

Sara didn't understand, and Karen whispered in her ear. She giggled as Griffith awkwardly dismounted, leaving Tito, holding his rifle, in command of the saddle.

He walked toward a wide swath of moonlight behind a stack of the logs and kicked some coke bottles and rusting tin cans out of his way. He set his pack down on the logs and dug through it for the white, plastic, first aid kit. He found the Neosporin, mostly by feel, squeezed some onto his fingers and reached down the back of his trousers to spread it on his saddle sores. He flinched when he touched the large, raw, wet abrasions. Gently, he smeared the ointment over the butterfly-shaped wound. After he closed his pack, he unzipped his trousers to relieve himself.

Once again, the sounds of the night forest returned to fill the frightened silence. Frogs peeped from some nearby wet spot, and a small jungle cat called like a child, its melancholic cry sliding up the scale. Another animal screamed once, silencing the jungle momentarily.

The heat from the fires pulled a current of cool night air off the mountainside across Griffith's face. He sniffed the breeze and caught a sweet scent reminding him of newly-mown grass. At his feet, the weeds rustled. A rodent raced from the logs and darted under his stream of urine. It disappeared into the taller grass where the horses were grazing.

He smiled, finished, and zipped his pants. As he turned, he

heard Bellota snort. Something dark slid through the grass near Karen's horse, but before Griffith could speak, Bellota reared and stomped her front hooves in the earth. She reared again, this time neighing loudly in pain. A long snake, dark and menacing, flew up, the fangs of its arrow-shaped head caught in Bellota's calf.

"Karen!" shouted Griffith over the piercing wails of the horse.

Still mounted on the panicked Bellota, Karen lifted Sara from the saddle. While the wounded horse kicked the air and bellowed in fear and pain, Karen lifted Sara's legs above Bellota's neck. She pushed the two of them backward off the stirrups and saddle. Twisting in the air under Sara, Karen hit the bare earth with a grunt. With Sara still in her arms, she rolled clear of the wild hooves.

Griffith stepped cautiously forward, trying to grab Bellota's reins as they flew past. Karen jumped up and took three fast steps to her horse. Pushing Griffith out of the way, she grabbed the whipping reins and pulled down as hard as she could, forcing Bellota to the ground. The neighing gasps were anguished and continuous.

Standing on the reins, Karen turned to Robledo, who was trying to back away, and yanked the rifle out of Tito's hands. She slammed the butt end to the ground and pinned the snake with its fangs still imbedded in Bellota's bleeding foreleg. Bellota's leg jerked forward, tearing the snake from her calf.

The snake's head twisted back and hit the ground at Karen's feet. She lifted the rifle. The reptile, its spine broken, reared its head back, ready to strike again. A streak of pale yellow hung momentarily in the shadows at Karen's feet. She drove the rifle butt toward it as hard as she could. The snake lunged forward and struck the butt. The force of the Karen's blow drove it back to the earth. Twice more she slammed the rifle at its head, and the viper lay dead.

Panting, Karen turned to Bellota. In the moonlight, the horse's leg wound was growing, the skin and muscle dissolving away in copious amounts of dark blood. Her legs twitched spasmodically, and blood splattered Karen's pants as she lifted the rifle to her shoulder.

Bellota's head stretched up and out, her neck muscles rigid as if she were trying to escape her body. Blood dripped from the corners of her eyes and flowed mucousy and red from her nostrils and mouth. Between the agonized cries roaring from deep within her, the horse desperately sucked in bubbles of breath over her swollen tongue. Sara shrieked.

Karen aimed the rifle at Bellota's head and pulled the trigger. Nothing. A wail, distressed and phlegmy, rose from Bellota's throat. Karen lowered the rifle, clicked the safety to single shot, and re-aimed. The bullet crashed into the horse's temple.

Bellota lay still, her leg muscles twitching.

Sara's piercing cry ended abruptly when she bent over and vomited in the grass. Karen clicked the safety on and lay the rifle on the ground. She went over to Sara and touched her shoulder. Sara turned, hugged her, and cried quietly into her embrace.

Griffith looked away, and Robledo paced nervously, side to side. Tito sat silently in the saddle, rocking with the motion of the horse as it stamped its hooves. After several moments, Griffith walked Robledo over and wrapped his arm around Karen's shoulder.

He leaned close to her and said softly, "We should go. We've made an awful lot of noise."

Karen nodded. Sara wiped her nose and face with the dirty sleeve of her dress, and looked up at Karen.

After a moment the girl said, "I'm ready to go."

"Okay," replied Karen quietly. "Let's get out of here. Sara, ride with Tito."

Karen looked up at Tito. He was very quiet.

"Are you okay, Tito?"

"*Sí*," was all he answered as he slid forward in the saddle.

Before she mounted Robledo, Sara stole a quick look at Bellota.

"Should we bury her?" she asked in a faint voice.

"I'm afraid that's not possible, Sara," Karen tried to explain. "We just have to tell ourselves she's not in any more pain. That's just her empty body. Nature will take care of that."

"*Es verdad*," agreed Sara.

The young girl crossed herself and mounted Robledo. Karen grabbed their pack and gave the rifle to Griffith who was still holding the reins.

"Grif," said Sara from behind him, "could I have the reins, *por favor?*"

"Of course. I'm sorry. I... yes, here you are."

He handed her the reins and forced a small smile.

Ahead of them, over the ridge, the moon poked holes in the canopy. Shafts of pale light filtered to the floor of the tropical forest. Holding hands, Karen and Griffith walked ahead of the children's horse. Up the trail into the deepening forest, the nocturnal shadows and feral choruses closed in and surrounded them.

CHAPTER EIGHT
INTO THE JUNGLE

Along the *Río La Revancha*
Tuesday dawn

> Hope is a good breakfast,
> but it is a bad supper.
>
> *Apothegms, No. 36*
> Francis Bacon
> 1561—1626

Shortly before sunrise, the deepest shadows of the jungle night began to retreat, and a pale green-gray mist grew out of the depths of the forest. As dawn crept under the canopy, the chirps and trills of birds tentatively emerged from the trees. The high-pitched whirr of the cicadas grew with the light until it became white noise behind the stirrings of the early morning jungle fauna. A howler monkey screeched through the canopy with a ferocious roar. Several more howlers returned his call. For the next several minutes, the trees came alive with the resonant, pulsating growl of territorial males, almost as if the forest itself were breathing. Then, abruptly, the monkeys fell silent.

Griffith had no idea how far they'd hiked overnight. With frequent rests since they'd left the clear-cut valley, they'd climbed steadily up the northern spine of *el Volteado* and over a long ridge dropping them into a narrow valley draining to the south.

Less than an hour after dawn, the first of the day's heavy showers pounded through the canopy. Within minutes they were soaked. The rain poured steadily without wind or letup for nearly half an hour. The footing got mushy as the steep trail wound its way off the mountain into the ravine. Karen walked Robledo over the most treacherous spots while the others slid and fell, often dunking themselves into the torrents of dark brown water rushing down the mountainside.

Had they decided to stop, they would undoubtedly have gotten chilled from the morning downpour. The children, unused to such extremes, shivered and suffered silently each time they slipped in the mud. They were descending from over three thousand feet in altitude, and even after the rain ceased, it took a while for them to warm up.

As the dawn filled the jungle with crystal streaks of light, Griffith thought about the kidnapping. Karen hadn't broached the subject with the children, and his imagination provided too much disturbing detail for him to ask them about it. Had he known the actual vivid and perverse facts of their abduction, the filth, the cold food, and the repeated gropings, his own fears might have multiplied out of control. Griffith didn't doubt the kidnapper's treatment of the children had been threatening, humiliating, and, at the very least, psychologically abusive. But when he considered the nature of their captors, thoughts of physical torment grew into the possibility the children were sexually abused as well. He shuddered and forced the horrific image from his mind.

Griffith's background, the comfortable, small town upbringing, university work, and the security of a tenure-track teaching position, made it difficult for him to even imagine such personal horror. Had Sara been willing or able to talk about it, he probably would have been too shocked to know how to respond. Additionally, Griffith suspected if he tried to engage Tito in conversation, the child's arrogant disdain for his and Karen's efforts would deafen him to whatever humiliation and guilt Tito was holding inside.

Griffith's complete lack of experience with that repulsive, dark threat of violation left him without any appropriate emotional responses. In fact, until now he'd given almost no thought to the children, content to let Karen do whatever nurturing was necessary. Although that seemed selfish to him, he just didn't want to think about the children who had ended his honeymoon with such perilous abruptness.

What was of more immediate concern to him was the future. It was difficult to admit, but he wasn't in shape for another long, physically draining day. Griffith's hips and hamstrings ached from the effort of hiking over continually rough terrain. Rather than silently dwell on something he could do little about, he fell back on his own training—as an observer. If nothing else, a greater awareness of his environment would distract his more fearful thoughts and concerns. And perhaps a bit of additional knowledge would aid them at some point.

To that end, he focused on the elements of his environment, whether or not he could identify them. The omnipresent hum of the insects hung in the background, varying in volume and intensity. Amphibious rhythms played in the trees and wherever marshy ground litter had accumulated. Spiders strung their webs across the wet spots along the trail. Mosquitoes filled the dawn with their incessant buzz. Except for an occasional brief waft of air that found its way below the canopy, the early morning hung still and humid.

The sun broke into the green dawn. Light sliced through the jungle canopy in narrow rays. A large flock of chachalacas—tall, brown birds—came scratching through the rot of the jungle floor looking and acting like dark, over-sized chickens. The numerous males of the flock kept up their monotonous "cha-cha-lac" so loudly and continuously the hikers still heard them long after the birds were lost to sight.

Later, high in the canopy, the high-pitched, descending scream of some predatory bird silenced the forest. Within a minute, a second piercing shriek rang down on Griffith. Then a third call in front of him was followed by the heavy whoosh of the raptor's wings. From the shadows, a large, red-tailed hawk materialized, speeding directly at his head. He ducked, and the downward rush of air from its wings smelled faintly of avian nests.

He spun around to see if the hawk had struck either of the children or Karen. Far behind him on the trail, Karen was pointing into the canopy where it had disappeared. The three of them seemed unaware he was so much farther down the trail. He stopped walking and waited for them.

When Karen and the children caught up, the bird had been forgotten. They continued down the trail, crossing a small stream, then turning southerly along the bed of a narrow, shadow-filled watershed, the headwaters of the *Río la Revancha*.

They stopped one more time to share the last of the raisins and give Robledo some corn. Karen filled their canteens through her purifier. They drank, and she filled the canteens again.

Reclining on his hip in the morning shadows, Griffith retreated into his study of the jungle. Karen had often seen him absorbed in such observation, and he appreciated this time she gave him by fretting over the children. He soon lost himself in tranquil observation. Around him, ferns filled the undergrowth, hiding their insect, lizard, arthropod, and crustacean life in perpetual shade. Thick mosses carpeted the tree trunks, and dense, viridian liverworts matted the deeply-shaded lower branches. Wrinkled, pale green lichens mottled the buttressed roots of the largest trees, and on a few, beach ball-sized termite nests swelled in the notches of the lowest branches. Spiraled trunks of lianas as big as his arm wound up from the ground like coils, climbing through the branches, weaving full the gaps between the tallest trees, and ending in long, tendril vines that hung limply above them like ropes. High in the canopy roof, epiphytes filled the upper branches, and the bright red flower spikes of innumerable bromeliads poked their bloody fingers from overlapping bowls of tightly bunched leaves.

The rapid growth and decay gave the jungle both intensity and fragility. The thin layer of humus, holding in the moisture and heat, produced a heavy, almost sweet odor of rotting vegetation. In most places, the root layer was interwoven tightly into a thick mat, taking up the nutrients directly and keeping the soil tenuous and infertile. The thin latisol soil was rust colored from excessive aluminum and iron oxides.

At Griffith's feet, two lines of small, reddish-brown leaf cutter ants marched along a minuscule trail worn into the clay. One column of ants carried tiny pennons of green leaf above their heads; from the opposite direction came their empty-armed comrades. Back and forth, thousands of ants shouldered their way through their miniature gully, trod deep by workers trudging to and from their one-pointed goal at the base of a huge, buttressed ceiba. The bare, light brown anthill of soft dirt hiding their unceasing industry covered two hundred square feet.

As the ants toiled in their endless diligence, they seemed unaware of the dark stream flowing by them. Griffith watched intently as the waters widened and began to lap at the edge of the worker's trail. Several ants were swept off the path where, still clutching their oversized bits of leaf, they scrambled to grab some root or twig. The stream expanded a few more inches washing a column of ants from their formic scented path. Others, stopped by the waters, frantically looked for ways above the deepening current, forging new trails into the undergrowth or turning back on themselves in confusion. Fascinated by the efforts of the ants, Griffith was slow to realize the obvious—the waters of the stream were rising.

"Time to go," he said, and he stood.

His muscles rebelled at the abrupt movement, and the seat of his pants stuck to his saddle sores. But he got up, stretched his aching muscles and popped his creaking joints. He pointed to the stream, now noticeably wider and faster.

"I think it must have rained again upstream of us."

"You're right, Grif," said Karen. "Let's get packed up. We'll find a village if we keep along this stream. Is everyone going to be okay for a few more hours?"

"*Sí*, Karen," replied Sara, "we will be fine. We are strong, and we will find a village, as you said."

With Tito in the saddle, Sara led Robledo by the reins. Karen walked in front, and Griffith fell in behind them all. For half an hour, they followed the seldom used, overgrown trail. The tumbling waters frequently ran over the trail, forcing them to wade through the gushing, ankle-deep current.

For the next hour, they followed the expanding stream as the ravine gradually opened into a small valley. More sunlight penetrated to the jungle floor. Between frequent low spots of rotting, black leaves and muck, grass grew over their path. The variety and intensity of the colors increased perceptibly as more light revealed the infinite shades of green, light siennas, and warm, dark umbers of the earth and its jungle.

Finally, their path merged with a dirt road, rutted and narrow, one direction leading south along the *Río la Revancha*, the other east into the jungle.

"Which way?" asked Griffith.

"Downstream," offered Karen.

No one objected, so they moved onto the dirt road. The mountain rose steeply on the far side of the river. The lowland jungle was denser. Stands of acacia reached into the road wherever pink flowering mimosas weren't crowding them out. A few nut palms stood above undergrowth thick with fiddlehead and elephant ferns. The dirt road remained shaded, but splashes of sunlight occasionally broke through and warmed them.

Walking was significantly easier, and they had only been on the road for twenty minutes when Sara pointed to a small clearing across the river. At the base of the mountain several papaya trees, with their small green, pear-shaped fruit, stood above the weeds.

"You're right, Sara," Karen said. "Somebody's been taking care of those. This is excellent."

Although they tried to hide their excitement, each one of them could feel it. Griffith took Karen's hand as they walked side by side, and they allowed themselves small smiles. Tito became more active, looking around and even taking the reins from Sara to ride slowly ahead. No one said a great deal, but every rotting fence post and overgrown fruit tree indicating human attention was pointed out.

Around a short bend, the mountain side took on a new appearance. In steep patches, some as large as an acre or two, the soil was blackened, with weeds and wild onion taking hold. Banana trees, with their small bunches of green fruit pointing upward, grew between charred stumps, but the hillside was so steep the fruit trees stood widely apart from each other.

After passing several of these steep, burned orchards, they saw their first *milpa*, the traditional Maya cornfield. The steep, blackened field was growing with waist-high corn. Bean runners wound their way up the corn stalks, and yams, their dark green tops still small, were interplanted in the rows. They passed another *milpa* containing the same corn and bean companions, but squash vines clung to the fragile soil, and garlic, with their tall white flowers, and peppers, short and not yet in flower, stood between the vines and corn rows.

"I can understand," said Griffith, "why we don't see folks tending their *milpas*—they're too damn steep to stand on—but why don't they clear some of the overgrown pasture there?" He pointed to the more level jungle fields to their left.

"Perhaps," offered Tito voluntarily for the first time since dawn, "the better land belongs to someone else."

The road turned to the left, continuing along *la Revancha* and skirting the mountain. Around the bend, Tito saw them first: two small children playing naked at the edge of the shallow river. They were dark-skinned with thick black hair, high round cheeks, and broad noses.

Hearing their playful shrieks, Griffith looked around and saw a tiny dwelling backed against the mountain. When Sara heard the children, who still hadn't noticed the strangers and their horse, she let out a small cry of relief and ran toward them.

The little girls, probably only five and six years old, heard her and stopped playing, obviously surprised to see anyone. Squealing excitedly, they scrambled up the opposite bank toward their plank and thatch home huddled against the mountain. As they dashed clumsily toward the shack, their high, wavering wail echoed back from the steep hillside.

A woman stepped from the shadows of the open doorway. She was young and her dark hair was tied back string. She wore a simple, pale white cotton dress with a faded pink, full apron covering her pregnancy. She was barefoot. The children ran up to her, and she pointed them inside while she stood in the doorway watching the strangers.

Sara ran to the edge of the river, waved, and called, "¡Hola!"

The young woman nodded slightly. Tito walked Robledo behind Karen and Griffith. As they approached the river, Karen waved and asked in Spanish if they could cross. The woman shrugged.

"I don't think she understood you," offered Griffith, not understanding her either.

"¿Habla Usted español, señora?" she asked.

This time the woman shook her head, so Karen pantomimed, with exaggerated, sweeping gestures, crossing the river. The woman allowed herself a tiny smile and nodded. She remained standing in her doorway, however, with her children squatting behind her, peering around their mother's ankle length dress.

Sara led Robledo and Tito across the shallowest part of the river. Karen and Griffith followed, wading through the cool waters to the worn, sunny, dirt path. The hut was tucked back against the eastern base of the mountain, and morning light had warmed the trees crowding this small plot of land.

For Griffith, this was every cliché about rural poverty he'd ever heard. Naked kids, dirt floors, an outdoor kitchen, no glass in the windows, no electricity, and certainly no sanitation facilities. Had he known the region, the nearest school was a three-day walk and the closest health clinic even farther. He felt an odd mix of sadness, resignation, and admiration for this family.

The young woman introduced herself as Margarita. Her eyes shifted between Karen and Griffith and the two Mexican children in their expensive but dirty and torn school clothes.

In Spanish, Karen tried to explain how they'd hiked over the mountain from Buenavista. Margarita looked incredulous, but Karen kept up her flow of words and barely comprehensible gestures.

From behind her Margarita's children giggled at Karen's efforts to make herself understood, and now Tito was having trouble restraining his own giggles. When Karen motioned for the location of a telephone, Margarita smiled and nodded vigorously. She pointed down the road they'd just left. Karen pointed the same way questioningly.

"*Sí, al rancho de don Pedro,*" replied Margarita.

Apparently she did have some rudimentary Spanish.

"How far?" asked Karen, pointing to her wristwatch. Margarita looked up for a moment and pointed to a spot in the western sky halfway to the horizon. A few hours.

"Can everyone make it a few more hours?" Karen asked the others. "We haven't anything left to eat, but the canteens are full. What do you say?"

"If there's nothing to eat," asked Tito holding his stomach, "can I have some of Robledo's corn?"

"Good idea," said Griffith chuckling.

Margarita whispered something to her children. They disappeared into the house.

A little indignantly, Sara said, "Tito, I'm sure we can make it without eating our horse's food."

"But can't he eat grass?" whined the boy. "I'm about to starve to death."

"You cannot eat Robledo's corn," she replied firmly.

"I wasn't serious, Sara," he sneered and then laughed. "But I am hungry."

Karen turned back to Margarita and smiled.

"*Muchas gracias, señora.*"

"De nada."

Karen turned to leave, but Margarita stopped her.

"Un momento," she said, and her children, now in worn tee-shirts much too large for them, came out of the doorway, one carrying a small, chipped ceramic bowl filled with soft corn *tortillas*, the other a bowl of mashed *frijoles refritos* and a few sprigs of fresh green onion. Margarita motioned for her guests to sit on the logs beside the open fire and took the *tortillas* from the child. She placed several of them onto a large flat rock half surrounded by the fire. A few seconds later she nimbly flipped them over.

All this happened so unexpectedly Griffith realized too late they should have refused this generous offer. Another few hours of fasting was hardly going to hurt them, or Tito or Sara. Eating now might mean Margarita's children go without food tonight. He looked helplessly at Karen who nodded and sat still.

Margarita picked up the first warm *tortilla* and handed it to Tito. The oldest girl then came up to him and offered him the bowl of beans and onion. He tore the *tortilla* in half and scooped out some of the contents. His mouth soon full, he smiled broadly at the child and took another bite.

Margarita's children served the others, offering a second *tortilla* as soon as they had each finished the first one. Refusing seconds, they all thanked Margarita and the girls in turn, but when Tito refused a second helping, Margarita filled one more *tortilla* with the last of the beans and handed it to him. The gesture and her voice were insistent, and her motherly command was understood even in her native Tzeltal tongue.

Tito smiled at her, took the *tortilla*, and quickly ate it.

When Margarita's children gathered their chipped, white metal cups and started toward the river, Karen motioned for them to sit down. She handed the canteen to Tito. He took a short swallow and passed it to the older girl who had been shyly watching him with sidelong glances. When she took it from him, she giggled and lifted it to her mouth. She spilled most of her gulp down her shirt and laughed so heartily everyone joined her. After the other girl tried drinking from the canteen, to the laughing accompaniment of her sister and Tito, Margarita took it from her, smiled, and handed it back to Karen.

Griffith touched Karen's arm and glanced at the other canteen hanging over Robledo's saddle horn. Nodding at him, Karen handed the canteen back to Margarita.

"*Muchas gracias,*" Margarita said proudly, holding up her modern, cloth insulated, Kevlar laminated, clip-on canteen.

More thanks were exchanged, and Margarita's girls escorted them to the river. They turned downstream, and the four children waved to each other until their arms tired.

Griffith was elated. They were headed toward a telephone.

CHAPTER NINE
THE PHONE CALL

Rancho Nuevo San Juan Bautista del Corazón
Tuesday

> It makes a difference whose ox is gored.
> *Works, Vol. LXII*
> Martin Luther
> 1483—1546

"No, I insist, you must stay here, shower, and refresh yourselves." *Don* Pedro seemed as surprised at their appearance on his ranch as he was engaging in his welcome. "I'll have snacks brought over, please have some, and then join me for something more hearty and elegant later this evening, after you've rested. If you leave your clothes outside, I'll have them washed for you.

"This is terrible," he went on, "what's happened to you. As soon as I return to my office at the *hacienda*, I'll notify the proper authorities, and we'll have you safely away. It may take a few days, perhaps, as we are very far from any officials out here on my little ranch, but consider this guest house yours until then. Now, if you'll excuse me to attend to my daily business. A ranch requires a great deal of attention, I'm afraid."

"Those were your Brahman we saw in the fields," asked Griffith.

"*Sí*," replied don Pedro. "You know cattle?"

"No, *señor*, but I was impressed with their size, much bigger than others I've seen."

"You have a good eye, *Señor* Grant. They're the best cattle in Chiapas. All ten thousand are Brahman/Senepol cross, especially adapted for this climate and your *norteamericano* tastes. As I said, they require much work, so if you will excuse me?"

He stepped off the porch and back into his new, white pickup truck. They watched him drive the loop around the horse pasture and out of sight.

The guest house was comfortable but small. Done in a bastardized Victorian decor, the cottage had a small kitchen and pantry on one side of the main room, two large beds, and a private bath with footed bathtub and porcelain fixtures. It was certainly comfortable enough for Griffith. He looked forward to untying the knots which had gripped his muscles and bowels since yesterday.

Not even two hours after they'd left Margarita's, they'd been picked up by two taciturn *campesinos* in a beat up, old, white, Ford pick-up. One of the *campesinos* drove them to the center of *don* Pedro's *Rancho Nuevo San Juan Bautista del Corazón*, a few miles past jungle pasture land filled with large herds of grazing cattle. The other rescuer rode Robledo in. The four of them weren't actually taken to *don* Pedro's *hacienda*, which was situated atop the highest point of land above the stables, horse pastures, and the guest house. They were too filthy for that, Griffith was sure.

Once *don* Pedro left his uninvited guests, Tito sprang for the bathroom. Sara sat in the corner wing chair, waiting for her turn to scrub off three days of mud and sweat. Karen stripped to her underwear and sports bra and tossed her clothes outside the door. She hugged Griffith, whispering how much she loved him and how anxious she was to resume their honeymoon. Stretching out on the far bed, she smiled at him before closing her eyes, and within thirty seconds, she was snoring gently on her back.

Griffith alone remained restless, impatient for the expected sense of relief to descend. He paced the room for minutes, knowing he was going to be the last one in the bathroom. He went outside and sat on the porch glider. He swung for a while, but soon got up, unable to figure out why he couldn't relax. He walked to the side of the cottage. A few monarch butterflies darted among the tea roses and hibiscus, and he paused to watch.

He looked down the dirt road, past the barns and cattle pastures to the dark green mountains they'd crossed. Staring into the distance, he wondered just how long it was going to take to assimilate this experience. He hadn't gotten over his fear for their lives yet, so the idea he might have participated in something heroic escaped him.

He blinked, refocusing his eyes on the folded green mountains in the distance. The dusty, lonely road they'd traveled disappeared in the shimmering vapors hanging over the jungle pastures. Funneled by steep, dense mountains, the intermittent breeze lifted scents of thick verdancy which cut through the earthy odors of manure and animals.

Time froze for him. Still shaken by their flight through the night, Griffith felt as fragile as this intense world that had engulfed him. Until now, frightened, frenzied activity had been the only way to survive. And that fear refused to loosen its grip on him.

Beside the nearest barn, another of the ubiquitous white pick-ups was parked. Several ranch hands stopped their work and looked toward him. Griffith saw them and glanced over his shoulder, hoping they were looking at something else.

His discomfort at this innocent moment confused him. Karen was much more open to strangers, and her confident manner had initially allowed him to relax amidst a language and culture he didn't understand. He wanted to blame his continued disquiet on their circumstances, but he supposed that was too easy. Nevertheless, he turned and walked the other way toward the horse pasture, wondering if the *campesinos* would think he was just another *gringo* snob.

He strolled beside the pasture fence, head down, lost in thought. Beyond the humbling reminders of his aching muscles and raw saddle sores, he wondered if his unease had another source. Despite the impetuous method Karen used to make decisions, he was certain she'd been right about heading this direction. They'd found some refuge, and within hours, perhaps a day or two, this ordeal would be over.

But something else was nagging at his thoughts: all the *campesinos* he'd seen around the ranch had been aloof—even their driver was oddly quiet. No one other than *don* Pedro had seemed at all surprised seeing the four of them walk out of the jungle.

Hadn't they heard of the kidnapping? He found that hard to believe. If they knew the situation, he wondered, what would explain their obvious reserve? Still walking, he passed a groom brushing a large, white Arabian in a small fenced pasture. The groom continued his vigorous strokes along the horse's flank, but he kept glancing back and forth between the *hacienda* and Griffith.

Griffith slowed, shaking his head. They had found a ranch and phone—Karen had been correct, of course—so why was he still edgy? Not a single, logical answer presented itself.

Long ago, however, Griffith had learned when answers were elusive, it was probably because he was asking the wrong questions. Unable to find a reason why he couldn't relax, he asked himself what would make him feel better. A shower and a hot meal would certainly ease the tension of the last twenty-four hours. And some sleep.

Then it struck him. Why did they come here in the first place? To use the phone, of course. He didn't know why, but he was sure just talking with someone he knew would soothe the frayed edges of his nerves. If anyone besides the authorities knew they were here and knew what had happened to them, he was certain he'd feel better.

He looked up. He'd walked around the pasture near the back of the *hacienda*. On the crest of the hill, breezeways connected the detached buildings. Griffith tilted his head at the odd architectural mixture. The *hacienda*, a large, ranch style farm house, with lots of red brick below white siding and numerous windows and breezeways to accommodate the climate, spread out on the hill. The lawn was surrounded by a simple, whitewashed, plank fence.

He thought for a moment about how to ask *don* Pedro to use his phone for a long distance call. Since he was filthy, however, and as malodorous as he'd ever been, he hesitated crossing into the man's house. He wasn't sure he'd want to go into his own home this way, let alone a beneficent stranger's.

He decided to return to the cottage and shower. As he turned, however, uncertainty filled him like the disturbing scent of ozone in the air before a thunderstorm. What was making him question everything? Was it because he felt as if he hadn't really accomplished anything? The thought that Karen had taken all the responsibility for their decisions generated some guilt. But she was more experienced, he rationalized. She was the teacher and outdoor enthusiast, wasn't she?

He paused and realized his thoughts were leading him away from the *hacienda* and its phone. In a fit of pique, he climbed over the plank fence onto the *hacienda*'s lawn. His muscles groaned. Too embarrassed to go ahead and use the front entrance, he headed toward the back breezeway. As he neared the covered walk, he became aware of someone moving behind him. The instant before he turned, he heard Tito's voice, out of breath, call to him in a stage whisper.

"Grif, *un momento, por favor.*"

Tito's urgency startled him. Griffith spun around and saw the boy who, although clean from his bath, was still wearing his dirty shorts and jacket. He was making an obvious effort to remain calm.

"Grif, we should go back to the house," said Tito, pulling nervously on his fingers tips.

"But why, Tito?' he asked. "I'm doing something. Wait. I'm glad you're here. I was just going to call home, and I could use your help. And you could call your father. Why don't you come with me?"

"But, Grif," he protested, "Karen said to find you now, and the *caballerizo*..."

"That's fine, Tito, but I want to make a call first. Come on. Help me."

"But Grif..."

From an open window, they heard a voice, raised in some anger. *Don* Pedro's, Griffith realized, and the man was on the phone. He turned around.

"Let's go to the front," he whispered to Tito.

As he started to tiptoe away, they heard *don* Pedro's voice again. He was clearly agitated. Griffith and Tito were out of sight of the window, but close enough for Griffith to pick the word "zapatista" from the flow of angry Spanish.

"Come on," he said to Tito.

He wanted to take the boy's hand and lead him away, but he hesitated. Besides being too uncomfortable for something so familiar as touching the President's son, he saw Tito's attention had shifted to *don* Pedro's conversation. Despite Griffith's inner voice admonishing him about eavesdropping, the obvious irritation in *don* Pedro's voice prompted him to ask Tito what was being said.

"He's talking about our horse." answered Tito. "He's angry, and... wait."

"Who cares?" *don* Pedro shouted with uncontrolled frustration.

Tito quickly translated for Griffith during the pauses.

"That's not the point. They were armed, and they said they'd been hiking through the jungle all night.... I ask again, why are the Zapatistas within striking distance of my ranch?... I said I'll hold the children until you arrive, but suppose the Zapatistas strike first?... As you say, but so will my *guardias blancas*.... Hurry, because I don't want these little time bombs, or their *gringo* friends, here any longer than necessary.... These children will create problems here, and somebody will have to eliminate... Isn't that what we paid for?... Quickly, then."

Griffith heard the click of plastic. Releasing his breath, he broke out in a sweat. *Don* Pedro's voice, menacing and tense, was such a contrast to what he'd heard earlier. Tito's translation simply reinforced what Griffith felt. Making as little noise as possible, he took Tito's hand, and the two of them stepped quietly across the lawn and over the paddock fence. Out of sight of the *hacienda*, they ran.

Don Pedro's tone had driven a spike into Griffith's gut. His earlier discomfort took on a much more fearful countenance. His mind raced with his feet as he tried to recall every word he'd heard from Tito. Was it possible "eliminated" had more than one connotation? His heart pumped fear into his extremities. Holding Tito's hand, they ran until it struck him they'd probably have to continue running for a while. The irony tripped him, and he stumbled to a halt.

Tito, gasping to regain his breath, stared at Griffith quizzically. Griffith realized how conspicuous they looked standing in the middle of the pasture, bent over, sucking for breath. He released Tito's hand.

"It's okay, Tito. Let's just keep walking. We'll get there. Just keep walking."

He repeated it to himself, hoping to ward off the chaos of panic. It was over a quarter mile back to the guest house. During the minutes it took them to get there, the adrenaline managed to make him nauseous. If he kept walking, he wouldn't throw up.

When he opened the door to the cottage, he saw a decision had already been made. Karen and Sara were both dressed; their clothes were no cleaner, but both of them had gotten showers. Sara was closing the day pack on the bed, and Karen was clipping the canteen onto her hip pouch.

"What's happened here?" he asked.

"Oh, Griffith," said Karen calmly. "Thank God you're back. We've got to keep moving."

"I know," he said.

"Tito told you?" she asked.

"Told me what? No, Tito didn't tell me anything." His voice was quivering despite his efforts to remain calm. His words came out in a rush. "I don't know how you knew this, but we're still in trouble, Karen. We overheard *don* Pedro on the telephone. He didn't call the police like he said. He called someone else... oh, God, you're not going to believe this. He told this guy to come here and eliminate us, the children and their *gringo* friends. That's us."

"'Eliminate us,'" Karen said, a little too calmly for Griffith. "He used those words?"

"Exactly those words. Right, Tito? You translated for me."

"*Sí*," he replied, "he said he was paying him to eliminate us."

"Karen, I couldn't believe it myself. He said the Zapatistas were about to strike here, and he was going to use the *guardias blancas* to defend himself. Do you remember what Esmeralda told us about them? Oh, Karen, you didn't hear his voice. It was not the same man."

"Okay, Griffith. I believe you. And it fits with what we heard."

"What? What *you* heard?"

"One of *don* Pedro's maids came by while you were out. She told us it wasn't safe to stay here. She said all the *campesinos* are returning to the mountains and jungle because a war is about to start. She packed us some food and left us this."

Karen held up an automobile key and nodded toward the back window. A white pick-up was parked behind the cottage.

"She thought it was important we leave real soon."

"What about Robledo?" asked Griffith.

"Griffith, how could we take him? We don't even know where he is, and…"

"But I do," answered Tito. "The *caballerizo*, the… ¿*cómo se dice, Sara?*"

"Groom," she answered.

"*Sí*, the groom in the pasture told me Robledo is in another pasture. He said he would take good care of him for me after we left."

"Excellent," said Karen. "He'll be okay, here, I'm sure. Are you ready to go, Grif?"

"Karen," he asked, "if there's supposed to be this war, maybe we should stay here? I mean, aren't we on one of the two sides?"

Griffith wondered if his reluctance to give in to the flight instinct was more from fatigue than anything else. And did the groom say to Tito 'after we left'? He had no idea what that meant.

"Do you want to stay?" Her question was sincere. "*Campesinos* or *guardias blancas?*"

"Well, I know how *don* Pedro sounded when we arrived, and that is not what Tito and I just heard. The man doesn't want us around. So I guess I'm not staying behind."

Griffith picked up the stuffed pack, noticing it was heavier than he remembered.

"What's in here, Sara?" he asked.

"Fruit, from the maid," she answered. "Mangoes, banana, papaya, some bread and cheese. Very nice. Your things, too, and some more toilet paper."

"I've got our passports and money here," said Karen with her hand on her fanny pouch.

"Well, then," he said, nodding to her, "let's get out of here."

Karen opened the door and led the way around back. She slid into the driver's seat as Griffith tossed the gear into the truck bed. He stepped on the back wheel and pulled himself over the sidewall. He landed with his kneecap on the raised metal groove running the length of the bed. He shifted his weight off that knee, and his hand touched a sheathed machete. He sighed at this world too full of weapons and pain.

Rubbing his knee, he watched the children scramble into the cab beside Karen. Karen looked back at Griffith's pained smile. His matted brown bangs framed his crooked glasses.

"Griffith, you should drive," she shouted. "You could pass for a *campesino*. From a distance, anyway."

He knew he could have, too. Two days in the tropical rain and mud had quite effectively effaced his *turista* veneer.

"Sara," she said getting out of the cab, "you and Tito stay down. Grif, I'll ride in the bed."

She jumped over the metal sidewall landing next to Griffith and lay down. Again, Griffith felt a nauseating disorientation. Without thinking, with hardly a grunt, he got up, sat on the sidewall, and slid to the ground.

"Which way?" he simply asked.

"Pick something unexpected," suggested Karen.

"Okay, but I'm going to take it easy for a while."

Griffith started the truck, shifted into first, and eased the clutch out. He smiled at the children as they scrunched on the dusty floorboards. Determined to drive to the nearest town, he drove around the house onto the dirt road heading toward the *hacienda*. He chose this way for a single reason: the road appeared to be wider.

They had three-quarters of a tank of gas, and the truck handled all right. Too much play in the steering wheel and the clutch was worn, but they both worked. Nobody would pay any attention to just another white pickup with a tired *campesino* driving lazily out to the fields.

So on he drove, steering carefully around the mud-filled ruts, past *don* Pedro's *hacienda* and his barns, and past his fat Brahman grazing indifferently in their fields. Beyond that, a series of bright yellow well caps hunkered close to the ground in *don* Pedro's southern fields.

Griffith could hardly believe it, but they were on their way again. Karen handed three bananas in through the passenger's window. Sara peeled them and handed Tito and him each one. He thanked her, took a bite, and drove on.

Shaking his head, he grinned tightly at the abiding absurdity of his honeymoon.

Tito looked at Griffith and Karen talking at the tailgate and let out a little huff.

"I'm hungry, Karen," he said, getting out of the cab and walking back to them.

Karen reached for the pack. On the open tailgate, she sorted out their food.

"Help yourself, Tito," she said.

Everyone reached for bread and cheese or a piece of fruit. Karen finished a banana and took their purifier and canteen to a clear running, natural spillway at the edge of the river.

"So, what do we do now?" asked Tito through a mouthful of papaya.

"Well, Tito," said Karen from the bank, "we still aren't sure where we are, but the plan is to find someone who does know. Unfortunately, it seems we've been running into more people willing to hurt you than help you. But don't worry, this road goes somewhere. They all do."

"I'm not scared," said Tito. "But they took my rifle, didn't they?"

"Maybe one of the *campesinos* will find a use for it," she replied. "Anyway, we'll find some kind of village before dark, and I still think a telephone is our best bet. We'll just call long distance to your folks. How does that sound?"

"We should have done that back at *don* Pedro's," lamented Sara.

"You're right, of course, Tito," agreed Karen.

"Actually," said Griffith, "that's what Tito and I were about to do when we overheard *don* Pedro."

"I guess it's a good thing you did overhear," said Karen. "So, for right now, children, you should be thinking about how to call your parents and what to say."

"*Sí*, that's right, Karen," piped in Tito. "I'll talk to my father when we find a telephone."

"Are you ready to continue?" she asked him.

"*Sí*, let's go now and find a telephone."

They packed up, squeezed together in the cab, and drove off. Griffith was still at the wheel, and Karen kept the mood positive with questions for the children about their friends and their lives as *el Presidente*'s kids.

Griffith was impressed with how articulate these two were. They attended the best Catholic school in México. Sara even mentioned going to school in Europe when she was older. They had been chauffeured and catered to, fawned over by obsequious adults currying the favor of their parents, and severely reprimanded by their parents whenever they stepped outside the established boundaries of their positions. High expectations had been placed on them early. As much as academic excellence was demanded, more of Sara than Tito, they'd also had to learn public behavior as a virtual discipline. It was obvious to Griffith they understood some of the prestige and the difficulties of their lifestyle.

"It was Father's idea," Sara explained, "to have Tito and me travel with him. 'To see *la República* and learn about our country,' he said. I've even been with my mother to the clinics in the *barrios* of México, but I don't think I want to become a doctor."

"This was our first trip to Chiapas," sighed Tito.

"You've never seen the rain forest, then?" asked Karen.

"No, and I don't think I like it."

"Well, I love the jungle," replied Karen, "but for your sake, I hope we can get you out of here soon."

The farther they drove, however, with no improvement in their road or situation, the more worried Griffith became. He did not want to spend another night in the jungle. If they had to, he thought, they could just keep driving until the road ended, *someplace*, he assumed. But evening was approaching and the tropical sky would soon deepen to indigo.

Around the next bend, however, the jungle opened up. Ahead of them, the rough, dusty road ended in another wider, graded, dirt road. At this lonely intersection stood several plank houses. The primary dirt road went east and west out of the village. Other than a rusting frame in the tall weeds, their truck was the only vehicle in sight.

They'd arrived in Amparo Agua Tinta, Black Water Mine, a village of eleven families in homes of plank siding and tin roofs. Time and activity were slow in this hour before sunset.

Karen stopped the first person they saw, a young man with long black hair, white cotton pants and shirt, a baseball cap turned backward on his head, and a machete hanging from his belt. She asked him if the village had a telephone.

"¿En Amparo? Sí, en la Cantina," he answered. He pointed toward the largest one story building at the intersection.

Griffith parked the truck on the grass beside the building. *La Cantina* was a home and attached open air store with a plank fence and corrugated tin roof protecting a few shelves of sugar, corn meal, flour, sodas, candy, and a limited choice of canned goods. It had the only electric hookup in the village. The single power line running from the *Lagunas de Montebello* ended here in Amparo, providing weak and irregular amperage. The store also had the only television, a tiny black and white model, and the only telephone.

Because everyone in the village stopped by at least once a day, it served a small menu, primarily variations on chicken, rice, or eggs for a few *pesos*. A small plate of fresh vegetables or fruit, depending on what had been gathered from the gardens out back, came on the side. Besides nurturing her six children, the owner was also the store manager and head cook. Her older children acted as cashiers, stockers, dishwashers, and waiters. There was too little work for too many people.

Under the tin roof, they found a table where they could see the TV. Layers of ghosts danced beside the actors of *Days of Our Lives*, and the dubbed Spanish was scratchy and thin. Several children who had been watching the TV, stared at Sara and Tito.

Karen went up to the woman at the glass-topped counter and asked if she could use their phone. The woman hesitated, but when Karen offered twenty *pesos*, she took her inside to an old, black rotary phone. Tito jumped up and followed them. When Griffith and Sara sat down, a girl about eleven-years-old came up to them and asked in Spanish if they would like something to drink. Griffith ordered four Cokes.

A small, mangy, arthritic dog with a deep, open sore in place of its left eye ambled toward Griffith. The mongrel sniffed and drooled about Griffith's feet. He wanted to shoo the mutt away; instead, he tucked his feet under seat as far as he could and patted him lightly on the rump. The dog eventually stopped sniffing and curled up on the dirt beside his sneakers.

While they waited for their *refrescas*, several heads popped over the fence to stare at the *gringo* with his Mexican child. When the young girl returned with their bottled drinks and straws, she said her mother would be right back. And more faces appeared. Sara smiled awkwardly at the first few, then ignored the rest. Griffith kept looking around, absorbing the slow pace of life in the jungle. He glanced over the fence down the road to the west, into the setting sun. More people were walking toward them.

Then it struck him. Of course the four of them would be more than *turista* curiosities. And they were becoming the center of too much attention for his comfort. His stomach twitched in tiny spasms. He sucked his Coke through the straw.

Behind him, Karen and Tito walked from the house. Their expressions made it clear they hadn't gotten through.

"The *señora* kept apologizing," Karen said. "I did get a dial tone, but the operator wouldn't answer. I dialed the number Tito gave me, still nothing. I let the *señora* dial it. Even less happened. Sorry. Maybe later. So, should we order something to eat and watch a little TV?"

Sara and Griffith nodded. Karen looked at the brown faces almost completely surrounding them, staring, peeking, and giggling quietly over the fence. She glanced back at Griffith, and he managed a small smile.

"Do you think they know who we are?" he asked.

"I really doubt it, Grif. Sure, they've probably heard about the kidnapping, but why would they associate that with us?"

"Then why are they all looking at us?"

The stares weren't impolite. On the contrary, the friendly, curious eyes and sideways glances blossomed into quick, shy smiles whenever eye contact was made. But for such a small village, he thought, it seemed a lot of people were gathering by the fence of this tiny *cantina*.

The mother came back out, kicked the yelping dog away from under the table, and smiled apologetically at them.

"*Más tarde, tal vez. Lo siento. ¿Comidas para todos?*"

"*Sí, gracias,*" replied Karen.

The mother went back inside the kitchen, and Karen turned to Griffith.

"She said to try the phone later, so I ordered dinner for us."

"Great," replied Griffith, "a hot meal."

"*Sí,* that would be *bueno,*" agreed Tito, casually mixing his languages.

Griffith kept glancing around, counting the increasing number of curious faces. In the far corner, by the open entrance, several heads turned away, not just from his eyes, but all the way around, looking back up the western road. He leaned out from his bench to look through the open gate. He stared for several seconds before he realized the men he saw striding through the dusk toward them were armed. They were at least a hundred yards away, silhouetted by a small cloud of burnt sienna dust glowing in the setting sun—five of them, rifles slung over their shoulders, barrels pointed up.

Griffith touched Karen's arm and nodded toward the road.

Karen turned and smiled, admiring the red and orange sunset.

"Beautiful, isn't it?" she said.

Griffith just looked at her.

"Karen," he finally said, "look again, please."

When Karen turned a second time, the whispering around them increased. Behind them, somebody said *"guardias blancas"*. Then she, too, saw the rifles and twisted back to Griffith, her eyes wide.

"I would guess," he said, "that's why everyone is leaving."

Everyone who'd been around the fence and at the tables was gone. Quietly and completely.

"I suppose," she said, "the phone will have to wait."

"All right, then," he said, sighing, "what now?"

"I want to eat," said Tito, unaware of their anxiety.

"Later, I'm afraid, Tito," said Griffith, still maintaining his calm pose. "I, for one, would like to follow everyone else's example and leave. Now, actually, if no one has any objections."

"I do," said Tito. "I want to eat first."

"Tito," said Sara firmly, "she's not serving anything right now. Everybody has left. I'm ready to go, too."

"All right, let's do it, then," said Karen, getting up from her chair.

"Stop!" demanded Tito.

"Wait," cautioned Griffith.

"Why? Let's go," Karen said and sat back down. She leaned forward toward Griffith.

He kept an eye toward the approaching men. Their pace had not changed, still slow and deliberate in the evaporating heat of sunset and dust.

"Let's not be hasty," he said. "The truck's right in view. Let me walk over to it and casually drive off the other way. You guys head into the house and out the far side. I can pick you up behind the store. Why make it obvious we're all leaving?"

"I want to stay," repeated Tito.

"Okay, Grif," said Karen, putting up her hand to quiet Tito, "but you be as invisible as you can."

"My best. See you all around back."

"But I want..." started Tito.

Griffith reeled around and leaned close to the boy's ear.

"Quiet!" His voice was firm and low. "We're leaving, Tito."

"But..."

"No more."

And Griffith walked out into the warm light of the jungle sunset. He realized he was giving in to the flight response again, but since the locals didn't seem to have a problem with it.... Without glancing toward the men, who were now within fifty yards of the *cantina*, he went to the truck and got in. Turning the ignition, he pushed in the clutch pedal and ground the shifter into reverse.

As he backed around and nudged the accelerator, he didn't see the men gesticulating in his direction. Trying to appear casual with his left elbow hanging out the window, he backed onto the narrow road. Out of the *guardias blancas'* sight, he drove along side the building in first gear, riding the clutch. The mother of Amparo's only business opened the side door, saw the truck, and gestured to the others inside. Griffith drove up just as Karen, Sara, and a smiling Tito, carrying a large pastry, came out.

As they climbed in, Griffith wondered which way to go. He looked behind him. When he turned back, the mother was shaking her head vigorously and pointing east, down the improved road, toward the night and farther into the jungle.

He eased the clutch pedal out, but his quivering leg slipped. The back tires spun noisily in the dirt. The truck lurched out into the dusty road. Griffith swung the steering wheel left, shifted into second, and popped the clutch clumsily. The transmission engaged with a clank, and pebbles and grit flew behind them as they roared off.

Tito scrambled to his knees, still clutching his pastry, and turned around. Flying bits of rock slowed the five men who were now not more than thirty feet behind them. Two of the men dropped to their knees to aim their rifles, and a third stopped and lifted his weapon to his shoulder. They held their fire as the last two ran in front of them after the truck, their hands protecting their faces from the flying gravel.

"I think they're going to shoot!" yelled Tito.

"Get down!" shouted Karen.

Reaching across Sara, she grabbed Tito and pulled both children onto the floor of the truck. Griffith leaned forward in his seat and almost stood on the accelerator. With his left elbow braced against the vent window, he shifted up with his right hand.

In the din of gravel ricocheting in the wheel wells and a screaming engine, they couldn't hear the rifles open fire. A slug hit the tailgate, however, and the concussion shook the cab. Griffith kept leaning into the wheel, trying to push the accelerator through the floorboard before he shifted again.

Suddenly, the large, side mirror by his left arm shattered, its glass and metal mangling with a horrendous crash. Simultaneously, Griffith's breath was ripped from him by a burning gash along his forearm. He let go of the wheel in mid-shift, and the truck careened to the right.

Air rushed over the exposed nerves, and Griffith screamed. He grabbed the wheel with his right hand. The truck skidded sideways toward the embankment and slammed into it, crushing the lower side panels and lifting the left wheels off the ground. Inside the cab, they were thrown into each other and then back again as the truck bounced down into the road.

Griffith pushed the accelerator to the floor and gritted his teeth, trying to catch a breath. Blood washed over his elbow. The pain was fierce, and his left hand was already numb with shock. Chancing a look in his rear view mirror, he saw a dense cloud of dust swirling across the road.

He breathed again. The raw pain of the wound intensified as blood dripped onto the door, his shirt, and pants. His eyes flooded, obscuring his vision. When he blinked, a tear splashed off his cheek.

"I've been shot," he said, his voice low and throaty.

Karen was already crawling over Tito, pushing him back against her door. She pulled her blouse out and began to tear at the bottom. She ripped it around her back nearly hitting Tito in the head with her wild elbow. Before she could finish tearing, Sara grabbed the loose end and tore it the rest of the way.

Lightheaded, Griffith held his arm across to her. Blood pooled in his lap. It was dark red and filled his head with its thick, metallic scent. His head nodded and his eyes began to roll as waves of copper nausea smothered him. The middle fingers of his left hand twitched, shooting darts into his forearm. The pain cleared his eyes.

He looked up and straightened the wheel. The engine screamed to be shifted into fourth. He ignored it, keeping the accelerator to the floor and his bloody arm held toward Karen. The uneaten pastry bounced on the dash board.

Karen wrapped the improvised bandage around the wound several times. She tore the end lengthwise with her teeth and knotted the two ends tightly over the wound. After Griffith shifted, she checked Tito and Sara. They were holding onto the seat, staring at Griffith's bandaged arm. Griffith's face was ashen.

"It must really hurt, Grif," said Karen. "God, I'm sorry."

It did hurt. A great deal. He never imagined a gunshot could hurt so much. He needed to stop. Another wave of nausea rippled through his intestines. He looked into the mirror and could see nothing of the shooters or Amparo Agua Tinta. If he didn't stop now, he'd vomit.

"Karen," whispered Griffith, "will you drive? I don't feel well."

"God, yes! Let me drive."

She got out of the truck before Griffith had completely stopped it. She ran around the back and opened his door, ready to catch him. He turned, smiling through his nausea, and braced himself with his right hand on her shoulder.

"Thanks," he said and got out of the cab.

She took his arm by the bloody elbow and cushioned it as they walked around the truck.

"Let me get a clean compress from our pack. I can fix this up better for you."

"Okay," he replied and leaned against the passenger's seat.

He lifted his head and took several slow breaths, willing the flow of saliva to stop. Long ago he'd learned the signs preceding regurgitation. Since childhood, his utter revulsion at the smells and taste of his own bile had forced him to discover ways to avoid that most repulsive bodily function. He wouldn't allow himself to throw up, now or ever. Slowly, he sucked cool air over his tongue, clearing the worst of the nausea.

Once Karen got the bandage unwound, the intense pain eased noticeably. She had wrapped it very tightly. She let the exposed wound bleed for a few moments, then squeezed a glob of antibiotic ointment into the gash. She laid several rumpled but clean gauze pads over it and retied her original bandage.

"Not so tight this time, please," asked Griffith.

"Sorry, love."

"I guess I wasn't invisible enough," he smiled weakly.

"Oh, Griffith," said Karen, tears filling her eyes, "you were so amazing. You saved our lives! God, the way you drove!"

She handed him three aspirin and the canteen and then laughed to keep from crying when she realized he had only one hand to use. She took the canteen back and opened it for him.

"We'll get that cleaned up properly once we get back. It's not as bad as, well, as the pain must be. Oh, Grif, I'm sorry."

"Karen, quit apologizing, please. I'll be okay. But we'd better keep going. I think the bad guys have a much better idea now of where we are."

Griffith slid onto the passenger's seat, holding his left arm under the elbow, and Karen shut the door for him.

"Are you okay, Griffith?" asked Sara.

"Yes, thanks, Sara. It hurts, but I'll make it. We need to keep driving."

"We'll find a telephone," she reassured him. "I'm sure. And a doctor to fix your arm. You were brave, Griffith."

Tito, his mouth open and eyes wide, was staring back and forth between the bloody arm and Griffith's pale face.

"Griffith," asked Tito, "would you like me to get in the back of the truck so you have more room?"

Karen and Sara looked at Tito in surprise.

"No, thank you, Tito. That's very kind, but let's just keep going."

"Okay, but let me know."

Karen released the brake, eased the clutch pedal out, and drove off.

"Well," she sighed as the evening shadows slipped steadily across the road, "at least we're on a better road. This has got to take us to another village. We'll just try again."

"Karen," said Griffith, his voice a little stronger, "should we consider alternative plans for the night?"

"Well, we have half a tank of gas left."

After several moments of silence, Sara cleared her throat.

"I know we're still in trouble, Karen," she said, "but it's okay if we talk."

Karen looked at her, and Griffith smiled weakly.

"Out of the mouths of babes," he chuckled.

"I'm not a baby, Griffith," protested Tito.

"Oh, sorry, Tito. It doesn't mean that. It means sometimes young people can be wiser than adults."

"Oh, *sí*, I know."

"Karen," asked Sara, her tone steady, "what if we can't find another phone this direction?"

"Do you suppose," asked Griffith, "this road could just end without another village, or... or anything. Just end?"

"In the jungle, maybe," replied Karen. "But why have this graded road if it doesn't go anywhere?"

"That makes sense," agreed Sara.

"So let's keep driving," said Griffith. "I don't particularly want to go back to our riflemen."

"Zapatistas, Griffith," said Tito.

"Oh, Tito, you don't know that," objected Sara.

"You don't know, either, Sara."

"Why do you say that, Tito?" asked Karen.

"I saw them close up, before they shot Griffith. They were not army or police."

"The people at the *cantina* called them *guardias blancas*," said Karen.

"White guards?" said Sara. "Who are they?"

"I heard *don* Pedro talk about them," said Tito.

"They work for the ranchers," said Karen.

"And it's pretty obvious the *campesinos* don't trust them," added Griffith.

"Well, they weren't wearing white," said Tito, "so I guess that's wrong. And they were wearing camouflage and maybe a scarf like the Zapatistas. I'm sure they were. You know, Griffith, if Marcos catches us again, he'll probably kill you and Karen."

"Tito," cried Sara, "that's a terrible thing to say."

"*Sí*, I'm sorry, but it's true. I thought we could talk about everything."

"You're right, Tito," agreed Karen. "We can. So tell us about this Marcos, okay?"

"*Sí*, he is the worst of the terrorists. He is called *Insurgente*, the rebel."

Sara obviously disagreed with him and sat silently, her arms crossed and breathing a little too heavily.

"Marcos," continued Tito, "commands their army. They live and train in the jungle. I heard he's so tough his men have to eat monkey and drink their own piss."

"Oh, Tito!" blurted Sara.

"No, it's true, Sara. They kill their enemies and destroy the land and houses of the ranchers. They say he's very handsome, and all the ladies fall in love with him. He has women in his army. That's why he can't take his ski-mask off."

"Tito," insisted Sara, "he can't take his mask off *in public*, because everybody would know who he is. They would assassinate him. You don't understand anything."

"Tell me more, Sara," encouraged Karen.

"Marcos would never allow what's happened to us. I don't care about politics, but everybody knows Marcos. He wears the ski-mask as a symbol of the invisible *indígena*. He writes poetry, and he teaches."

"But Sara," interrupted Tito, "you know they kidnap important people like Father. They've kidnapped police before."

"I don't believe he would kidnap us. It was somebody else."

"Oh, Sara, you're the one who doesn't understand anything. You even said you don't understand politics."

"At least I admit when I don't know something instead of making up some story."

"But our kidnappers said they were Zapatistas."

"*Sí*, and they joked about it."

"Well, whoever it was," said Karen, "somebody wants you out of the way. So it's even more important we stick together. We need to be very careful from now on."

"Karen," asked Sara again, "what if we can't find a phone this way?"

"I don't know, Sara. But I'd be surprised if we didn't."

"But there's only jungle this way," said Tito.

"Not forever. We'll find another road through the jungle or south to Guatemala. I don't think we're going to run out of options to save you guys."

"What about me, Karen?" asked Sara. "I'm not a guy."

"Oh, sorry, girl. That's North American slang. Sometimes, it's neuter."

"So you're a guy?" Tito asked Karen. "You act like one."

"Thank you, Tito," she replied. "But no, I'm not a guy. When it's plural, it means everyone."

"Okay, guys," announced Tito, "then let's find Grif a doctor, too."

"Good idea, Tito," said Karen.

Karen continued driving east. After only five miles, however, they met the *Río la Revancha* for the third and final time. This time the road abruptly ended. Directly across the river, a wide cart trail, rutted and overhung with jungle, disappeared into the foliage.

Karen slowed the truck, and she and Griffith looked at each other without speaking. She downshifted and eased forward into the river. When the truck reached the middle of the water, the engine coughed and tried to stall.

"Hold on," she warned.

Karen gunned the engine, and they bounced across onto the narrow, washed-out road. The thick jungle closed in on them, cloaking the last of the evening light. The temperature dropped, and the sounds of the night came alive around them. The pain in Griffith's arm was numbing. Unable to sleep, he stared at the truck lights bouncing off the swathing, dark jungle.

Wounded, tired, and hungry, he saw nothing beyond the small, yellow cones their headlights cut in the darkness.

CHAPTER ELEVEN
TARGET PRACTICE

Rancho Nuevo San Juan Bautista del Corazón
Tuesday afternoon

> Among other evils which being unarmed brings you, it causes you to be despised.
> *The Prince*
> Niccolo Machiavelli
> 1469—1527

Two men, dressed in fatigues without identification, their automatic rifles ready, crossed to the corners of the Victorian guest house and positioned themselves in range of the door. *Comandante* Bicho, flanked by two black-uniformed *judiciales*, strode onto the porch and knocked on the door.

No one answered.

He knocked again, louder. He waited a few seconds and stepped back. He nodded to the men behind him.

One held the screen door, and the other raised his boot and kicked the door open, splintering the latch and frame. They darted in, weapons ready, and scanned the room. With one of the *judiciales* as back up, the other checked the bathroom.

"*Comandante* Bicho," protested *don* Pedro from the yard, "why didn't you just open the door? I'm sure it was unlocked, and they are no longer armed."

Bicho ignored him and followed his men into the cottage.

Inside, his head jerked from side to side, noting a papaya on the floor by the bed and the sheets of the far bed pulled back. He sniffed the rumpled pillow and then stalked back out to the front porch, pulling the door shut. It clattered against its broken frame.

"*Don* Pedro," he said evenly, "your guests seemed to have left."

"What? I don't understand," said *don* Pedro.

"It seems simple enough. You said they were here. Now they are not. We must find them. Again."

Don Pedro called to the groom tending the Arabian.

"Esteban, have you seen the *gringos* and their children recently?" he asked.

"Yes, *don* Pedro," he replied. "The *gringo* was on the porch swing, but it was hours ago. I've been here with *el Sultán*."

"And they didn't leave?" he asked.

"No, *don* Pedro," he lied, "I didn't see them leave."

"Is their horse still here, do you know?"

"Yes, *don* Pedro," said Esteban, pointing toward another pasture.

"And their tack?"

"I don't know."

"Find out. Check our horses, too."

"Yes, *don* Pedro."

Esteban took the tall Arabian by the halter and headed to the barns. Because of the afternoon heat, or perhaps because of the missing children, nobody paid any attention to how much time he took getting to the barn.

Bicho walked to the white pickup which had brought him from his helicopter and opened the passenger door.

"Valdéz," he said to the nearest of his men, "stay here. Find out what you can. If they happen to fall into *don* Pedro's hands again, make sure they don't leave this time."

"Yes, *Comandante.*"

"*Don* Pedro," he said, "where do these roads lead?"

He flicked his eyes both ways, north, the direction from which the four fugitives had walked out of the jungle, and south around the main house.

"That way," answered *don* Pedro, pointing past his home, "is the difficult way to the main road, through Amparo. To the north is longer but faster, through the village of Río Blanco, then south and west to the *Lagunas.*"

"There is no other way out?"

"Not out, no. It's possible to continue east into the lowlands. But there's no way out of the jungle for hundreds of miles, except west to the main road."

"Excellent."

He ordered *don* Pedro's *guardias blancas* to drive one of the ranch's trucks on the narrow road to Amparo as quickly as they could. If they happened to catch up with the four who fled, they were to detain them until he arrived.

"*Don* Pedro," he continued without facing him, "this is unfortunate. Everything fell into our hands. All you had to do was hold onto the children until I got here. We could have ended the Zapatista threat and then returned the children to the President. Your money, and that of your fellow *latifundistas*, would never have been touched.

"Now, who knows what will happen? Without his children, the President must approve armed intervention. At least we can rid ourselves of this terrorist threat. I am less sure, however, of the fate of the children. And now, even the billions of *pesos* in your *latifundista* fund are in jeopardy.

"Alvarado, drive us back to the Huey," he ordered and then

turned to face the rancher. "*Don* Pedro, I don't want my work wasted because you got careless."

"Of course not," agreed *don* Pedro. "I still don't understand how..."

"Yes," interrupted Bicho. "But we'll find them, nevertheless."

Bicho waved his hand at his driver/pilot, and they drove off. He doubted if *don* Pedro would ever figure out how the *gringos* escaped with the children. But unless they were completely ignorant, which seemed unlikely given what they'd accomplished so far, Bicho assumed they simply took one of *don* Pedro's trucks.

Once in the air, Bicho told Alvarado to fly toward Río Blanco, the easiest and most likely escape route. Since the sun would be setting within the hour, he wanted to check it first. He also radioed his regional headquarters to contact all field squads, *judicial* and *guardias blancas* alike, with instructions to detain any *gringo* couple, especially if children were with them. And, he added, all white pickup trucks were to be stopped.

Flying less than two hundred feet above the forest canopy, they traced the road north and west, past Margarita's little home hidden against the mountainside and toward the last extension of the all-weather road to Río Blanco. They saw some foot traffic, a *campesino* and his family Bicho ordered Alvarado to buzz. He descended to under a hundred feet, over the narrow cut at the top of the canopy. The parents grabbed their children and darted into the brush.

"Didn't look like them," commented Bicho casually.

They flew on to Río Blanco, a small village similar to Amparo. Two white pickups were parked in the road surrounded by several dozen people, including four of the local *guardias blancas*.

"Take her down," ordered Bicho.

They landed in the road. Motioning for Alvarado to stay aboard, Bicho got out and walked over to the crowd.

"Who owns these trucks?" he asked.

The trucks were parked side by side in the middle of the road. The older truck had rusted panels, a cracked windshield, and four bald tires.

"I own this one, *Señor Capitán*," volunteered a sere, old *campesino*, pointing to the rickety pick-up.

Bicho looked down at him.

"*Comandante*," he corrected. "Where are your ownership papers and registration for this truck?"

"I've had this truck a very long time. I don't know where my papers are, *Señor Capitán*."

"*Comandante*," he repeated more loudly to the tiny, frail man. "And the other truck?"

"Yes, *Comandante*, it's mine," said a young *indígena*, dressed in white cotton shirt and pants.

"Your papers," demanded Bicho brusquely.

"They're at home. I don't have them with me. I'm sorry."

"I'm sure you are. I suppose that means you expect me, without any proof, to believe you own this truck?"

"Yes, *Comandante*. That's right."

"It would be a mistake to be impudent with me, *indio*."

He almost spat the last word.

"I'm sorry, *Comandante*. Impudence was not intended."

Bicho, unsure if he was being mocked, turned away and strode back to his helicopter. As he passed one of the *guardias blancas*, he stopped and spoke quietly.

"Are these all the vehicles around here?"

"I believe so, sir."

"Good. Clear this area, soldier. Leave the trucks there."

"Yes, sir."

Bicho climbed aboard and showed Alvarado a thumb up. Once Alvarado got the Huey over the village, Bicho pointed down at the trucks. The squad moved the people back, but the *indígena* refused to leave his truck. Alvarado swung the Huey around so the nose pointed down at the trucks in the road. Bicho flicked on the loudspeaker switch.

"Stand clear!"

Bicho's voice boomed down on the crowd from the speaker mounted under the nose.

The *indígena* broke free from the *guardia blanca* holding him.

"Halt!" blasted the voice again.

But everyone kept backing away even further. Some ran into buildings and others across the fields. A few just moved out of range, watching the confrontation. Everyone except the *indígena* truck owner. He got into his truck, slammed the door, and sped away, kicking up dust and gravel.

Bicho pointed with his chin, and Alvarado flew in behind the fleeing truck. Bicho took the machine gun grip and lined up his fleeing target. He squeezed off a two-second burst. The 7.62 mm, armor piercing shells ripped through the body of the truck, almost cutting it in half. The truck skidded off the road, tripped sideways in a ditch, and flipped into the meadow, rupturing the gas tank. Bicho squeezed off another short burst, igniting the truck in a fireball.

"Zapatista, no doubt," said Bicho.

Alvarado shoved the rudder over, and they spun around. He headed back toward the other truck, alone now in the middle of the road. One more burst from the machine gun and the other truck rocked and shivered. Bullets tore the hood open, blew apart the engine, shattered the windshield, and penetrated the bed. Gas and oil flowed into the dust as the Huey left Rio Blanco behind.

Bicho directed Alvarado to fly southeast along the new, all-season road the government, in its Sisyphean efforts against the annual rains, was perpetually working on. These roads were intended to give the *campesinos* and *indígena* of the jungle greater access to schools and clinics. Whether they even made those long trips to the few schools and clinics scattered through the jungle, Bicho didn't know or care. These new roads, however, did make it easier to move troops on the ground, especially during the rainy season.

Flying low, not much above stall speed, they reached San Vicente twenty-three minutes later. The local *guardias blancas* had parked the village's three trucks in the middle of the dirt road. One of them was pale blue. Rather than land, Bicho used his loudspeaker to clear everyone of the area. He repeated the strafing procedure, destroying any means of escape this village might provide for the children and their abductors.

Alvarado banked the Huey east toward Amparo. The mountains dropped quickly toward the lowland jungle, and a wide, low valley opened up. Shortly, the road split, east toward Amparo and the jungle, and west back to the *Lagunas*. Bicho pointed east, and Alvarado banked left. Within minutes, their radio crackled with the excited voice of a *guardias blancas'* squad leader in Amparo.

"Yes, *Comandante*, they were at the *cantina*, but they left in a white truck and drove east into the jungle. Over."

"Did you see them? Over?"

"Oh, yes, *Comandante*. The blonde *gringa*, a dark haired man, and the children. And the white truck. Over."

"Very good. Post a guard. Detain them if they return this way. And torch the *cantina*. Over. Alvarado, boost it. Let's get to Amparo and find their trail."

Alvarado bore east, and Bicho keyed the GPS navigation

box for the coordinates of Amparo. Too small to be listed, the screen blinked "no results". Nevertheless, following the improved road, they flew over Amparo within minutes. A small fire licked at the corner of *la Cantina*. No one was around. They continued southeast along the extension of the new road.

As they reached the *Río la Revancha*, the sun was down, and the jungle stretched a deep blue-green eastward, disappearing into the emerging darkness. Alvarado slowed the aircraft. With the searchlight on, the road was impossible to pick out through the canopy's brilliant reflection. They turned it off, and Alvarado followed the shadowy cut in the canopy. The jungle grew more tightly over the road until they lost it altogether in the evening shades.

Finally, Bicho cocked his wrist up and twisted his forefinger in a small circle. Alvarado hovered over the jungle, scanning for the flicker of headlights. The helicopter drifted slowly east. After several more minutes, Bicho spotted their target: headlights flickering off distant tree trunks.

Alvarado brought the helicopter nearer the canopy. From this lower angle, the foliage below them was awash from the downblast, but they could follow the headlight reflections. As they flew nearer, Bicho caught glimpses of the red taillights.

Alvarado eased the Huey closer to the truck. Bicho held the machine gun grip and waited. When they were within a hundred feet, Bicho switched on the thousand-watt, narrow beam searchlight, aimed the machine gun, and squeezed the trigger for nearly three seconds.

The pick-up truck shuddered under the sustained barrage and careened out of control into the undergrowth. Abruptly, the headlights flashed off a huge tree trunk and bent upward as the truck skidded onto the buttressed roots. The screech of wrenching metal cut through the night as the truck twisted upward, became airborne for an instant, and slammed back to the earth on its cab. The pick-up vibrated from the impact, and the lights flickered. When the gas from the ruptured fuel line vaporized over the hot exhaust manifold, the truck exploded into flames. The leaves and nearby brush crackled in the heat and caught fire.

"Good shooting, *Comandante*," complimented Alvarado.

"Excellent flying, Alvarado. It's a pity they got in the way, but I believe we are now ready to eradicate the Zapatistas." He jerked his head sideways. "Head back to *don* Pedro's, and let's have some tequila."

Their GPS located the coordinates and flashed the bearing. While the jungle burned with petroleum-fed intensity, Alvarado pulled the elevators and gunned the engine into a climb. They'd be drinking shots of Hornito's within thirty minutes.

CHAPTER TWELVE
UNEXPECTED DIRECTIONS

La Selva Lacandona
Tuesday night

> Like one that on a lonesome road
> Doth walk in fear and dread,
> And having once turned round walks on,
> And turns no more his head;
> Because he knows a frightful fiend
> Doth close behind him tread.
>
> *Rime of the Ancient Mariner*
> S. T. Coleridge
> 1772—1834

Karen drove slowly through the jungle—Griffith doubted they were being followed—and after nearly an hour, night enveloped them. The headlights carved out their tiny patch of light, exaggerating the darkness around them. Driving toward the rising moon, the jungle crowded the road, and the canopy closed over their heads. Huge, buttressed trees shouldered their way into their path. Liana vines dangled like curtains above them.

Tito and Sara were dozing, and Griffith kept his face toward the cool air blowing in his window. In worried silence, he watched for any sign of habitation as Karen drove them deeper into the jungle. They passed no one and saw no lights.

Karen slowed the truck and steered onto a large, half-buried rock to avoid a wide hole. The rear bell housing screeched as it dragged over the boulder. She swung the truck back into the center of the road and glanced at the rear view mirror.

The possibility of having to spend a second night, alone in the jungle, was beginning to unnerve Griffith. He held his throbbing arm close to him and considered how to get through the next few hours. He really didn't believe they'd find a telephone in this direction, but other than turning back and facing the *guardias blancas*, what choice did they have? They had to keep driving east. Something would happen. They'd just have to improvise when it did.

Griffith sighed quietly to himself. Unlike Karen, improvisation was not a talent he nurtured. Although he'd never thought himself reluctant to act, he was certainly reflective. That habit of reflection had come during the struggle over his parents' deaths. Even before he and Karen married, he'd spent hours trying to figure out why he loved this woman. The two of them were so different. He understood the physical attraction and had overcome his inherent shyness to appreciate it. But that wasn't what bound him to her. It wasn't even her confidence and capabilities, as great as they were. What Karen possessed, what she had brought to him, was the spontaneity to act—something he hadn't realized he'd lost until he fell in love.

In the faint light of the cab Karen looked again into the mirror. The lines around her eyes wrinkled in shadow as she squinted.

Someone's behind us, Griffith realized.

Bile soured his stomach.

He turned around trying not to disturb the children in their sleep and saw headlights, far behind them, blinking through the trees. Since leaving *Na-Bolom* thirty-six hours ago, everything, from the first random police search to his gunshot wound, had reconditioned his fear and flight responses. And now, less than an hour after sunset, along a narrow jungle road miles from the nearest village, a set of headlights was triggering the same response once again. He wanted Karen to drive faster, to lose the vehicle behind them as quickly as possible.

"Are they gaining on us?" he asked softly, hoping not to wake the children.

"Who?" asked Sara sleepily.

"The car behind us, Sara," replied Karen. "And yes, Griffith, I think so."

"Do you want to lose them?" asked Griffith.

"What about your arm?"

"I'll hold on."

Karen smiled at him and nodded. Tito was still asleep against Sara's shoulder.

"Should we wake him?" Sara asked.

"Does he always sleep this soundly?" asked Griffith.

"*Sí*, always."

"No, don't wake him," said Karen. "This may be nothing at all. Let him sleep if he can."

Karen gave the truck more gas. She kept to as straight a line as possible, looking for level road, driving through water holes and ruts, and bouncing over rocks and fallen branches. The truck rattled and shook as its worn springs transferred every bang and jolt to their spines.

"I think they're gaining on us, Karen," said Griffith looking back. He was sitting sideways against the door, his left arm protected against his body, his right hand braced on the dash.

"Shit," whispered Karen under her breath.

Sara smiled at the profanity.

"How far back?" asked Karen

"Hard to tell," he answered. "Quarter of a mile, maybe more. Is there anywhere to turn off, or hide, or..."

"I haven't seen anything. Do you think I can get the truck off the road, maybe behind one of those huge trees?"

"We'd end up on foot because I don't think you'd get it back on the road. What if we just pull over in the next wide spot, turn our lights down, and let them pass?"

"Suppose they stop?" she suggested.

"Take off like a hitchhiker's bad dream?"

"And if they pull in front of us and stop?"

"Christ, Karen, I don't know."

"Sorry, Grif. Just being paranoid."

"I wonder why?" he replied sarcastically.

In the rattling cab, Griffith mulled over their limited options. Keep driving was about it, he figured. Then, at the edge of his hearing, a different noise, a new sound, above and behind them, caught his attention.

"Oh, Christ on a cross," he muttered.

The distant thrum of a helicopter droned in his ears and jaw.

"Do you hear that?" he asked.

"Oh, not again," moaned Karen.

She pushed the truck a little harder, skimming over the ruts, skiing through the mud, and slamming over the rocks. The thump of helicopter rotors grew heavier.

"Let's confuse them," announced Karen. "Brace yourselves."

Ahead of them, the road bent to the left around a huge, buttressed ceiba tree. She lifted her foot off the accelerator and waited as the truck coasted forward. Ten feet before the tree, she slammed on the brakes and steered into the turn. As they slid past the ceiba, she punched off the headlight button.

Everything went black as the rear end skidded past them. Leaves and branches slapped the back panels, and darkness spun around them. The truck rocked sideways to a stop, blocking the road. The engine stalled.

Stunned into silence, Griffith looked across the seat out Karen's window at the headlights bouncing toward the sharp turn. Tito sat up, rubbing his eyes. Karen cranked the ignition, and the engine jumped back to life. She ground the gears into reverse. Before she could release the clutch, an intense white light cut the night and spotlighted the other truck, a few hundred feet away and closing.

The terrifying, explosive shock of repeated, high-powered machine gun fire burst through the night. The truck in the spotlight careened across the road toward the ceiba as slug after slug ripped into its metal hide. Griffith stared dumbly at the outline of two passengers tossed about the back-lit cab. The truck skidded off the road and up the long buttressed roots until it flipped backwards. The grating twist of metal tore into his ears as the truck slammed onto its roof.

An instant later, it burst into flames. With the thrashing rotors above them swamping the incandescent explosion, the concussion rocked their truck. The wash of the blades buffeted black smoke and vapors over them. The helicopter rounded up and flew off.

Griffith sat still, blinking his eyes. The heat through Karen's window warmed his cheeks as the other truck belched smoke and flames into the treetops. The smell of burning rubber and the popping of flesh sizzling in the inferno spread through the canopied forest. He tried to shake his head clear, but the repugnant odors hung acrid in his nose.

Nobody spoke.

Then Karen turned on the headlights. She backed around,

shifted into first, and accelerated, driving farther into the night and deeper into the jungle.

***

By ten o'clock they had arrived at a clearing above the village of la Fortuna Gallo Giro, the first wide spot along the *Río Lacantún*. La Fortuna was clustered on the other side of the river, but the road ended in this clearing at the top of a steep, muddy hill. Below, a foot bridge with thin cables bolted around the largest trees on each side was suspended above the river. Muddy leaves, branches, and plastic debris caught by the bridge during the frequent high waters hung from the narrow boards.

Across the river, lantern light glowed in a few of the rough plank buildings. On this side, the orange-yellow flame of another lantern flickered in the trees. Three men were stretched out under the trees, talking, drinking, and watching fishing poles balanced over the ends of several small dugout launches beached at their feet. Karen stopped the truck and turned off the lights. The men looked up at them.

"Well, guys," said Karen, her voice tired, "I guess the road does end."

Across the river, the road began again beyond the last thatched home. From there, in good weather, during the dry season, it was possible to pick a tortuous path several hundred miles north and west out of *la Selva Lacandona*. In four-wheel drive, carrying extra canisters of gasoline, it was possible, but not during the rainy season.

Besides, they couldn't get across the river.

"Any ideas?" asked Karen.

"If there's a truck in that village," suggested Tito, "maybe we could trade."

"Why would they trade for a truck on the wrong side of the river?" asked Sara.

"If they won't trade for a truck" said Griffith, "maybe we can get something else."

"Go down the river?" asked Sara.

"Rivers get wider," he replied, "villages become towns, and towns usually have telephones."

"And I bet this pick-up has some value," added Karen, "even on this side of the river."

"Okay," agreed Griffith. "Odysseus didn't turned back, right?"

"Who's he?" asked Tito, getting out of the truck.

"Oh, Tito," replied his sister, "don't you know anything? He's from *La Odisea* by Homer. He had a long, terrible sea voyage after the Trojan War."

"You've been in school longer than I," he protested and ran off toward the hillside.

At the top of the hill, Tito glanced back to make sure the others were coming and disappeared over the edge. First a squeal and then peals of laughter went rolling down the hill as Tito discovered it had rained here before they arrived. He slid and tumbled, rolling over in the mud until he found his balance and rode giggling to the bottom on his back. Legs in the air, he slid to a halt in front of the smiling fishermen. He stood, covered in red mud, and waved.

Karen and Sara waved back. Karen had the gear: the small backpack with their sundries, toilet paper, and the last of their fruit and bread, and the purifier, canteen, and fanny pack. She hung the sheathed machete from her belt, leaving her hands free.

"Who's next," she asked.

Griffith looked down the trail. The moon shadows were sharp, but the trees growing beside the steep trail blocked most of the lambent light. Narrow shafts of pale blue spackled the trail, altering the depth perception and confusing the eye. It was well over a hundred feet to the bottom. This wasn't going to be easy, he thought, especially trying to protect his sore, swollen forearm.

"I'm not taking Tito's route," he said.

He glanced from side to side for a path down. The trail was ten or twelve feet wide, bare of any vegetation, and eroded away in long gullies. At the bottom, one of the men pointed to the left side of the trail. Griffith looked and saw nothing but shadowed trees. He shook his head, held out his right arm, and shrugged.

The fisherman walked over, reached down, and picked up the bitter end of a heavy, one inch, hemp line tied to a tree. In the dense foliage, Griffith discerned the shadow of a rope, tied from tree to tree at banister height. He smiled and waved.

"I'll take the rope," he said.

With his good right hand gripping the rope, he turned around so he faced the hill. Holding his left arm tightly against his chest, he stepped back. The footing was slick, but the rain-worn gullies and small, grassy clumps along the edge gave him some confidence. He took his time reaching the bottom, feeling for the firmest tussocks and pausing several times to catch his breath.

Once he was standing next to Tito, he relaxed and gestured for Sara and Karen to follow. With more than a few slips onto the muddy trail, they got down. Filthy again, Karen smiled at the astounded fishermen.

"¿Hablan Ustedes español, señores?" she asked.

"Sí, señora," said one of them removing his straw hat. The man wore calf-length trousers, old *huaraches*, and a wool *serape*.

"Karen," announced Tito, "I've already talked with José. His name is José. They don't have a telephone or any trucks or cars across the river."

"*Me llamo* Karen," replied Karen extending her hand, "*y* Griffith *y Sara.*"

José nodded at her and smiled at the others.

"I told him you and Griffith wanted to trade our truck for his boat," said Tito. "Look, it has a motor."

Each of the three, eighteen-foot launches had a small outboard mounted on the back transom. The moonlight wasn't strong enough to reveal all the rust and wear, but these boats were more than dugouts. They were planked and roughly painted, with narrow thwarts for seats. Each had a gas can in the stern connected to its outboard. In addition to the fishing poles off the transoms, nets lay in the bottoms.

"*¿Vuestra camioneta?*" José asked, looking at Griffith.

"*¿Por la lancha, sí?*" answered Karen.

She smiled at Tito and looked at Griffith, who half shrugged and nodded agreement.

What the hell, he thought. They'd already lost one horse, left another behind, and stolen this truck. At least this fisherman might make out all right on the deal.

Karen held up the key. José looked at his friends maintaining as indifferent a mien as possible. He turned back to Karen, smiled, nodded, and then spoke to Griffith.

"*Sí, señor,*" he said. "Okay."

Griffith understood the last part and looked at Karen just as she tossed him the key. He handed it to José who pointed to the middle launch.

"*Muchas gracias,*" the fisherman said with a big smile and held the key up for his friends to see. He grabbed the rope and started up the hill. His friends followed enthusiastically, climbing nimbly behind him.

"*De nada,*" Griffith called after them.

"Let's go," cried Tito, running toward their new boat.

At the river's edge, he slid feet first into the river, then stood in knee-deep water. He grabbed the rough gunwale and scrambled into the launch. Griffith stepped aboard, placing his foot unsteadily in the center of the boat. Balancing himself on the port gunwale, he crawled over Tito hunkering down amidships. He slowly made his way to the stern, pulled in the fishing line, and placed the pole in the next launch. Sara followed him aboard, sitting forward.

Holding the muddy painter at the bow, Karen waited until everyone was evenly seated. She then tossed the line aboard, shoved the bow through the mud into the gentle current, and jumped lightly into the launch. She stepped around each of them to the stern without rocking the boat and picked up the only oar—a long, heavy, wooden blade.

She spun the launch around, pointing the bow downstream. Turning to the outboard, a very old, three-horse, two-stroke Evinrude, she found the shutoff valve, opened it, checked the fuel line, and shook the rusty, three gallon tank. It was mostly full, so she lowered the engine's propeller into the water. She located the pull cord and gave it a slow, preliminary tug. The piston moved, so she pulled harder. It coughed once. Two more yanks and the old engine belched, sputtered, and caught. Karen twisted the throttle gently a couple of times, and the engine smoothed out.

Holding the gunwale firmly, Griffith sat in amazement. Just like that, in the middle of nowhere, they were motoring downstream.

On the slow, wide river, the launch moved easily. Every mile or so, another stream, sometimes large and swollen from localized rains, would join the *Río Lacantún*, altering its current in various ways. By midnight the moon was well past its zenith, glittering off the river. Except for the occasional small clearing hacked and burned out of the dense cover, the jungle grew thick, hanging its limbs far over the river. Through the quiet night, the soft, omnipresent hum of insects whirred in the trees. A fish broke the surface with a slap. Then the eerily human-like cry of a nocturnal wild cat silenced the forest. Minutes later, the gurgle of water covered something sliding from the shore into the water.

They passed a small, unlighted village on the left bank and waved to several late-night fishermen reclining on the grassy bank by a fire. The cedar-scented smoke from the small fire curled into the branches and leaves. Wispy, ghost-like tendrils illuminated by moonbeams reached across the water's surface.

Sara, curled against the forward thwart, watched the bow slice through the smoky apparitions and listened to the gentle susurration of the water flowing by the hull. Tito, awake for the first hour until the rhythmic motions of the boat lulled him to sleep, lay in a ball on the fishing nets.

In the stern, Karen sat on the thwart with one hand on the tiller and the other on Griffith's shoulder. Griffith sat on more nets, his back between Karen's legs, his head leaning against her arm. His left arm was swollen and tender to the touch. But with the jungle night isolating them, the wide, gentle river bathed in moonlight, and a cool breeze across their cheeks, Griffith savored these few quiet hours.

Since *Na-Bolom*, their honeymoon had lost its romance for him, but the quiet, nighttime beauty of this rain forest river soothed him. At times his thoughts wandered away, but the presence of Karen and the children, all of them lost deep in the rain forest of southern Mexico, kept tugging it back. He had rarely thought of children before. Although he and Karen had talked around the subject prior to their wedding, both their lives were too busy to have considered it seriously. He contemplated the inescapable bond being forged among the four of them.

"Karen," he said softly.

"Yes, love?" she whispered.

"Do you think you want to have children? I mean, of our own?"

"Griffith, what a lovely thought. But maybe we shouldn't base our decision on this particular child-rearing experience."

"These kids are okay, I guess. They're a bit spoiled, but who am I to say. If they were ours, I'd probably spoil them, too. I've got to admit though, I'm real ignorant. Not just about children, but all this."

"Oh, Griffith," she replied, "I do love you. You've been so steady. Thank you. I think you're the reason these kids have handled all this so well. They're feeding off your strength. They even seem stronger than when we found them."

"They do, don't they? I wish I felt as strong right now." He paused. "Karen?"

"Yes, Grif."

"We need to get out of here soon."

"I know. I'm worried, too. You need a doctor."

"A doctor would help. Karen...," Griffith hesitated, unsure how to express his thought, "we can do this. I mean, we'll do all right... together, you know. But unfortunately, I'm not prepared for any of this. I need you, Karen."

"We need each other, Grif."

He twisted around to look up at his bride. The moonlight glinted off the dark quetzal feather still braided in her hair. He reached up to touch it and struck the end of his left elbow against the thwart. He stifled a groan.

"Oh, how is your arm?"

She massaged his left shoulder and neck, working her fingers along the knotted muscles.

"It's still sore. Bearable, considering. I had no idea a gunshot could hurt so much. It burned and, God, it was like… like the top of my forearm exploded."

Karen winced audibly.

"Oh, it's not so bad now. If I don't move my arm. It's sort of numb, but my fingers still work."

He moved his left fingers slightly, and muscles twitched with painful darts. Karen rubbed his shoulder and neck again.

"Oh, Karen, I love you so much. I bet I haven't told you that enough today."

"Ah, and I love you, too. But, really, since the kids arrived, who's had time?"

Griffith laughed and then, caught up in the absurdity, he found himself trapped in his laughter. His arm hurt, but he needed the relief. He laughed so hard when he finally inhaled, he snorted. And Karen laughed with him.

Sara turned around and waved. Griffith caught his breath and waved back. He nestled himself deeper between Karen's warm thighs and sighed, enjoying the sound of laughter.

"Kids might be nice," he mused.

Karen rubbed his shoulder. For the first time since *Na-Bolom*, Griffith closed his eyes and slept. Above the steady putter of the tiny outboard, the nocturnal voices of the jungle drifted across the water. The moon crept slowly toward the horizon. The river wound around gentle bends, first north, then again south, but always working its way eastward, deeper into *la Selva Lacandona*.

***

It was after four a.m. when the weather changed. Within minutes, the air changed from quiet and cool to heavy and moist. A warm, soft wind, thick with verdant scent, wafted across the jungle. Distant thunder rolled, long and low on the increasing wind. The river's current increased, and the surface broke with tiny, white-capped wavelets.

A towering, splintered bolt of lightning tore open the sky, illuminating the jungle. Simultaneously, a tremendous crack boxed their ears. Griffith awoke with a start. The first, large drops of rain plunked into the water.

Karen steered the launch closer to the lee shore on their right where the sloping riverbanks rose into hills. She'd been staying in the middle to keep away from the insects, but the approaching rain would drive the mosquitoes away. And the overhanging trees might afford some protection from the weather.

Just as the launch slid under the nearest trees, the rain came down in earnest. Under the low canopy, darkness engulfed them. The rain was loud, smacking the water in millions of staccato hits and slapping the leaves until they released their sopping contents in miniature torrents. An overburdened elephant fern released its wet load onto Tito.

"Oh, that's cold," he protested sleepily. "Where am I?"

"We're still on the river, Tito," said Karen over the puttering engine.

"Oh, sorry," he said and lay back down, curling himself into a ball.

The current increased under their keel. Griffith wanted Karen to slow even more, but he knew they'd lose steerage if they did. In utter black, Karen leaned into him and shouted over the rain.

"We need to get back out into the river where I can see a little."

Tito sat up in the bottom of the boat.

"You'll get wet," he said matter-of-factly.

Suddenly, from the darkness in front of them, Sara screamed. The bow of the launch careened off a house-sized boulder jutting from the steep bank. From the stern, they saw the faint white ghost of Sara's dress as she was thrown forward into the bow. The current shoved the launch's starboard gunwale against the boulder and pinned it there. The wind and the force of the current bounced waves off the boulder, rocking the long, narrow-beamed launch, banging it against the rock, and splashing water over the outboard gunwale.

"Griffith," shouted Karen, leaning over his ear, "take the throttle. Move us out into the current."

"Yes," he shouted back. "Go check Sara. I'll be okay."

Karen crawled over Tito to the bow. Griffith tested the throttle gingerly. More water splashed over the gunwales, chilling his ankles. When Karen faded into the darkness forward, he opened the throttle. The launch didn't move. Each wave hit the launch broadside, holding it against the boulder. He gave it more gas. The launch, straining against the force of the current, inched forward momentarily, then slid back against the boulder.

Holding the throttle with his right hand and protecting his left arm, he leaned his back against the port gunwale and braced his feet on the face of the face of the rock.

Tito got on his knees to push with his hands.

"Be careful, Tito," shouted Griffith.

"*Sí*," he called back, and leaned into the rock.

"Wait a moment, Tito. Watch me."

Tito turned and Griffith pointed to his feet against the boulder. The boy repositioned himself. Griffith nodded in rhythm to the crests and troughs of the waves. When the next wave lifted them, Griffith nodded vigorously and gunned the engine. They both pushed.

The launch slid down the receding surface of the wave, and the little two-bladed prop strained. The bow edged past the rock and balanced there. Again they were lifted. At the crest, instead of being knocked back into the rock wall, they remained half a foot out.

"Now!" shouted Griffith.

They both pushed again with their feet. Griffith lifted himself off the thwart, balancing on his shoulders, straining his legs against the rock. The force of the current grabbed the bow, and his feet were yanked away from the wall. He fell back into the boat, jarring his left elbow against the gas can. Tears filled his eyes as he sat up to steer.

Pulled into the current, the launch moved away from the boulder, out into the cresting waves and racing torrent. The stern quickly spun around, and the launch sped into the rain and river. Griffith backed off the throttle and pulled it over to straighten their downstream momentum. It wasn't as dark away from the trees, but the heavy downpour, much louder in the middle of the river, pounded on them.

A new sound lay under the roar of the rain and river. Lower and deeper, it surrounded them. Griffith looked around. On both sides of the river, the shore line was growing taller, hills becoming walls. They'd entered a canyon, and the racing waters echoed from its walls.

Running with the current, the narrow boat pitched and rocked. In addition to the water shipped into the launch, the confused waves made it difficult to steer. When the launch slid down the face of a breaking wave, however, and began to surf along a trough, the pitching motion eased. They sped forward into the night.

Tito moved back and sat on the bottom at Grif's feet. Behind him came Sara, crawling on her hands and knees with

Karen holding her hips, balancing her from behind. Karen pointed to the shore and nodded.

He pulled the rudder to port and raced the tiny engine, but the launch was unable to clear the crests and get out of the current. He shook his head, trying to clear the water from his glasses. The force of the current kept them moving downstream. A long wall of waves between them and the rocky cliffs denied Griffith's efforts to steer out of the maelstrom into the relative peace of the protected cliffs.

Again, he gunned the engine. The bow cut through the crest of the wave, but the current caught the stern, twisting the launch sideways. Just before they presented their beam to the current—where they would have broached and sunk very quickly—he released the throttle and swung the rudder back to regain control. The current refused to release the captive launch.

Karen sat up, looking around at their predicament. She leaned forward and lifted up the long oar. She told the children to move forward, and slid the blade port side deep. She signaled Griffith to make another attempt to cross the wave barrier.

He twisted the throttle full open and pulled the tiller toward him. Karen held the blade as hard as she could against the current, forcing the stern to stay behind them. The launch shot through a narrow gap at the top of the waves, first lifting its bow out of the water, then slamming it down. The bow sliced the calmer water as it raced toward the cliff wall.

"Brace yourselves," shouted Griffith, pushing the tiller away from him.

He got the bow headed back downstream, and the launch slid toward the cliff, slowed, and tapped the wall with the starboard gunwale. Karen shipped the oar. They started to bail the excess water out with their cupped hands while Griffith steered.

The shoreline was a high cliff giving them a rain shadow. By the time each wave reached them, the sheltered walls had reduced its power, shortening its period and diminishing its amplitude. The ride, almost as fast, was considerably less turbulent.

Griffith's left arm ached. A fresh stain of blood dotted his wet bandage. As he sat back to catch his breath, the little engine sputtered. He turned the throttle. The motor hesitated and stopped. He kicked the gas can, and it echoed empty. He breathed deeply, glad they hadn't run out of gas in the middle of the rapids.

Karen pulled the oar back out. Standing, she sculled slowly with the current, keeping them pointed downstream. As the river widened, the boat slowed and drifted sideways. They glided along within twenty feet of the cliff which was now broken up into boulders, ledges, and small talus beaches. Griffith sat up expectantly, peering into the shadows.

The shower tapered to a drizzle. The night was growing lighter, and shadows began to take shape along the shore. Dark patches of vegetation softened the rocky outcroppings. Ahead of them, a fog bank glistened opaquely above the widening river.

"Look," cried Tito, excitedly pointing to a very faint, diffuse glow high within the fog. "A light."

"That's the moon," disagreed Sara.

Griffith looked around him, certain the moon had already set.

"Tito's probably right, Sara," said Griffith. "The moon went down a while ago, I think. Let's head into shore, Karen."

A real light, especially one they could see at this distance, meant more than a single electric line. The children sat up, staring anxiously into the darkness, while Karen sculled a meandering course toward the near shore. Unwilling to let any premature excitement take hold of him, Griffith peered into the darkness and listened.

To his right, beyond the water lapping against the rocky shore, the soft swish of moving leaves drifted to him. He lifted his head, but it had passed, leaving only moist, quiet air. He turned his ear to the shore, but the leaves were now silent.

Then, out of the night, too near and too loud, boots scrambled across gravel.

"*¡Alto!*" a man's voice echoed from the rocks.

Griffith froze. Karen, still on her feet, stopped sculling.

"*¡Deténganse!*" shouted one of them, ordering them to halt.

Several dark figures materialized from the shadowy background. The faint glint of rifle barrels caught Griffith's eye. His skin went cold.

"*Deténganse, por favor,*" the voice repeated.

The bow scraped over the scree and jerked to a halt. Three men crunched over the gravel and pulled the launch farther onto the beach. Karen sighed, handed the pack to Griffith and strapped the canteen, purifier, and machete over her fanny pack.

"Quietly, please," the man commanded in Spanish. "Out of the boat."

Karen stepped past the children onto the rocky shore. After the children climbed from the launch, she took their hands. Griffith got out and stood behind them.

"This way," they were ordered.

The men were dressed in black cotton pants, dark shirts, Sam Brown belts, and handkerchiefs tied around their necks. Their hair was thick and roughly cut. And they were all armed with rifles

"*¿Adonde vamos?*" asked Karen.

"*Silencio, por favor,*" said the leader.

He began to climb the rocks. She risked repeating her question.

"Where are we going?"

He ignored her and kept climbing. The two men standing behind them nudged Karen and Griffith forward with their rifle stocks. The steepness of the rocky climb forced Karen to release the children's hands. With just a look to Griffith, she took the lead, and Griffith fell in behind the children.

No one spoke as they climbed the rugged trail, twisting between boulders and around scrub cedars and shrubs growing in every cranny and bit of earth left behind during the rains. Holding his left arm against his side, Griffith climbed with deliberate caution. Twice he motioned to stop so he could catch his breath and rest his burning hamstrings and buttocks.

When they reached the top, the armed men gathered in a narrow copse of trees overlooking the cliff. The leader took something out of his back pocket and waved it at the other two. They pulled their dark ski-masks over their heads.

Zapatistas! The bile churned in Griffith's stomach.

The leader motioned everyone forward. Beyond the trees, the distant light of civilization glowed through the night fog. Griffith, caught between his fear and a rising anger, ground his teeth. What now lay ahead loomed larger and more terrifying than the threat chasing them. Their immediate future had become the barrel of a rifle.

CHAPTER THIRTEEN
THE ZAPATISTAS

Hydroelectric Station #371 at Neuva San Andres
El Río Lacantún
Wednesday, before dawn

> Nor dread nor hope attend
> A dying animal;
> A man awaits his end
> Dreading and hoping all.
> Death
W. B. Yeats
1865—1939

The gunmen led them along the cliff line toward the lights glimmering in the fog at the mouth of the canyon. Beads of sweat ran down Griffith's ribs, and his left arm throbbed. The quiet, moist air under the trees matted the dark hair on his arms, and his shirt clung to him. A medley of odors filled his head. Mold and rotting leaves under foot, the tingle of cedar around him, and the damp river below assaulted his nose. Even his own body smelled of animal fear, and his mouth tasted of coppery anxiety.

For fifteen minutes they walked quietly in single file. Karen often turned to touch each child reassuringly on the shoulder and make eye contact with Griffith. They hiked in silence along the cliff, marching toward lights. The lights obviously meant people. If it were a rebel camp, Griffith doubted whether there was anything they could do. But their captor's insistence on silence suggested otherwise. So did the lights mean something else? If so, could they find a way to escape? Or get someone's attention? Without any answers, the questions ran in circles around his head.

Finally, the trees ended, and their trail was blocked by a chain link fence. The fence, topped with two rows of razor wire, tapered to anchor bolts at the edge of the cliff. It ran perpendicular from the cliff and disappeared into the night fog rolling across a meadow. Beyond the fence, a hundred yards across the field, several large block buildings were lit up by long rows of outdoor utility lights. Each light pole burned 8,000 watts of sodium vapor energy through crystalline reflections of moisture, bathing the buildings in artificial and perpetual daylight.

Through the fog, Griffith made out the initial letters, *C F E*, of the long name painted on the nearest building. Beyond, the tops of large, metal towers with their suspended high tension lines marched in a line down the mountain toward Guatemala. This was the government's Hydroelectric Station #371 at Neuva San Andres, one of dozens of earthen, electricity-generating dams which sold virtually their entire output to Guatemala.

The leader turned to them and said in a whisper, "*Silencio, por favor.*"

His comrades squatted on their haunches, their rifles leaning against their shoulders. Silhouetted against the distant lights, the leader took a small black box from his belt and held it to his mouth.

"Nest," he whispered into his radio. "Nest, this is *Guacamaya*. Nest, this is *Guacamaya*."

Karen started to translate for Griffith, but Tito, who was standing beside him, held up his hand and whispered the translations in Griffith's ear.

"*Guacamaya* is a bird," he explained to Griffith.

After several seconds, the radio clicked.

"*Guacamaya*, go ahead. Over."

"We have found the nestlings and are ready to make our approach. Over."

"Repeat, *Guacamaya*. Please repeat."

"We have found the nestlings and are ready to make our approach. Over."

"Excellent, *Guacamaya*. Return to the nest immediately. We will be ready to fly. Good work. Over."

The leader put the radio away and turned back to them.

"You must follow me. Be careful. On the other side of the fence, we must stay close to it. It will be very dangerous if we are seen."

He stepped to the edge of the cliff, held onto the chain link, and let himself down over a three-foot drop to exposed rock. He turned and extended his hand to Karen. Ignoring it, she grabbed the fence, followed him onto the rock, and then helped Sara down. Tito climbed down the fence by himself. Griffith followed slowly, very conscious of his wound.

One of the men grabbed a section of links at ground level and pulled up. He motioned for them to crawl to the other side. Karen led the way, maneuvering under the fence on her hands and knees. Once they were all on the other side, the leader took off at a brisk pace. They hurried to keep up as he pressed along the fence line.

For a thousand yards or more they followed him through the darkness and mist, away from the buildings. Then, out of the fog, drifted the distant drone of an engine.

Griffith squinted past the leader into the nebulous vapors of the moist night. Was it possible they were going to be driven somewhere? Finally, an easy ride. The thought amused him with its grim irony. Easier, sure. Easier to get them some place they'd never be seen again.

After another few minutes of rapid walking, Griffith made out the vague shape of a small plane. Flying, he thought, to take them even farther from escape or rescue.

A hundred feet from the single engine plane, the leader stopped them.

"You must now run to the airplane, quickly."

They stood there, waiting for him to lead them.

"Go," he repeated. "Now!"

Karen put her hand on Sara's and Tito's shoulders, and they started out into the field.

"Why didn't they follow us?" said Tito turning to Griffith.

"Good question. Karen, should we make a run for those buildings?"

The buildings were more than a half mile behind them, bathed in yellow fog.

"I bet they've got people watching us," added Karen.

"What if we made some noise," suggested Sara. "You know, attracted somebody's attention."

"Unfortunately, I couldn't see anybody in any of those buildings," said Karen.

"No, neither could I," agreed Griffith.

Before any decision was made, however, a man jumped from the plane and ran out of the fog toward them. He was short, and he carried a shotgun and bandoleer filled with shells. He also wore a black ski-mask. He beckoned for them to follow him back to the little, yellow airplane with the letters *CFE* stenciled on the sides and wings. The hard, plastic canopy was up, and another ski-masked figure sat at the controls. An unlit pipe hung from his mouth.

An older man stood on the ground by the pilot's side. He was neither armed nor dressed as the others but wore slacks frayed at the cuff and a blue cotton, short sleeve shirt with a *CFE* patch on the sleeve. Pointing to his watch and then to the distant buildings still shrouded in the pre-dawn fog, his gestures were urgent and worried. The pilot spoke gently to the man on the ground.

"It is okay, Miguel. We're ready to leave. Go back, now. And thank you very much. Go with God."

Their armed escort waited as the four prisoners helped each other onto the wing of the American Aviation-built Traveler AA5, the forerunner of the Grumman Cheetah and Tiger aircraft. There were only four seats in this thirty-five year old plane. The pilot turned to them and took the pipe from his mouth. He pointed to the back seats with his pipe and spoke in a quiet baritone. His English was clearly enunciated and well-pronounced, although the Mexican accent was apparent.

"Take the children on your laps, and strap yourselves in, please," he said.

Sara sat between Karen's legs, and Tito squeezed next to Griffith on the narrow seat. The other soldier climbed into the copilot's seat and lowered the canopy over them. While he strapped himself in, the pilot pulled the throttle out. Holding the wheel and working the differential brakes of the fixed nose-wheel plane with his feet, they headed down the meadow toward the cliff.

Fog poured past the nose and windows. The lights of the *CFE* buildings loomed ahead on the right. When his speed was up, the pilot pulled the wheel column. The light airplane lurched off the ground, bouncing the tail skeg off the grass. He eased the column back. The nose dipped, and the wheels collided solidly with the grass, jarring his passengers.

Before he had time to figure out exactly how sensitive the elevator on this light-weight Traveler was, he had gotten himself into a pilot-induced oscillation, lifting and then bouncing the plane down the last hundred yards of meadow. He managed to avoid striking the propeller on the ground each time, but when they reached the cliff line, the last bounce took them beyond the precipice. The plane soared off the cliff, dropping through the fog.

In the back, the jostled and cramped passengers sat wide-eyed as the plane broke from the fog bank. It dove toward the dark river hundreds of feet below. While the copilot took out a chart and notebook, the pilot pulled the wheel back, banked left, and brought the plane neatly up into a course above the Colorado Canyon. Holding a small flashlight on a chart, the copilot checked some figures in the bouncing light.

"Bearing three-one-zero," he said.

His voice was young and high. He sounded like a teenager.

"Time check, oh-five-thirty-eight," he continued. "After ten minutes, turn up to a course of three-four-five to the *Laguna*. Twenty more minutes at ninety knots."

"Three-one-zero until oh-five-forty-eight, then three-four-five," replied the pilot. "Thank you."

He turned to face his passengers and waved his pipe in the air as he spoke.

"Welcome aboard. I'm sorry there will be no in-flight service."

"Where are you taking us?" asked Karen.

"Somewhere you'll be safe until we can reunite the children with their family."

"Right," snapped Tito sarcastically. "After you ransom us."

"Ransom, child?" replied the pilot. "No, that's not our intention."

"Would you mind telling us your intentions, then?" asked Karen.

"Certainly, my lovely *rubia*," he replied, "but we intend to accomplish so much, I'm not sure where to begin."

"How about with the children?" suggested Karen. "That should be easy enough."

"But I told you. We intend to reunite them with their parents when it is safe."

"Safe for whom?" she asked.

"For them, of course."

Griffith was confused by the tone and direction of this conversation. The pilot sounded calm to him, non-threatening, and even sincere, despite his macho flirting. But here they were, against their wills and literally under the gun, in an airplane apparently stolen from the government with a pilot who was evading Karen's questions.

"Why have you kidnapped us?" asked Griffith

"Ah, *señor*, we have not kidnapped you. But you have been in grave danger alone in the jungle."

"What do you call this?" demanded Karen.

"A rescue," replied the pilot.

"Right," said Tito again. "By Zapatista terrorists."

"Tito, be quiet," shushed his sister.

"Ah, *sí*, the children of our *Presidente* Patrillo."

"Are you not Zapatista?" asked Karen.

"*Sí, señora*. And you are the *norteamericanos* who stole the children from their abductors."

"And now you have them back," said Karen, the edge of anger in her voice. "Are you happy?"

"Have them back, *señora*? No, no, you are mistaken. We never *had* the children in the first place. But what you did was very dangerous. And very brave."

"You didn't kidnap them?"

"No, *señora*."

"Bullshit," spat Tito.

"Tito!" cried Sara. "Stop that!"

"He's lying. He's probably Marcos himself, the big liar."

"A liar?" said the copilot, his young voice high with laughter. "Well, that *is* what all the women say about Marcos, so it must be true."

"If you didn't kidnap the children, *señor*, who did?" asked Karen.

"We don't know. But since three villages were destroyed and a half dozen *campesinos* killed yesterday, apparently in the search for you four, I have my suspicions."

"What?" gasped Karen. "What did you say? Where?"

"*Sí, señora*. West of here."

"Amparo? Was Amparo one?" she asked.

He looked at his copilot who nodded.

"Oh, God, Griffith."

"Yeah, and apparently two more villages we haven't had the opportunity to visit yet," replied Griffith cynically.

"Driving here, we were chased by a helicopter," she said. "It blew up a truck behind us."

"We didn't hear about that, but *sí*, helicopters attacked the villages."

"Whose helicopters?" asked Griffith. "Certainly not the military."

"Don't be so certain, *amigo*. They have before. But no, not this time, I think."

"Then who?" he repeated.

"Unfortunately, it has the signature of the *PJF* and their *guardias blancas* cohorts."

"Karen, that's the…"

"Yes, what we heard in Amparo."

"And during dinner at *Na-Bolom*."

"You're right," she agreed.

"You've been to *Na-Bolom*?" asked the pilot.

"Yes, it was lovely," said Griffith, fondly remembering the start of their honeymoon. "Very romantic."

"*Señora* Blom disapproved of our approach to our common problems, but she brought a great energy and spirit to the struggle. The House of the Jaguar hasn't been the same these years since her death. As you say, however, it is very romantic, and it's a powerful symbol for the Lacandones."

"The Lacandones," said Griffith. "Yes, the *indígena*. But who are these *guardias blancas*?"

"The hired thugs of the *latifundistas*," he answered in a steely voice.

"Yes, we've heard of them, but what do these *latifundistas* do that's so bad?" continued Griffith.

"*Señor*, perhaps a brief history would be easier. If you would not be offended by that, or by my obvious bias."

"No," replied Griffith, "I'll listen to anyone who admits his biases up front."

"The first step in shedding our ignorance, no? I will be brief, then, but everything I tell you and your lovely wife and you, as well, *niños*, is verifiable in media files, in libraries, on-line, and here in the jungle."

The pilot looked at his black Casio watch and tilted the wheel to his new heading. To their right, beyond the horizon, the eastern sky glowed with a hint of false dawn. In front of them clouds had built a towering wall; below, lay the ebon canopy of the jungle.

"The people of Chiapas," he started, "live in the state richest in natural resources, but we have the lowest standard of living in all of the Western Hemisphere. The trees, the land, and the oil reserves are traded in the back rooms of the *Palacio Naciona* by a few very powerful, very wealthy people. The best land in Chiapas was given to the *latifundistas* by the government. Through their *guardias blancas*, they enforce their version of law and order. They control the elections, the distribution of the remaining land, the local taxes, everything.

"The *indígena* throughout Chiapas are the epitome of the disenfranchised. Their votes mean nothing, and their voices are unheard. Their wealth is stolen from them, leaving them in poverty, disease, and ignorance. Did I say this would be brief?" He looked at his copilot. "How long to *la Laguna*?"

"Seventeen minutes, then bear off to two-nine-seven."

"*Gracias*. So for the Zapatistas as you call us, for the EZLN, our goals, in addition to ensuring the legitimacy of local elections, are primarily economic, social, medical, and educational.

"And now, as if the *indígena's* total disenfranchisement weren't enough, NAFTA has sounded their death knell. You are familiar with NAFTA, our so-called free trade agreement? Since our country is indebted to the banking interests of our northern neighbors and the international market place, NAFTA has continued to guarantee the continued dominance of the entrenched power structure."

Sara had been listening closely to this man with the sincere, impassioned voice. She leaned forward to speak.

"*Señor*," she ventured.

"*Sí*, little one," he replied.

"My name is Sara," she said a little indignantly.

"*Sí*, I know. And your brother is Tito. But I must apologize.

We do not yet know your friends' names. Very impolite of me."

"They are Karen and Griffith," said Sara for them.

"Griffith Grant. And you are?" asked Griffith quickly.

"Ah, *sí, señor*," he answered. "My name is Rafael. Our copilot is Mario. Any more, I'm afraid, is not yet possible. I apologize for that and for these uncomfortable masks we must wear."

"He's Marcos," announced Tito once again. "I don't think we should trust him."

"Very good attitude, young man," replied the pilot, "but as Marcos himself has said, 'Everyone is Marcos'."

"I have a name," said Tito exaggerating his sister's indignation.

"*Sí*, Tito, and you're wise not to trust anyone too soon," cautioned Rafael. "First let them prove themselves to you. You must always remember your position and never let anyone take advantage of your power."

"Now you sound like my father."

"Perhaps he is wiser than most people think. But Sara, you were going to ask a question?"

"*Sí, gracias*. We've seen this poverty, *señor*, but how will starting a war help?"

"It probably won't, you're correct. And I don't think any village would support a war. But troops are being moved into eastern Chiapas, ostensibly to rescue you and your brother. Unfortunately, it's been at the cost of other children's lives."

"You talk very well, *señor*," Griffith said to Rafael, "but we'll take your advice about trust until these children are home. So, I'll ask again, where are you taking us?"

They flew into a cloud bank and lost sight of the faint horizon. Rafael checked his altimeter and descended. It began to rain, but the clouds thinned as they dropped.

"*Señor*, bear with me, *por favor*. We're flying to a camp, but I cannot tell you where. It will be safe and a little more comfortable."

"Are you going to make us drink piss?" asked Tito.

"Tito!" cried Sara, slapping him on the arm.

"You've heard stories about this Marcos."

"He makes his men drink their own…"

"Tito," interrupted Sara, hitting him again. "Stop that."

"Tito," said the pilot chuckling, "I was with Marcos on that bivouac. He had read a book about a man lost at sea who drank his own urine to save himself. He wanted us to try it. Just in case. But no one volunteered to be the first to drink from his own cup. So Marcos decided we should all try it. Together, at the same time. We each pissed, er, *perdóneme*, urinated into our cups. Watching each other, we quickly gulped it down."

Next to him, Mario shook his head in muted laughter.

"The sight of two dozen vicious guerrillas, the government's worst nightmare, all bent over, vomiting on themselves is much funnier now than it was at the time. So no, Tito, we will not be drinking any more of that. But after we land, Griffith, we must inform the village leaders of your rescue and then wait for them to send their decision. I wouldn't worry, but it may take a few days."

"I don't understand," said Griffith. "What decision?"

"The EZLN is both the representative arm and the army command of the indigenous people, but the people make all the decisions—whether to go to war or negotiate to keep the military and police out of the villages. Each village decides what action to take. I and the rest of the Zapatista army follow their orders. Even Marcos does not make those decisions."

"I don't see the problem. You said we're not prisoners. Just let us make a phone call to their parents. If we can find a working phone, that is."

"It is complicated, I'm afraid. The police, the media, and even *el Presidente* are blaming the EZLN for the kidnapping. You can see the problem."

"No," interrupted Sara, "I can't."

"The EZLN can hardly return you to your family saying we had nothing to do with the kidnapping."

"I see that," said Sara. "I'm not stupid. I'll just tell them the truth, that's all."

"The logistics are difficult, Sara. That's what the villages will have to decide."

"I still don't understand something," questioned Griffith. "Well, lots of things, but tell me why you kidna… wrong word, 'rescued' us from a government installation."

"You would have been turned over to the *guardias blancas*, I believe. You saw how they behaved. They have their eyes and guns everywhere, especially since your escape. Everyone is afraid of them and of the *judiciales* and the military, and…"

"… and the Zapatistas," added Tito.

"*Sí*, there are those who should be afraid, those who have abused their power and stolen privilege."

"My father has not abused his power," said Tito defensively.

"Excuse me, again, *señor*," continued Griffith. "Why are the *guardias blancas* trying to kill us? That doesn't make sense."

"A most difficult question. We don't know why, for sure. Since the EZLN has been falsely connected to the children's disappearance, some believe if the children die during this crisis, it will give the *guardias blancas* an excuse to break the truce and hunt us down. The *indígena* fear the consequences of such a sacrifice."

"So the accused Zapatistas decided to rescue us from the *guardias blancas*," said Griffith. "As you implied, difficult to believe."

"This was not an EZLN decision, actually. Our villages started blowing up. When we heard about two children with a *norteamericano* couple in the jungle, we made a local decision to find you. It has yet to be approved, but more than *your* lives are at stake."

"Seems very convenient," said Griffith, "how you found us just before you say the *guardias blancas* would have."

"The trail of smoke and fire was easy to follow to the river. After that, to be honest, we were surprised to find you with all the rain and fog tonight. But we had several squads along the river looking for you. I'd like to hear the story of your escape and journey. You have impressed and confounded many people. The jungle is vast, but the gods were smiling on you."

"Your gods have not been particularly kind to us yet," said Griffith, "so perhaps we're due for a change."

"It sounds like a string of very fortunate occurrences to me. Certainly for the children. How were you hurt?"

"When we were leaving Amparo. We'd tried to call their parents, but the phone was dead. When the *guardias blancas* showed up, everybody disappeared. We decided to leave, too. They objected."

"You were very lucky."

"Yeah, my first gunshot wound. Very lucky."

"We'll have our *bruja* look at that for you when we land."

"What's a *bruja*," he asked.

"A witch," said Sara.

"What?"

Rafael and Mario laughed.

"Most of the villages have no Western medicine of any sort. *Las brujas* use traditional remedies and medicines. I hope you can set aside your prejudices. She can be sensitive to non-believers."

"I don't think it's a question of non-belief for me. If she

knows what she's doing, yeah, I'll let her look at it. I'm mostly concerned about infection. I can handle the pain until I can get a real doctor to stitch it up."

The rain picked up, forcing drops through the canopy seals, but the plane held steady. In the distance, clouds flickered with buried lightning.

"How far to the *Laguna*?" Rafael asked his copilot.

"Four minutes."

"Already. I love how quickly time passes during good conversation."

A gust of wind shook the plane, rattling the canopy. Lightning flashed again behind the clouds, and a few seconds later, the rumble of muted thunder rolled over them. Another gust rocked the small plane.

"I think I'll take her down some more," Rafael said, mostly to himself.

"You're the pilot," said his companion.

"I only want to see the lake. Make sure we're in the right place."

"It'll be there," replied Mario. "It's nearly ten kilometers wide."

They were flying through the back of a thunderstorm, one of a line of heavy, warm Pacific lows. These thunderhead clouds, thousands of feet high, were part of the same storm line they'd boated through in the Colorado Canyon of the *Río Lacantún*.

Rafael took his cold pipe from his mouth and put it in his shirt pocket.

"The pilot has turned on the no smoking sign," he joked. "We may experience a little turbulence, so please make sure your seat belts are buckled and your seat backs are in their upright position."

Everyone except Griffith laughed tensely. He listened to the continuous rumble. Another jagged bolt of lightning, sharp and brilliant, lit up an open expanse of water a hundred feet below them. The thunder cracked their ears. The wind buffeted the little 1,300 pound airplane, and tiny drops of rain water flew about the cabin.

"Bearing off to two-nine-seven," said Rafael calmly.

He banked left, and the wings tilted through a blind horizon of rain. As he centered the wheel, a blast of wind slammed down on the body and wings of the plane, rattling it and lifting the passengers against their seat belts. Somebody screamed. Rafael struggled to hold the nose up as the wind vibrated the entire airplane, forcing it toward the water. The wind shear coming off the mountain at the north end of *Laguna Miramar* drove the shuddering plane toward the storm-driven waves of the lake.

The plane shook violently. Yards above the water, the left wing suddenly buckled at the support strut. With a crack, it flew past them and smashed into Rafael's side of the canopy sending shards of thick plastic across the cockpit. The nose corkscrewed wildly. The right wing tip caught the water, crushing the propeller against the surface. The plane tumbled over its broken wing, tripped over the tail section, and landed belly first.

Amid grunts and cries, they slammed back into their seats. Tito landed hard on Griffith's left thigh, bruising it deeply. Sara bounced between Karen's wide-stretched legs. Their seat belts had kept the six of them from bouncing around the tiny cabin and had probably saved their lives. All the same, Griffith's spine was jarred and his stomach quivered with disorientation.

"Quickly," shouted Mario, unbuckling his harness, "we've got to get out before we sink."

The young copilot lifted the canopy while the others struggled from their harnesses. Water splashed in from both the waves and rain. As Mario climbed onto the wing, he shouted back at Karen.

"Life raft behind you!"

Griffith, his left arm soaked in fresh blood, lifted Tito off his lap into Mario's arms, and then he grabbed Sara's hands and helped her out. As she scrambled over him, her foot pressed down on his wound. He screamed and pushed her out into Mario's arms. Nausea swept through his gut. He turned to Karen.

"Go!" she shouted, crawling around her seat to find the life raft.

The nose tilted forward a few degrees and water rushed past Griffith's ankles. Struggling with nausea, he lifted himself from his seat and looked over at Rafael. He was unconscious, so Griffith reached down and unlatched his harness before climbing onto the wing.

The wing was awash. As he stepped onto it, his sneaker slipped out from under him. One leg still inside, he fell forward, out of the plane. He was about to slam his hip into the side of the fuselage when he instinctively grabbed the metal edge with his left hand. His grip broke his fall, but as he spun sideways, the torque on his arm yanked his shoulder out of its socket with a pop. He let go, screaming in pain. He landed in the water, holding his left arm against his body.

Karen heard his scream just as she found the life raft canister. She looked up. Mario was kneeling on the wing above him, holding Griffith's head out of the water. Karen turned back to the canister and released the latch holding it to the fuselage. The canister fell forward, wedging itself against the seat. She twisted, lifted, pried, and, finally, broke it free.

She pushed it through the canopy opening onto the wing. Mario was pulling Griffith back onto the sloping wing, so Karen held the canister against the fuselage and turned around for the pack and belts.

In the water, Griffith shook the spray from his glasses and reached up with his right hand for Mario's arm. He looked up through a shattered left lens and hesitated. Another wave boarded, and the wing canted as he groped for Mario's arm. Disoriented, he grabbed a softer, fleshier rib cage than he expected and let go. He slid back into the water, fingers clawing the air, until he caught Mario's collar and ski-mask. And held on.

The mask twisted over the copilot's eyes and mouth. In one rapid movement, Mario ripped the mask off and grabbed Griffith's wrist. Through his fogged, cracked glasses Griffith saw her dark tresses blow free in the gusting winds. She bent over and grabbed his right shoulder. With one heave, she stood, lifting with the strength of her thighs and back. Her left foot slipped, and, still pulling on Griffith's shoulder, she fell under him.

The tip of his left elbow struck the wing hard. Again, he screamed. But this time the pain swiftly disappeared to be replaced by a monstrous ache enveloping his entire shoulder. The ball of the humerus had been jammed back into its socket.

The copilot, still under him, was using her legs to lift them both farther onto the wing. Griffith rolled onto the cold metal. Sara and Tito knelt beside him, holding him as the wing slowly shifted. Mario turned her attention to the life raft canister.

Seeing that Griffith and the children were safe, at least for the moment, Karen smiled at the surprising sight of their rescuer. She then spun around in calf-deep water toward Rafael who had fallen forward onto the wheel column. She strapped on her fanny pack and threw the backpack onto the wing. She reached over the seat and grabbed Rafael under the shoulders. Karen pulled his shoulders up, but she couldn't lift him. When his head tilted back, she saw blood and rain water running down his forehead.

The plane jerked forward a few more degrees. Karen braced one knee on the instrument panel, but she still couldn't pull him loose. She dropped him and lowered her shoulders over his lap. Stretching one arm between his legs, she gripped his left knee and pulled. His boot was caught.

Cold water, which had already filled most of the cockpit nose, rushed in faster. She took a deep breath and plunged her face underwater. She grabbed his knee with both hands. Still caught. Jammed between his body and the wheel column, her leverage was limited. She couldn't find a good angle to pull. Upside down, her head under water, the plane lurched and shuddered for a moment. Slowly, it turned on its side, lifting its wing tip clear of the water before the nose pulled it down. As the cockpit sank under the dark waters, Rafael fell forward over Karen.

On the surface, the other four clambered into the inflated life raft as the sinking plane lifted its wing from the water. The life raft slid off into the roiling lake. The air was filled with foam and mares' tails. Waves sloshed over them, and the wind chilled them through their wet clothes.

Inside, Karen pulled and yanked on his leg, and the water got colder. She reached farther down to the boot pinned by twisted metal. The plane slid deeper into the water. It convulsed once, burping out the air trapped in the broken tail section, and gained momentum. In the chilling darkness, she held on, pulling on his leg and pleading silently in her head.

Moments later, the instrument lights flickered out.

Screaming into the storm, Griffith scrambled to the side of the raft on his knees. He reached for the wing, trying to keep the raft from being blown across the churning lake. As his fingers brushed the cold metal, his weak shoulder collapsed on the soft gunwale, and he fell forward. His terrified cries were flayed to nothing by the ferocity of the wind.

In agonized gasps, he watched the plane turn and slide under the water. He could see Karen squeezed head-first between the pilot and the column, her legs kicking the dash. The wing tip twisted away from him, its green light shining.

Out of reach, the wing sank in front of him, twisting into the dark maelstrom. He plunged his right arm into the cold water. The yellow plane faded into the depths. The green wing light dimmed and blinked out. He stared into the water, watching for her, waiting for her to break the surface gasping for breath.

He waited. The wind drove the raft across the lake away from her, and he waited. A knot of monstrous denial choked him. Lifting his one good arm above his head, he howled to the indifferent black sky.

"No-o-o-o!"

CHAPTER FOURTEEN
THROUGH THE SWAMP

Laguna Miramar
Early Wednesday morning

> And as he, who with laboring breath has escaped
> from the deep to the shore,
> turns to the perilous waters and gazes.
> *The Divine Comedy*
> Dante Alighieri
> 1265—1321

Griffith clung to the side of the raft as the soft, rubber floor rolled in the waves under him. Spray flew into his face, stinging his cheeks and spattering his glasses. He peered into the darkness for Karen, certain she would appear, willing her to the surface.

"We're getting blown away," he shouted

The wind tore his voice from him, scattering it before the others heard. The woman Mario motioned for the children to stay low in the raft while she sat opposite Griffith, counterbalancing his weight.

"Where's an oar?" yelled Griffith.

He turned and scanned the small raft.

"*No hay remos,*" she shouted. "No paddles."

On his knees, he turned back to his desperate vigil, fighting the waves and wind for balance. He stared into the darkness, refusing to believe the obvious. She simply could not have drowned. Not Karen. Not on their honeymoon... in a foreign country... not here, not now!

"Stop raining, goddamn it!" he screamed.

He didn't know what to do. It couldn't end this way. Every choice they'd made seemed so right at the time. And every one led to this incomprehensible moment. She could not have drowned, and he would find her, that's all.

"Just stop raining," he whispered.

Tito crawled to Griffith's side.

"Can she swim, Griffith?" he asked.

"Huh?" said Griffith. "Oh, Tito. Yes, she can. Very well."

"Then she can swim to shore," said Tito hopefully.

"Yes, Tito, she could."

Even if they'd crashed in the middle of lake, she could swim across it. But in a storm? With an injured man? Griffith had to assume she could. He wasn't going to believe anything else. No other alternative existed for him. He had to resist the future's dreadful maw opening wide to swallow him. His mind chanted *Find her, just find her*, blocking out any other reality. The ache in his shoulder moaned for her. The sopping bandage now twisted around his swollen forearm begged for her attention. *Find her.* The mantra slowed the onslaught of his terrified imagination.

All his limitations loomed before him: the languages he didn't speak, the rain forest where every direction seemed more deadly than the last, and the vigilante force in lethal pursuit. Regardless, his goal, the only future he would consider, was clear to him. He would find Karen. He'd find a way. Then together, they would get the children to safety.

He sucked in his breath, tucked his aching left arm against his chest, and sat on his haunches to watch and wait. He turned his face into the wind, noting it had weakened. The crests of dark, green waves broke less frequently. The raindrops were smaller, stinging his cheeks and hands. He looked around, trying to orient himself to the dawn. The entire sky was thick with leaden clouds. He couldn't see any hint of a shoreline. He checked his watch. Six-fifteen. He turned back into the wind, staring once again across the breaking water.

Over the next hour, the rain drizzled to a stop. The wind gave way to a chilly, early morning mist that rose spectrally from the lake's surface. The deep, green waters now lay placid, no hint of the earlier turmoil remaining. The sun, finally up, was too weak to burn through the fog.

Enveloped in a cloud of shifting gray vapors, sitting motionless out of sight of any land, Griffith waited, struggling for patience. His stomach was empty and tense. When the drone of a helicopter, muffled by the fog, passed over them, bile soured the back of his throat.

He turned and made eye contact with Mario—*or whatever her real name is*—and she lowered her eyes. The children, however, looked up at him with open sympathy.

"I wish there were something I could do," said Sara. Enclosed in walls of mist, her soft voice was unexpectedly loud.

Griffith looked at her, wanting to say "thank you" but found himself unable to form the words. His lips quivered and parted. All he could manage was a tiny nod.

"Grif," said Tito, "perhaps we can swim the raft to shore. It's no good sitting here. Look." Tito pushed on the upper tube. The raft was slowly losing air.

Griffith looked around at the fog. The winds had been westerly before, blowing them toward the dawn. Away from the nearest shore—perhaps—not toward it. Closed in by the morning fog, sitting motionless on glassy water, every direction was the same.

"I think," said the young woman looking down at the still water, "Tito is correct."

She began to unlace her boots.

Behind the fog, no hint of a shore line was visible. In the reluctant dawn, the deep, viridian hue of the water had lightened to a sullen green. How, Griffith wondered, could someone swim, hauling a life raft, without any direction? And she was so tiny, he realized, with broader shoulders and hips than Karen, but still several inches shorter.

Unsure what she intended, he surprised himself by asking, "What's your real name?"

She put her boots in the middle of the raft, unbuckled her belt, and unbuttoned her work shirt. Stripped to her tee-shirt and khaki pants, she ran her fingers through the green water. For a moment, Griffith's eyes drifted to her nipples, rigid under the damp, white cotton. He closed his eyes and pictured Karen's small, pale breasts, how warm and firm they were. He shivered.

"My name is Marina, Griffith."

"So, Marina, which way are you going to swim?" asked Griffith.

"That direction," she said, pointing over her shoulder. "I think the shore is that way."

If she intended to pull the raft behind her, Griffith doubted her chances of success. After all, three others were still in the raft. He could swim, slowly, he supposed, but he was disinclined to get his wound soaked again and uncertain of his own strength. And he didn't think either of the children could or should swim any great distance.

"Should we wait until this mist burns off a little more?" asked Griffith. "You know, so we can find the shore."

"Perhaps that would take too long," she said.

She grabbed the hemp line snubbed at the bow ring and swung her legs over the side.

"I will go slowly," she said and slid into the water.

She stroked gently forward with one arm, gradually overcoming the raft's inertia. When Griffith saw Sara and Tito reach into the water and start paddling with their hands, he joined them. Keeping his left arm snug to his chest, he pulled his right hand through the cool waters of *Laguna Miramar*.

Within a few minutes he warmed. This little effort was enough to resist the tangle of questions for which he had no answers. If nothing more could be done right now, he would rely on his own training to steady his besieged emotions. His ability to observe and to become detached while observing might give him some sense of control, however hollow and false.

He lifted his nose and sniffed the air. Around them, the wispy tendrils and curling vapors had homogenized into a uniform cloud. It smelled faintly of lavender. The gentle shushing of the children's strokes, their even breathing and easy efforts, and the soft rhythmic ripple of Marina's slow, steady sidestroke filled the ghostly mist. In the diffuse light of dawn, the green, bright water reminded Griffith of the fluorescent lakes he'd seen with Karen at the *Lagunas de Montebello*, at the start of their honeymoon.

Staring into the gray emptiness, his heart swelled with disbelief.

Out of the vaporous morning fog, an image of Karen coalesced. She was kneeling at the edge of *Laguna Tziscao*, marveling at the bright tropical fishes. Griffith blinked. The reflection of his desire remained so precise and detailed, he stopped paddling and lifted his wet hand toward her. His eyes became distant, and he followed her into the void of fog and memory. He loved the way her body moved so easily, so comfortably. When she pointed at the small fish by the shore, simple awe animated her body. God, how he wanted her.

The plash of a fish breaking the surface startled his full heart. The vision of Karen faded into the mist. In the next moment, an ache clamped down on his chest, gripping his heart with cold, bony fingers. In frigid reality, he realized he couldn't even assure himself she was still alive.

He stroked his hand again through the cool, green water. In front of the raft, Marina rose up, standing chest-deep in water. Without looking back, she began to slog through the bottom mud toward the trees and lianas gradually forming out of the mist.

"Look," said Tito, "we're here." His small voice died at the wall of vegetation.

Marina had gotten them to the edge of the lake, but there was no way to get ashore. The jungle, in its relentless effort to fill as much space as possible, had extended its reach several yards over the water. Mist filled every gap between the leaves and branches of an impenetrable wall of verdancy. Marina stopped pulling the raft and looked up and down the shoreline for an opening. She then turned to the right and once again dragged her feet through the thick muck. The raft drifted behind her.

Griffith wondered why she chose to turn this way. He now realized she had understood the earlier change in water color—not that the sun had risen but the lighter the color, the shallower the depth. But what else had she seen? He didn't know, and to him the implication was simple—he still had no idea what he was doing in this environment. He could see what was going on around him, but he was unable to comprehend what it meant.

If he were going to find Karen, then he and the children needed Marina. He knew that. He had no problem being dependent on a woman. Another woman, he reminded himself. Especially one who knew this jungle. And he'd find out soon enough whether Marina's politics were going to get in his way.

"Could I help?" he offered.

"If we don't find a way ashore soon, perhaps. But, no, *gracias*."

For nearly fifteen minutes, Marina hauled the raft along the tree line. Above the fog, the chop of several more helicopters flew from the west and then faded to the north without passing over them.

From the edge of the dense jungle, a quick splash startled them. Marina stopped, and the raft bumped silently against her. She stared under the outstretched limbs and foliage into the deep shadows obscuring the shore line. Holding a finger to her lips, she pointed toward the shore beneath a thick, vine-covered trunk growing horizontally for a dozen feet from the bank before righting itself. Griffith couldn't see anything in the shadows.

Then from the gray-green fog of the awakening jungle, several small snorts and a shallow splash were followed by a very loud and startling "Wooph!" Instantly, the forest was filled with barks and grunts. The brush exploded with crashing and snapping as a dozen shadows took flight into the depths of the jungle.

"Wild dogs?" asked Griffith catching his breath.

"No. Peccaries," answered Marina. "Wild pigs. Very good eating."

She turned toward the shore and ducked under the large tree and vines. Submerged to her shoulders, she headed ashore with the raft slowly turning to follow.

"Are we going to hunt pigs?" asked Tito.

From under the trees Marina laughed.

"No, Tito, but I think we can get ashore where the peccaries were drinking. Keep down."

Lying on the cool rubber, darkness enveloped them. As Marina dragged them beneath the foliage, leaves, twigs, spider webs, and insects caught on their clothes and in their hair. At the muddy bank, the children scrambled from the raft into the trampled undergrowth and brushed themselves off. Carefully, and perhaps from exhaustion, Griffith crawled slowly from the soft raft.

Marina dragged the raft completely out of the water. The children unloaded what they'd gotten out of the plane: the small pack and canteen, Marina's clothes and boots, and her belt with its machete and small side packs.

Around them, the grasses and ferns had been pounded into a rough clearing. Numerous small paths disappeared into the thick jungle. The heavy scent of musk hung in the moist vapors, mingling with the rotting humus, fresh excrement, and flowering vegetation. Griffith, picking the cobwebs from his hair, peered down the wildlife trails into the undergrowth.

"Where to from here?" he asked. "How are we going to find her? Them."

Marina stopped lacing her boots and looked up at him.

"Griffith," she said softly, "do you think they're alive?"

Griffith didn't answer immediately. Sara and Tito, surprised at Marina's bluntness, stared at Griffith in silence. He sighed deeply.

"Either way," he finally said, "I've got to find her."

"I believe they're both alive," said Tito.

"And we'll help you find them," agreed Sara.

"Thank you, both," said Griffith. "And we'll all get out of this jungle together. Unless Marina feels she must do something else. Are you going to help us, Marina?"

"*Sí*, Griffith, of course. I'll finish what I started, but I…," her small voice vulnerable for a moment, "I don't believe they're alive. I'm sorry. This is difficult for me, as well."

Griffith was moved by her intensity, and by the implications of what she revealed.

"Were you close to Rafael?" he asked.

She swallowed and took a breath.

"*Sí*. He taught me a great deal. And he was important to others."

"But why don't you believe he and Karen… made it?

"Rafael couldn't swim," she said in a rush. "He made all of us learn to swim—it was part of our training—but he never learned. A childhood fear, he said. Oh, *Dios*, what are we going to do without him?"

"You loved him, didn't you?" said Sara.

"Oh, Sara, *sí*, but you don't understand."

"Marina," said Griffith, "even if Rafael's afraid of the water, Karen is an excellent swimmer. Very strong. She could easily have swum to shore with him."

"You don't understand," she repeated. "I am very sorry you've lost your wife, a great tragedy. But all of *la República* has lost a hero."

Her eyes teared in the pale light that filtered through the canopy.

"You mean…" Griffith hesitated at the thought, "that was…"

"Marcos!" exclaimed Tito. "I knew it. That was *Insurgente* Marcos."

"You weren't supposed to know that," said Marina, "but *sí*, Rafael is Marcos."

"Oh, Christ on a bloody cross," moaned Griffith. "This is unbelievable. It just can't be. And all I wanted was to be alone with Karen, with my…

He took a breath and blinked away a tear.

"All right, goddammit," he continued, "we'll find them both. And if my honeymoon ends up on the cover of *Newsweek*, well, screw 'em. No one's going to believe it anyway. So, like I said, where to from here? Will your people, your army, send someone to look for us when we don't show up?"

"I'm not sure they know we were coming. When you were found, our arrangements were made very quickly. It's more likely the *guardias blancas*, or the *judiciales*, will be sending search parties."

"The helicopters we heard?" asked Griffith. "Because the plane was stolen from a government facility."

"The intention was to borrow it, but, *sí*, that's correct."

"So why can't we just wave a white flag?" he asked.

"The danger," said Marina, "is the appearance of surrendering and the implied admission of culpability. Even with the children's testimony, it might be very difficult to secure our own freedom once we turn ourselves in. I have learned not to presume the inevitability of justice."

"So we need to keep out of sight?"

"It would be a good idea," agreed Marina.

"If it'll help us find Karen and Marcos, and if…."

"Griffith, *por favor*," she interrupted, "you must not use that name. His name is Rafael."

"Oh, yes, *sí*, I'm sorry."

"*Gracias*. May I suggest another path?" asked Marina. "I think if we move east, we'll find a small village with a contact who can help us."

"But that's away from the lake, isn't it?"

"Griffith," said Sara, "it's help."

"I'll search the lake with Griffith," offered Tito. "You two go for help."

"The *Laguna* is large," said Marina, "a hundred kilometers or more around, without trails. And mountains block the north and south shores."

"Marina," replied Griffith anxiously, "I can't leave the lake. Karen's gotten ashore, I'm sure of it. If Rafael's with her, she'll probably stay put. She knows what she's doing. I have to find her."

"If she can take care of them both," countered Marina, "shouldn't we see to the children's safety first?"

"So you can clear your Zapatista's name?"

She paused and lowered her eyes for a moment.

"Your distrust is misplaced," she replied quietly. "But *sí*, that would be one result of getting the children home. But the children would be safe. And another result might be additional resources to search for your wife. And a doctor for you."

Her patience and logic in the face of Griffith's insult shamed him. He wasn't at all sure he could find Karen on his own. His arm hurt, and it had gotten more tender to the touch. The bandage was soaked and tight under the swelling, and his shoulder ached. They had no food and little water. He did need her help.

"How far is this village?" he asked.

"I'm not sure, but *Nuevo Huitiupan* is only three or four kilometers east of the *Laguna*. And we are on the eastern shore, *sí?*"

"What kind of help?"

"A man who can assist us to our original destination."

"Which is where?"

"Northwest, sixty kilometers, maybe more."

"Sixty kilometers! No, I can't go that far. That's too far away."

"Griffith," she replied "it's a camp where we have resources to find Karen and Rafael. And to turn the children safely over to their parents. Hopefully, without a war."

"Without a war," he repeated. "Yes, so I understand. Children, what do you think? We're in this together."

"I'll go with you, Grif," said Tito.

"And I, as well," agreed Sara.

"All right, then, Marina, we'll accompany you. At least as far as Nuebo Weety, or whatever. I'm sorry, my Spanish is nonexistent, I'm afraid."

"*De nada. Y gracias*, Griffith. I think this will be best. At *Nuevo Huitiupan* people will help us."

"Yes, I hope so."

Griffith and the children needed the help. He knew that. Wandering around the jungle, he certainly wasn't going to stumble over Karen. So why was he hesitant to accept Marina's assistance? The left side of his body ached with abuse. They were being hunted, apparently by more than one armed group. And the dark spectre of death stalked them with relentless disdain. That was why he hesitated. People were dying all around him. For no reason. He feared that the path back to his wife was going to become bloodier.

"Marina, you realize people have gotten killed helping us?"

"*Si*. It is difficult for all of us. Life and death are very close neighbors in Chiapas."

"Yes, I've noticed."

"We sometimes have few choices in life, but if we don't help, then what are we?"

"Come on, let's go," said Tito, swatting at a mosquito. "This place is awful, and I'm hungry."

"*Sí, niño, claro que sí.* We'll find some food at *Nuevo Huitiupan*. It won't be long."

Hacking a path through the brush with the machete, Marina led them along one of the peccaries' narrow, muddy trails. Under the canopy, weak light sparkled in faint droplets of moisture. The heat and humidity within the dank jungle were overpowering, and the farther from the lake they hiked, the more the temperature rose. The stink of unwashed fear clung to Griffith's clothes. Sweat glistened unevaporated on his skin. Within minutes, he was sucking in draughts of thick, damp air.

They hadn't been hiking long when the dense jungle abruptly ended. Ahead of them, flat, open savannah stretched several miles across a wet valley toward the *Sierra San Felipe* mountains.

"On the far side of the valley," said Marina, "a road connects several small villages."

"Is that *Nuevo Huitiupan*?" asked Sara, pointing to a thin column of dark smoke across the valley. It rose narrow and vertical for hundreds of feet before the light airs dispersed it.

"It's a cooking fire, isn't it?" said Tito.

"Perhaps," answered Marina, "but the fire is all the way across the valley, and the smoke is the wrong color for a cooking fire, I think. Let's find out."

Griffith wiped the sweat from his forehead. He and the children followed her out onto the soft ground beyond the forest. The savannah at the northern end of this valley was water-logged, and the terrain, although flat and open, was mucky and foul. The air hung quiet and heavy over this damp basin, and small, black flies swarmed in thick clouds over the wettest sedges and choked-out lagoons.

Marina followed a path of grassy clumps, moving from tussock to thicket. From small stands of palmettos crowded together, past scrawny live oaks scattered on a few small prominences, they worked their way across the valley, swatting flies and mosquitoes and dripping with sweat. Slogging through soaked, heavy soils wore on them all.

The effort to keep moving forced Griffith's doubts about leaving the lake to recede. His shoulder ached into his chest, and his forearm had started throbbing again. His dark hair clung matted and filthy against his damp neck and forehead. Breathing heavily in the humid air, he struggled through the muck. Black mud splattered his pants and shirt. Through his cracked glasses, fogged with the humidity and heat, the others were ghostly forms at the edge of his vision. His energy waned in the sucking heat, and the dull blade of nausea mocked his frailties.

It took over three hours to cross the savannah. Half a mile from *Nuevo Huitiupan*, still out of sight beyond the tall grasses and palmettos, the *Río Azul*, a small, dark river whose course and banks changed with each thunderstorm, stopped them. Copses of thorny palms with long, thick needles protecting their trunks dotted both river banks. From their soggy depression, thin, wispy trails of smoke could be seen drifting over the village.

"Let's stay to this side," suggested Marina. "It will take us around the village."

"Marina," asked Tito as they continued, "is this your home?"

"No, no, Tito. But my home is in the jungle, north of here."

"Then you're not from the city like Mar… Rafael?" asked Sara.

"No, but like many in our army, I met him when he brought his hopes and ideals to the jungle."

"Are you Lacandon? " asked Sara.

"*Sí*, I am southern Lacandon. My family lives in Lacanjá. But I have not seen them for many months. They do not approve."

"Of fighting?" asked Tito. "Women shouldn't fight."

"Ah, Tito, you're so very young," she said smiling, "but many people think the same way. Even my father. Very few of us understand the need to drive the ranchers and loggers, and the *evangelistas*, from our land. We do not want them, we did not invite them, and we get nothing from them to improve our lives. So, if I had married like the other young women in my village, I would never have left there. One day, however, I'll be able to go back and teach what I've learned about education and power."

"*Sí*, women should be teachers," decided Tito.

"Tito!" exclaimed Sara. "Don't be so stupid."

"I'm not stupid, and you shouldn't call me that."

"Well, that's a stupid thing to say, Tito. Why should women only be teachers?"

"And nurses," he replied.

Behind them, Griffith's step was deliberate and focused. Exhaustion masked his irritation over this sibling bickering. Their voices became background. Fearful of a clumsy fall, he moved slowly and carefully.

"Actually, Tito," interrupted Marina, "everyone should teach."

"But you're an *insurgenta*," he insisted. "You don't teach."

"Teaching is the most important thing we do, Tito. Whether it's Spanish or arithmetic or how to rotate crops or build a *sanitario*, Rafael has always said the true revolution is education. Each one must teach one."

"But you kill people."

"When someone threatens your life, you must make a choice."

"To live or die?" he offered.

"If we're honest with ourselves, the choice is sometimes to kill or die."

"Have you killed anyone, Marina," asked Sara bluntly.

"I don't know."

"How can you not know?" demanded Tito.

"You misunderstand. I've been in two firefights, but *en la selva*, it's impossible to see who's shooting at you. So you shoot in the direction of the incoming fire. It's terrifying and impersonal. I don't want to do it again."

"But you would," said Tito.

"I would rather teach. My dreams are better when I am teaching."

Griffith tried to listen, but the burden of pushing himself forward demanded an inordinate amount of his attention. Light-headed and short of breath, he staggered to the meager shade of a small palm tree. Flies buzzed too loudly. Each one he swatted left a small streak of dark crimson on his skin. Blood pulsed at his temples and churned past his eardrums. His arms and legs tingled. He tried taking a deep breath, but short, gasping pants were all he could manage. He wondered if one could drown in this damp air. He needed to sit. He looked around for a dry spot, trying to focus through his cracked lens.

Looking down, the ground rushed up at him. He collapsed into a stagnant backwash, grabbing the trunk of the thorny palm. A large black thorn at the base of the tree penetrated his left palm. Unconscious of his pain and suffering, he lay still, eyes rolling back. His breathing slowed.

Minutes later, he awoke, lying on his back, blinking up at three strange, brown faces staring at him. He didn't recognize the woman in fatigues or these filthy children with their concerned expressions. He looked around for Karen.

"Grif?" asked Sara.

When he heard 'grief' in her accent, however, the present came rushing back to overwhelm him with its familiar terror.

Karen was still gone! And he had to find her. And lead these children somewhere.

His head ached, and his mouth tasted foul. Trying to lift himself, he pulled his left hand protectively against his abdomen and caught the broken end of the embedded thorn on his shirt. He stared down at his palm.

"Grif, are you all right?" she asked.

He looked up at her and nodded with a twitch. He pushed himself up with his right arm so he could sit. When he tried to speak, another wave of nausea rose from his stomach. He rolled to his side, too weak to resist the spasm and opened his mouth. He gagged once and held his breath.

Nothing happened. The bile receded, and he released the tension in his abdomen. He wiped the saliva from the side of his mouth, grateful he hadn't vomited, and swallowed back the rank taste.

"I'm sorry," he said weakly. "I don't feel very well."

"I'll go to the village," said Marina, "and get some help. Stay here and rest. I won't be long."

"Okay, I'll stay with Grif," said Tito.

"Please hurry," added Sara.

"Of course. Half an hour, no more."

He recognized something important was happening, but the nausea and heat muddled his thinking. He nodded without understanding. Marina stood, smiled at Sara and Tito, and disappeared into the tall grasses along the river. The children helped Griffith to a dry hummock where he leaned back in the thin shade of several young palmettos.

"You'll feel better after you eat, Griffith," said Sara.

"Thank you, Sara." The thought of food did not appeal to his nervous stomach.

"I think Marina will find a way to help us," she added.

"But she's an *insurgenta*, Sara," protested Tito. "She's not going to help us."

"How can you say that, Tito, after what she's done already."

"Yeah? We were doing okay until she captured us and wrecked the plane. Now she's leading us farther away from Karen."

While the children bickered, Griffith tried to focus his thoughts. His shoulder ached, but he could move it a bit. The throbbing in his forearm was worse, and the swelling had tightened the skin. The pulled rib cage muscle and the saddle sores were forgotten irritants. But when he looked at the thorn embedded in his palm, and the red, swollen skin surrounding it, he tried to remember... something.

What was it? Find Karen, yes, but then what? No, it was how... how can... he lost the thought. It was something *he* had to do. Or read. Or e-mail? No, he did that before he left Charlottesville. Maybe it was the children?

He wiggled the broken end of the thorn. It didn't hurt. That was a surprise. Everything else certainly hurt. He tried to pull it out with his right thumb and forefinger, but he couldn't get a grip. With his teeth, he bit the extrusion, lifted it from his palm, and spit out the bitter, black tip. Within the small, red circle, a tiny, black dot remained below the skin, a spot of blood where the sharp tip had left a miniature bull's-eye.

He stared at his palm. The cracked left lens of his glasses scattered his vision, and the other remained fogged in the humidity. Sweat dripped from his beard and pooled in his open palm. He couldn't understand why he felt as if he were missing something important. He took his bent frames off, set them down, and wiped the sweat from his forehead and eyes. In cautious increments, he lifted his palm away from his chest and tilted his head back to focus on the tiny target again.

"Oh, Tito," continued Sara, "you're wrong. She'll be back with food and help. You'll see."

"Yeah, with some more Zapatistas, too."

"Children?" asked Griffith softly. "Could you not argue, please. ¿*Por favor*?"

"We weren't arguing," replied Tito.

Sara clenched her teeth and glared at him.

"The Zapatistas," whispered Sara angrily, "are the ones who are going to get us out of here."

"Griffith is getting us out of here, not some woman."

"Children," pleaded Griffith.

"*Sí, lo siento*, Grif," apologized Tito.

The children pouted at each other in silence. Griffith stared at the dot of blood on his palm, wanting to remember. He swatted another black fly and wiped fresh blood from his face.

Thirty minutes later, as abruptly as she had left, Marina reappeared from the grasses, carrying a burlap sack.

"This is what I found," she said, and opened the sack on the ground.

Fresh corn still in the husk, some dark red yams, dirt clinging to them, and several papayas and plantains fell out. She handed Griffith her canteen. He took several tentative sips of warm water. When his stomach accepted the new sensation, he allowed himself a longer, slow drink. Marina was quiet as she handed each of them a papaya.

"What's wrong?" asked Sara.

"The village is empty," replied Marina.

"Where are they?" asked Sara.

"I don't know."

"And the fire?" asked Tito.

"It was the village."

"Their village caught fire?" asked Griffith incredulously.

"There was help."

"I don't understand?"

"I could still smell the cordite where explosions had started the fires. Several of the villagers are dead. I hope the rest fled to the jungle. I took the vegetables from a garden."

"What now?" asked Tito, peeling the skin from his fruit. "Can we eat?"

"I think we should head north, along the mountains," said Marina. "Once we get past *Huitiupan* and into the forest, we can build a fire, Tito."

"You said there were other villages in this valley?" asked Sara.

"*Si*, but I'm afraid we'll find the same thing."

"Any telephones?"

She shook her head. "Not in this valley."

"No trucks?"

"Perhaps. And perhaps they were destroyed, as the one in *Huitiupan* was. But even if we found one, the road doesn't leave the valley."

That didn't make sense to Griffith. The road didn't leave the valley. Was that possible? So how were they supposed to get help in this swamp? Karen, he hoped, was somewhere behind them, and there was nothing but jungle in front of them. His breath came in short gasps.

"What's that way?" asked Tito pointing north.

"Over this *sierra*, maybe fifty kilometers, there is a Lacandon village."

I'll never make that, Griffith admitted to himself.

"What if they attack that one, too," asked Tito.

"We have never fought the ranchers or their *guardias blancas*.

"But they burned this village?"

"The villages in this valley are not Lacandon. For centuries, our only resistance has been to remain hidden in the jungle away from everyone."

"But you're fighting," insisted Tito.

"Few know or care about one woman."

Their words buzzed in Griffith's ears. He shook his head trying to refocus. He needed to find Karen. Squinting at the mountain range rising steeply beyond the smoke of *Huitiupan*, he sighed deeply at the prospect of climbing. He took a small bite of the papaya. The juice soothed his throat, but he struggled to swallow the tiny piece of pulp.

"There's a pass," said Marina, "north of that peak. Once we're in the forest, we'll go slowly."

"How long will it take to get to that village?" Sara asked.

"A few days."

Griffith groaned.

"But what about food?" asked Tito. He threw the empty peel down. "This won't be enough."

"*La Selva* will provide for us."

Tito frowned and said, "You're going to make us eat monkey, aren't you? Well, I won't eat monkey meat."

"Perhaps we won't need to, *niño*," answered Marina.

"Not if I were starving."

"Okay, then," interrupted Griffith softly. "I think I'm ready."

With Marina leading the way, they headed slowly north, bypassing the smoldering *Nuevo Huitiupan*. Climbing back into the rain forest, they followed the *Río Azul* as it narrowed. Along one of the tiny feeder streams, a trail ran up the western face of *Cerro San Felipe*, the last mountain overlooking the vast lowland rain forest. Marina turned up that way.

Once in the shelter of the jungle canopy, they stopped. Marina hacked some brush into kindling. Shredding the long, white fibers from the open seed pod of a nearby ceiba, she built a fire. She took a worn piece of flint from one of her belt pouches and with her machete, chipped sparks into the silky, dry tinder. The fire grew quickly. When the first coals appeared, she peeled back the corn husks and placed the exposed yellow ears on the fire. After the corn had blackened, she gave them each an ear.

Unable to develop a coherent thought, Griffith ate quietly. The little food he did swallow, he didn't taste. The water and food soothed his nausea, but his strength continued to wane. In the growing haze of his wounds and fears, he fretted over some vague goal drifting just out of reach.

On his palm, the red target remained unchanged with its tiny, black bull's-eye. Turning his wrist, his whole arm ached. When he stroked his elbow, it was warm to the touch. Blood pounded hot at his temples. Under the clotted rag of Karen's bandage, a fever had begun its fight against the infection eating at his gunshot wound.

CHAPTER FIFTEEN
SEPARATION

Laguna Miramar
Early Wednesday morning

> I hate causes, and if I had to choose between
> betraying my country and betraying my friend,
> I should hope I have the guts to betray my country.
> *What I Believe*
> E. M. Forster
> 1879—1970

Karen broke the surface of the roiling lake with Rafael in her arms. Where they had crashed into the laguna had been surprisingly shallow. When the small plane drove its nose into the muck just thirty feet down, the impact had been hard enough to crumple the nose section and free Rafael's wedged boot. With the last bubbles from the cockpit, Karen kicked them to the surface.

Holding Rafael's head above the water, she looked around as the waves broke over them. The raft was nowhere in sight. It couldn't have drifted too far, but only the breaking crests of the nearest waves glimmered in the pre-dawn darkness. She yelled Griffith's name once. The wind tore her voice away.

She decided to save her strength. She had no doubt that, by herself, she could have outlasted the storm by treading water, but with Rafael now conscious and in a great deal of pain, she had to find the shore.

With nothing but confused waves and shifting winds to guide her, she just began swimming. She swam slowly with Rafael under her arm, trying to keep both their heads above the breaking waves. Within minutes, however, the surface calmed, and she could make out a line of trees through the drizzle. She looked around again for the raft. She saw nothing, and the possibility of the raft having been blown away from this cove worried her.

Nearing the tree-lined shore, the exposed roots of a mangrove stand reached out into the water, giving her a place to rest with the now conscious Rafael. It also blocked their way to the shore.

For over and hour they struggled trough the maze of tangled roots, branches, and mud protecting the shoreline. Rafael's ankle hurt a great deal, and Karen spent as much energy lifting and protecting his ankle as she did climbing over, through and around each standing root.

Finally, they dragged themselves to a scrape of dirt above the water line. The rain had been replaced by a dense fog, and the sun had risen ashen and obscured. They lay back for several minutes, recovering their breaths.

Karen's mind raced, going over one option after another. It seemed likely that Rafael's ankle was broken. That would have to be dealt with before they could even think of moving.

"Rafael," she said. Her voice was hushed in the fog and thick brush blocking their way inland. "I'll have to splint your ankle if we're going to move from here."

"Karen," he replied weakly, "I think we should consider staying here for a while. I believe it will be easier for the others to find us than if we moved."

"But how would they know we got out of the plane?" she asked.

"If not," he agreed, "perhaps they will assume we drowned. And I would have drowned if not for you. *Muchas gracias.*"

He smiled through his pain and nodded toward the distant thrum of blades flying across the lake toward them.

"Perhaps we can get a ride with that helicopter," he chuckled. "I'd rather not walk out."

"How do you always managed to make light of everything?" asked Karen.

"I apologize for my levity. It's how I react when I have no answers. So many people simply expect me to know what to do. Most of the time I'm relying on smarter and better people than I."

At that moment, Karen realized what she had suspected all along. Perhaps she didn't really suspect it, but in her heart the possibility that this was *the* Marcos, *Subcomandante* of the Zapatistas, excited her.

"You're Marcos," she ventured, "aren't you?"

"*Sí*, Karen, but that's merely a name for the public. I am Rafael. And I don't know what we should do."

"Well, let me splint your ankle first. Then we'll decide."

She found no trace of blood on his boot or sock and decided to leave it on. She splinted his lower leg and foot with some stout dead wood branches. If Griffith and the others had been nearby, they might have heard Rafael's agonized screams as she straightened his foot and tightened the splints with strips torn from his fatigue shirt.

"I'm not going anywhere for a little while," he groaned after she was finished.

"You rest a while. We have other options. We could camp here. Build a fire and get a little more comfortable. I could explore some; see what's around us. Or we could wait to see if the others find us. They do have all the equipment from the life raft and packs. And I don't think Griffith will believe we drowned. He'd want to know for sure before acting on the belief that I, that we, drowned. That's just the way he is."

"And Marina knows the jungle as well as anyone."

"That's her name? She fooled me."

"The less beauty she reveals, the less trouble she seems to have from those under her command. At least until they learn of her intelligence and strength. She quickly earns their respect. Whatever Marina and Griffith decide to do, she'll find a way to protect them, I'm sure."

"Well, then, let me make us a little more comfortable. After I get a fire going, I think I'll explore the area. Maybe I can find us some help."

Clearing their small beach, she made Rafael a smooth spot to lie down while she gathered deadwood. Her hip pouch had gotten soaked, leaving her passport, checks, and pesos wrinkled and soggy, but the wax coating on her waterproof matches was unbroken. And it took just one of them to get a small, warming fire started. Even though another helicopter passed near them, Karen thought the canopy above their fire would break up the little smoke it was producing.

"We're going to need some food and water soon, Rafael," she said. "I want to find out more about where we are. I'll be back within thirty minutes."

"Karen," said Rafael, "please be careful. The jungle has its dangers, but they can be avoided. The perils of man are more insidious, however."

She smiled in appreciation.

"Thank you, I will," she said. "You know, Rafael, you speak like a poet."

"My one strength," he grinned.

"See if you can rest. I'll be back soon."

Once out of the mangrove, Karen followed the first game trail she found. Another helicopter passed overhead, but the brush hid her movement. Less than a quarter mile inland, she found a dirt road.

Just as she squeezed though the thick growth of saplings lining the shoulder of the road, she heard a frightened gasp. Twisting around, she met the wild-eyed gaze of a boy, barely seventeen. Sweat dripped profusely from his forehead, and the barrel of his automatic weapon quivered with his own terror. Dressed all in black, including his helmet, heavy boots, and Kevlar flak vest, he was weighted down with grenades and ammo clips hanging from his pockets and belt. The bright, yellow letters of the *PJF* adorned his breast pocket.

She smiled and held her hands out, palms up, to show he had nothing to fear. He didn't say anything, eyes darting from her blonde hair to her filthy clothes. Karen kept smiling, but before she had time to sort through her options, including testing herself physically against this frightened teenager, his squad leader drove up in a black *PJF* jeep. She was taken to a helicopter in a clear-cut not far away.

She never saw Rafael again.

CHAPTER SIXTEEN
LA BRUJA

La Selva Lacandona
Wednesday

> Aye on the shores of darkness there is light,
> And precipices show untrodden green.
> There is budding morrow in midnight;
> There is triple sight in blindness keen.
> *To Homer*
> John Keats
> 1795—1821

Throughout the afternoon Griffith, the children, and Marina hiked upward, toward the northern pass around *Cerro San Filipe*. Their trail was narrow, forcing them to walk single file. They climbed from the tropical lushness of the low-lying jungle into the montane rain forest with its cedars, strangler figs, and tall ferns. The shade held the temperature in the high eighties. Occasional breezes coming off the mountain cooled them, but the humidity remained high.

Griffith kept a measured pace. The throbbing in his forearm had expanded to his shoulder, his arteries pounded in his temples and neck, and his fever climbed. With his visual attention tunneled to the ground immediately under him, the chatter of the rain forest fauna and the trudging of feet lost their clarity and droned in his ears.

It was difficult to keep his thoughts focused. He tried to think about Karen, what she would do here, what she was doing wherever she was, but then he'd lose the thought before it could lead anywhere. He knew he was in some physical danger, but that realization led nowhere, as well.

And on it went for him. The children kept close, one or the other turning back every minute or so to check on him. They would stop Marina frequently and carry the canteen back to Griffith for a few small sips. He neither remembered drinking nor answering their concerned questions.

During the afternoon, they covered a difficult three miles, climbing slowly up and around the base of the mountain. Several hundred feet below the summit, the rough trail leveled out. The sun was behind them, and angled beams of light pierced the canopy, dancing kaleidoscopically over the intense green of the deep forest.

Griffith kept trying to focus on a goal, something he knew he had to do, some target which kept moving out of range. He stopped and peered at the tiny mark on his palm. Just another wound, but he struggled to make any connection between his injuries and his needs.

When Sara couldn't hear his labored breathing, she turned and came back to urge him forward. He moved but only after she touched his back, so she decided to hike behind him. With the effort of hiking, Griffith became less and less aware of his surroundings. His vaporous thoughts incinerated in the hot flashes of fear tumbling through his head. The chaos in his mind wore on him, and the fever drained his body. He stumbled on.

In the distance, he heard Karen's voice, indistinct but insistent. He cocked his head side to side, seeking its direction. He wondered at the improbability of actually hearing her. He knew her voice had to be an auditory hallucination, but it was so real it distracted him. He stopped moving. Not knowing what his next step needed to be, he got lost in the metaphor, unsure why one step kept interfering with the other.

Sara touched his back lightly, and he mumbled an apology. He remembered he had something specific he needed to figure out. Once again, he began his slow measured pace, head down, eyes on the ground, trying to focus his hazy thoughts.

Out of the hum of the jungle, three notes of a small bird—rapid, hard calls, repeated twice—penetrated his fevered silence. He forgot about his next step and looked up through a narrow gap in the understory of the jungle. Although overgrown and barely passable, what looked like a path led up the side of the mountain. He was awed by its shrouded and forgotten purpose. Farther up, the flutter of wings and another trill filtered through the brush. Without a thought, he shouldered his way through the untrammeled growth blocking this steep gap in the forest and started climbing.

"Griffith," called Sara from behind, "this way."

"Yes, I know," he said over his left shoulder.

"No, Griffith, this way," she repeated.

Marina and Tito turned around and saw Sara looking up into the jungle.

"Where's Griffith?" asked Tito.

Sara pointed toward Griffith's path.

"But why?" asked Marina. "That's not even a trail. It's just a wash for the rain coming off the mountain."

From above, they heard Griffith's excited voice.

"Sara. Tito. This way."

"But Griffith," called Sara, "why? Where are you going?"

"To find Karen?"

"What?"

"Come on, children. This way." His voice was farther up the trail.

"I'd better follow him," said Marina.

"I'll go with you," offered Tito. "Sara, you come, too. Griffith! Wait for us."

They scrambled up the wash after him. The rain had swept away most of the soil and humus, leaving a mat of interwoven roots over the dark, bare rock. Where the climb was too steep, the roots provided hand and foot holds. Between the steepest inclines, on sections of level, exposed limestone, they'd catch sight of Griffith, grunting and struggling upward with his one-armed efforts.

"Look!" he said. "These stairs are for us." He pointed to the rough rock under his feet. "See. This is the way."

"But, Grif," whined Tito, "where are you going?"

"To find Karen," he repeated.

"But she's not up there."

"I know."

"He doesn't make sense," said Tito.

"Is he sick?" asked Sara.

"*Sí, niños*, I think so. It's my fault. I wasn't paying enough attention."

"It's his arm, isn't it?" said Tito.

"Perhaps we should stop him," suggested Sara.

"More stairs," called Griffith. "Come on, children."

His trail was no more than the widest gap between the ferns, saplings, and laurel breaks crowding each other for the available space and light. His stairs were rough, broad-shouldered rocks of uneven height whose placement and generally level tops approximated the idea of steps.

Against all his scientific training, his feverish intuition drove him. Unable to see where he was going, or understand why this felt so imperative, he just kept climbing. And each time his ascent was blocked by the forest or a wall of rough, dark limestone, he would twist and shove his way to the right until he could climb again.

His path ended in a laurel thicket below the wide summit of the mountain three thousand feet above the valley of the *Río Azul*. With Marina and the children behind him, Griffith stopped to catch his breath. Ahead of him, the maze-like laurel blocked his way. Behind him, the trees, giant ferns, and innumerable lianas obstructed the view. Nevertheless, Griffith was sure once he got high enough, he'd be able to see more clearly.

Marina was about to protest, but Griffith held his finger to his mouth for silence. Listening intently, his eyes unfocused, he tilted his head sideways. Seconds later, the fluttering of wings brought his head up. He pointed into the treetops. A small, dull green bird, no more than ten inches long, flew from a cluster of epiphytes high in a tree. Twittering "cow, cow, cow", the bird darted across the trail over their heads where it snatched an insect out of the air and veered up the trail into the canopy.

"Oh, look," said Sara. *"Muy bonita."*

Griffith held up his right hand, forefinger in the air. From the same tree, flew the bird's mate, slightly larger. Its emerald green feathers glistened in a ray of sunlight, and its bright scarlet breast caught the eye. When it flew completely into view, however, all four of them gasped. Streaming for nearly two feet behind the stubby, white tail coverts were the most magnificent emerald plumes, undulating slowly and majestically in the air. The deep green male, with his red breast and long, iridescent tail feathers glinting in each shaft of sunlight, followed the female up the mountain and into the canopy.

"Dios," whispered Marina. "A quetzal and his mate."

"How did you know, Grif?" asked Tito.

"Huh? I... I didn't know. I heard it."

Griffith turned and crawled on his knees and good hand into the dense thicket.

"*Un momento*, Griffith," called Marina after him.

She pulled her machete from its canvas sheath, but he had already disappeared. She held the children back and began to hack at the tough stalks and branches of the laurel. Beyond the laurel, some bare limestone boulders showed where Griffith had already climbed out of view. Marina and the children followed.

Within minutes, Griffith broke through the last of the laurel. The top of *Cerro San Filipe* was a plateau a few dozen acres wide. Several small, overgrown mounds stood above the flattened peak. In the center of the plateau, another mound, taller and wider, thrust its crown above the scrub trees. Without brushing any of the dirt, leaves, or webs from his filthy clothes, he squinted across the thin stands of saplings and brush. He shaded his eyes and nodded.

"There!" he said breathing heavily. He pointed to the central mound.

"But Griffith," said Sara behind him, "nothing's here."

"You'll see," he panted, and started through the brush along a small deer trail.

"But Griffith..."

Tito and Sara took off after Griffith. They swatted aside leaves and branches, ducked under large ferns crowding the path, and followed him across the plateau. When they got to the central hill, it rose twenty feet above them, and its base stretched off into the brush in either direction. The hillside was less dense, and scrawny cecropias and taller ferns stood above the thick grasses.

Griffith climbed to the top, followed by the children and Marina. Sweating profusely, he leaned against a thick sapling.

Curling his left arm protectively against his damp shirt, he grinned. He reached up to remove his glasses so he could wipe his stinging eyes. When his fingers touched his wet eyebrows, he realized his glasses were gone. He'd left them somewhere, or they were knocked off—he didn't know. His carelessness should have bothered him, but other than driving and reading, he concluded without much guilt he didn't need them to actually see. In the jungle, anyway.

"I've lost my glasses," he announced as the sapling bent with his weight.

"Oh, Grif," cried Sara, "how can you see?"

"No, it's okay," gasped Griffith blinking away the sweat.

Griffith inhaled the fragrant air freshened by the open skies. A gentle breeze, steady and cool, dried the sweat on his forehead. In the bright sunlight, lichen-covered limestone reflected the light. Daisies and wild Mexican sunflowers blossomed in the crevices. He staggered across the grassy tussocks and rocky outcroppings, past a mound of crumbled, weather-darkened stones to the edge of the small hill and stood facing the sun.

For the first time in days, he could see beyond the next giant fern. He was no longer blinded by mist. The claustrophobic isolation of the swamps and forests disappeared. Across the valley, all the way to the horizon, everything was soft and indistinct. But even without his glasses, he could see.

The sun was an hour or more from setting, and the western highlands shone blue-green in the distance. To his left, the damp, green valley of the *Río Azul* stretched to the southern mountains where he'd spent last night with Karen. Three thousand feet below him and miles across the valley lay *Laguna Miramar*, sparkling like a small, silver coin in the sunlight.

"There," he said to himself.

The children walked to the edge and flanked him, and Marina stood behind them.

"Griffith, *cuidado, por favor*," she said. "Be careful."

"But she can see me now," he replied.

"Who?" asked Tito. "Karen?"

He didn't reply. Tito looked up at him. Griffith's face was ashen. Gazing across the valley to the distant lake, he swayed slightly and spread his feet to keep his balance.

"Grif," said Tito, "can we sit down?"

Griffith nodded and kept staring. Tito tugged on his right hand.

"Yes, Tito," mumbled Griffith, "sit down."

Tito looked at his sister, and she motioned for them to sit. Together, they pulled him to the ground between them where he slouched cross-legged, still staring at the lake.

Marina brought him the canteen. He took it from her, making an obvious effort not to spill it. They waited for him to take a drink, but he just sat there, cradling it in his lap, his left arm held rigidly against him. When Marina reached for it, he handed it back to her but kept his eyes on the lake. She held the canteen to his mouth. He tilted his head enough for her to pour several small sips into his mouth.

"*Niños*," said Marina softly, "I think we should camp here tonight." They looked up at her and nodded. "Will one of you help set up?"

"*Sí*," said Sara, "I will. But will Griffith be all right? I think he's very sick."

"I'm worried, too, Sara. Perhaps some hot food will help him."

"But he's not going to die," said Tito urgently. "I know. We've got to help him so he doesn't."

"We will, Tito," she reassured him. "You stay with Griffith, okay, and Sara and I will prepare a camp and our dinner."

For the next hour, Tito sat with Griffith. Several times,

Griffith's eyes glazed unfocused and then closed. After a few minutes, he would abruptly pop them open and stare again across the valley. This went on until he started to mumble. Tito thought he was trying to tell him something at first, but Griffith's responses didn't make any sense to him. So he just listened while Griffith slurred and murmured incoherent phrases and words.

Marina and Sara worked steadily in the late afternoon sun. Finding plenty of deadfall, they hauled firewood for the night. Then Marina cut palm fronds and sapling stakes for a shelter, and Sara hauled the material for her. They cleared an area below the central mound where Marina found two saplings, each over a dozen feet tall and about ten feet apart. Using her weight to pull one over, she brought its crown to the ground. With Sara holding the top, she levered a large rock onto it, pinning it down. After repeating that with the second one, they laid the cut branches crosswise between the saplings, using the live branches to hold them in place. Finally, she showed Sara how to weave palm fronds, base up, between the cross ties until the lean-to was covered on three sides.

While Sara worked on their shelter, Marina started a small, protected fire. She then she excused herself, disappearing off the plateau and into the jungle. When she returned thirty minutes later, she was carrying a gutted, young peccary over her shoulder. Its head had been removed, and blood stained the back of her shirt.

She set the carcass down and looked around for Sara. On the hilltop, Sara called and waved frantically to her. Tito was kneeling over Griffith who lay on his right side. Marina ran up the small hill to them.

"What's wrong?" she asked.

"We don't know," said Sara. Her voice was high and throaty.

Tito looked up at Marina from his knees and spoke rapidly. "He was okay. He was. He was mumbling, and... and... words I couldn't understand, and he was okay, Marina, but then he said 'I should sleep', and he fell over."

"It's all right, Tito."

"He's still breathing, I checked, I did, but his skin is cold. Look at his elbow. It's very hot. Is he okay, Marina?"

She knelt down beside Tito and laid her hand on his shoulder.

"Sh-h-h, *niño*. Let me look."

She reached over and caressed Griffith's elbow. It was warm and had swollen so that the joint could no longer be seen. His filthy bandage was twisted down around his wrist, exposing the raw, tumescent wound. She placed her palm on his cool, dry forehead.

"Let's move him under Sara's shelter."

"Don't hurt his arm," said Tito protectively.

"We'll be careful. Here, Tito, you brace his wrist while I roll him on his back."

As soon as she touched Griffith's shoulders, he began muttering. She lifted him, and his voice steadied, deep and resonant. When she realized what he said, she almost dropped him. In oddly accented Mayan, in the dialect of the Lacandon, he repeated the words clearly.

"*Hach pixan*," he intoned.

"What's the matter?" asked Sara when Marina hesitated.

"Nothing, *niña. Nada.*"

She lifted his right shoulder again, and supporting his weight, she staggered off the hill down toward the make-shift lean-to. Halfway, Marina had to rest, and set him down. Once again he spoke.

"*Hach pixan.*"

"What did he say, Marina?" asked Sara.

"It's not a word many people know. Perhaps he slurred an English word like 'hospital'."

"I don't think so," said Tito. "He said *'hach pixan,'* and you understood him. What does it mean?"

"If that's what you heard, Tito, it means 'soul dream' in Lacandon Mayan. But it would be impossible for him to know that. Only the *hach winik* dream *hach pixan*."

"Marina," said Tito, "I don't understand."

"I'm sorry, Tito. I was surprised for a moment, that's all. The *hach winik* are the true people—our name for ourselves. In a true dream, you speak with the soul of another, perhaps a person you once knew or maybe an animal. A *hach pixan* is rare and very important to the *hach winik*."

"Have you dreamed a *hach pixan*, Marina?" asked Tito.

"Only two."

"And…"

"When I was your age, Tito, I met the animal who gave me my name."

"Marina?"

"No. That's my Christian name. My family name comes from the Raccoon lineage. In my dream, I talked with K'ek'en the peccary and was told where I could make my first hunt. My father refused to believe me and wouldn't allow me to hunt."

"Is that why you left your family?" asked Tito.

"Tito!" exclaimed Sara. "That's impolite."

"It's okay," said Marina. "No, Tito, but I did take my bow and arrows and sneak away. When I returned with the young peccary I had slain for our family, my father wouldn't speak to me for days. Everyone in my village calls me K'ek, except my father. It was later that I left. Please, let's finish moving Griffith to Sara's shelter."

She carried him the final yards down the hill and propped him up in the lean-to in front of the fire. While Griffith nodded in and out of consciousness, the small blaze crackled and spit.

"*Niños*," Marina said after some minutes of contemplation, "Griffith is going to need some help."

"We know," said Sara. She was almost in tears, and her voice was frightened and urgent. "But we can't move him."

"Can you get him a doctor, Marina?" asked Tito. "We'll stay with him, won't we, Sara?"

"Your concern for this man is... impressive, but it would take many days to bring a doctor here."

"He could fly in a helicopter," offered Tito.

"There is a *bruja*," she said, ignoring Tito's plea, "who lives in a small *caribal*, our name for village, called *Xamansaswich*, maybe twenty kilometers northeast, if I can find the right tributary, and if..."

"Will you get her now?" asked Tito abruptly.

"It's night, Tito," she replied with a little surprise in her voice.

"But he needs help."

"Tito," she explained, "at night, the jungle is a very different world. The *hach winik* don't walk in the jungle at night because many kinds of death hunt in the shadows. The moon animals, the owls and the great cats, judge the balance of your life in the dark."

"You're afraid," Tito said bluntly. "Griffith led us through the jungle at night, and he wasn't afraid. We hiked all night, even after that snake killed our horse."

"What's this?" she asked.

"It's true, Marina," replied Sara. "*La barba amarilla* did bite Bellota."

"*Dios*, child." Marina's voice was a whisper. "The *nauyaca!*"

"The what?" asked Tito.

"The *hach winik* name." She glanced at Griffith reclined in the firelight. His lips trembled, and the sweat on his face glistened in the firelight. "And Griffith did this?"

"And Karen," said Sara. "That's why they love each other, and why he has to find her."

"I think he's very brave," said Tito.

"That may not be the only word to describe him, Tito. I will find *la bruja* for Griffith, *sí*, although I don't think we can return before tomorrow evening."

"We'll be okay," said Tito.

"You'll need some things. Before I go, I'll get more firewood."

"Marina," said Sara, "we can get the firewood. You showed me, remember?"

"*Sí*, Sara, I did. But let me cut up the meat for you. You should roast all of it. Don't leave any fresh. Keep the roasted meat close to the fire, and bury the rest away from here. You don't want to attract any animals, especially in the dark."

"We'll keep the fire going all the time," suggested Tito.

"*Sí*, that would be good, but keep the fire low. I'll leave my machete. You'll need it to get water."

"With your machete?" asked Tito.

"*Sí*, Tito. Cut the liana vines near the base. You'll be able to fill the canteen with water."

Before she left them, she cut the haunches and hams free, spitted them, and split the back and ribs. The children gathered more firewood in the quickening dusk while she checked their remaining food, the yams, plantains, and a few ears of corn.

Satisfied with her preparations, she wished them God's protective veil. She touched Griffith's forehead one more time—it was warmer—and then stood silently by the fire for a few moments.

"Watch over Griffith, and each other," she said finally, holding each child by the shoulder, "and I'll return soon." She gave them the traditional farewell of the *hach winik*. "*Bin in kah*. I go, now."

With *Akna*, the moon, and *Uayeb*, the north star, to guide her, she found the narrow path down the northern side of the mountain to Griffith's trail and headed east into the dark jungle. As the sun's light faded over the western highlands, the children sat quietly by the fire, near Griffith's feet, and turned the spitted meat.

That night, they regularly poured sips of water into Griffith's mouth. Once they got him to chew a small piece of roasted pork which he spit out before swallowing. Sara cooked a plantain, mashed it up with one of the baked yams, and fed him a small amount with her fingers. Later, all three slept, although Griffith's moaning outbursts woke the children so often it was easy to keep the fire glowing. Between fitful bouts of sleep, he rambled unintelligibly, mixing bits of English, Spanish, and Mayan.

The next morning, the children discovered he'd soiled himself. After a short debate, Sara and Tito reluctantly forced themselves to clean him. Without another word between them, they undressed him. Tito took his pants to a small rain pool, and Sara got the toilet paper from Griffith's pack and washed him like an infant. They knew Griffith was unaware of what he'd done or what they were doing, but whether out of embarrassment or for Griffith's pride, they agreed to keep this to themselves.

During the day, Thursday, the seventh of Griffith's honeymoon, the children explored the plateau. At the top of the central mound above Griffith's lean-to, the jungle spread below them in every direction, broken only by low mountain ranges, a few rivers, and the valley they'd left. From this height, the scars of human habitation and exploitation blurred into insignificance.

When they exhausted the search of their aerie, boredom led them to Griffith's pack. They dug out his travel guide to southern Mexico. For most of the day they took turns reading aloud the tourist information about Chiapas' cities and towns, *la Selva Lacandona*, several short chapters on the numerous Maya ruins, and the myriad ethnic groups along *la Ruta Maya*, the ancient, white limestone roads called *sacbeob*.

Between practicing their English and reading to Griffith, they gathered more firewood, ate some, fed Griffith whatever little he'd swallow, and listened for Marina. The entire time she was gone, neither Sara nor Tito mentioned their fears, and not once did they bicker over any task or opinion.

Throughout that day, Griffith's fever continued unabated. His elbow was so swollen his arm lay nearly straight along his side, and the redness extended to his wrist and upper arm. He remained semi-conscious, babbling under his breath while the children read and played. To Sara and Tito, he seemed neither better nor worse, so, with youthful innocence, they accepted their situation with equanimity.

As the evening shadows lengthened, however, Griffith grew agitated. He began to sweat profusely. Several times, unable to sit up, he shook with palsied frustration. When he spoke, his voice was noticeably louder and so filled with pain the children tried to wake him from his delirium.

Less than an hour after the sun had set, Griffith began to rant feverishly about the mountain, grumbling over somebody he was supposed to meet. Sara and Tito sat close by, unsure what to do.

Then, from beyond the fire, out of the shadows of the

rising moon, stepped Marina. Because her passage had been muffled by Griffith's ravings, the children were unaware of her until she cleared her throat.

Unable to handle his surprise, Tito blurted, "You came back."

"*Sí, niños, con la bruja,*" she said smiling.

Out of the jungle, an older woman and a young man, both as short and dark-haired as Marina, stepped into the light of the fire. They carried woven backpacks, and the young man had an extra, oversized cotton bag he set by the fire.

Sara and Tito gazed at these faces from their history books. Flickering, yellow light from the low fire danced over their dark, deeply-lined cheeks. Their long, ebon hair was center-parted. They wore identical *xikuls*—calf-length, white tunics—and both of them stood evenly balanced over their feet. The two *indígena* silently stared back.

The trip had not been as difficult or frightening as Marina had imagined. Twice, she had gotten lost and had to calm herself by singing under her breath. After the moon set, she crossed the *Río Negro*, looking for the tributary that led up to *Xamansaswich*. Uncertain of its direction, she stood in doubt until a jaguar, downstream of her, howled its warning. She turned upstream, found the tributary, and entered the tiny Lacandon *caribal* shortly after dawn. Five extended families, sixty-three people, lived in a dozen plank and thatched houses along a small stream. Their dogs and chickens outnumbered them.

The *indígena* of *Xamansaswich* had heard of this Lacandon woman who fought like a man—Marina was notorious among the few hundred surviving Lacandones. When she identified herself, she was shown the home of their *bruja* Chan Nuk and her son, José Pepe.

It took her over an hour to convince Chan Nuk to return

with her, primarily because *la bruja* had no intention of getting involved with the Zapatistas. When Marina mentioned how Griffith had followed the quetzal pair to the top of the mountain and his delirious references to a *hach pixan*, Chan Nuk scoffed, but abruptly agreed to follow Marina. Out of humanitarian curiosity, she said.

The entire village gathered as their *bruja* and her son left with this *hach winik* woman in the fighting clothes of the Zapatistas. With José Pepe loaded down with food, jugs, jars, herbs, roots, and powders, they returned to *Cerro San Felipe*, arriving just after sunset.

"How is Griffith?" asked Marina.

"Oh, Marina," said Sara, "he's not well. He barely eats or drinks, and his arm is so hot. Can *la bruja* help? Can you help him?"

"I do not know," said Chan Nuk in rudimentary Spanish. She looked at Griffith, lying in the shadows under the lean-to. "Is this the *gringo* who speaks Mayan?"

"*Sí*," said Sara, walking over to Griffith and kneeling beside him, "this is Griffith."

"A difficult name to pronounce," said Chan Nuk.

"Karen calls him 'Grif'," suggested Tito.

"And who are you?" asked Chan Nuk.

"I'm Tito. That's Sara, my sister. Who are you?"

Chan Nuk turned to Marina and asked in their native Mayan dialect, "Did he learn his manners from you?"

"It is his concern for the *gringo*," she replied softly, "which speaks through his mouth, *bruja*."

"Karen is his wife," said Sara.

"I see, *niña*. And you are the children of *el Presidente*?"

"*Sí*. And Griffith rescued us, with Karen," said Tito.

"*Sí*, will you look at him, *por favor*?" asked Sara.

"Since I am here, I will look at him."

Chan Nuk knelt under the lean-to. Griffith was mumbling, his head rocking slowly side to side. She listened to his breathing and felt his wet brow. When she touched his swollen left forearm, he flinched. She sniffed the air around his head, then his arm, and down to his legs. Getting up, she asked them to move him out of the lean-to into the light of the fire and the moon.

"He is dying," she said, matter-of-factly.

"You must save him," said Tito firmly.

"That is not for me to decide, boy who talks like a man."

"But you must!"

"He might be able to save himself," she conceded, "with some help, but it is his decision. Perhaps it is his time."

Sending José Pepe to collect water to boil, she unwrapped Griffith's useless bandage and threw it on the fire. She wiggled the dark clot of blood in the center of the wound. Sliding a fingernail under one end, she peeled the clot free.

The odor of rotten flesh assailed them. Thick, yellow pus flecked with dark brown streaks oozed from the wound, gagging them with its malignant, festering stench. Chan Nuk let the pus drain while she listened to Griffith's soft mutterings. Then she squeezed out some more, wringing a loud groan from him.

José Pepe returned, set the water on the fire, and retrieved Chan Nuk's medicine bag. She took out several pouches, laid them beside her, and then handed José Pepe a large gourd.

"Your water, please. And each of you," she said turning to the others, "please add your water?" When she saw their expressions, she added, "To cleanse his wound."

While they each stepped into the nearby shadows to take their turn, Chan Nuk picked through her herbs and roots. Holding each one up to the firelight, she placed some in small piles on a cloth. Marina returned with the half-filled gourd.

Chan Nuk asked her to hold Griffith's injured left arm by the wrist. When Marina gripped his forearm and turned it a few degrees at the wrist, Griffith again mumbled his incoherent mixture of three languages. While José Pepe poured the warm urine down the angle of Griffith's wound, Chan Nuk massaged the muscle around the wound to keep it open.

Griffith struggled weakly for a moment and then lay still. His muscles relaxed and his eyes opened. He spoke, this time clearly and distinctly.

"*Xu'tan!*" he said, the incredulity clear in his voice. "Now?"

Chan Nuk paused for a moment and looked at him. His skin was feverish and pale. His eyes stared blankly into another world, but he was no longer a tight little wad of knotted muscles and joints. His body had relaxed, and he seemed larger and more comfortable.

She finished cleansing the wound and motioned for her son to set the gourd down. She picked up several large balsam leaves from the nearest pile and submerged them in the water pot on the fire.

Without a blink or twitch, Griffith spoke again, deep from his diaphragm.

"*Xu'tan!*"

Chan Nuk jerked her attention back to her dying patient.

"What's the matter?" asked Sara.

"Shush, *niña*," quieted Chan Nuk.

"*Xu'tan*," he uttered one last time, denial thick in his voice. "*Kinich ahau* does not believe it."

He fell silent, his breathing deep and thick.

"What's the other language?" asked Chan Nuk.

"English," answered Tito. "He said he didn't…"

"*Sí, sí*," she interrupted, waving her hand for silence.

He lay in the light of the fire, sweat glistening on his skin. His eyebrows knitted for several seconds and then relaxed, as if he were listening to some nether voice.

"Who's *Kinich ahau*?" asked Sara.

"And what's *xu'tan*," added Tito quietly.

Chan Nuk looked at them momentarily.

"*Niños*," she finally answered, her voice low and apprehensive. "*Kinich ahau* means Lord of the Sun. The *hach winik* have not had an *ahau* for many centuries. Our legends say our last *ahau* was called the Destroyer of Temples."

"And *xu'tan*?" repeated Tito.

"It is Mayan, too."

"But Griffith," said Sara, "doesn't know any Mayan, I think."

"What does it mean?" asked Tito for the third time.

"It is a very old word, not heard very often. Perhaps we didn't hear it correctly."

"*Bruja* Chan Nuk," demanded Tito, "what does *xu'tan* mean?"

She looked at the precocious boy without smiling.

"It means the end of the world. Now be quiet, *niños*. I must hear what he says."

CHAPTER SEVENTEEN
DREAMS

Popol na Puuc Witz *Cerro San Felipe*
Valley of the Hero Twins *La Selva Lacandona*
Imix 12 Kayab A.D. June 5, 1525

> *Ki'iba'a wilik.*
> (Be careful what you see in your dreams.)
> A Lacandon parting before sleep.

"*Xu'tan!*" *I couldn't believe this former Lord of Texcoco below me was serious. I repeated the apocalyptic word.* "Xu'tan. *Lord Cohuanacox brings us Word of the end of the world?*"

The Lord of the ruins of Texcoco stood still, his western-styled pati, *with its shiny beads and metal, knotted across his shoulders. My attendant had positioned Cohuanacox so the Sun shone in his eyes from behind me. He wore none of the jewelry which should have accompanied him except for a small cross hanging around his neck by a thong.*

Nevertheless, out of respect for his former authority, I had Cohuanacox raised to a stone below my throne, and other than my priest also a stone below, I had given him private audience. My batabob *from the villages and my* nacomob, *ceremonially armed, were a full level below, an ear away.*

At least Cohuanacox still understood when to remain silent.

I used my Jaguar voice so that my batabob *would hear this. I wanted Word of this meeting to cover the Valley before this traitor Lord even left our realm. My village chiefs would eagerly share any new knowledge throughout the*

Valley. I dropped the back of my jaw and relaxed my vocal cords so my pitch remained low. I balanced the force of air from my diaphragm, placing my voice above Cohuanacox's head.

"How can the Lord Cohuanacox," I pronounced, "come to Popol na Puuc Witz, to the Mountain of Our Sacred Counsel, with words of the xu'tan? Just because his city has abandoned the gods of the Three Worlds, does he believe we will also destroy our god-pots as capriciously? Why does he want Word with us?"

I lowered my eyes to his so that Cohuanacox, if he did indeed remember his discipline, would recognize it was time for him to speak.

"My Lord Kinich," he began.

He neither looked at my face, nor at my feet, settling his focus on the green feathered *pati* covering my bare shoulders. This audience did not warrant any ceremonial headdress or even my more elaborate *ex* that hung between my bare legs from my waist to my sandals. *Honor your enemy, but do not flatter him.*

"I have come at a momentous turn," he continued. "The gods have given us a new warrior class of powerful lords in our World."

Rather than point out the insultingly obvious—the impossibility of knowing the will of any gods you have forsaken—I let my body speak nothing.

"A great warrior, a leader of many warriors, Capitán Hernán Cortés wishes to meet the great Lord Kinich of the *hach winik*."

"And this," I asked in my bird voice, "is the xu'tan you so blithely relay to us?"

"My Lord Kinich, rather than listen to the stories of the powerful Lord Cortés and his capitáns—certainly rumors have reached you before I—Lord Cortés, himself, wishes to reassure you he seeks only allies to defeat our common enemies."

Of course I'd heard stories of the enemies this Cortés has already accumulated.

"At certain turns," I replied, "it is most difficult to know who the enemy is."

"And that is the reason he requests your most eminent presence at his camp, to show you both his strengths and weaknesses."

Why would this warrior lord ask for such an unseemly audience? To reveal weaknesses in the forest where the light is not welcome is absurd. The forest hides, so he has something to hide, not reveal. And what is Cohuanacox hiding? Rather, what has been kept hidden from him by this Cortés who would invite me into the shadows?

"Does this new lord of yours," I asked, "intend to introduce us to his new god, as well?"

I could be blunt in my own city.

"If you wish, my Lord Kinich, his priest will speak of their Lord Jesús Cristo."

"Perhaps you would tell us of your introduction to their Lord."

"My Lord, I am not a priest. I am not able to look into the Invisible World, but I have seen the power of Lord Cristo."

"Power enough for you to forsake the gods of the Three Worlds?"

I was incredulous.

"I believe these are the true gods, my Lord."

"There is more than one?"

"Lord Cristo's Father of the Celestial World and the god they call the Spirit."

"From Xibalba's Underworld?"

"Again, my Lord, I am not a priest. I am not sure."

No, but this new god has made you arrogant enough to repeat yourself.

"Then the City of Texcoco still burns incense in their god-pots?" I asked.

"We burn the incense, yes. You have heard differently, My Lord?"

"Many stories are heard in the forest during this turning. And your people?"

"They are prosperous."

I was confused. Prosperity meant the gods favored his people. Why then would they need to find new gods? Besides, wouldn't his people replace their leaders before they abandoned their gods.

Is it possible that Cohuanacox has learned to speak a not-Truth? The very concept was staggering. In all my years I had yet to meet the man who could hide a not-Truth. I had never even considered the possibility. But if this were so, then I could learn little else from this man. I did, however, have one more question.

"And your allies, the High Lord Cuauhtemoc of the Mexica Aztec and his ally Tetlepanquetzal, they are also well?" I had heard conflicting stories.

"Both Lords have left the Light World," said Cohuanacox, his voice less steady than it should have been. "I also bring this Word to you."

I was shocked, not because I either knew or particularly cared for these lords from the volcanoes of Tenochtitlan far to the west, but they had been allies of this Lord standing below me. So why was this difficult for him to tell me? Did they not die well?

"Their deaths were ritualized?" I asked.

"They were beheaded." His voice was steady that time.

So they died in disgrace and without the rituals to take protect them in the Dark World.

"This Lord of yours, this Cristo, could not save them from their enemies?"

He was silent for a single moment, but I saw faint, unexpected movement in his eyes. The question surprised him.

"They betrayed their Word to Lord Capitán Cortés."

The effort it took to keep his voice in Truth betrayed him. So their own ally spilled their Blood. Interesting. A stone below, to my right, in my peripheral vision, my Jaguar Priest, Bahlum Ek ahaucan, turned just enough so the blue feathers on the knot of his pati were visible to me—our signal that he wished to speak silent words with me. Without looking at Bahlum, I spoke.

"Bahlum Ek ahaucan, you have Word from the gods for your Lord Kinich." I made it a statement.

"My Lord Kinich, if I may?"

I nodded to him, and Bahlum Ek took the high step that ceremonially separated me, the ahau of Popol na Puuc Witz, from those below. He lifted himself to my level, his back to the audience of petitioners and advisors. When he turned to Cohuanacox below us, he rotated in my direction with his head down, meaning the stars were positioned to accept the invitation.

BLOOD OF THE EARTH

It was customary for Bahlum Ek to stand to my right so no symbolic significance could be misinterpreted by blocking the view of my withered left arm and shoulder. Since I had been crippled by a jaguar when I was thirteen, leaving me with a useless left arm, I've allowed that side of my body to become deified by the people, the yalba winik. *Public focus on my left side, aided by the priests who communicate with the Dark World, has become a powerful image for me.*

Turning to the audience below, Bahlum Ek lifted his head, making sure his shadow fell over Cohuanacox, and then shut his eyes. The cobalt blue makeup on his closed eyelids became empty sockets. I also closed my eyes, knowing my lids would sparkle with the ground quetzal feathers in my iridescent green eye makeup.

Bahlum Ek ahaucan, *Jaguar High Priest and Word of the Gods, raised his arms. In a voice trained since puberty, his words resonated from the mountain below his feet. It was a very effective technique, his lips trembling but his voice emanating from below us.*

*"*Kinich ahau, tal in wilech,*" he intoned in his deep and resonant* Puuc *voice. "Lord Kinich, I have come to you."*

With practiced timing, we both counted silently to ten. Our eyes still closed, we turned toward each other. The people at public court were always impressed by the harmony of our movement, certain it represented a closer bond with the god-worlds. After counting to ten once more, we turned away and faced the people. We opened our eyes simultaneously. Bahlum then looked directly into Cohuanacox's eyes for a five count, providing me with the rest of the information I needed, and then stepped back down one stone to my right.

When he had retaken his position, I leveled my gaze above Cohuanacox. I spoke quickly to him.

"You may say to your Lord Capitán Cortés we will attend his camp in five days when the Sun has completed half its Turn. Our Western Sacbe *passes by his camp near the* Ix Chel *Temple, the Rainbow House, on the Red Shore of the Lake."*

Then in my Jaguar voice, I said for all to hear, "Tell the Lords Cortés and Cristo it is not yet time for the world to end."

✯✯✯

Thursday night

"José Pepe," said Chan Nuk, "you must go to Na'ha and find old Chan K'in."

"Will he make Griffith better," asked Tito impatiently.

"Quiet, *niño*," she said softly.

Griffith's fever raged through his body as he lay sweating and pale by the fire. For nearly twenty minutes they had listened to him mumble his distressing words from three worlds.

"Now, 'SePepe," Chan Nuk went on, "listen carefully. Tell Chan K'in I have heard the Destroyer of Temples speak through this *gringo*."

"What?" protested her son. "But, Mother, he won't believe me. I'll sound foolish."

"Yes, of course. But tell him exactly what I said. Now you must hurry."

"Yes, Mother." His shoulders dropped. He glanced toward the shadowed forest that stretched off the mountain deep into the night. "It will take several days to get there. I should sleep so I'll be strong in the morning"

"José Pepe," replied Chan Nuk quietly, "you must be back here with Chan K'in in three days."

"Three days! But I'll have to leave tonight."

From the other side of the fire, Marina stood. Her small frame was dwarfed by the darkness behind her.

"I'll go with you, José Pepe," she offered unexpectedly.

His eyes widened with surprise. He looked to his mother.

"Marina," she said, "you must remain here with Griffith. Your path is with him and the children. 'SePepe will be our messenger to Chan K'in."

"But Na'ha is so far," she protested, but only with half a heart. "And you want the *t'o'ohil* to hear Griffith?"

"What's a…" started Tito.

"If this *gringo* chooses to live," Chan Nuk replied holding her palm up toward Tito, "how can anyone but the Preserver of our Knowledge know what must be done?"

"I understand," said Marina, and turned her attention to helping José Pepe gather some food for his pack.

"Is the Preserver important?" asked Tito.

"Yes, *niño*," answered Chan Nuk. "José Pepe will tell Chan K'in our story. We will see if he returns."

After José Pepe left, Chan Nuk kept the children busy boiling water and heating *piñon* pine resin for a poultice. She showed Sara how to change Griffith's balsam dressing. Periodically, Tito spooned him some tea brewed from wormwood leaves, bark, and root, known among the healers as *iztauhuatl*.

"*Bruja*," said Marina, "if you cannot heal Griffith's wound…"

"Please, I am Chan. It may be your friend needs more than a simple *bruja* can provide."

"I'm sorry, Chan. I'm so worried about the children and Griffith I forget myself. I didn't mean to suggest you can't…"

"You've been misjudged, I think," she interrupted. "You've chosen a different direction, a path which brings tomorrow into our lives. I cannot decide if that is good since I only know what I know today. Chan K'in has said he fears he will not live until the end of the Fourth Age. If this *gringo*'s dreams mean something, I would like Chan K'in to hear them before he or the *gringo* dies."

Tito sat up from his mat.

"His name is Griffith," he said to her.

"*Sí, niño*, but as a *gringo*, Griffith should not know our ancient beliefs."

"But Griffith is a scientist," said Tito. "He studies invisible things."

"Tito," corrected his sister, "Griffith is a physicist. He studies atoms."

"Sí, niños," said Chan Nuk. "And I would like Chan K'in, who understands our ancient Knowledge, to hear him. I cannot judge the importance of Griffith's dreams."

"But Chan," said Sara, "Griffith is sick. His dreams are—oh, what's the word?—hallucinations, aren't they? Because he's sick."

"Perhaps, niña. But that doesn't mean his dreams are unimportant."

***

The lively conversations of frogs filled the warm evening air around the central Temple of Xibalba. The torches cast surreal shadows which flickered in the gentle night breeze rising from the valley floor. I entered the Temple of the Underworld carrying a small flame in a dish of oil. At the far wall I descended the steep, uneven steps into Xibalba's mouth.

My tiny firelight touched the sloped walls of the vaulted ceiling, bringing to life the nine Lords of the Underworld. Our ancestors' images, carved and painted on the damp walls to protect this sacred entrance to Xibalba's cave, danced in my light. With each step deeper into the earth, they greeted me one by one. Although I wasn't a priest, my Divinity allowed me access to the Turnings of the Dark Realm. Unfortunately, permission to walk and talk among the dream souls didn't make it any less frightening.

The walls narrowed as I stepped deeper into Xibalba. As I neared the bottom, a full three levels down, my wavering flame gave me more comfort than light. I shivered in the cool, moist air, but I wasn't going to set my light down just to pull my pati *tighter around my shoulders.*

At the bottom of the third staircase, I reached the small death room of my ancestor Pacal Sac Kuk. The ceiling brushed my hair, and his sarcophagus almost filled the room. Its carvings told of Pacal's descent into Xibalba. Through the roots of the Ceiba, he left the Light World with its jade-encrusted branches and double-headed serpent wearing a quetzal-feathered crown. Into Xibalba he passed, under the sky band which recorded the starry placement of each of our ancestral deities.

At the back of the death room was Pacal's path to Xibalba, open only to those worthy enough to enter the black and invisible Underworld. I had to squeeze between the sloped walls and this elaborately carved bed for Pacal's Light World body to reach the entrance.

Behind the sarcophagus, at floor level, I found the sacred cave. I slid my flame-bowl into the Dark World, thanked Pacal for showing me the way, and welcomed any night souls who might wish to converse. Cool air stroked my face, and cold spiders ran up my spine. My heart felt thin and weak against my ribs.

The opening was barely large enough to crawl through, so using my good elbow and knees, with my face just fingers above the floor, I crawled into Xibalba's cave, blind and with my head bowed.

Once I was all the way in, I sat with the flame-bowl at my feet. It illuminated little more than a small bit of the cold, muddy floor under me. The walls stretched away into darkness. My eyes flashed with minute bursts of light sent by the guardian souls to keep me blind.

I waited. My own fears beat at my heart, and cool vapors gripped my back with tension. I forced down a breath to calm my bones. My stomach churned in anxiety. The sacred xibalbaj okox I had eaten before entering the temple knotted my intestines with cramps. With the ingestion of the Death Mushrooms in this sacred cave, I was stepping into the Three Worlds simultaneously. Unsure whether the xibalbaj okox had yet opened my spirit walls, I started a breathing exercise at my toes.

Before I could even get my knees to breath, however, my body slipped through a dark opening into the Underworld. Faintly at first, I heard the brush of clothing as some soul passed by. Tiny splashes in small puddles, and susurrant breath, hollow and wispy, fed my eager senses.

The pulsing vibration of Xibalba's rivers rumbled with the flow of Earth Blood through the Underworld. The walls, breathing with the earth, shifted in crystalline light. The slow turning of the wheels echoed with the groans and creaks of the growing earth.

Somewhere in Xibalba's *passageways,* hach balum, *Lord of the Night, purred contentedly in his lair. I inhaled, seeking the familiar odor of death in the jaws of Lord Jaguar, but only the thick, earthy smell of the cave reached me. He must be far away.*

My legs and buttocks lost contact with the cold stone and mud beneath me. The cold lights of the Soul World blinked in the darkness, and I was no longer sure if my eyes were open or shut. Several spirits came and sat down nearby. I heard the sibilant shush of their xikuls *as they settled on their haunches.*

I waited. I wasn't going to speak or look at them without their permission. I knew if I tried verbalizing my needs, if I didn't understand the needs of the people well enough to simply wait, the demon Souls would rip at me in derision. The answer would come, but only if I did nothing more to seek it.

Since the wheels never stop turning, I did what little was left to me. I quieted my heart with all its noisy fears and hopes, readying myself for a spirit to walk with me through this hach pixan. *I did not expect Lord Kinich to be ignored for long.*

I waited.

Suspended in the Underworld, with its ethereal lights, memory smells, and surreal sounds, I fought the expectation that every sensation held some message for me. No longer able to tell the difference between waiting and waiting expectantly, I ached for what I did not know.

The world, the life I was born into, was changing. New gods appeared in the north, new kinds of death had entered the Light World, and all that was, was shifting. That knowledge, however, meant I knew nothing. Wanting answers, needing someone, some animal or human spirit to share what I was blind to, I finally accepted my ignorance.

Then, without warning, at that most fragile moment of emptiness, a great fear grew from the ground beneath me. It rushed from the cold earth, driving through my body like a spike. I shook feverishly. My breath bubbled in rales. Dread strangled my throat and smothered my heart. My muscles twitched uncontrollably. The urge to flee burned in my chest, and I ached to give in to the heat of panic.

Then from deep within the turmoil of my heart, the faintest Word took shape—the tiniest encouragement, the sweetest desire to surrender. Oh, if this were a True Voice in the chaos, I had to cling to it.

I closed my heart to the demon-fears of thought. All I believed, everything I thought I knew, bled from my heart. Layers of terror peeled away like an onion. Breath after breath, the wishes vanished, desire dissolved, and love and pain lifted away until, once again, I could see.

Below me I saw the Valley of the Hero Twins with its tall, green fields of maize between every village stretched to the far horizons. High in the air above the Valley, a hundred columns of smoke rose from all the hundred villages. My vision narrowed and I shuddered. Every village belched yellow flames and fiery ashes into the skies. The women and children screamed soundlessly in the fires. Monstrous four-legged, two-headed warriors, covered in metal and fur and consumed with the fever of Blood, rode through the smoke and ashes, slashing at the terrified women with their great swords and impaling the children with their lances.

Shocked and nauseated, unable to watch the slaughter, I turned away and looked up at Puuc Witz. *My vision tunneled until I was on the sacred mountain. Like an apparition, I stood helpless among my people. Beaten and enslaved, they were being forced to tear down their temples, stone by stone, and throw them from the mountain top. The stelae recording my family's history lay broken and crushed at my feet. Shards of god-pots, empty of their incense, were scattered in the dust. One of these* conquistadores *laughed as he set torch to my bird house. Two of my precious, frightened birds struggled through the mayhem to reach the trees below us.*

In the middle of the limestone rubble, more conquistadores *ordered the People to erect a crude, wooden cross, the height of two men. One of their red priests sprinkled water on the ground. My dizzy head reeled with incongruity and chaos. Their death priest, dressed in the rain red of our chac priests, spilled lifeless water over the ruins of our gods while the* yalba winik, *the innocents of the Valley, had their holy Blood released unsanctified onto the earth. My heart screamed for an answer.*

Its hollow voice echoed weakly against my ribs.

Then out of the smoke and blood, curtains of faint phosphorescent pastels folded together. I squinted at the distant image of someone I knew. But something was terribly wrong. She was upside down, suspended by her feet. I could barely see through the vapors, and, oh, Itzamna, what have you brought me? This is not an answer!

I closed my eyes, but still I saw her—my Lady Caran Koh, her dainty hands and feet bound, hanging from a branch high in a sacred ceiba. I opened my eyes, and she was closer still. Her warm Blood dripped unsanctified from her headless body.

My heart screamed, and my eyes burst with water. The one love in my life, this noble woman who sacrificed her Blood so quietly, the woman who gave children to the People, remained before me, horribly destroyed, headless, hanging by her feet, her soul lost in mutilation.

This cannot be. This must not be! On the verge of vomiting, I swallowed back my horror, vowing this sickness within me would not escape.

✻✻✻

Friday

"Is he better, yet," asked Tito as soon as he awoke.

He and Sara had finally slept, but the periodic outbursts from Griffith's fevered dreams had wakened them several times. During the night, Chan Nuk and Marina had either dozed or listened to Griffith's terrified dreams. They had continued to pour tea into him, and three times they had changed the dressing on his forearm, replacing the steeped *iztauhuatl* leaf over the gunshot wound. The hot pine poultice on his left palm had opened the tiny puncture wound.

Earlier, before sunrise, when Marina cleaned another of Griffith's watery evacuations, she found his saddle sores, still raw and running. Chan gave her some blanched lizard's tail herb, *yerba de manzo*, to make a dressing for the open sores. When the children woke, Marina was washing the bile off his beard where he'd tried to throw up.

"He's no worse, I think," answered Chan.

"He had bad dreams," asked Sara, "didn't he?"

"Difficult dreams, *sí*, but perhaps they were not bad."

"When will he get better?" asked Tito.

"I do not know. Last night, he walked beside death."

"I heard him crying once," said Sara.

Tito looked at her in obvious disagreement.

"He wasn't crying, Sara," he said. "Griffith wouldn't cry."

"Tito, that's not true," she said.

"Did he cry when the Zapatistas shot him?"

"They weren't Zapatistas, Tito."

"I know, but did he cry? No."

"Tito, I heard him. That doesn't make him bad just because he cries."

"Perhaps," interrupted Marina, "he was crying for someone else."

"*Sí*, for Karen," agreed Sara. "He misses her. Before he got sick, all he wanted to do was find her."

"Well, I still don't think he was crying," said Tito. "I heard him, too, and he talked about some battle." He glanced at Chan. "You said he almost died."

She looked up from Griffith's pale, tormented face.

"He had a struggle last night. But he's sleeping now, so maybe he won his battle. We will see."

"*Niños*," said Marina, "let's fix something to eat. Then we can clean away some of this brush and give ourselves more room today."

Tito stood up and stretched.

"Good idea," he said. "I'm hungry."

He looked around. The early sun was burning away

the mist from the eastern rain forest. On the mountain top everything was damp and cool. He listened to chachalacas in the jungle far below, disrupting the early silence with their loud, repetitive clucking.

"I think I like camping," announced Tito, "and I like it here. Let's stay for a while. Will you teach me to hunt, Marina?"

"Tito," said Sara, "if we don't get home, soon, there may be a war. Didn't you hear anything Marina or Marcos told us?"

Chan Nuk looked up at the name, her eyes wide for a moment. She fixed her stare on Marina. Tito spun around. Glaring at Sara, he posed with arms akimbo. She was about to get indignant when she realized her error.

"Oh! I'm sorry, Marina. His name is Rafael, I know."

Chan Nuk lowered her eyes and sat back. Marina nodded curtly at Sara's apology and turned to Chan Nuk.

"Chan Nuk," said Marina, looking for an explanation, "I didn't think it was important to mention him. Griffith and the children needed help, and because Rafael and Karen... perhaps they drowned, and you were the only one I could... and... I'm sorry."

"Marina," answered Chan Nuk after a few seconds, "I'm no one to judge. I am worried this is a very important turning, and I myself don't see a clear path. I'm not so worried, however, about your vision. You have chosen your path."

"I should have told you. I apologize."

"Is there more to tell? Is there going to be a war in the forest?"

"I don't know. The *guardias blancas* have been burning the villages, and the EZLN believes the *judiciales* are bringing an army into the jungle. We knew this before we found Karen and Griffith with the children. I should have told you."

"Where is this battle supposed to be?" asked Chan.

"Troops and supplies have been moving toward the Guatemalan border."

"Here?"

"Close, *sí*."

"That's the direction we came from," asked Sara, "isn't it?"

"*Sí*," said Marina.

"Will they be able to find us?" asked Tito.

"I'm sure, *niño*," she answered.

"They're burning the villages," said Chan Nuk, "to find the children. And now they are going to kill all the Zapatistas and all the *indígena* who are in their way because you have the children. Why would men go to war over two children?"

"And why would they frame the EZLN?" replied Marina. "These are questions to which I haven't any answers. But the four of them were lost in the jungle, and we found them before the *guardias blancas* did. What were we supposed to do? Send them back into the jungle? Hand them over to the people who claim we kidnapped them?"

"*Perdóneme*," interjected Tito, "but she's right about the *guardias blancas*. We were at *don* Pedro's ranch. I heard his order to kill us. We escaped and drove and took a boat and flew, and Marina and Karen and Griffith saved our lives. This is the only time I've felt safe since we were kidnapped."

Chan Nuk listened quietly and smiled when Tito finished.

"I understand, *niño*. And we'll keep you safe if we can. But now, there may be a war because people think Marina and her soldiers kidnapped you. And since you are with them... for most people, what they think is true becomes their truth."

"That's what Marc... uh, Rafael said," added Sara, "but all I have to do is tell them Griffith and Karen saved us. Why wouldn't they believe me?"

"You may have to do that, Sara. But until that time..." she

turned to the young Zapatista *indígena*, "have you figured out how to prevent this war?"

"Perhaps when Chan K'in arrives, he'll help us," she ventured.

"This is your plan?" Chan Nuk indulged a wry smile. "Why would the *hach winik* fight? Our bows and arrows and our little rifles against the *judiciales*? When have we ever fought anyone? Not the ranchers or loggers or squatters or even the *evangelistas*. No, Marina, we know we can die as easily as your Zapatista soldiers."

"Chan Nuk," said Marina, "I don't wish to sound stupid or thoughtless. I apologize if my arrogance has insulted you, but none of this was anticipated. None of our plans have worked. What's happening now is beyond my control. Maybe beyond everyone's control. I don't know how to stop this war."

"Chan K'in has been saying for years," replied Chan Nuk quietly, "the *xu'tan* was coming and the *hach winik* would leave this World. Whether we are to have a place in the Fifth World or not, Marina, your ignorance is no greater or less than anyone's."

Neither of them said anything further. Marina knelt by the fire, her back to the rising sun, stirring the dying embers. Sara got up and walked to the edge of the field overlooking the valley. After a few moments, she turned back to them excitedly and pointed down the mountain side.

"What is it?" Tito yelled. He got up and ran across the plateau to her.

"Shhh," hushed Sara as she waved him over. "Shh!"

From the canopy, flying up and over Sara's head, were a quetzal pair, perhaps the same birds Griffith had followed onto this mountain. The female chirped her plain song and flew over their camp toward the morning sun. Her mate, his long, royal plumage iridescent in the early sunlight, darted back and forth across her path.

Running and giggling across the hilltop, Tito chased after them, dashing past the lean-to where Griffith slept quietly, searching for their nest on the eastern edge of the plateau.

***

I turned from my Lady and listened to the simple song of my quetzals. The Royal Birdhouse was my favorite place, and my connection to the quetzal was well known by all the People of the Valley. My mother, the Lady Evening Star, began the practice of keeping a mating pair of our sacred birds following my attack by the jaguar. It's said that a quetzal led her to where I had been carried in the jaws of hach balum. *She found me, still conscious and bleeding, by the lake shore where Lord Jaguar had left me, apparently not ready to take me below to* Xibalba.

Ah, Itzamna, how I love your birds. How can I repay you for sending them to my rescue? At my installation nineteen years ago, I decreed as Word that no more quetzals were to be killed for their royal plumage. The feather hunters, of course, soon learned to trap the long-tailed quetzal and his mate.

Despite this, our hunters have reported fewer numbers again this year. Oh, my birds, won't you tell me why you're leaving this World?

Regardless, we try to preserve those who guide us. For these past nineteen years, the trapped and clipped birds have been given to the villages for perpetual protection. Each village batab *honors a chosen family with the responsibility of caring for the bird.*

To receive a mating pair has become such a great symbol of respect, especially for those families blessed with hatchlings, the entire village supports the family as long as the birds live. But the numbers of our great birds, the souls of those who connect us to the thirteen levels of our Celestial World, are still declining.

It has become difficult for me to accept that my actions, whether our Priests declare them as Word or not, might not make any difference in the Light World. If the common people, the yalba winik *who are unable to look into the Celestial World, if they fail to see the positive effects of their* ahau's *actions in their World,* how can I legitimately claim my sovereignty? Doubting myself was new to me, and I did not like it. Nevertheless, I had made my decision about this Cortés and his new gods.

"That is my Word, My Lady," I said to her with a good deal more formality than was necessary.

"Kinich," she replied, sensitive to my shift in tone, "My Lord, this is so... so drastic."

"You have no more choice in this than I."

"But how can a True Dream require such action?"

She was obviously confused by my order to leave the city and take our Royal Children with her into the primeval forest. The very idea of abandoning the city for the perilous jungle was foolhardy, but to commit our Quetzal lineage to the uncontrollable forces outside civilization was absurd in the extreme. Still, it had to be done.

"You will leave in four days, after the Renewal Ceremony. I'll ask Bahlum Ek to go with you. Nacom Bolay will personally oversee your warrior guard. You and the children will be safe."

"And you, My Lord?"

"I will find you."

"What does that mean, Kinich?" she asked. "When will we return to Puuc Witz?"

Her voice was more urgent than was becoming, and I had little time for discussion. The priests and batabob would be arriving soon. I had to address them.

"Caran Koh," I said softly. "Our Blood is part of this mountain. We will return, but for now, I need your help. You must trust my Dream, just as I must."

"Kin, of course I trust you. I just don't understand why you leave me in shadows. Why can't I know where we're going or when we're returning?"

Knowing my explanation would be unacceptable, I remained silent.

"But," she finished, "if I must remain blind, then so be it. Am I allowed to fear for you? Or the children?"

"Oh, Caran, my beautiful Lady."

I took hold of her left hand. She squeezed back with her thumb and two long fingers. Even after all these years, whenever I touch her regal, exotic left hand, the first knuckle ceremonially cut from each of her middle fingers over fifteen years ago, I feel a surge of pride and at times like this, a powerful lust for her. With the Blood she has given to the earth, the gods would gladly escort us all the long way to the final turning of our Fourth Age.

"My love," I said, "the gods have given us the responsibility to protect the People. When we do, the gods protect us. And remember, until the Renewal Ceremony, we have these few days together to... strengthen the Blood between us."

A smile broke at the edges of her lips. She lowered her eyes provocatively. Placing the two fingertips of her left hand on the skin around my birth knot, she gently pushed. Long ago, she learned how easily I was aroused by any connection to the Blood. As ahau, my duties to the People included initiating every Sacrifice. The pleasure I derived from serving when the Blood flowed had become visceral as well as heart-centered. Caran knew this, and the few quick turnings we managed to get alone were often spent in erotic play.

I looked down at my Lady's ebony hair, straight and lustrous, and slid my fingers through her thick tresses. Surprisingly, she looked up at that moment, making eye contact and breaking the mood instantly and intentionally. Startled, I was about to speak when she stepped back and cast her eyes to the floor. What god's mischief was this?

I spun around, expecting to see some child or farm animal pulling at our privacy curtain. Bahlum Ek was standing in the doorway—I'd neglected to drop the curtain—and at the sight of the Blue Priest, the front of my ex hiding my embarrassed arousal sagged.

"Bahlum," I smiled awkwardly, "I thought you could read my thoughts. Certainly everyone else believes that."

"I'm sorry, my Lord Kinich." Noticing my Lady, he returned the smile. "Perhaps I was preoccupied."

I don't think he intended that as a rebuke, but he was correct—we both had a great deal to do. I nodded.

"The batabob will arrive for their audience shortly."

"Bahlum, I know that." *I was miffed he'd think I'd let my play insult my village chiefs.*

"Of course. I only bring you fore-knowledge you might find useful."

Now I was abashed, having presumed an ignoble thought about my own Blood Priest. Last night in Xibalba's World, *I discovered my heart might cloak thoughts which could lead to impotent madness. Now this unfamiliar doubt entered my heart again. Am I strong enough to save the People? Or is this Death God of Cortés more powerful? I was grateful for any additional knowledge.* I nodded to Bahlum again.

"Your nacom Bolay," he continued, "does not trust that Azteca Cohuanacox. Consequently, he has pledged his warriors to the batabob in exchange for the additional village warriors they will provide. Led by Bolay, they are going to Voice articles of attack and defense for you to approve."

So they've heard the stories of the pagan brutality of the conquistadores. *That was necessary for my plan to work.*

"Thank you, Bahlum."

I expected him to exit after the dismissal. He didn't, and I gave in to him. He was, after all, the one who had let my own Blood in the Temple more than once.

"What else?" I asked.

"They've heard you had a True Dream in Xibalba's cave."

"Then perhaps we can save them."

"But they fear you'll negotiate with these invaders rather than sacrifice your warriors in battle."

"I'll reassure them my Dream was otherwise."

"Will you, at least, give me knowledge of your dream before the meeting?"

"No, Bahlum. And not to my batabob, either."

"Kinich, why will you not share your hach pixan with me?"

He'd asked me that three times since I'd stumbled out of Xibalba's *Temple just after dawn this morning. I should tell him something.*

"All right, Bahlum, since you are so insistent, I will tell you why I can't share my conversations in Xibalba with anyone. I can't... because I didn't have any. There was no one who would talk with me, Bahlum."

"A hach pixan *without a person or animal to talk with. I don't understand. Didn't the mushrooms work? Or did you vomit too soon?"*

"No, but I needed to."

Bahlum Ek wanted more from me. Usually a priest would never seek information reluctantly given, but Bahlum believed he was capable of bearing the darkness others released. Given our family and Blood ties, he directed most of his priestly curiosity at me. He understood the need to vomit out the evil—there are not many ways to release the darkness which can fester inside—but the lack of Souls in a True Dream needed clarification. He stood there silently, waiting for more. I wished he wouldn't press me with my Lady here.

"Bahlum, I will tell you this. In Xibalba, I..."—*I was not sure how to describe a world which is not*—"I saw the Valley that is and the Valley that is not. I saw many People and many strangers, but neither was in this World. I think I walked out of time."

Unable to keep the awe out of his voice, he said, "You walked where the Wheel hasn't turned, and you won't share that Vision with your Blood Priest?"

I did owe him more, and my Lady, as well, both of whom had listened to my evasions with patient acceptance. My arrogance in attempting to change the World distressed me enough. How could I reveal a horror not yet part of the Wheel?

"Bahlum, let me tell you what I do know. We were once the greatest people all the way to both seas. Our sacbeob *stretched to the corner stars so our merchants could trade with every city and our warriors could fight and drink with everyone else's warriors. Our artists carved our history in the great stelae here and in Palenque and Yaxchilan. Your priesthood once had many great astronomers who set down all the knowledge of the Wheels of the Worlds and the stars of the sky.*

"I do not mean to insult you, Bahlum. You know this. But now, everything has changed. Where are the People in this World? Here in our Valley, but nowhere else. The Itzas, the Toltecas, and the Quiche overran the other Maya cities years ago. And now even the lowly Aztecas threaten us with these strange warriors and priests who revel in slaughter and destroy all that is sacred. How can this be, Bahlum? You taught me that the Wheels are not finished turning on Us. Yet we are the last of the People."

"Whatever your Vision," protested Bahlum, "it cannot mean Cohuanacox and his pagan ally Cortés are going to destroy us. Use the thought patterns you were taught, Kinich."

"But what if you're wrong, Bahlum? What if we can be destroyed? Are you sure we can defeat such unholy killers? They have huge, four-legged warriors who can't be killed because their skin cannot be pierced. And what about this new fever from the Yucatán, mayacimil, the 'easy death' where the skin explodes leaving the few survivors scarred for life? What if our healers can't cure the mayacimil? Are we strong enough to defeat two enemies—one we can't kill and another we can't see?"

"Kinich, we did not make the Wheels, and we cannot stop their turning. You know the calendar even if the illiterate warriors and merchants do not. The Wheels have nearly five hundred more years to turn. How can they be stopped? How can the Fourth World end before it ends? I don't understand you."

"I have seen it destroyed, Bahlum."

"This is your True Dream?"

"Bahlum. I will not let them crush our city and slaughter our People."

"Was this your hach pixan, Kinich?"

"My hach pixan! I will change my hach pixan, Bahlum! By all the gods who wander the darkness of Xibalba, I will not let our enemies tear down Puuc Witz and destroy the last of the Maya. Not the Quiche, or the Itzas, and certainly not these conquistadores from their obscene, new World.

I will give the People their five hundred years so we can meet the end of our World together.

"That is my True Word to you, Bahlum, and to you, my Lady, and to my People!"

Behind me, Caran Koh placed her cool, left palm on my back between my shoulder blades and pressed with her two Royal fingertips. She accepted my Word.

✸✸✸

Saturday

"Has the Lord of Light spoken again?" asked a small *hach winik* man, dressed in his calf-length *xikul*.

"Will he speak to us?" asked another.

A half dozen men, all *hach winik* with thick, black hair, and similar pale *xikuls*, stood near Chan Nuk and her *gringo* patient, close enough to shade them from the afternoon sun. Sara and Tito stayed inside their recently enlarged shelter where Griffith slept evenly. Marina, still in her fatigues, stood protectively by Griffith's side.

His arm remained swollen, but the red, infected areas had been contained. His temperature still swung wildly over the hours, but Chan Nuk was comfortable with his struggle, feeding him tea, and helping Sara change his bandages. Chan Nuk was comfortable, that is, until the arrival of these *hach winik* from a village to the north.

"Chan Nuk," inquired another, "what has the Lord of Light told you?"

Chan stood and walked away from Griffith. They turned to listen to her but kept their focus on this strange, weak *gringo*. She motioned for them to follow her. They did, reluctantly, only because they knew Chan Nuk would tell them nothing otherwise.

"Why are you here?" she asked the eldest of the men.

"The Destroyer of Temples has returned," he replied as if she were ignorant.

"Where did you hear this?"

"From José Pepe, your own son. He told us Chan K'in from Na'ha was coming to confirm his dreams."

"Tell us what the Lord of Light has told you," piped in another.

"Yes, what do you know?" from still another.

"Is that the 'woman called soldier'?" asked the youngest man in the group, glancing at Marina.

"Please," said Chan Nuk quietly, "until Chan K'in arrives, there is nothing to tell. With Marina, this *gringo* has rescued these two children and come to this mountain. As you can..."

"We heard a quetzal mating pair led him up the mountain." interrupted one of the younger men.

Chan Nuk looked at him a long moment before answering. He lowered his eyes.

"If this man came here seeking counsel about his wife and these children, I do not know. Perhaps Chan K'in will know. If the *gringo* lives."

Two of the men gasped.

"Yes," she said, "he is very sick. If you wish to help, you may stay."

So until it got dark, the six men worked to clear more of the brush away from the mountain, prepare more camps, and collect firewood. Behind Griffith's shelter two of the men cut saplings and undergrowth away from the mound of limestone rock. Pointing out the weathered edges, they concluded these rocks were the foundation of an ancient Maya temple and Griffith was led here intentionally by the quetzals.

One of men then left to return to his village, saying the people needed to know what was happening here.

After sunset, they returned to the fire, close enough to overhear if Griffith spoke. The children, oddly shy, appeared before dinner and were warmly greeted by the new arrivals. Several of the men had brought food with them and declared it would be their honor if the children shared the evening meal they had prepared. When Sara and Tito smelled the large, roasted turkey—one of the men had shot a wild, blue-headed, ocellated turkey in the lower jungle—and the plates of yams, beans, *chiles*, and fruit, their shyness evaporated in the aromas of their first real meal in days.

With Marina translating, the new arrivals began to ask questions of Sara and Tito. As children of *el Presidente*, they kept personal information to themselves, but while they ate, they were drawn into lengthy conversation about the heroics of Griffith, Karen, and Marina. These *indígena* from the rain forest were enthralled by the children's story of this *gringo* who spoke from their past.

After everyone had eaten, including a few fingers of fruit and warm yam for Griffith from Sara, the *hach winik* remained, allowing their own small fires to burn to embers. The rest of the night they stayed near this mysterious man from another world, waiting for his dreams to speak again. One of the men voiced the hope this *gringo*'s dreams might bring all the *hach winik* together in their poor threatened world.

※※※

From the High Throne, the Honored Sacrifice was led to the red-stained Temple of the Rain overlooking the eastern expanse of the Forest. Naked, except for the small ceremonial ex covering his genitals, the Sacrifice was painted in wide, black and white vertical stripes. He knelt on the stone between his escorts, similarly naked but painted a pale blue. He lifted his eyes to the blue chac *priest standing in front of him. The* chac, *several shades deeper than the escorts, lifted the Frog knife from his elaborate jade-encrusted, blue-feathered waistband. Holding the left ear of the Sacrifice, he placed the tip of the obsidian blade against the lobe.*

"Kinich *ahau, Lord of the Sun," intoned the priest so that I and those gathered below could hear the first moment, "our Sacrifice freely gives his Blood to anoint the Temple of the Rain."*

With a single, swift downward stroke, the blue chac *slit open the Sacrifice's earlobe, replaced his knife, and caught the flow of the Sanctified Blood in his Blood Bowl. The Sacrifice did not flinch. After several moments, the* chac *turned to the east and lifted the blue tripod bowl above his head.*

The arrhythmic chanting of thousands of yalba winik *who had gathered all morning rose over* Puuc Witz *into the sky. During a Renewal Ceremony only the priests, lords, and* batabob *were allowed among the high temples. The rest of our People stood shoulder to shoulder filling the white stone Royal* Sacbe *encircling the Holy Mountain. The overflow clogged the numerous access* sacbeob *and clambered among the trees and* milpaob *terracing the lower slopes. From the Five Temples of the World atop* Puuc Witz, *the energy of the mountain, renewed by the taste of Blood, would flow through them this day.*

The People needed this Blood and Feast Day because the sacrifice I was asking them to make after the Feasting would be the greatest challenge any Maya city ever confronted. Since I had convinced the batabob *of my plan, the tension from the massive preparations the last four days had grown palpable.*

My own anxieties from these days of change were now lost in excitement as the chac *dipped his fingers in the bowl and smeared his chest and stomach, streaking his blue makeup with dark crimson lines. He turned and walked around the silent, bleeding Sacrifice to the Red Temple. Still holding the Blood Bowl above him, he poured a thick stream of the Life Force onto the ancient, red-stained stairs leading into the temple. In his bare, blue feet he stepped onto* the bloody stones and turned back to the East. Leaving a trail of dark footprints, the chac walked past the Sacrifice, this time around the other side completing the circle. He stopped at the top of the eastern Red Stairs, high above the People who continued their chanting.

He held the Blood Bowl out to them. Their voices came together, rapidly crescendoing until all along the Royal Sacbe, encircling the mountain, the ten thousand or more who had come up from the Valley raised their voices in unified Renewal. With the Blood Bowl steady, the chac kept the Voice of the People at a peak for several moments. He then hurled the Sacred Bowl down, smashing it on the stone stairway and splattering the last drops of the Blood out toward the People.

Their Voice broke into chaotic screams.

The chac and escorts waited with their Sacrifice until the Voice of the crowd below us began a slow retreat. The escorts lifted the Sacrifice to his feet and led him, in full view of the People, along the edges of the High Terrace to the Yellow Temple above the southern exposure of Puuc Witz. Our Sacrifice, the son of a servant captured during the Quiche Wars long ago, was doing well. He kept his poise, and it seemed to me he had already moved into the Blood Dream. Certainly the sacred mushrooms that Bahlum had fed him earlier, the same xibalbaj okox I had consumed days before, were opening his spirit to the Journey of Sacrifice.

Thankfully, it had been many years since a Sacrifice had disgraced us with too obvious a reaction to the pain of giving. That one's terrified screams had ruined the season's maize crop, threatening the People with starvation and my rulership with chaos. But this servant, our Sacrifice, had eagerly volunteered to give his Blood to the Renewal. I was starting to feel some little pride in him.

At the Yellow Temple, a second blue chac stepped out to join his brother in attending the Sacrifice. The Sacrifice opened his mouth, and the chac grasped his lower lip. His jade knife was carved into an ear of maize. With the tip of his dark green blade ready to pierce the Sacrifice's lip, the chac spoke.

"Kinich ahau, Lord of the Sun, our Sacrifice freely gives his Blood to anoint the Temple of Yum Kaax, God of the Yellow Maize."

The priest punched the blade through the lower lip and slid it back out. He fed a thin braid of maize silk through the hole and knotted it. Again, the Sacrifice remained motionless, although his escorts held him securely by his upper arms. The pale, green silk was soon gouted with Blood which dripped slowly into the chac's *Blood Bowl.*

The chac *finalized the Maize ritual, bloodying himself, the Temple, and then smashing the Bowl for the People below. Again the People responded with a Voice of high energy and earthy enthusiasm. My heart pounded in my chest. The gods were with us, the Blood flowed, and the back of my neck itched with excitement.*

Our Sacrifice was now escorted to the western temple, the black-painted House of Balum, the Ebon Jaguar. A third blue chac *appeared and led the offering of Blood to the rare, black cat. One of the escorts removed the Sacrifice's* ex, *exposing his penis. The* chac *lifted his ebony jaguar knife, its tail sharpened to a thin point, and placed the tip under the foreskin. He spoke his offering to me and pierced the foreskin. The dark Blood flowed freely.*

From the vantage of my Throne, I looked for signs of frailty. Our sacrifice didn't struggle, showing a worthiness and strength which honored us. If he were weakening, I couldn't detect it. Everyone else, from the Royalty to the blessed yalba winik *gathered below us today, had to be feeling the same thrill as their* ahau. *And I felt it from my dry mouth to my growing erection.*

The chac *repeated the ritual, anointing himself, the temple, and then smashing the Bowl. Rather than wait for the sustained cheers and chants of the People to lessen, the escorts following the three blue* chacob, *walked the Sacrifice to the fourth temple, the nothern White temple of the Sun, the House of Kin.*

Here, a fourth chac *used the curved beak of his hummingbird blade to ceremonially drain the Blood from the nasal septum of the Sacrifice. This time, however, after the* chac's *ritual smashing of the Blood Bowl, the Sacrifice honored himself, and astounded the People, by refusing any further assistance from his escorts. With the Voice of the People mounting, he straightened himself and staggered toward the central Altar of the Heart below* Xibalba's *Temple. Their Voice vibrated in my heart with its power.*

BLOOD OF THE EARTH

From my throne above the center of the plaza, I watched, enthralled. I silently urged the escorts to stay close to our Sacrifice. He made it to the base of the huge, carved Altar and waited for his escorts. They then helped him ascend the final, steep Jaguar Stairs to the top. The Sacrifice, Blood still oozing from his cuttings, stretched himself out on the mottled, brown stone. The four chacob *stepped to their stations on the Altar's corner steps. The Voice of the people drove the Ritual toward its climax, and I had to control my breathing to stay above my own eagerness.*

The great Bahlum Ek ahaucan *appeared in the entrance of* Xibalba's *Blue Temple, above all others in the center of the plaza. One slow step at a time, he descended to his Sacrificing Stone beside the Altar. Dressed in his most exquisite blue raiment, his* pati *hung to his waist, heavy with jade, spondylus shells, leather, and indigo feathers glinting in the sunlight and fluttering in the gentle breeze. For the Renewal, he wore the his most regal Blue Jaguar headdress with its open jaws and ivory teeth poised to strike. It had taken his artisans months to meticulously weave the various shades of ten thousand, tiny blue feathers, each barb individually sewn in place to resemble the spotted fur of the jaguar.*

Bahlum Ek's personal chac *and three naked, blue attendants paraded from the Temple, each of them carrying a Prayer Board. The* chac *carried the Heart Knife on his Board, and the attendants separately carried the Blood Bowl, the Skinning Knife, and the god-pot smoking with copal incense.*

They stepped onto the Sacrificing Stone with Bahlum. The Sacrifice lay before them. The four chacob *who had let the first Blood grasped the Sacrifice's extremities. He remained still, his breathing heavy and slow.*

The Altar itself was raised high enough for many of the People to have some glimpse of the ritual above them. They chanted and danced. Many of them shrieked and swooned. The air above Puuc Witz *vibrated with the strength of their Voice.*

Bahlum's chac *handed him the thick obsidian knife, hilt first. When Bahlum raised the knife over his head, the People within view grew quiet. He held the sacrificial knife steady while the silence expanded like a flood through the People, encircling the mountain and swallowing all noise. At the moment of complete silence, the Jaguar Priest spoke in his most powerful* Puuc *Voice. Out of the mountain, shattering the silence, the Voice of the Creator Hachakyum spoke through Bahlum Ek ahaucan.*

"Kinich ahau, Lord of the Sun, our Sacrifice freely gives his Blood to renew the People."

With both hands, Bahlum drove the knife downward into the chest just below the left nipple, shattering the fourth and fifth ribs where they attached to the sternum. My heart almost choked me with the force of the blow. The initial blow spasmed the Sacrifice, causing his legs and arms to twitch. But not a Word escaped with the rush of air from his punctured, crushed lung. I leaned forward, rapt with the power of Blood, holding my breath, anticipating the Release.

Bahlum twisted the knife once and worked his hand into the gaping wound. Puuc Witz and all its People remained silent. With two more quick cuts, Bahlum pulled the dark Heart free from the Sacrifice and thrust it above his head. Brilliant, deep red Blood covered his hand and poured in thick streams over his feathered wristband and down his blue arm.

The response was instantaneous. Cheers and shouts cracked the air as the people erupted with Voice and movement. Jumping and pushing, shouting and crying, their energy poured over my skin. The Earth trembled.

My own breath returned in gasps, and my heart pounded in my ears. Sweat broke out over my entire body, and my fingers relaxed their grip on the stone arms of my throne.

The nearest attendant stepped forward with the Blood Bowl on his Prayer Board. Bahlum laid the Heart in the Bowl. He placed his bloody hand on the Sacrifice's forehead, anointing him, and closed his blank eyes. He then smeared the Altar and himself and moved back to observe the completion of the ritual.

The second attendant stepped up with the thin, keenly sharp Skinning Knife and held the Board out for Bahlum's chac. The chac took the knife and inserted the tip of the black blade under the skin at the lower edge of the chest wound. With rapid, deft movements, he sliced open the abdomen to the groin and ran the knife around the hips, cutting the Skin away. He girded the shoulders and neck and sliced the skin of the torso off with practiced efficiency. The third attendant approached the stripped corpse and laid the smoldering god-pot in the vacant Heart space.

The bloody chac *draped the sloppy hide around his shoulders and danced, his steps high and noble, to the edge of the darkened stones of the western terrace, three levels above the crowd. He spun several times, dizzying himself. Then under specific and secret instructions from me through Bahlum, he grabbed the Skin and spun one more time, hurling it through the air, off the terrace, and down on the People below.*

The People roared with excitement. Never before had anyone other than a sanctified chac *danced with the Skin. The blessed* yalba winik *who ended up with the Sacrificial Skin landing on him, reverently covered his back with the sticky hide. He was abruptly hoisted in the air. The wild crowd paraded him along the Royal* Sacbe *completely around* Puuc Witz.

For the first time in days, I felt optimistic about our future. The People would now feast and drink throughout the afternoon and evening, gorging themselves until they fell or vomited. Tomorrow, while I was to be carried across the Valley for my audience with the barbarian Cortés, the People would complete the work of their salvation.

✸✸✸

Sunday

By noon, several more groups of *hach winik* from another two villages had arrived on the mountain plateau. They, too, brought stories they'd heard about the return of the Lord of Light. Sara and Tito, who were now often sought for information and confirmation, were amused by the attention and occasionally corrected the wildest exaggerations. Marina remained by Griffith's side, keeping the curious and reverent visitors from crowding his shelter.

Chan Nuk, worrying over the effects of her son's willingness to discuss his errand at every village, kept the three dozen *hach winik* busy. Some cleared away more undergrowth from the mountain top. Others hunted, gathered wood, or built temporary wattle, daub, and thatch houses. A few, considering it quite an honor, were selected to improve the shelter protecting Griffith from the summer sun and the evening thunderstorms.

Several of the men began to separate and organize the central ruins on the hill above Griffith's shelter. Someone noticed the four smaller mounds at the edges of the plateau were aligned on the cardinal compass points. They dug, uncovering worn, cut limestone at each site.

With the discovery of the ruins, the myth around Griffith grew. With each new influx of villagers, with each retelling of recent events, Griffith's story was embellished. The quetzals leading them to the ruins became Griffith's Light on the path to the past. Some said his fever was self-induced to give him access to the Underworld where he, as the Last Lord of Light, could instruct his present body. Many of those who'd actually heard José Pepe on his journey to fetch the venerable Chan K'in believed Griffith returned to this mountain as the *ahau* of the *hach winik*. He was Kinich *ahau*, Destroyer of Temples, who sacrificed himself four and a half centuries ago to ensure the survival of his people. A few of these pilgrims, mixing Maya, Christian, and New Age mythology, even expressed the belief Griffith reincarnated specifically to lead them through the *xu'tan* to their Fifth World.

Throughout the day, more *hach winik*, including women and children, arrived in small groups from villages deeper in the rain forest. Many brought what belongings they could carry, as if they intended to make new homes here. Others even burned off sections of ground cover for *milpas*.

Because Griffith had referred to this mountain as *Puuc Witz* in his dreams, that replaced *Cerro San Felipe* as its common name. And *Puuc Witz* was rapidly becoming a small village with new houses, gardens, and expanding excavations.

Later that evening, as the small cooking fires and quiet

conversations transformed this ancient mountain peak into a community, Griffith's fever rose again. When Marina sent for Chan Nuk at her new house, a hundred or so *hach winik* gathered near Griffith's shelter to keep vigil the rest of the night. Marina's connections to Griffith tied her into the new myth, and the *hach winik* now viewed her as the guardian of their lost Lord. Her requests to remain back from the shelter were effectively orders.

The children were by his side, and his maiden guardian stood over him while Chan Nuk attended his fever. In the shadows, Griffith moaned. The crowd quieted, inching slowly forward like an incoming tide. They awaited the voice of this powerful Lord who walked in the darkness.

※※※

The Rainbow Temple was set back from the shore, above the flood line, but Cortés' men had carved out a hasty camp nearer the water. The great forest stood in shadow around his camp. Besides the impractical camp site, all their garbage, food animals, carcasses, and even their excrement lay within a nose of everyone.

My litter bearers set me down in front of the Capitán *of the* conquistadores. *They moved behind me and sat on their haunches. My two warrior escorts stood to my flanks. In defensive posture, they were allowed to protect my sacred left side. My warriors must have been as disgusted at what they saw as I, but they knew quite well only I was allowed to show any reaction to these disturbing images. I chose not to reveal my own revulsion.*

This Cortés was a big man, well over fifteen hands tall with filthy hair hanging on his shoulders and covering the lower half of his face. Even his eyebrows were thick. I knew this was ignoble of me, but he looked like one of the wooden men from the Third World who survived the Flood to return as monkeys. I must watch my heart so I don't reveal such thoughts.

He was dressed in a dull, metal chest plate over layers of clothes, thick leggings, and cuts of leather covering his feet and calves. I assumed his repulsive smell was due the absurd amount of clothing he wore. A large, golden cross bearing a likeness of a naked Sacrifice hung about his neck. He wore a long knife in its ceremonial sheath, but the sheath was stained from use. Didn't his priests wipe the knife clean before bedding it? In fact, everything about him was dirty.

Cohuanacox stood behind Cortés and his attendants. Whether Cohuanacox knew it or not, his lack of standing among these heathens was apparent. Even the small Yucatecan woman by Cortés's side was granted higher respect.

Grazing along the shore were the great four-legged beasts they called Horse, taller than a man. I felt foolish when I realized it was just a large animal the conquistadores *rode into battle. The power of fear and superstition on illiterate warriors must be part of their strategy. My* nacomob *would be most interested in such a tactic.*

Since these bearded conquistadores *first appeared in the north, I'd heard many stories of this Cortés. His quick subjugation of Motecuhzoma's people in the Aztec west was surprising, even with all the enemies the Aztecas had accumulated over the years. The subsequent slaughter of more than ten thousand commoners at Tenochtitlan, however, is difficult to believe. What god requires so much Blood?*

I'm told this disease called the Easy Death, mayacimil, *which killed so many Itzas in the Yucatán, came from the same god of Cortés. He must be a very powerful death deity if he's capable of killing in so many ways. Perhaps that's why they carry him nailed to a cross.*

It surprised me when Cortés rose from his small, wooden throne. Self-respect and honor must not be part of their ritual meetings. I could see the sweat on his forehead, about the only part of his body visible. Here in the depths of the forest, in this clumsily hacked-out camp along the banks of the Lake, the man remained hidden. I would wait for him to reveal himself.

"Kinich ahau,*" he said with an accent unlike any I'd heard, "welcome to my camp. My ally Cohuanacox speaks highly of you."*

So either Cortés or Cohuanacox had learned to speak not-Truth. Until now, I was not convinced one could speak something that is not. I wonder if such a person also lives in a World out of time. My ears must be very sharp to know which words from this Cortés were Word. The standard ceremonial greeting would cover my surprise.

"Lord Cortés, we honor you with our presence."

The small, dark woman from the Yucatán stepped forward and whispered to Cortés. He raised his bushy eyebrows at me. I had no idea what that meant.

"We have come into this land," Cortés said, "to help you against your enemies. As we battle our common foes, we are also desirous of your allegiance to defeat the forces of evil overrunning New Spain."

New Spain? Where was that?

"Lord Cortés," I said, "you honor our People of the Valley of the Hero Twins with your desires. Should 'our common foes' threaten us, we will surely send our warriors in defense."

Again the young woman spoke to Cortés. This time he looked at me with dancing eyes. Why the growing agitation?

"You do not understand, I'm afraid," he said.

It was certain I didn't understand this man, but his idiom of fear seemed as inappropriate as his clothing. Why would he express fear?

"Either we are allies in the same battle," he continued, "or we are enemies."

"Lord Cortés, my People have always been ready to battle those who would destroy us, but it has been many years since we were last threatened. We would, however, honor you with an invitation to enter Popol na Puuc Witz. Dine with us, and tell us of this place you call New Spain."

I had no expectation that such would happen. In fact, I had staked our future on something entirely different. But, despite his crude and filthy manner, I did wonder for a moment whether allying with this warrior and his deadly god could help to secure our future? If such an alliance with these strange and powerful warriors were possible, then I have made a devastating and unforgivable mistake. Seeds of uncertainty sprouted in my heart. Nevertheless, I remained confident in my bearing before this man in his miserable camp with a Yucatecan woman for an advisor and a fallen Azteca lord for an ally.

When the Yucatecan woman finished whispering to him, his eyes flared, and he paced like a yalba winik *before he spoke.*

"This is New Spain!" He was nearly shouting. "All the land from sunrise to sunset and from ocean to ocean. And yes, I will enter your city, and you will show your people why you have chosen to ally with me. But first, I will have Bishop Bartóleme baptize you in the name of Jesús Cristo so you may travel with us under the eyes of God in Heaven."

How can he name a land already named? These language differences were difficult. And did he think I had accepted him as an ally? In his heart, had he misinterpreted my invitation? If he had, then his unritualized allegiances were made too easily and probably broken just as quickly. But he was going to show me one of their rituals, giving me some better understanding of this Lord Cristo they follow so zealously. I decided to extract more information. I found my hummingbird voice and spoke.

"Ritual should be honored in a more civilized setting, Lord Cortés. Perhaps you will return with us to Puuc Witz *to ritualize your baptize ceremony with a welcoming ceremony?"*

He stopped pacing and looked down at me reclined on my litter seat. I watched him struggle with his response. A strong mind, but no discipline. His eyes quivered ever so slightly as they focused on me. Under his beard, his jaw muscles flexed and knotted. His back teeth must be worn flat.

"Understand me, indio*..."*

Within his voice, I heard emotions unworthy of a warrior leader. Certainly if any of my nacomob *had as much anger and fear as Cortés was trying to dissemble, I would end his appointment prematurely.*

"... you must be baptized before you can even talk to me. It is only through the grace of God I don't..."

He lost his thought! Amazing. His mouth was speaking differently than his heart. Suddenly, he turned to one of his nacomob *and spat out his anger.*

"Will somebody please do something about this... this cripple's insults? My God, what I have to tolerate!"

Cortés turned his back. Before I overcame my astonishment at his outrageous behavior, his nacom *nodded toward two of his warriors. They stepped nervously forward. Open-handed, their long knives still sheathed, they fixed their eyes on my warriors. Their reaction, I thought, was more from fear of Cortés than any intent to harm me.*

As his warriors neared my litter, mine stepped forward. I gave them no signal to act, so they assumed a Stone Stance in front of me.

His warriors gesticulated an intention to approach. The uncertainty of miscommunication and the fear of unforeseen consequences clouded my ability to absorb meaning. My heart rate increased but not in my breath. With neither threat nor signal from me, my warriors maintained their rigid attitude.

The others looked to their nacom. *His nervousness revealed his doubt. The least fearful of Cortés's men took a tentative step toward me. My warriors flipped their jaguar axes into Stalking Position and held them steady.*

Cortés's nacom *shouted a command. Instantly, it was chaos. Cortés darted into the shelter of the forest, followed by his priest, the woman, and the coward Cohuanacox. His warriors unsheathed their weapons but held their positions. Three more warriors leaped from the brush not ten paces from us, lifting long, strange spears at odd throwing angles.*

When my guards saw the additional fighters, they mounted a Monkey Defense. Swinging their axes wildly, they severed the legs from the nearest two. They ordered the litter bearers to get me out. As they lifted my litter, I braced myself with my good arm to keep from falling.

One of my warriors opened his mouth to bark another order. His voice was blasted out of existence with a monstrous clap of thunder and lightening that exploded from one of the long spears. The face of my warrior burst apart, splattering blood and bits of bone on my bare legs. Two more explosions aimed at my other warrior knocked him screaming to the ground. He landed on his shattered, bleeding hip and lay writhing in twisted agony beside my litter.

Three more warriors leapt from the cover of the forest slashing their great knives at my helpless bearers. When the first bearer died under a deep blow embedded in his skull, the litter fell. I rolled face down over my useless arm.

The savagery of the attack drove the other bearers tripping over the litter and crashing down heavily on me, crushing the breath from my lungs. Several ribs snapped. One of my bearers struggled to lift himself off me. A tremendous blow to his neck silenced his terrified screams. His head rolled off the litter, and his warm water splashed on my legs

The sharp odor of blood filled my nostrils.

In silence, I waited for my passage into the night. I recognized Cortés's heavy step as he approached.

"Get this heathen on his feet."

The bearers were dragged off. I was grabbed under my arms and lifted roughly to my feet. The broken ribs dug into my lung. Bone ground against bone. I couldn't get enough breath to show him the terror he wanted to see. With blood in my mouth and eyes, and numbing pain lifting me out of my body, I struggled to stay upright.

"Listen to me, indio." I couldn't see him through the blood. "I will have your head and carry it into your Puuc Witz so you can watch as we destroy all that affronts us. You have one chance to live. Understand?"

I acknowledged my understanding with silence.

"I said, 'Do you understand?'"

He placed the tip of his long knife against my sternum and pushed. My own warm blood traced a wet line down my abdomen as I staggered to maintain my balance. Two warriors caught my wrists and pulled in opposite directions, holding me on my feet.

"Kneel, indio, and renounce your pagan religion before the one true God, in the name of the Father, his son Jesús Cristo, and the Holy Spirit. Only that will save you and your city."

I smiled through my pain, knowing I truly had changed my hach pixan. I had walked in Xibalba's World, and I had altered the Time That Was Not. I was satisfied.

His warriors forced me to my knees. Still firmly held by my wrists, I hardened myself for the final journey. I leaned toward the barbarian who would free me. Blood from my split lip pooled under my tongue. Bent over before this unworthy warrior, I lifted my head and spat my own unsanctified blood at him. A few, small drops landed on his boot.

BLOOD OF THE EARTH

An angry scream caught in the throat of the death Lord Cortés. I blinked my bearer's blood from my eyes and watched Cortés swing his great knife at my neck. As the long blade cut through the air, I saw the Sun glint its last light off the tarnished metal. I smiled again and...

I floated above his horse-soldiers as they rode through the Valley of the Hero Twins. Fearful of ambush, Cortés was flanked by his horsemen and two files of foot soldiers. Walking beside Cortés, a groundling carried my bloody head on a pike. They marched slowly east toward Puuc Witz.

Passing rows of maize, all cut and stripped, they saw no one. Each wattle and thatch home stood empty, every stone meeting house destroyed and left in rubble. Shards of broken pottery were scattered thickly across the raised sacbe, *forcing the horses down off the road. Silent villages, slashed fields, and useless fragments were all that greeted them. Cortés' foot soldiers torched the empty homes.*

When they reached the Royal Sacbe, *Cortés sent his men around the mountain top. Building stones had been rolled down the mountain, blocking their passage. Posting a guard, they cleared a course up the Ek staircase. Up the thirteen steps of each level, past each stripped terrace, they made a path to the Five Temples of the World.*

At the top, not a Temple was standing. Not a Maya remained. My People had destroyed their own city. Every sacred stone had been torn down, our incensarios *lay shattered on the ground, and the entrance to the* Xibalba's World *remained hidden beneath the ruins.*

Nothing was left. And that was all that Cortés found.

Drifting over the ruins, I smiled. For the first time, the conquistador *had failed to conquer. The People, by fleeing to the depths of the vast, impenetrable forest, had avoided annihilation at this barbarian's hands. More importantly, they had secured their future in the Fourth World.*

Cortés stalked the destruction, venting his frustrated impotence at his gods. He cursed his men and lashed his venom at a stunned and silent Cohuanacox. In angry defeat, Cortés urinated on the lifeless head of the 'indio.' He then ordered the wet trophy of his hollow victory thrown over the mountain side.

CRAIG GOHEEN

I watched my head arc downward, my long, black hair spiraling behind. The iridescent green makeup over my closed, dead eyes sparkled in the Sun. At the thought of my Lady, our children, and all the hach winik *free in the forest, I dissolved into wisps of fragrant air wafting over our beautiful, green World.*

The People will learn to survive in the jungle.

CHAPTER EIGHTEEN
THE BALCHE CEREMONY

Puuc Witz (formerly *Cerro San Felipe*)
Monday

A man gradually identifies himself with the
    form of his fate; a man is, in the long run,
    his own circumstances.

El Aleph
Jorge Luis Borges
1899—1986

"Look, he's smiling," said Sara. "I think he's better, Chan Nuk."

Griffith heard her voice but couldn't place it. He had awakened without opening his eyes. Keeping his eyes closed, he lay still, breathing evenly. This young girl's voice disturbed him.

"Oh, Chan," called Tito, "come look, please."

Another voice he didn't know. Sleep memories floated through his cloudiness and filled him with vague images of flying, blood, and death. Disquiet tugged at the edges of his consciousness, some distant fear. And a sense of loss. He wanted to ask Karen and wondered if she'd left for school yet.

He took a deep breath and opened his eyes. His expectations were overwhelmed by the sight of a half dozen people, two of them children, and all but one of them dressed in similar—oddly familiar—off-white tunics. Beautiful, rich brown faces stood out from the long white gowns. They all had dark hair, nearly black, and most of them wore it long and parted in the middle. And they were all staring at him.

He reached for his glasses and couldn't find them, but he did glimpse the fabric of his own clothing. He was dressed in a rough cotton, knee-length white tunic, like everyone else. His disorientation shook him. Behind the two children stood a short woman in military fatigues, the only one dressed differently. She looked concerned, her eyes flicking between the small crowd and himself. Next to her stood a tiny, old woman, smiling and nodding.

He'd lost his glasses and apparently his clothes. He remembered nothing. The humidity felt like Charlottesville, but that was all. He glanced out the front of his pole shelter. Bright green grass, reflecting an intense sun, stretched beyond the small crowd. The open field was filling with more *indígena*, all walking toward his shelter.

He hoped he was still dreaming.

The old woman smiled and then asked him something in an unfamiliar language. He stared at her for a few moments before shaking his head in confusion. She turned to the soldier-woman and said something. The younger woman knelt beside Griffith. He knew her without understanding how.

"Griffith," she asked in a soft, accented voice, "how are you feeling?"

And she knew him. He looked up at her, saw the tight lines of concern around her dark eyes, and heard the warmth in her voice.

"I'm fine," he said slowly.

He tried to sit up. When he moved his left arm to brace

himself, an old, deep ache grabbed his shoulder and shot down to his forearm. He gritted his teeth and lay back down.

As the intensity subsided, images streamed into him, flooding his memory. The pain of the gunshot tore through his arm again, and Karen bound his wound with cloth from her blouse. The chaos of the escape in the truck and then Sara and Tito, these children, sitting with him, bickering under a tree in a swamp, tripped him in time. Then, in a thunderstorm, silent lightning flashed in his head, and their crowded little plane crashed in the roiling waters of the *Laguna*. And the young woman, a Zapatista guerrilla, pulling their raft ashore under the trees, this was her.

"Where's Karen?" he asked weakly.

"Caran Koh?" the old woman asked Marina.

She shook her head.

"Marina?" said Griffith. "That's your name. Is Karen here?"

"No, Griffith," she answered.

"Where are we? Why are we here?" He wasn't sure which question made more sense.

"We're on *Puuc Witz*. Where you led us."

Puuc Witz—something that sounded familiar, at least. But what did she mean he led them? The memories didn't connect. After sitting in the swamp with these kids, it was a blank. Nothing. And before that, all he remembered was…

The realization grabbed his heart in its fist and squeezed. His breath caught in his throat. He'd lost Karen. He had to find her. And together they had to take the children, Sara and Tito… where?

"Are the children…." He stopped and looked over at them. Their eyes were wet, and their smiles crooked. "Are you two okay?"

"Griffith!" Tito jumped forward and landed next to him. "*Sí*, we're fine. I knew you'd win the battle. Tell me about your dreams. Everybody's talking."

Dreams. And a battle. How could he have forgotten so much?

"Tito," admonished Sara. "Don't ask too many questions. Griffith hasn't recovered completely. He must be tired."

"Sara, excuse me," he said, "my memory's a little slow coming back. Who are all these people?"

"That's Chan Nuk," introduced Sara. "Your *bruja* who healed you."

He nodded at her and smiled. Chan Nuk took that as a signal to look over his injuries. She reached for his left wrist. Without volition, Griffith pulled his arm closer to him. She smiled and reached for his wrist again. This time, he let her take it and watched as she unwrapped the cotton bandage on his arm.

That's not Karen's bandage. He remembered the sound of her blouse being torn and her wrapping his wound. He wondered where the bandage was.

When Chan Nuk lifted the brown, sticky leaves from his wound, she smiled. The infection had been brought to the surface and released. She hadn't wanted to stitch the wound closed with the infection so rampant. It seemed to be healing. If he kept it clean, it would close, albeit with a wide scar.

She pointed to his left shoulder. Griffith hesitated and then stretched it out slightly. It was too sore to roll much either way, but he did manage to lift his elbow almost forty-five degrees.

Chan Nuk nodded, first at him, and then at Marina. At that, everyone in the crowd outside smiled excitedly at each other.

"Would you like something to eat, Griffith?" asked Marina.

Griffith tried to smile, but worry gnawed at him. Among all these strangers watching him like eager puppies, he knew he needed to find Karen, and they needed to save the children. But it did feel like he hadn't eaten for days.

"Yes, *sí*, please. Food would be good. *Gracias*, Marina."

Within minutes, plates of warm *tortillas*, hot scrambled eggs and *chiles*, grilled venison in tomatoes, fresh papaya, and melon, sliced and cut from their rinds, surrounded him. At least a dozen different people brought meals to share.

Chan Nuk said something to Marina. She turned to Griffith.

"Chan Nuk," she said, "suggests you should only eat a little of this at first."

Griffith chuckled at the thought of trying to eat all this food, probably more than he could consume in a week. He nodded.

"Sara and Tito," he said, "have some breakfast with me. We haven't seen food like this for days, huh?"

Tito smiled and leaned forward. He lifted a *tortilla* and scooped up some eggs.

"Tito," said Sara, "we've already eaten. Be polite."

"But I'm hungry, Sara," he replied handing the *tortilla* to Griffith. "Besides, I want to eat with Griffith."

"It's okay, Sara," smiled Griffith. "Have some if you like. Marina?" he asked, nodding to the food. "Chan Nuk, I'm sorry, is that correct? Please." He looked out at the crowd and shrugged. *"Por favor,"* he said to them and gestured with his right hand over the plates of food.

Marina smiled and stepped behind him into their shelter. She sat on a crude bench where she could see the crowd. Chan Nuk squatted on her haunches at Griffith's feet and filled a *tortilla*. To Griffith's surprise, all the people outside stepped back and either sat in the grass or stood in small groups.

After a few minutes, Marina spoke.

"Griffith, if it would be okay with you, there is a man who would like to meet you. His name is Chan K'in, and he is coming from a small village call Na'ha, many kilometers north."

Griffith turned toward her, grimacing from his stiffness and aches.

"Marina," he asked, "could you sit over here so I can see you? Thanks. Now why would this Chan K'in want to speak with me. I don't even know why we're here. What's happened?"

In small, out-of-sequence bits and with frequent interruptions and embellishments from Tito, Marina explained what he had missed since they left the *Laguna* five days ago. Slowly eating his *tortilla*, Griffith listened in amazed silence while this story unfolded.

When he heard how everyone had reacted to his fevered, ranting hallucinations, he put the unfinished *tortilla* down and sat quietly in disbelief. He had no idea he'd lost five days—he could adjust to that—but during that time, the world had become a vastly different place for him.

Troops were moving into the jungle, apparently to start a war over the children. Virtually every *hach winik* still alive, including those converted by the *evangelistas*, was either on this mountain or coming to it. Their traditional chief, what Marina called the *t'o'ohil*, the guardian of Maya ritual, wanted to meet him. And rumors of the Lord of Light calling his people to *Puuc Witz* were spreading beyond the rain forest.

In the time it took Marina to reveal his missing days, Griffith's world disintegrated before him. He'd been dumped into the chaos of a civil war, with two children dependent on him, and without his wife. Distraught, he just wanted to find Karen.

He looked outside at the crowd of people. They kept

their distance, out of earshot, but their numbers continued to swell. Perhaps two hundred *hach winik* had now gathered around Griffith's make-shift home.

"How can these people think I'm some reincarnated Maya?" pleaded Griffith. "That was just a dream, hallucinations from my fever. Even you said that. What do they expect? I don't know anything. I don't even remember the dreams."

That was not entirely true, he knew. Images of birds and bloody knives flew by. Gruesome flashes of pulsating caves darted through the darker regions of his memory.

"Griffith," said Marina, trying to reassure him, "these stories of your dreams, don't worry about them. The *hach winik* respect their dreams, but only Chan K'in can interpret the most important ones accurately."

"So this Chan K'in will be able to tell them they were only fever dreams?"

"Griffith, don't worry, please. I believe Chan K'in will agree to shelter you and the children until we can contact their parents."

"Well, then," decided Griffith, "I'll have to talk to this man, won't I? Tito, Sara, perhaps we *can* get this straightened out, find Karen, and finally get out of here."

***

It was dusk before José Pepe arrived with Chan K'in and the last of the villagers from Na'ha. Chan K'in was short, like most *hach winik*. His thick, black hair was parted in the middle with his bangs cut straight. Deep creases radiated from his eyes, and long furrows outlined his smile. He chewed on an unlit, hand-rolled cigar, and his teeth were stained brown. He was uncertain of his age, but he remembered events in the forest others had traced back ninety years.

Through Marina, he was introduced to Griffith. He spoke neither Spanish nor English. Without discussion, he and Griffith were escorted to the new *balche* house. Several men offered to carry Griffith and Chan K'in in litters some of the women had woven, but Griffith insisted he was perfectly able to walk, and Chan K'in just laughed.

Inside the wattle and mud *balche* house, a dozen *hach winik* men from different villages relaxed around a small fire. A few of them had lit their home-made cigars. Tobacco and wood smoke drifted thick and aromatic over their heads. A dugout log, brimming with crushed and fermented *balche* bark and honey, was warming by the fire. Griffith sat on a long woven mat.

Around the fire squatted eight, red clay bowls. The bowls were ring-based and unpainted. Molded on the sides and rims were a variety of crude effigies with grinning wide mouths, bulging eyes, cat's ears, and other likenesses of their gods. These god-pots, the traditional Lacandon *incensarios*, were clean and unused.

Sitting next to Griffith, Chan K'in removed his own new *incensario* from his woven backpack and set it by the fire. He smiled broadly at Griffith, then at each of the other men. He spoke a few words, and then, lifting one more god-pot from his pack, he held it up. It was blackened from regular use, and the molded effigy of a cat on the rim had its ears broken off.

Chan K'in stood and set his used god-pot inside the new ones, closer to the fire. He spoke for some moments, his voice almost a song. Then he abruptly stamped his foot down onto his old *incensario*, crushing it to shards and dust.

One of the men reached behind him and lifted a long wooden platter on which small hand-formed balls of blue painted *pom* were laid out. Chan K'in took one of the balls, made from the resin of the copal tree, and crumbled some of it into his new god-pot. He passed the platter to the next man. When all the *incensarios* were ready, Chan K'in took a burning stick from the fire, lit his incense, and passed the torch. While the others lit the incense in their own god-pots, he sang softly, almost to himself. By the time all the *pom* was lit, the sweet, heavy scent had cut through the cigar and wood smoke.

Olfactory familiarity tugged at Griffith's memories. Incense and smoke drew back the veil of nepenthe, and half-remembered images gathered in the dark recesses of his consciousness. A deep foreboding filled him as tendrils of suffering crept into view.

A young *hach winik* beside the dugout filled a wooden cup with *balche*. He handed it to Chan K'in who then offered it to Griffith. Griffith waited while the rest of the cups were filled. When everyone had their cup, Chan K'in took a sip and smiled. The others tasted their brew. The *balche* was warm. The thick, brown drink was much heartier than any micro-brewed ale Griffith had ever had back home. This tasted raw and very potent, with just enough honey to cut the edge from the bitterness.

Through the smoke of the fire, incense, and cigars, he looked around. Shadows danced in the corners. The hut murmured with the hiss of the small blaze and the soft sounds of men drinking and puffing. As if sitting in another century, this communion of men enfolded Griffith in its sincerity. Despite his anxiety to find his wife and the fearful apparitions from his dreams, the gentle, unhurried pace of the *hach winik* slowed his blood and cooled his apprehension.

He took another sip. Except for one younger man with a crooked jaw who was sitting half in shadow by the *balche* dugout, everyone was smiling. When this man looked up from the dugout, Griffith caught his eye. The young man beamed, showing most of his yellow teeth in a lop-sided grin. Unable to contain himself, Griffith smiled broadly.

Chan K'in finished his *balche*. When the young man tending the *balche* dugout received the cup, he turned to Griffith and asked him something. Not understanding him, Griffith shrugged and passed his empty cup. Chan K'in nodded and chuckled.

They were all glancing at him, apparently waiting for him to do or say something. Without a hint as to what they might want or expect, Griffith sat still, staring into his refilled cup. He took another sip and decided he needed some help. Getting up, he excused himself amid their smiles and went to the open doorway to look for Marina. She was standing near the hut, her back to it. He gestured for her to come inside.

"Griffith," she protested, "the *balche* hut is for the men."

"But Marina," he explained, "I need help in here. The ceremony was fascinating, but it was short, and it's over. We're just drinking now, and they want to talk. I think they want me to say something, but I'm completely lost. Come in and translate for me? *¿Por favor?*"

"Griffith," she replied, "I would, but I don't think the men would accept me."

"Would you ask them?" he wondered.

"Perhaps you should."

"Oh, no," he said. "Just stand in the door and tell me what's going on?"

"Griffith, I'm not sure."

"Oh, please? What's the difference? You've been standing outside."

"I'm on watch, not listening to you and the other men."

"I'm sorry, Marina. I didn't mean that. Please, let's try this."

"I'll stand in the doorway. Behind you."

"Thank you." He turned around, facing back inside the hut. "Okay, Marina, tell them I need you to translate."

She stood behind him where she couldn't see into the hut and hesitated.

"Go ahead," prompted Griffith.

In a voice hardly above a whisper, she translated Griffith's words over his shoulder into the hut. Several of the older men objected before Chan K'in could answer, but the wrinkled, old man lifted his arthritic hand. They fell silent.

"We have finished the Renewal of our God-pots," Chan K'in told them, "and we have tasted our *balche*. Now I would like to hear what this man has to say. Since he must speak through Marina…"

He lowered his hand, and they started to argue about whether to let her in or move outside themselves. The young man by the dugout even suggested they break with tradition and offer her some *balche*. In the midst of this, Chan K'in motioned for Griffith and Marina to come in. The men fell silent when they saw her. As invisibly as she could, she sat on the dirt floor to Griffith's right.

Chan K'in was the first to make eye contact with her. He gave her a quick smile, and then he spoke to the men.

"This world is ending,"—Marina translated his words in Griffith's ear—"and since everyone has traveled so far, everyone is welcome to stay and drink with me and the *norteamericano*. We are going to share some dreams."

They all stayed, of course, wanting to hear Chan K'in's interpretation of the dreams, but even more, they were eager to hear the words from Griffith himself.

"But it was just a lot of confusing dreams," protested Griffith.

Following Marina's translation, Chan K'in smiled, nodded,

but said nothing. Griffith was frustrated. And it wasn't because he was confused. He knew what they wanted. All day the *hach winik* had shown him such deference and... awe. That's what it felt like, he admitted. And that scared him.

No, it was even more than that. What really frightened him was his own ignorance. If these people expected anything from him, they were going to be disappointed. How could they base a belief system on these dreams, he wondered. On dreams perhaps. He could understand that. But on his dreams? He was a *gringo* who'd lost his wife because he didn't know what he was doing. Just a miserable, ignorant *turista*, lost in a country about to go to war with itself. With these poor people trapped in the middle. He believed he had little to say to the *hach winik*.

Chan K'in cleared his throat. He spoke, his voice rhythmic and melodious.

"One night, a young wife dreamed her husband Kin Bol failed to return from a hunting trip he was planning for the next day. In the dream, her husband's favorite hunting dog returned without him. Because the dog had barked during the night and awakened her from the dream, she believed it to be a *hach pixan*. She feared if she didn't tell him about it, she would never see him again. But she also knew if she did tell him, he might not go. Then her hungry children would have no meat."

Chan K'in paused and relit his cigar from the fire. After Marina finished her soft translation, Griffith smiled. He could hardly pretend he understood the culture, but if a lesson were being relayed, he wanted to be receptive. His needs, as anxiously as they strove for attention, could wait a while longer.

After several minutes of smoking and drinking in silence, the young man by the dugout gestured to refill Griffith's cup. When Griffith got his cup back, one of the older men spoke to Chan K'in.

"Did the woman tell her husband about her *hach pixan*?"

"Oh, yes," replied Chan K'in. "Of course. She said, 'Kin Bol, my husband, I dreamed you did not return from your hunt, and the children and I were left alone.'"

Chan K'in paused and smiled broadly, showing his tobacco stained teeth. Griffith sat up and nodded expectantly.

"But," answered Chan K'in, "the husband still went hunting, and he and his dog returned safely."

"But without any meat?" ventured Griffith.

"Yes, of course. You see, you do understand dreams have a true meaning."

He didn't. He had no idea what Chan K'in's story meant. Should the wife have told her husband or not? It made no difference either way. What did feel certain, however, was Griffith's reluctance to share his own dreams. Even though he needed their help, trading his dreams for their assistance was not going to help anyone. It felt too much like condescension. He tried to explain.

"Chan K'in, I was very sick. Chan Nuk said my fever was extremely high for several days."

Chan K'in just smiled. The others nodded at Marina's translation as if they understood his fever was both necessary and something to grin about.

"Chan K'in, sir, I did some reading before my wife and I came here, and while I've been here, too. Perhaps that would explain..." Griffith paused, realizing he was trying to rationalize away what he hadn't even described yet. "My dreams were a result of an infected wound. I got shot, we think by *guardias blancas*, when we ran with the children. And then the plane crashed, and... oh Christ, I don't want to talk about this. You've heard it, I'm sure."

"Marina told me," said Chan K'in, "your wife is a very strong woman."

Griffith was surprised, both at the Chan K'in's transition and his thoughtful reference to Karen.

"Thank you," said Griffith quietly.

"You will hear more from her," predicted Chan K'in.

Griffith suddenly felt arrogant. And ashamed of himself. The Lacandones, the *hach winik*, had given everything they had to help him and the children. And he was too proud to accept their gifts. He realized he was going tell Chan K'in everything he remembered from his dreams. He owed them that much.

He took a sip of *balche* and sighed. Even though the memories were tenuous and difficult to describe, he began his story. Slowly, from one image to the next, the dreams crept from the darkness of his memory. Moving down a shadowy, narrowing staircase toward a sepulchral cave, he remembered the fear he associated with the word *Xibalba*. He recalled the disorientation of the mushroom dream within the cave, and the frightful dissonance clinging to the edges of his memory. Inside in the cave, he heard the Blood of the earth and felt an uncomfortable sense of displacement. He didn't belong there in the darkness, hiding from some somber and gruesome outcome he couldn't face and didn't want to remember. A powerful urge to alter his dream surfaced.

At times he would pause, sipping his *balche* absentmindedly, letting some distant image take shape. He told them of his beautiful Lady in the birdhouse and their aborted love-making. When he remembered Marina was translating this to a group of men, he blushed and stammered in mid-sentence.

At other times, the story gushed out of him uninterrupted. The fear for his family and the survival of the People drove his dreams. But the Renewal Ceremony, from the painted, naked

Sacrifice to Bahlum's magnificent jaguar headdress, overwhelmed his memory with the exuberant Voice of the People and the power of the Blood. Griffith's account of the ecstatic, almost sexual release when the sacrifice gave up his heart captivated his silent audience.

Marina's voice reminded him of the young Yucatecan translator with Cortés by the lake. Why was she with him? Visceral repugnance churned in his stomach at the disgust these *conquistadores* generated in him. Odors of excrement and stinking men drifted across his memory. He wanted to stop these invaders.

Finally, in both victory and defeat, Kinich *ahau*'s grand scheme unfolded between Cortés' filthy camp and the enlightened beauty of the Five Temples. When Griffith recalled the destroyed city, he hesitated. His words stumbled over the birdhouse lying broken and unrecognizable. The ruined temples and the scorched valley homes felt so desolate, so absolute.

Then it struck him. His dreams had neatly filled in the missing details of the last days of Maya history. Until that moment, their implication had escaped him. His fevered mind had invented its own story of how these civilized people had avoided extermination at the hands of Western exploiters by returning to the savagery of the jungle four and a half centuries ago. His hallucinated version of history gave the *hach winik* a potent tale of their own missing history. Knowing the rational cause of his hallucinations, however, seemed treacherously insignificant compared to the power of their vision.

He fell silent and held out his empty cup. The hiss of the fire and the soft plunk of his cup dipped in the *balche* filled the hut. Some of the men were nodding, others had their heads bowed, and the rest were staring at Griffith.

From the back one of them spoke softly, almost to himself.

"Kinich *ahau*."

When Griffith looked up at the voice, everyone was nodding. After a moment, he realized what they meant.

"No, please. I am not Kinich *ahau*. I dreamed about him, that's all. Tell them, Marina. Tell them I'd done some reading, some studying about this area, the history, and I must have read about him."

She translated what he said, and once again they all nodded their agreement.

"Did you tell them? Why are they smiling?"

"Griffith," said Marina, "I told them, and they believe your dream."

"But why did they nod when he said 'Kinich *ahau*'?"

"They believe you. They will accept your Word."

"They don't think I'm him, do they? You know, the reincarnation or whatever of this Lord, do they? Ask Chan K'in?"

"Griffith," said Marina, "we don't have any records of the last lords. And the idea of reincarnation is not even a Mayan concept. In the oral tradition handed down to Chan K'in, our dreams can connect us to our past, among other things."

"Ask him, please."

After she asked his question, Chan K'in smiled and nodded at Griffith.

"Griffith," he began while Marina translated softly, "this is what I believe. I accept your dream as a true dream. On this day, near the end of the Fourth World, you have brought us Word from our past. Because many other signs have come together here on this mountain, I will trust you as we cross to the next world."

"Oh, Chan K'in, I'm no prophet. I can't lead you anywhere. I don't even know where I am myself."

Chan K'in smiled and nodded again. Unable to help himself, Griffith smiled back, laughing gently at the absurdity.

"Chan K'in," he continued, "I respect your beliefs, and I understand dreams can be important. But anybody from anywhere could have read what I did and dreamed a wild, hallucinatory dream. Some people overheard it, and exaggerated its significance. To think I'm some kind of... oh, that doesn't make any sense."

"But it does make sense, Griffith," replied Chan K'in. "I have seen the signs for many years. The forest disappears to the loggers and ranchers, and the game leaves. Soldiers fight in the jungle, and the *evangelistas* tell us of their apocalypse. Soon our people will be no more. With these two children, you have brought your dreams to us."

"Chan K'in, I didn't come here to do that. I can't lead anybody anywhere—I'm the one who needs leading. I've no experience at all in the jungle. Surviving was almost too hard for me. Now, with everything else, the kidnapping, the terrorism," he sighed, "and with Karen missing, I just want to find her and get out of here. I can't help anyone."

He felt like crying.

Chan K'in looked away and passed his empty cup along. Relighting his cigar from the glowing end of a stick, the old man puffed billowing, gray clouds into the air above him. When his cup was returned, he sipped several times. Then to no one in particular, he spoke softly.

"One night," he began, his voice once again song-like, "many turnings ago, a *hach winik* named K'ayum dreamed of a man whose skin was light and whose face was hairy like yours, Griffith. This man was sitting on his verandah watching his cattle graze in large pastures, letting his horses work the *milpas*, and admiring his wives bending over to collect eggs from the chickens. In K'ayum's dream, this light-skinned man told him that Akyantho, the god who invented money for soft-handed foreigners, gave him these animals so his pale skin would not burn in the *milpas*.

"The next morning, K'ayum begged this god to give him some money to buy cattle, horses, and chickens. 'Look how hard I must work,' K'ayum pleaded to Akyantho, 'to find food for my skinny wife and my children and for my poor dog who must hunt with me every day in the forest.'

"So Akyantho took pity on poor K'ayum and gave him money to buy cattle, horses, and chickens. K'ayum was very happy because he had listened to his dream, and now his life was easy. He slept all day and took another wife to make love with all night.

"After many days like this, K'ayum awoke one morning very hungry. He sent his second wife to get some corn and eggs for their meal. She returned empty-handed. She told him the horses had trampled the *milpas* and the cattle had eaten all the corn and wandered off into the jungle. Even the chickens were living in the trees and had forgotten where to lay their eggs.

"Upset from his comfort, K'ayum called his dog to help him find their animals. The dog, who had also grown fat and lazy, didn't want to get up. K'ayum became angry and kicked his dog. He then sulked off into the forest to look for the animals himself."

Chan K'in paused to sip from his cup and puff on his cigar. Getting to the point seemed to take a while among the *hach winik*, so Griffith sat patiently and drank down the last of his *balche*. Drinking probably wasn't real good for him anyway, he realized, but since he wasn't going anywhere tonight, he held out his empty cup.

Chan K'in emptied his cup with a gulp and passed it along. He sat up, inhaling deeply, and opened his mouth. A deep, liquid belch rose proudly from his stomach. Everyone grinned and nodded. Griffith chuckled quietly, waiting to see who would follow with their own variations of complimenting the brewmaster. Several others managed some impressive displays, but Griffith, fearing more than a burp might arise, chose not to stir up his stomach.

One of the men got up and left the hut. The sound of urine splashing on the ground outside prompted several others to join him. Unsure how impolite it might be to talk with people out of the hut, Griffith just looked at Chan K'in stirring the small fire with a stick and smiling gently.

These folks really do smile a lot, he thought.

Chan K'in lifted his head and asked Griffith what he did before coming to the forest. When Griffith told him he was a physicist, Marina paused in her translation.

"Griffith," she said, "there is no word for 'physicist' in our language."

"Oh, okay, that makes sense. Tell him I'm a scientist; that I work in a university and study very small particles of matter."

Marina looked at him quizzically for a moment, and then translated what he said. Chan K'in nodded, obviously impressed. He picked up a pinch of dirt and held it up as a question.

"No, Chan K'in. Very much smaller. Invisible, actually. We can learn about our world, and the entire universe, really, if we understand how the smallest particles behave."

"And what do you see in the Invisible World?" asked Chan K'in.

"Basically, I look at the predicted effects these particles

have on their environments. I then formulate further hypotheses to test, and ultimately we learn just a little more about how the universe works."

He knew Marina wasn't entirely sure of her translations—which made sense—but Chan K'in smiled at some subtle humor in Griffith's words. The others wandered in, and Chan K'in began to speak before they were seated.

"We have come to the last turnings of the Fourth World. This is recorded, but even without that knowledge, we would still know the end is near. We have watched our forest cut down and our jungle made pasture. With the game driven away, we are now hunted in our *milpas* by the *nauyaca*. Even the *evangelistas* tell us the end is coming, and to be saved, we must forget our past. Their world is difficult to comprehend.

"Now, when any man or woman can see what's happening to our forest, this *gringo* comes from Akyantho's world bringing children to these ruins which have remained hidden from all but the quetzals. Why would this happen? Just to remind us our world is ending?"

"No," protested Griffith. "No, I didn't come here for any purpose. This was my honeymoon. Really. I can't teach you anything or to lead you anywhere. Believe me, Chan K'in, I'm completely ignorant about the rain forest. I know next to nothing of your people. I don't even understand the politics of this country. I did a little reading, and I came here on my honeymoon with..."

His voice cracked with frustration.

"Damn it! I just want to find Karen. That's all. And get these kids back to their parents. Can't anyone see we don't need this. Who wants a civil war, or a holocaust, or anybody killed over any of this? We don't need a goddamned apocalypse." His voice tightened in his throat. "They're just kids, for Christ's sake! And I'm *not* your prophet. I'm an ignorant tourist. Why can't I just go home?"

Everyone was quiet. Even the final, translated words from Marina were soft and understated. When she finished, only Griffith's tired breathing was heard. Chan K'in puffed on his cigar for several moments and then sat up.

"So K'ayum," he continued as if his story tied seamlessly and melodically to Griffith's pain, "who was still hungry, left his dog and family to search for his cattle and horses. He wandered the jungle for many days unable to find them. Finally, he became so weak from hunger he had to return home. But without his dog, he was lost. He had walked many miles, after all.

"To find his way, K'ayum climbed the tallest tree." Chan K'in's voice deepened and the rhythms quickened. "At the top, he disturbed a gang of monkeys living there. They shouted and screamed at him, and some of them spit on him. The largest, bravest male edged toward K'ayum and exposed his fangs, trying to drive the intruder back down the tree. K'ayum, who used to be a great hunter, bared his teeth back at the monkey.

"This angered the monkey. When he jumped at K'ayum, they locked arms and began wrestling in the branches. K'ayum's hunger drove him. Just as he twisted the monkey's neck and broke it, he lost his balance, and they both fell out of the tree."

Chan K'in exhaled a narrow stream of smoke and paused a moment. Just as Griffith wondered if Chan K'in's stories ever actually ended, the old man smiled at him. And then, with a grin, he told the punch line.

"K'ayum had his monkey to eat, but the fall killed him."

Marina finished translating through everyone's laughter, and even Griffith laughed. He felt about as capable as K'ayum. Fulfilling the mythic need of a dying culture was so far beyond him, the simple thought of it was absurd. And the very idea of following a stranger from an alien culture simply because of a dream seemed wrong to him. He knew his own cultural biases were preventing him from understanding the *hach winik* and how they viewed this world, but shouldn't these people despise the foreigners responsible for their destruction?

"Chan K'in," he said, "may I ask something I'm uncertain about?"

"Yes, yes," he replied, waving his empty cup in the smoky air. "Only the man who comes in search of counsel will make good use of it. Ask questions, even if you don't have answers."

An interesting way to look at it, Griffith thought.

"Chan K'in, this story suggests if K'ayum had never listened to his dream, none of this would have happened to him. He did ask for help from this god of foreigners, didn't he?"

"Akyantho, yes. But his dream was not the same as yours."

"Is that the point?"

"No," laughed Chan K'in. "I don't know. I do know because we were lazy in the past and wanted to sleep and make love all the time, we never learned anything. Even today, our pigs and cows wander out of their pens into the jungle, and our chickens lay their eggs in the grass and trees for the rats and snakes. All we can do is hunt the little game left and make love to our wives. We are the ignorant ones, Griffith."

Griffith sighed. He supposed all kinds of ignorance must exist, but sitting here miles from anywhere, away from cities, doctors, the media—in the absolute center of nowhere—everyone could die. Especially if people were dependent on him. He looked down into the thick, brown brew, feeling more vulnerable than the day he and Karen arrived in this country.

"Chan K'in," he finally said, "whatever you think of me and my hallucinations, it's utter folly to believe I can help your people. But, given that Marina and Chan Nuk saved my life, our lives, I will say this."

His own voice sounded so authoritarian to him.

"This is it," he repeated more quietly. "I... have no idea what I'm doing."

Marina hesitated a moment before translating. When she finished, everyone remained exactly as they were. No one changed expression or position.

"And this is what I'm going to do," continued Griffith. "Right now, I'm going outside. I need to piss, and... excuse me, relieve myself, and then I'm going to walk around in the air. And think. So, if you'll excuse me, please, *por favor*, I'll be going out for a little while."

He drank the rest of his *balche* and set his cup down. As he stood, his head tried to float away. He leaned over, and a small burp gurgled from his throat. It tasted awful. He straightened himself and staggered to the doorway.

Outside, the cool air bathed his forehead. The moon rose orange and full in the east. Small campfires twinkled around him. Balancing himself awkwardly over his feet, he breathed the moist air. His head cleared for a moment and he looked around.

Behind him stretched the impenetrable rain forest, the last home of a dying people overcome with the inexorable surge of a technological world—their urge to survive destroyed by cultural ennui. In front of him, the distant *Laguna*, the last place he saw Karen, lay hidden under the indigo blanket of night. Armies were moving under a shadowless galaxy, converging on this mountain with their modern weapons and lethal intent. Out there, lay only burdens and blood of which he wanted no part.

He shook his head, inarticulate at the combination of choices and chance which had placed him here. Unanswerable questions and fragments of inchoate ideas floated in his *balche* haze. He lurched forward toward a shadowy bush. Reaching for his zipper, he found the cloth of his *xikul*. Much easier, he thought, lifting the hem.

His urine puddled at his feet. Swaying in the gentle breeze rising off the mountain, he admired and feared these kind, primitive people who so desperately wanted messianic deliverance from their inevitable extinction. Deep within his inebriation, cradled within his heart where he was unwilling to verbalize his passion or express his most profound fears, he tightened his grip on his own acute need, his only need, he told himself—to find his wife.

Determined to make them understand, he shook himself dry, dropped his tunic, and spun around. Staggering as he turned on the uneven ground, he swung his arms wildly in the air and stopped himself with a few flatfooted steps. He sighed, and a wave of nausea rippled up from his stomach. Annoyed, he took a slow breath to quell the gurgling queasiness.

He looked up, and standing in front of him, only a few steps away, was Marina, silhouetted in the dim light from the *balche* house. Surprised, he stumbled backward. He opened his mouth to excuse himself. A loud pocket of gas rumbled up from his stomach, filling the air with its expansive belch and rank odor.

Embarrassed, he swallowed back the nauseous grumblings. He wiped a spot of saliva from the corner of his mouth. He was about to excuse himself when his stomach suddenly spasmed in a wrenching cramp, doubling him over. He reached out for Marina's shoulder to steady himself and stumbled clumsily forward. He fell to his knees and bent over until his forehead touched her feet.

Mewling little squeaks caught in his throat. Unable to

catch his breath and stave off dizziness, he grabbed the back of Marina's ankle with his right hand and held on. His stomach twisted into an angry fist. In a single, violent gout, he threw up the *balche* and everything else he'd consumed that day.

Just as quickly, the knot uncoiled its grip on his stomach, and the nausea passed. Without a sound, he rolled to his side and closed his eyes, grateful to have finally found a place to rest... to sleep... to forget.

CHAPTER NINETEEN
CHOICES

Puuc Witz
Tuesday morning

> The gods will not do for a man what he should do for himself. The gods do not like lazy people.
> Chan K'in of Na'ha
> 1908? -

When Griffith awoke the next morning, Marina was sitting beside his rough bed, looking outside. She had changed to a *xikul*, but had kept her ammo belt and pouches cinched around her waist. She didn't see his eyes open. His sour mouth and thick tongue brought last night's embarrassment back. He closed his eyes.

Since *Na-Bolom*, his honeymoon had been destroyed, blown away in the winds of cultural disintegration. Every hope lay twisted in horrific fear, his life irrevocably scarred by others' irreconcilable conflicts. And what had he done about it? Gotten drunk and thrown up—for the first time in his life. And then passed out at the feet of the one person who'd done more for him and the children than anyone. Unable to answer these people's needs, he couldn't even muster the strength to deal with his own fears.

He opened his eyes. Marina was watching him, smiling

softly in the morning shadows. He tried to sit up. A wave of sour nausea swept over him. He leaned back on his right elbow and let it pass.

"Are you all right?" asked Marina.

He looked up at her, and their dark eyes met for an instant. His cheeks flushed with abashed warmth. He wanted to apologize for last night, for embarrassing her, and himself.

"May I do anything for you, Griffith *ahau*?"

When he heard her attach *"ahau"* to his name, his heart sank. They were not going to let him out of this myth-making. Not even Marina. He had hoped that she, at least, was on his side. Didn't she know him for what he was—a weak, ignorant *gringo*?

Anger swelled in his heart. She didn't have any right to expect him to fulfill some legend from her past.

"Yes. Yes there is, Marina. For one thing, don't call me *ahau*. I'm not your *ahau*, okay? I don't want to be your *ahau*. Or anybody's. Okay? So stop calling me that."

He struggled to his feet. Swooning with lightheadedness, he grabbed the pole siding.

"Do you feel all right?" she asked. "Shall I send for Chan Nuk?"

"Oh Marina," he said without lifting his head, "don't you understand? I can't do this. Everything you and the others have done, I'm grateful. Hell, you saved my life, but don't you understand? Everybody's treating me like I'm special, as if I can save their lives. But I can't, Marina. I'm lost, and I've… goddamn it, I've lost my wife. I've lost Karen, and I… I don't know what to do."

His eyes burned. Giving in to the waves surging from his heart, the words poured from him unrestrained.

"I hate everything that's happened—I do—but I'm helpless

to change anything. I despise the violence and the fear, and I hate what these children have seen. But I don't belong here. I want to go home, and I don't know what... or how... I *don't* know.

"I'm sorry. God, I think I even hate myself."

Not wanting to cry, he stepped past her and stared out the door. Surrounded by the rough community growing on this mountain, he was trapped inside the twin spirals of their expectations and his self-loathing. These people, in some racial desperation, had come here for answers, for help. In tragic, mythological irony, they had come to him, and he couldn't even give them hope.

"Griffith?"

Marina's voice was soft and open.

"Leave me alone," he whispered and walked out the doorway into the intense morning light.

With his head down he strode around the central temple mound to its north side. Along the trail ahead of him, he sensed someone. He glanced up. One of the villagers, a tiny, young woman with an infant on each hip smiled at him. She stepped to the side of the narrow trail. He looked around, avoiding her eyes, and turned onto a small path recently cut to his right.

Not wanting to see or talk to anyone, he followed the narrow path across the plateau. At the edge of the mountaintop, hidden from view by the undergrowth, was a small clearing surrounded by numerous pink-flowered, pale green mimosas. It was shaded by the branches of a twisted, old live oak. This isolated, natural garden overlooked the unbroken, green carpet of the rain forest stretching from the base of *Puuc Witz* to the eastern horizon.

Under the branches of the live oak, he sat on the musty, soft brown earth and crossed his legs on the cool ground. He sighed and lowered his face into his palms. Alone, he was ready to cry. He waited, but the tears wouldn't come. A knot of self-pity balled its fist against his diaphragm, stifling his breath. He swallowed and gasped, sucking in a draught of warm, moist air.

He felt so lost, so alone. Unable to loosen his gnarled emotions, he sat insensate. He couldn't breathe. He couldn't cry. He couldn't even face his benefactors. His denials grew larger and more hollow. Within the emptiness, the demon fear roamed, waiting for him to confront the one reality he'd refused to acknowledge.

He lifted his head from his hands and sighed. Here, in this magnificent jungle of wild orchids and ferns, where change and growth were the only constant, he was incapable of lifting himself from his morass of self-pity. Frozen in the onslaught of annihilation, he stared into a blank future, silent tears filling his vision.

What if she *is* dead?

From the darkness of his denials, the question stepped into the light. What if he was refusing to believe the obvious? First his parents had died. The only way he'd been able to control that torrent of loneliness was by virtually sequestering himself in an academic environment. Then Karen showed up and gave him a new life. She led him out of the laboratory and into the world. And now... so fast... all this. How was he supposed to cope? His life had been so secure and neatly boxed. Why did he leave his lab and computers in the first place? It was so safe, he repeated to himself.

Tears finally slipped down his cheeks into his beard. Except for the tiny sobs sucking at his abdomen, he sat perfectly still, neither fighting nor encouraging the flow from his eyes. His volition had been vaporized. Inertia grew like roots in fertile earth.

Then from outside the soundless, black vacuum of his self-contempt, a faint song, the "cow! cow! cow!" of a single bird, filtered through the leaves above him. Sniffing away the tears and mucous, he heard it again, oddly joyful and melancholic. From over the edge of the plateau, down in the receding jungle, another bird answered her call and flew from the understory. When it banked toward the crown of the live oak, Griffith saw the magnificent, iridescent tail feathers undulate in rainbow streaks of sunlight. The moment the quetzal disappeared into the upper foliage, his mate flew out, dropped past Griffith's head, and darted into the forest below.

The children had told him how the quetzals had caught his attention and led them onto *Puuc Witz*. Where he didn't belong. This was not his world. Trapped here, amidst all this fleeting beauty, he felt so dirty. And it wasn't just the lack of bathrooms and showers, either. He felt dirty inside. He and Karen had come with the best intentions, but everything, their honeymoon, the lives of these few surviving Lacandones and their magnificent jungle, and Karen's life, had all been destroyed by this world.

He glanced down and squinted his eyes. Under the wide branches of the live oak, soft mounds of dried guano had built up over the seasons to a gray-brown mat. A few fresh, white smears were splattered about.

Perfect, he thought. No answers. Just a pile of bird shit. If this were what his life had come to, well, maybe everything became simple. Perhaps this *was* all there was—living in shit until they come after you. Everyone was going to die, weren't they? Some, it was hideously apparent, sooner than others. And like individuals, civilizations died just as miserably, their sad remnants unseen and forgotten. Caught in the slaughter, his future was as grim as any poor *indígena's*.

But he couldn't sit here forever. He had to do something, even if he simply got out of everyone's way. Now this was the forbidden thought, wasn't it? The one with the most fearful countenance of all. Why shouldn't he end it right here? This was really the question he had avoided. If they were all going to die anyway, why should he be part of the bloody mess someone else was going to make of it? At least he'd be making the choice.

In blackest irony he wished he could e-mail the world his message of futility and surrender. By refusing to see it through to the grotesque end so inescapable for all the other helpless victims, he could tell everyone how utterly ineffective one individual is—one final act to show how meaningless any act was, right or wrong.

But who would even care about one man? For that matter, who would even concern themselves with the obliteration of one more small, impoverished tribe. If he were going to choose that path, then escape from his misery could be its only purpose. And since e-mail was obviously out of the question, he could hardly make some ultimate statement of personal angst for the world to remember, anyway.

Then, in the rich soil of his self-pity, the tiniest germ of an idea seeded itself. Was it possible, he wondered. A simple idea, he told himself. However unlikely and incongruous it seemed sitting on a mountain awash in the relentless forces of the primeval *Selva Lacandona*, he wanted to believe it was simple enough to work. The urge to survive tantalized him.

He would need help. And the *hach winik* were so eager to give it. But that very thought gave him pause. What hidden costs would he accrue by accepting their assistance? They acknowledged his dreams and wanted to believe this role they assumed for him, their *ahau*, their lost lord, of all things. Would he have to allow that mantle, or could he find a way around that responsibility, a responsibility he was certain he wasn't able to fulfill?

Believing Karen was alive might be evil dressed as sweet hope, but to find her, he would have to open that box. Like Pandora, he had to know. He would tell the *hach winik* his idea and simply deal with the consequences. And in his gut, he knew there would be some. Nevertheless, he would ask for their help.

Satisfied with his decision, he waited for the release of tension and anxiety. But there was none. He wanted this newly-found resolve to provide some lift from his self-indulgent swamp, but he was still as frightened and despondent as ever. All he'd actually accomplished, he realized, was making the decision. The easy part.

He stood up. Hangover spins rushed around his head. He took a deep breath. As his head cleared, he brushed the leaves and flecks of brown and gray from his *xikul*. Time for the hard part, he told himself. As he left the clearing, heading back to his hut below *Xibalba*'s ruined temple, the rustle of his departure disturbed the quetzal in the tree above him, and the bird, the ancient symbol of light to these people, flew from his nest and disappeared in the jungle below.

※※※

"Marina." He took a breath, unsure how to approach his question. "Would you ask Tito and Sara to come here, please?"

Marina sat erect on her stool.

"*Sí, claro.*"

She stood a bit more stiffly than before although Griffith was too preoccupied to notice. As she turned to leave, he cleared his throat and continued.

"Marina, would you also bring some breakfast for the four of us? I think I'm hungry. Oh, and could you get me something to drink, too? A lot of it, please. *Gracias*, Marina."

"*De nada,*" she whispered.

Within a minute, Tito and Sara came into his shelter, smiling and excited. They, too, were now dressed in *xikuls*. One of the women had embroidered a simple repetitive bird motif around the hem and sleeves of Sara's tunic. Like the men, Tito wore his unadorned. Their dark hair was shiny and straight, and their faces were scrubbed clean. They both had a small, dark green feather tied into their hair. Tito came up to Griffith and held out a third feather.

"This is for you, Griffith," announced Tito. "Sara said she would braid it into your hair."

"Well, thank you, both of you," answered Griffith, "but I've never worn anything in my hair before. Besides, what kind of a feather is that?"

"Oh, Griffith, you know," teased Tito.

"Aren't quetzals endangered? Where'd you find it, Tito?"

"One of the women found it."

"Those same birds, the ones you said I followed? You say she found them?"

"Oh, yes, Griffith," said Sara. "It was so strange. This woman said your quetzals had a nest in a tree near the eastern edge. She found their feathers on the ground and decided it was her job to protect your birds. She's cleaned the brush away and keeps watch so no one disturbs them. Do you believe what's happening up here?"

"I'm trying to," said Griffith. "And I think I know the tree she's talking about."

"The *hach winik* keep finding more ruins," added Tito. "Everywhere they look, they uncover something. And you led us up here, Griffith."

"Children, please. I was sick. I don't remember any of that. It's all just a lot of jumbled images to me. Don't interpret what I did as anything special. It's all coincidence."

"Griffith," said Sara, lowering her young voice to effect a

more sincere tone, "you are special to these people. And to Tito and me even more. You brought us here. You saved our lives."

She knelt down beside him, and Tito handed her the dark, emerald green feather.

"May I?" she asked, holding the feather toward his hair. "*¿Por favor?*"

"Oh, all right, Sara. But both of you must understand we've got to get *you* to your parents, and *I've* got to find Karen. You do understand?"

"*Claro*, Griffith," said Tito as Sara braided the feather into Griffith's hair. "*Comprendemos*, but we have many friends here who will help us. They think you're from the past, Griffith. One of them told me you're going to save us all."

"Tito, listen to me." Griffith's voice was firm. "I'm not from the past. You know that. I'm just a *gringo* who's lucky to be alive right now. Don't make this any more difficult for us. We're not here to save the world."

"But Griffith," protested Tito, "you *are* special. And not just because you saved us. We all heard your dreams."

"Tito, stop that! The only way we can get out of this is to stick together and stay focused on getting you home. Understand?"

"But Griffith…"

"Tito," interrupted Sara, "it's okay. Remember?"

"But Sara… oh, okay, *sí, hermana*, I remember."

"Remember what?" asked Griffith.

"We talked to Marina before you woke up this morning. She made us understand how you feel."

"*Sí*, Griffith," added Tito, "we understand."

"Understand what?" asked Griffith,

"That we have to go home."

"And don't we? A war is about to start because your parents can't find you. Don't you think we should?"

"Of course, Griffith," she replied.

"*Claro*," agreed Tito.

Marina appeared in the door, and Griffith motioned to her to come in. Chan K'in and Chan Nuk followed. Behind them a half dozen women entered carrying bowls of steaming eggs and *chiles*, fried yams with turkey strips, and gourds of fresh water and papaya juice. After setting their food down, they left. The leaders of the villages who'd drunk with him last night crowded into the front of his hut.

Griffith smiled nervously at the crowd. He looked around at all the food and then at the men who were smiling back at him. Chan Nuk knelt beside him on the left and checked his wound. She looked into his eyes and massaged his shoulder firmly until he grimaced. She then nodded to Chan K'in and stepped back.

"You're feeling better, Griffith *ahau*?" asked Chan K'in through Marina.

"Yes, a little. Thank you, Chan K'in. I'm sorry I didn't return to the *balche* house last night. I, uh, I think I... I passed out."

"There was much inside you needed to get out."

"I've never done that before. I guess I misjudged how much I was able to drink. Still too weak, probably."

"It is good to rid yourself of the evil which grows inside," said Chan K'in. "I have been sick many times, though not so much since I've gotten too old to be bad. Griffith *ahau*, we will not stay while you eat, but I wanted to tell you we will give our help in whatever way you would have it."

Griffith considered asking them not to call him *"ahau"*, but before he could respond, Chan K'in rose and ushered everyone out of the small shelter. The children dished out food onto four plates, and they began eating. Marina handed Griffith a cup filled with pulpy juice.

"Okay then, Marina," he said, "tell me about these armies heading our way. What's going to happen?"

"While you were dreaming, many stories came with the *hach winik* to *Puuc Witz*. The *PJF*, the *guardias blancas*, and perhaps the military are moving toward us through *el Valle de Río Jatate*, burning each village they find."

"But they were burning the villages before Griffith *ahau* brought us here," said Tito.

"More villages? Did we see that?" asked Griffith.

"*Sí*," answered Tito, "crossing the valley while you were sick."

"And the *PJF* is here, in that valley to our west?" asked Griffith.

"No," replied Marina, "not their soldiers and equipment. Just the *guardias blancas*, although an army is gathering on the western shore of the *Laguna*. Initially, they wanted to drive you and the children into the open."

"By burning villages."

"To scare the *campesinos* and *indígena* into turning you in, perhaps, or to leave you no place to hide."

"Do they know we're here?" asked Griffith.

"I don't know. From what our runners report, they may."

"Runners?"

"*Sí*, a few of the hunters came to me, and I've been teaching organization and defense. They call themselves *Haawo*, the *hach winik* name for the coatimundi. Some believe the *haawo* can travel the jungle unseen if he chooses; others that he can speak with the souls of the Invisible World. I didn't think you would object."

"No, no, of course not. That was a good idea. So do you know what's happening with the Zapatistas, too?"

"No, I'm sorry. We've not made any contact with them. I'm sure they know of the troop movements because they were on alert before we found you. They may be headed this way."

"To engage the military, do you think?" he asked.

"I don't know. Only if all the villages throughout Chiapas approve, something they may not be willing to do. But if they do, I fear they may end up in a trap between the *judiciales* and the military."

"Where we are."

"*Sí*, where we are."

"Okay, then, since it appears we're not moving," he began, "it seems to me we need to bring help to us."

"How?" asked Tito.

"We've got to make our location known."

"What?" exclaimed a surprised Tito.

"Griffith," said Marina, "you want to give away our position? I don't understand. It may be our only advantage."

"I agree with you, Marina, and I want to use it. But I don't want to give anybody a reason to start shooting, so you're going to have to help while we become visible."

"Griffith, I'm back with my people, and they have accepted me. We will keep you and Sara and Tito safe."

"What's your plan?" asked Sara.

"I have an idea," said Griffith, "but all of us will have to make it work. The idea is to tell everybody we can, including your parents, what's happened to you."

"From here?"

"That's right, Sara, from here."

"Griffith," she asked, "do you think they would stop fighting if they knew we were safe?"

"I don't know, but I think they would if your father knew. He could stop the fighting if he wanted."

"I don't think *el Presidente* is with the troops in the jungle," offered Marina.

"I agree, Marina. But he doesn't have to be. Sara, do you use computers in your school?"

"What?"

"Computers. Do you have one?"

"*Sí, claro*. Our school is very good, and we have computers at home, too."

"Do you know how to link up with your father through his computer at work?"

"*Sí*, when he's not traveling or in meetings."

"Do you have special access?"

"*Sí*. Both Tito and I have passwords."

"Excellent. This might work. Marina, let's send a message with one of your runners to that army by the lake. We need to tell them the children are safe and they would like to talk with their father."

"How will that be possible?" she asked.

"Your message will have to include a request for a computer with an up-to-date processor. Let's see, what else?"

"Excuse me, Griffith, should I write this down?"

"How much can you trust your runner to remember."

"Everything, if you tell him to. But in case the *judiciales* only speak Spanish, a list would help."

"I like the idea of an oral message, but you're right. We should do both."

Marina nodded and tore a sheet of ruled paper from a small notebook she carried in one of her pouches.

"Before you give the *Haawo* your message, Griffith, may I make a suggestion... if you wouldn't be offended?"

"No, please," he said, "go ahead."

"We should send three runners separately. A safe number.

And if you want them to remember, you must speak as their *ahau*. Is that okay?"

He was uncomfortable at the pose—it still felt arrogant to him—but he expected that. He nodded.

She went to the doorway and stepped outside. When she turned back in, and two men and a woman, dressed in their white *xikuls* and calf-height, black rubber rain boots, followed her in. They set their quivers and bows inside the doorway. They stood relaxed and confident, not making eye contact with anyone. They were wiry and short and looked like they could run all day.

"Griffith *ahau*," she said, "your *Haawo* runners."

Marina's soldiers, he thought with some admiration. He took a deep breath and assumed what he thought sounded like a professorial voice. Marina translated behind him.

"Take these words to the general of the army by the *Laguna*. Sara and Tito Patrillo are safe and wish to speak with their father immediately. To do this, they require a laptop computer with the following: Pentium processor, high resolution video card with eight or more megabytes of memory..."

Marina printed his instructions as she translated. The runners listened intently, taking much of it in phonetically.

"An internal fax/modem. Additionally, a cellular phone, a video camcorder and blank tape, and cables to connect each to the computer. And extra batteries for everything.

"Until the children receive all of the above, they will not speak to anyone. This is their choice."

He looked at each of them. Then, as an afterthought, he added, "That is my Word."

The three *Haawo* nodded when Marina finished translating. They turned and left, picking up their weapons at the door. Marina followed them outside, spoke quietly to them, and gave one of them the note before they trotted out of Griffith's view. She returned and sat on the right side of Griffith with the children.

"This is a very good idea to use the computer to contact their father," said Marina, some pride evident in her voice.

"*Gracias*, Marina," he replied softly. He admitted to himself he really had no idea if this would work.

"Are you going to make a tape of us, Griffith?" asked Tito.

"Yes, *sí*, we'll be using the camera."

"And the phone?" asked Sara. "Are we going to call our father?"

"Backup systems, Sara," interjected Marina, "are always a good strategy."

Griffith realized his plan, which wasn't exactly what the others thought, didn't have a backup. He supposed they might buy some time if his idea failed, but all he wanted right now was to get off this mountain, someplace safe and comfortable, as quickly as they could manage.

"We probably ought to plan for the worst," worried Griffith, "like if they won't give us the equipment, or your runners don't return."

"Griffith," said Marina, trying to reassure him, "that's why I sent three. They'll watch out for each other. If they get the equipment, they'll return with it."

"And if they're followed?" asked Griffith.

"I suspect they will be," she answered.

"Everything's going to be fine," added Sara.

"I hope you're right, Sara," replied Griffith with a sigh. "We are still a long way from home."

CHAPTER TWENTY
THE CAMP

Laguna Miramar
Tuesday

> Cruelty has a human heart,
> And Jealousy a human face;
> Terror, the human form divine,
> And Secrecy, the human dress.
>
> *A Divine Image*
> William Blake
> 1757—1827

When *Comandante* Bicho's personal helicopter landed at the camp west of *Laguna Miramar*, his headquarters had already been set up. Two batteries of mobile armor had arrived, and several companies of infantry were encamped along side a battalion of *PJF* troops. The jungle had been cleared for more helicopter troop carriers. Portable tracking dishes and a relay station surrounded the communications tent. Inside the open-sided tent, computers, monitors, printers, and phones filled several tables in the center. More electronic gear, including extra phones, laptops, and cameras, was stacked at the rear.

Since *Presidente* Patrillo believed the children were still captive, Bicho continued to control his hand. To that end, the President had given Bicho command powers over an additional complement of military equipment and support. Although not everything had gone as Bicho had planned, he felt confident the end was near. The unanticipated arrival of the children at *don* Pedro's ranch last week had nearly ended the crisis prematurely, but *don* Pedro's clumsiness had given Bicho a final opportunity to fulfill all his plans.

With the children no longer a worry, an unfortunate but acceptable loss, and the ransom paid and untraceable, it was time to finish this, to finally avenge himself for the degradation he'd suffered as the Zapatistas' hostage. The unbearable heat, the horrible food, and the diarrhea, all his suffering at the hands of the Zapatistas, had remained a visceral memory these long years he'd planned his revenge. This would pay back everyone for those humiliating six weeks he's been blindfolded in their filthy camp.

Even the mortification of being dumped on a jungle road when these unwashed *indios* and rebel Zapatistas were done with him, as if he were worthless as they, would no longer eat at him. More than that, the ignominy of being abandoned by his own government—not even a single rescue attempt during his forty days of captivity—would no longer have to be endured.

He would allow no peace between these terrorists and the government. Past debts were now due. In more ways than anyone imagined.

The officers were gathered in the com tent when he arrived.

"Gentlemen," he began, "I bring word from *el Presidente*. He is pleased with our efforts to track the hostages. From your satellite and reconnaissance reports, it seems obvious the terrorists have taken the high ground east of us. I understand there are several hundred rebels dug in on *Cerro San Felipe*. With nothing but jungle behind them, the valley between us is their only means of support. We now control the valley.

"Since the ransom was paid electronically last Friday, the kidnappers have not contacted us. Therefore, *el Presidente* has directed me to secure his children by any means necessary. I will do that. Unless we hear from the kidnappers, an air assault will commence tomorrow at dawn with six helicopter gunships.

"To that end, I want recon squads to cross the valley today and locate likely escape routes through the jungle. We'll control these routes with the additional helicopters scheduled to arrive tonight. All aircraft will remain on alert, and all infantry platoons and armor units should be readied within twenty-four hours.

"On the initial assault, I will lead the extraction team in my helicopter. If we don't secure the children quickly, I want backup helicopters dropping their teams around the base of the mountain. No one must be allowed to escape."

A soldier approached the tent and whispered to one of the com detail guarding the entrance. Motioning for the soldier to wait, the guard entered the tent. Bicho pivoted his head in the guard's direction and nodded.

"*Comandante*," said the guard, "an *indio* has walked into camp. He claims to have a message from *el Presidente*'s children."

The children? They're alive? That was unexpected. But whatever their message might be, it most certainly meant he'd found the rebels. Bicho smiled. And if the children lived through this after all, fine. But he would have his revenge either way. Too bad the trail of the ransom money had grown cold. Too bad for *el Presidente* and the *latifundistas*, anyway.

"Excellent," he said to the guard. "I'll take the message in my tent."

CHAPTER TWENTY-ONE
A LINK HOME

Puuc Witz
Tuesday afternoon

> I will show you fear in a handful of dust.
> *The Waste Land*
> T. S. Eliot
> 1888—1965

Throughout the day, the *hach winik* continued creating their small village and temple site from these abandoned ruins. Their impoverished villages back in the jungle were forgotten in their energy to rebuild *Puuc Witz*. The nearly three hundred *hach winik* who'd arrived on the mountain worked with an intensity and cooperation uncommon to their *caribals* spread across thousands of square miles of jungle.

Proudly, the people exhibited their communal efforts to Griffith and the children. Through Marina, they bragged of their efforts to come to *Puuc Witz* through miles of unmarked jungle. They showed off their new garden plots and went into detailed explanations of how they were building their homes.

But the work on the ancient ruins of *Puuc Witz* dominated their efforts. With only primitive tools, the *hach winik* cut and cleared around the five temple sites. Each block they freed from the jungle's cover was admired, discussed, and numbered.

Across the plateau at the western staircase, Chan K'in was

watching the ongoing excavations when Griffith and the others came over late that afternoon. The top landing had been cleared of the primary growth. Although the width and incline of the staircase were evident from their work, the paving and stepping stones still lay twisted from their beds by the jungle's incessant, centuries-old efforts.

They sat on the top stones. Chan K'in took the unlit cigar from his mouth and pointed over the valley to the west. Griffith looked, but without his glasses, the colors of the jungle blurred into a soft blanket of textures. The sunlight reflected off *Laguna Miramar*, but the savannah which lay between him and the *Laguna* was only miles of dark green and dappled brown splotches.

"Akyantho," began Chan K'in, "the god from the West who brought the foreigners and their money to the jungle, has become the strongest god in our world. The *xu'tan* your dreams spoke of will arrive only when he decrees, but the final turning of the wheels in the Fourth World is within our sight."

"What's the *xu'tan* supposed to be like, Chan K'in?" asked Tito through Marina.

"No one knows, Tito," he replied. "In my years, and the years of my father, we have seen many terrible calamities. The jungle has been cut and burned with so much smoke the sun could not find the day. Without the trees, the game left, and the soil stained the rivers brown. The ranchers and the *evangelistas* brought their foreign money and their rules. Now the *hach winik* buy trucks to drive to the great cities like San Cristóbal and Comitán where they sell their work to *turistas* to pay for gasoline to drive their trucks. This world has grown very cold."

"Will the *xu'tan* change that?"

"Certainly, young hunter. Since Akyantho sent Griffith *ahau* into the jungle, everything will be much different."

"Predicting change," said Griffith cynically, "is usually a good bet."

Chan K'in smiled and nodded. He held his rough cigar in front of him for a moment before continuing.

"When K'ayum was killed in the fall from the tree," he said switching to his more melodic, story-telling voice, "he knew he was dead."

Griffith smiled, remembering last night. So the story continues, he laughed to himself. He wasn't surprised.

"To begin his soul journey through the Dark World, he took some of the dead monkey so he could distract the vicious dogs who were hunting their abusive masters. He threw the monkey's hair around for the swarms of lice infesting the Dark World.

"After a long journey, he arrived at a very wide and dangerous river filled with many crocodiles. From the other side he heard his favorite dog barking. His heart pounded in relief when he saw his old hunting companion. He called his dog to him, but the dog, remembering the last time his master had kicked him, hesitated.

"K'ayum, who was surrounded by crocodiles and wild dogs, was upset his own dog would not jump in the river to save him. He took his last piece of monkey from his pack and held it up, again calling his dog. Recalling the good hunting with his master, the dog jumped into the river and swam to him. Leading his master back across, he kept the hungry crocodiles away.

"Still angry at his dog for hesitating to save him, K'ayum didn't even take the time to shake the water from his long hair. He threw the meat into the river where the crocs fought over it and kicked his dog to remind him to obey. He then told his dog to lead him away from Metlan, the place the *evangelistas* call Hell, to the heaven he deserved.

"After hiking many miles in the darkness among the man-eating demons and the poisonous snake-gods and spider-lords,

K'ayum needed to rest. He lay down under a ceiba and told his dog to guard him while he slept for a few hours."

Down in the valley, the faint crack from a rifle interrupted Chan K'in's story. They all looked, but no one could see anything. Griffith searched for some blue smoke wafting into the air. Seeing nothing, he suspected he'd seen too many movies in his youth. A second shot echoed up to them.

Chan K'in pointed to where he thought the sniper was located.

"I agree," said Marina. "Before I came up here, I was told our runners are returning. I think the sniper fire is behind them. Perhaps the *Haawo* are distracting the hunters."

"Marina," he asked, "how do you know all this?"

"We've kept reconnaissance lines spread across the valley. We'd also be tracking the EZLN if I had any idea where they were. I apologize. I should know that."

"No," replied Griffith, "that's all right. *De nada*. But how did you know what was going on with that sniper fire?"

"An assumption. Our runners have been relaying information about the soldiers who are trying to track your message bearers."

"Trying to?" asked Griffith.

"They get lost easily. Too much activity confuses them."

"Marina," he said, "I really hope,... that is, I really want us..."

He stopped, not wanting to stutter his thoughts in fragments at her.

"Marina," he began again, "I don't want anybody killed, anyone else. We'll get out of here without that." He paused, not nearly as certain as he sounded. "Won't we?"

"I think we can," she said. "We still have the strategic advantage."

Griffith listened to the confidence in her voice and realized he liked her. He watched her as she talked, noticing how attractive she really was, especially with her thick, dark hair tied back and her tunic cinched about her waist. She was intelligent and determined, and not afraid to use her strengths.

Just like Karen.

On the heels of that thought, however, an ache swelled in his chest until the pain was physical. It wasn't guilt over Marina. Innocent admiration didn't produce such distress. And he understood how random thoughts could easily trigger the agonizing reminder of his loss. But this crippling pain he felt each time Karen came to mind was now accompanied by a dreadful apprehension. If he was unable to handle his own emotions, how could he make his plan work? Trained to use his mind, it was his weak and fearful heart which controlled him.

"We know the terrain," she continued, "and we control the upper ground. They don't know our exact position, but when they do find out, they still won't know the terrain any better. And Sara and Tito, you both know your importance to them."

Griffith was taken aback by Marina's last statement. Was Marina thinking of the children as strategic advantages? He looked down, unsure how to react.

Sara stretched her hand toward him.

"It's okay, Griffith," she said. "Marina has already talked with us, and we understand."

"*Si*, Griffith," added Tito. "We've decided what to say to our father."

"So he'll know it's you two?" he asked.

"*Si*, that, too. Don't worry, Griffith, your plan will work."

"Thank you. Both of you."

"That's good," interrupted Tito, "but could we hear the end of Chan K'in's story?"

"But the story is over, Tito," said Chan K'in with a grin. "When K'ayum awoke, his dog had left him."

"So was he stuck in Hell?" asked Tito, shaking his head. "He shouldn't have kicked his dog."

Below them, people were moving through the brush. The wide staircase had been roughly cleared fifty feet down, and when the first *Haawo* runner appeared from the edge of the cover with a box under her arm, she looked up smiling. As she raced up the uneven stairs, several more *Haawo*, two of them carrying boxes, left the jungle and climbed the stairs. Marina checked her perimeter. More of her guard came from the dense cover and took up positions protecting the staircase.

Griffith's heart pounded against his ribs, and his breath quickened. He started to rise, but Chan K'in put his callused hand on top of Griffith's. Griffith looked at him, still resistant to the implied respect and responsibility his new role carried. Nevertheless, he remained seated.

He opened his diaphragm and took several slow, deep breaths. Remaining calm made sense, so he straightened his spine and closed his eyes. Assuming they got the equipment he needed, he allowed himself a small bit of optimism. Of course, not only was he in a foreign country, he was about as far as from civilization as he could get. The odds were hardly in his favor.

He opened his eyes. The runners climbed the last steps. Without looking at Griffith, they set the packages at his feet. One of them stepped up another flight, and keeping her eyes leveled at Griffith's chest, he waited.

The dream memory of being deferred to like this filled him. He wondered who was using whom here? At some point, he realized, he was going to have to confront this myth-making. But not now. He nodded at the *Haawo*.

"Griffith *ahau*," she began as Marina translated, "this is the word from the *Comandante* of the *PJF* forces: 'You are surrounded by troops. We will not attack for twenty-four hours if you return the children, unharmed, to us. If you return the ransom money and surrender, we will not attack. The children may talk to their father.'"

The message bearer turned to Marina and said, "Our shadows were redirected."

She stepped down, and everyone moved out of Griffith's line of vision.

"Okay, then, let's get started," said Griffith.

No one moved, apparently expecting Griffith to tell them what to do. He realized his reluctance to take charge was pointless. At least for now, he was going to have to accept the role he was given.

"Marina," he said, "open the boxes and spread out what we've got."

She nodded and opened the largest box. She handed the separate pieces to Sara and Tito. When it was all laid out, Griffith smiled tightly, a little surprised—everything he needed was here.

"We'll want a shelter, Marina," he said, "but keep it open all around. Just a roof."

"Griffith *ahau*," said Marina softly so they wouldn't be overheard, "this is a little exposed up here."

"No, this'll be fine," he replied. "They said we had twenty-four hours. That's plenty of time."

Marina nodded, obviously less confident of the word of the *PJF* than Griffith. She turned to a waiting squad, conveying the *ahau*'s orders for a shelter. She also sent two workers to build a table for the equipment.

With the assistance of Sara and Tito, they found the connections and jacks, plugged the camera into the video port, and turned everything on. While the computer booted, Griffith outlined his plan to the children.

"First of all, one of you needs to call your father on the cellular. Like you did in Amparo, Tito. Just a minute," he paused, squinting at the monitor. "I can't read this."

For just a moment he wished he hadn't lost his glasses. He moved back a few inches from the screen.

"Let's see," he mumbled, "enough volume, speed okay. Once this boots, kids, we'll know what's been downloaded. Then we'll be ready for the second part. Now Tito, if you'll try the phone, I'll type out an Internet address for your father."

"Are we going to use e-mail?" asked Tito.

"Yes, very good, Tito," said Griffith. "Your father will be able to verify your phone message by going to the Website I give you."

"Somebody's homepage?"

"Right, again."

"If there's a chat room," interjected Sara, "anybody can link up."

"Exactly, Sara."

"Even the newspapers."

"Especially the media. Since I'm tired of being alone out here, if enough people know what's happened to you... well, it's kind of like turning up the lights so we don't have to sneak home in the dark."

"That's brilliant, Griffith *ahau*," said Marina.

"*Sí*," agreed Tito. "You *are* going to fix everything."

"Well, not yet," replied Griffith. "And anybody could have thought of it. Let's just make sure the equipment works first."

He tapped a few keys and handed the phone to Tito.

"Phone home, Tito," he said with a smile.

Tito punched in the children's private number and waited.

"Are we on line, yet?" asked Tito after a few moments.

"No, you're just using the phone, right now. Any luck?"

"No. Lots of noises, and, oh wait. *Sí*, it's ringing!"

Griffith's heart pounded. The opportunity to get through to someone who could help them had finally arrived. He needed to believe the days and nights of running in fear were nearly over. And his search for Karen was about to begin.

Tito's eyes lit up, and he boomed excited Spanish into the tiny cell phone.

"This is Tito Patrillo... Yes, Tito San Miguel Lopez Patrillo... Yes, and I'm calling for my sister and me... Yes, we're safe. We need to talk with our father... For how long?"

Griffith pointed to the address he'd typed onto the screen, and Tito nodded.

"Give Father this address: *pluva@academ.uva.edu*. Understand?"

"Tell him we're okay," said Sara.

"Again?" asked Tito, still holding the phone to his mouth. "Should I tell them our plan?"

Sara shook her head emphatically.

"Okay. Tell Father," he said into the phone, "we are both okay, please. Thank you. Remember, it's *pluva@academ.uva.edu*. P—L—U—.... He hung up."

"What did he say, Tito?" asked Sara. "Who'd you talk to?"

"I don't know. Someone. He said Papá was away."

"For how long?" asked Griffith. He feared the first problem had just arisen.

"A few hours. But he said he'd give him the message. He sounded strange. I don't think he believed me."

"Didn't believe you?" questioned Sara. "Why not?"

"I don't think that matters, yet, Sara" said Griffith. "You'll convince them. Don't worry. We got through, and that's exciting. You did very well, Tito."

Tito beamed.

Griffith plugged the phone jack into the modem port and tapped in the long distance number of his computer network at the University of Virginia. After several excruciatingly slow and silent minutes, the computer came alive with a dozen seconds of screeches, beeps, and static. When that ended, a new screen blinked onto the monitor. From the top of the screen, in horizontal strips, a picture slowly emerged, line by line, orange and blue overlaid with the Rotunda Seal of Jefferson's University.

His breathing slowed. He felt like his entire bloodstream had just been washed clean. The children were almost jumping with excitement, shuffling their feet and leaning against Griffith's shoulders. Ignoring Tito's fidgety weight on his sore shoulder, he navigated to the Physics Lab homepage. Clicking on the names of everyone in the department he thought might be in their offices, he quickly sent them e-mails asking each of them to go to the department chat room. He then entered the chat room. Even though summer classes hadn't started, he was sure someone would be home. And that might be all he needed to get started. Fired with the realization he had just linked home, he rapidly composed his ideas as he typed.

```
Pluvarats, this is the Grantman, from the
Lacandon rain forest. I have an extremely
important message which must get out. I mean
OUT! I need help.
Who's home?
G-man.
```

He hit 'Send' and waited. From the length of time it took

to flash "message sent", Griffith suspected the software they'd given him was slower than anything he'd used at the physics lab for years.

He waited some more. Impatient, he looked up. From the top of the staircase, he squinted at the wide, blurry expanse of the valley. All around him, the men and women of the *bach winik* were quietly and efficiently proceeding with their work, finishing his shelter, excavating the ruins, and homesteading. The tranquil songs of the birds and insects, the fragrant, earthy odors, and the moist, clean air bathed him in their quiet luxuriance. This verdant world feigned peace and serenity.

The screen flashed and blinked. The chat room came alive with silent conversation. Several older messages scrolled before Griffith's plea appeared. Then after another few minutes, the first reply forced its way onto the screen.

> Grantman, great to hear from you. What a honeymoon you guys must be having. I suppose even there you've heard about the great Mexican kidnapping? So, what's this important message? Decide to resign your position on the faculty and stay in a tropical paradise, or what?
> TOAST.

"Toast?" asked Sara.

"A student assistant. Let's read the others."

"You know him?" Tito asked.

"Yes, Tito," replied Griffith. "And I'm hoping a few others, as well. Lots of gray matter to tap into."

"Huh?" grunted Tito.

"They're are all very smart. Let's read this one."

> G-man. So what's your story? The rain

```
forest sounds cool, dude, but people are
getting killed down there. The jungle is
alive with rumors of a messiah and his army.
Is your message from him?
    psidkik
```

"That's no help," said Griffith. "Don't know him."

```
G-Man: I hear you. Whatchaneed?"
Fizzle
```

"Hmm," he murmured. "Oh, wait, look here."

```
Grantman. Digger here, buddy. Everyone's
actually in the lab and working. Well, not
everyone. Ralph and Elaine aren't back yet
for summer session. We've been taking bets
whether you're going to come back now that
Karen's got you out of the lab.
    TD
```

Griffith took a deep breath. No time to think about that now.

"Okay, kids," he said, "let's see if the next part works. Do either of you know how to run this camera?"

"*Sí*, Griffith," volunteered Sara. "I've used ours before."

"Great. Then while I'm doing this, Sara, you check out the camcorder. Tito, help me here."

He stroked several keys, clicking on menus and looking into windows for the audio and video links. After several dead ends, he found the right one and began typing again.

```
    Digger. I've got an audio link here.
Can you plug us in? Anyone else in this
room please link up a/v if you can. This is
important.
```

> If we are going to prevent a war here in the jungle, notify all the addresses and hackers you know, especially the media.
> G-Man

He double clicked the audio link. Again they had to wait for it to boot. Impatient, Griffith opened the e-mail directory.

"While we're waiting, let's see if we can get your father to link up to my home page. Tito, you called your father, so, Sara, do you want to e-mail him?"

She nodded and began typing.

> Hope you received our telephone message, Papá. Tito and I are safe. Griffith *ahau* and the *hach winik* rescued us. We have to talk to you before your army attacks us. Please link up to the pluva@academ.uva.edu chat room. Link up to us now, Papá.
> *cinderella y caballero*

She turned to Griffith, and he nodded. She clicked 'Send'.

"Cinderella *y caballero*?" asked Griffith.

"*Sí*," she answered, "special names from our childhood."

"Pet names."

"*Sí*, that's what you call them. We're not supposed to say, but these are our passwords, too. I think he'll know us."

"I hope so. Well, let's return to Virginia."

Stepping between the children to the keyboard, he minimized the mail directory. The audio software was still booting. For anxious minutes, they stood in silence. Tito glanced up at Griffith several times. Just as he started to ask Griffith something, a burst of static erupted from the laptop's speaker. From two thousand miles away, the electronic clamor of a new age cut through centuries of half-remembered history and eons of geological indifference. *Puuc Witz*, the Mountain of Our Sacred Counsel, leapt noisily into the modern world.

All work around their shelter stopped. Thatch was dropped, bare poles laid down, and machetes sheathed as the *hach winik* gathered to hear the metallic, computerized sounds from the invisible future. Across the mountain top, word spread quickly. The rest of the *hach winik* halted their work and headed to the western staircase.

Some had heard of computers, and Chan K'in had even seen a laptop once when an eco-tourist writer visited him several years ago. But since the language of the *hach winik* lacked literal translations to explain what was happening, the unintentional consequence of this barrier was exaggeration of metaphoric proportions. To some, their *ahau* was talking to all the people of *Los Estado Unidos*, calling to them from the sky. To more than a few, these were voices speaking to him from the future.

"Griffith," came Digger's voice from the small speaker, "we're linked here. Can you hear me? This is amazing. Can you hear me, Griffith?"

Griffith smiled and took a breath. He'd done it. He'd established a real-time audio link with his university lab. This might actually work.

"Digger," he said toward the laptop's microphone, "you have no idea what it feels like to hear your voice. We're in big trouble down here, and we need your help. And everybody else who's linked up."

"We're here, Griffith. What's the prob?"

"Digger, before I say anymore, please, listen carefully. We may get cut off at any time, and I need you to keep this link open. If we do get cut, we'll be trying to get back to you, so stay on line. And ask everyone else in the lab to call the newspapers,

TV, congressmen, anybody who can get on-line. People need to hear this."

"Sure, Griffith. Toast and Annie are working the lines already."

Griffith nodded to the camera in Tito's hands. Tito held it steady, pointing it at them while Sara traced the cord to the back of the laptop, making sure it was secure.

"Digger," continued Griffith, "I want to try something. I've got a camcorder here, and I think the video card in this laptop can handle the load. Can we get a video hook-up at your end? I want to try a real-time link."

"Wow, Griffith, from the jungle. Very cool. We can do it, but this could tie up the University's server. The Dean'll shit."

Sara pulled gently on the sleeve of Griffith's tunic and whispered to him. Griffith smiled and nodded.

"Don't worry about that, Digger," Griffith said. "This is important. Besides, I've just been told the Mexican government will pick up the tab."

"Your call, Grantman. Let's see, uh, wait a second... yeah, the lines are clear here. I'm ready to check your vids now. You transmitting?"

"Are you ready, Tito?" asked Griffith.

"*Sí*, I've got a picture here," he replied.

He double clicked the video icon. One more click at "view" and their screen went blank. Sara sucked in a breath and looked at Griffith, who was staring at the empty screen.

When the screen finally blinked its pixals of light and color, Sara gasped again, this time much more loudly. A real-time, live picture of the two of them stared back from the monitor. On the screen, for anyone in the world to see by simply linking up to the PhysicsLabUVA homepage, stood Griffith, in his white *xikul*, a single, dark green feather braided into his thick, black hair. Next to him was Sara, similarly dressed and feathered. In the background stood old Chan K'in, smiling broadly, with virtually the entire Lacandon nation behind him. The dramatic, green backdrop of *Puuc Witz*, its new village, and the azure summer sky framed the white dress and brown faces of the remnants of the only Maya people to have successfully resisted the centuries of Western invasions.

"Griffith," exclaimed Digger, "I've got your vids. Kind of fuzzy... wait. Wow! Griffith, what's going on there? Lord, you look different."

Sara looked up at Griffith.

"Digger, I'd rather you didn't use the word 'lord'," asked Griffith. "A cultural thing, you understand."

Griffith turned to Marina and gestured for her to take the camera from Tito so he could join them at the computer.

"Digger," announced Griffith, "and everyone else out there on line, I'd like you to meet Sara and Tito Patrillo, daughter and son of President Patrillo of Mexico."

"Griffith, that's ridiculous," replied Digger.

"Digger," insisted Griffith, "listen. Over a week ago, these children were kidnapped, and Karen and I rescued them, well, accidentally rescued them."

"You what? Accidentally rescued?"

"Listen to me, Digger! We've been running from people trying to kill us ever since. The *hach winik*—excuse me, they're also known as the Lacandones—they've kept us safe. We've got to get this message out because the Mexican army is ready to go to war over the children."

"Griffith," interrupted Digger, "Griffith. Wait a minute. You haven't heard?"

"Heard what?"

"Jesus, Griffith, where the hell have you been? It's been on the news here in the states. The army has already captured the kidnappers in the middle of some Indian rebellion."

"What? Digger, what are you talking about?"

"Marcos! The leader of the rebel army, what's it called?"

"Zapatistas," said Griffith fighting the flood of emotions about to burst over him.

"Yeah, the Zapatistas. They captured him and some American woman. They haven't found the children or the ransom, but Griffith, they've confessed. The President already gave the order to destroy the rebels."

An American woman! It had to be Karen. Which meant she hadn't drowned. And she saved Rafael. She was alive! But why would they confess to the kidnapping? And what else did he say? Destroy the rebels?

"That would explain why the EZLN isn't around," said Marina quietly.

"Griffith, am I missing something?" asked Digger.

"Yeah, Digger, you are."

"If those are really the children," continued Digger, "then what's happened? Uh, Griffith, where's Karen?"

"She's... there was a plane wreck. We got separated. I... I thought she drowned."

"Oh, God, Griffith, I'm sorry. I can't believe that."

"But now, you say... Digger, before I explain, I need to know if you're getting any hits, particularly from... just a minute, Digger."

He turned his back to the camera and whispered to the children.

"I'd like to give Digger your father's Internet address. I know it's private, but it'll help us find out if he's linked to the site. If he is, this information could convince him your message is genuine."

"And," added Sara with a grin, "everybody else will also know his address. I think that will help, don't you, Tito?"

"Let's do it," declared Tito.

Griffith turned around, but before he could spoke, Tito announced his father's personal Internet address to the numerous surfers already connected to this story.

"My father's homepage," stated Tito, "is *www.ejecl.eumfed.gob.mx*, and his personal email address is *raul@psis.net*. Please write to him."

He repeated it in Spanish.

"Griffith," responded Digger, "Toast just told me we've gotten some international hits, including a number from Mexico. He says we're going to overload our server soon. What? Pardon me a second, Grif. Huh? Okay. Annie says several news agencies have also called us asking about stories of some messiah who's supposed to be leading an Indian uprising in the jungle down there? What's going on?"

"Digger," began Griffith with a small sigh, "that story is not very accurate. Monday before last, while Karen and I were camping, we stumbled across Sara and Tito in an abandoned logging camp. They asked us to help them, and for better or worse, we did. Believe it or not, we escaped on horseback, dodging bullets and helicopter rockets. At one point we were rescued by... some people who had a small plane to fly us to safety.

"Digger, the plane crashed into a lake during a storm, and I thought Karen had drowned. We had to keep running, and for nearly a week now, we've been with the *hach winik* in the rain forest.

"We're on the highest mountain northeast of *Laguna Miramar*, *Puuc Witz*. This is our location, so everyone will know we're not hiding. But we're surrounded by troops who want to kill everyone they think has helped the children.

"I know you believe me, Digger. And to their father, *el Presidente de Los Estados Unidos Mexicanos*, here are your children. They want to say something to you."

He stepped back. Almost as if they'd choreographed it, Sara and Tito filled the space in front of him. They both smiled broadly.

"Father," said Sara in Spanish, "I hope your picture is clear so you can see we are fine." She repeated it in English.

"*Sí*, Papá," agreed Tito, "we're safe here with Griffith *ahau* and our *hach winik* friends."

As Tito repeated himself in English, he gestured behind them where the *hach winik* had gathered to glimpse the screen and eavesdrop on languages they didn't understand.

"Father," said Sara, "please listen closely. You know we're safe. We don't know who kidnapped us, but it wasn't the Zapatistas, and it certainly wasn't Karen and Griffith *ahau*. They saved our lives, many times. Everything Griffith *ahau* has said is true. Look behind us. Nobody has any weapons, not the men or their wives and children. We're happy with these people. But, Father, we're unhappy about some things.

"All of the *hach winik*," she continued and pointed behind her, "led by Chan K'in, there, helped us because of Griffith *ahau*. He has sacrificed everything to bring us here, and he was even shot saving our lives. So this is our Word, Father. We are going to remain on *Puuc Witz* until the following has been done: first, your armies are threatening us. We want you to order them to leave the jungle. They scare us, and, Father, they're burning villages looking for us."

Griffith was stunned. What did these children think they were doing? They were not in any position to make demands. They were supposed to convince the President and his advisors everything was fine. How could threats accomplish that?

Remembering he was on camera, he hid his shocked amazement. But other than that, he had no idea what to do.

Sara leaned over to Tito and whispered in his ear for several seconds.

"Second," announced Tito, "we have been told the *Policía Judicial Federal* have Griffith *ahau*'s wife, Karen Grant, and a man named Rafael. They are innocent, and both of them risked their lives to save us. Father, you must release them immediately."

"And third," said Sara, "our most important point. All of this land around us belongs to the *hach winik*. They have lived here since before the *conquistadores*. Now, Griffith *ahau* has brought their past back to them. So according to prophecy, and in the name of Chan K'in, *t'o'ohil* of all the *hach winik*, we want you to order the ranchers, the *evangelistas*, and everybody else, including the Zapatistas, to leave the rain forest. The land, the trees, the water, the oil, the quetzal, the jaguar, and even the air, are rightfully the *hach winik's* to protect and use. *Puuc Witz* is where we will stand. The *hach winik*, following the dreams of their *ahau*, will control their land into the next age."

Griffith couldn't accept that these cosmopolitan children actually believed this myth-making they were abetting. How could they do this? They were surrounded by guns—and a great deal more modern weaponry, he suspected. How was this supposed to help them? He wondered whether Marina's hand was in this, but as upset as he was, he knew he couldn't let it show.

"Papá," continued Tito, "you can contact us at this address. Then you must come here after you send the army away. We want you to meet everybody, especially Griffith *ahau*, Marina, Chan Nuk, who saved Griffith when he almost died and had his dreams, and old Chan K'in who said Griffith's dreams meant he was the *ahau*."

"Tito," interrupted Sara politely, "is getting ahead of himself. Father, our line may be cut, but we'd like to stay online and show you everything up here: the ruins Griffith *ahau* led us to..."

"He followed a pair of quetzals," said Tito.

"...and their nest where these feathers were found and given to us. Oh, Papá, once we got to this mountain and Griffith *ahau* started to get better, this has been so exciting. We've learned so much; you'd be very proud of us. Tito went turkey hunting yesterday, and we've learned how to build and cook and find medicines in the jungle. Marina, show everybody where we are."

Marina panned across the beaming faces of the *hach winik*, who were much too shy and naïve about the camera to wave. Their smiles, however, and their attention to Sara, Tito, and Griffith were so sincere that the hundreds of surfers now linked to the Pluva home page were captivated. These gentle people in their simple white *xikuls*, and the three who stood with them, filled computer monitors with real-time pictures which sparked the imagination and conscience of a growing number of viewers. Through cyberspace, slowly and inexorably, word and picture began to spread around the globe.

Unaware of the effect his plan was having, however, Griffith dissembled his heart-threatening dread over Sara and Tito's audacity. He forced himself not to pace. As Marina continued to pan the camcorder across the mountain top, showing the world the beginnings of primitive excavations and the small village, Griffith turned back to the computer. He wanted to revel in the knowledge Karen was alive, but how could he ignore the obvious? She was a captive of the Mexican authorities along with the most famous revolutionary since Ché Guevara. Now with the children's surprise demands, home videos suddenly seemed futile.

He needed to keep busy. He minimized the video screen and typed in *http:\\www.ejec1.eumfed.gob.mx*. When he got in, he entered "cinderella" at the password prompt, and waited again. Once inside, everything he saw, the abbreviations and computer shorthand, all looked intriguing, but everything was in Spanish. He clicked on several whose Latin cognates he thought he recognized and found the typical links to government regulations, names of offices and agencies, and various information outlets. Even in Spanish, nothing looked out of the ordinary to him. He kept opening and closing files and didn't notice Marina give the camcorder to Sara and walk over to him. Mumbling to himself, he rubbed his aching eyes and sighed.

"Try *'inquis*,'" suggested Marina from behind him. "It may be about the investigation."

"Oh, God, Marina!" exclaimed Griffith. "You surprised me. I thought you were with... never mind. What did you say? 'Inkiss'. Yes, of course, the inquisition."

He wanted to say something to Marina—maybe ask her where the kids got this outrageous idea of theirs—but his anger was flustered with her sudden appearance by his side. Later, he decided, he'd confront her.

He clicked, and the screen requested a password. Neither *cinderella* nor *caballero* gave him access. He checked the file menu and clicked 'doc info'. Statistics, volume, and a brief description box appeared, but nothing to reveal a way into the file. He altered their properties and changed the extensions, but they were all dead ends.

"I don't know how to get in," he said. "Anything else look good to you?"

"Oh, there," she said as Griffith scrolled the screen. She pointed to *'rescate.'* "Ransom."

He clicked, and the original ransom note blinked onto the screen, just as it was saved and reloaded by Ramirez, the President's computer aide.

"Wow, $250 million!" gasped Griffith as he read. "And Digger said it was paid."

"To the ones who really kidnapped the children," added Marina.

"That's brazen. They didn't even have the kids to bargain with, and they got the ransom. I can understand their father's reaction to giving up that kind of money without getting his children back."

He paused, staring at the end of the message. A long row of numbers blurred and ran together, fifty or more, he estimated. Instead of a long list of single integers, however, Griffith saw small sets of numbers strung together. And something about them struck a distinct memory chord.

"Marina," he asked, "do you still have your pencil?"

"Sí."

"Will you copy that list of numbers. In case we get snipped."

She raised her eyebrows in question and then began writing.

"Curious, that's all," he said.

She copied the fifty-six integers while Griffith got busy at the keyboard. Within a minute, he found a list of prime numbers on some homepage called 'the prime source for prime information'.

"Would you copy the first, say the first forty numbers, too, please? If they're using more than that, we don't stand a chance."

"For what?" asked Marina.

"I'm not sure." he said.

Marina finished the two lists and gave them to Griffith. Several dozen *hach winik* had stopped working and were gathering near them on the western ridge. One of her *Haawo* was running up the staircase. Griffith, still focused on the screen, restored the video window. The camcorder was following the crowd to the western staircase. Everyone stood peering into the west across the valley toward *Laguna Miramar*. As Griffith turned to tell Marina, the screen lost its picture and then its link-up.

"We've been cut off," he said.

"Look," responded Marina laconically. She pointed toward the distant *laguna*.

Griffith squinted into the sun but saw only the wide, damp savannah they'd crossed. Beyond the swamp, a flash of reflected light twinkled over the *laguna*. His fear instinct tingled. Helicopters were out there. He was certain.

As he spun around to look for the children, they ran up to him, pointing across the valley. He looked again in the direction of their gestures and caught another tiny glint of sunlight moving above the lake. In moments, a half dozen bright glitters crossed the *laguna*, their invisible blades slicing the light.

When Griffith looked back, Sara and Tito were shutting down the equipment, and Marina was signaling to several of her *Haawo*.

"You'd better follow me, Griffith," she said.

"Why?" asked Griffith. "They must have seen the children's video. They're coming to get us, don't you think?"

"In case they're not friendly about it, I believe we should get to safer ground."

She spoke quickly to a nearby *Haawo*. He nodded and disappeared into the crowd. Tito disconnected the cellular phone, Sara closed the laptop, and they were ready to leave.

"Where's it any safer?" asked Griffith.

"A passage was found under the central temple that will provide you and the children temporary shelter. I think we should set up your base there."

"That's what you wanted earlier, isn't it, Marina," he asked.

"*Sí*, but, now, I think we should."

"Lead on," said Griffith.

As they hustled across the open plateau to the central hill, an eerily familiar vibration touched his skin and burrowed into his flesh. His heart started to pound, his stomach knotted, and the sweat on his forehead chilled in the gentle, mountaintop breeze.

He craned his neck around as he strode with his escorts, a *Haawo* squad that included two women. For the first time, Griffith saw how this tiny defense was armed—bows and arrows, a few .22 caliber rifles, and one ancient sidearm he couldn't identify. Chan K'in was gone, apparently with everyone else who'd disappeared into the surrounding jungle.

"Should we wait to see what they're going to do?" Griffith asked Marina as they climbed among the rocks and ruins up the central hilltop.

She nodded to two of the *Haawo*, handing one of them the camcorder. Then to Griffith she said, "Perhaps. We have a few minutes. Your shelter is nearby."

The *Haawo* took the rest of the equipment from the children, walked around the largest pile of limestone blocks, and disappeared. As the helicopters neared, the air currents lifted the drone of the engines and the beat of the blades up the side of the mountain. The vibrations throbbed more heavily on Griffith's eardrums, and the burn of adrenaline tensed his muscles. He looked across the slope, past the green of newly-thatched huts, toward the western staircase where several *Haawo* knelt in the brush.

Within the increasing roar of the rising helicopters, a substantial thump pounded the ground and vibrated to his feet. Then two more shook the earth, and Griffith gave into his urge to flee. He turned to the children, and they were already crawling toward the rocks behind them. The tremors under them grew into explosions on the mountain side. The staccato of rapid-fire weapons pierced the heavy thunder of the noisy aircraft. Columns of intensely-heated smoke billowed up the western slope of *Puuc Witz.*

Between rocks and ruins, Griffith rushed behind Tito and Sara. He glanced back and saw two swirling sets of blades rise above the western staircase. The wash from the blades drove the acrid smell of exploded cordite toward them. He looked around for Marina. She was directing her remaining *Haawo* with hand signals. As the lead helicopter hovered, scanning the terrain, she raised her hand above her head. The dozen *Haawo* who had flanked them to the central ruins disappeared, each in a different direction down the hill and across the plateau toward the uncut jungle.

Marina looked at Griffith, still standing among the ruins, and thrust her forefinger toward the ground several times. He fell to his knees and covered his head with his right arm, expecting to hear shells suddenly explode around him. Broken limestone chunks and pebbles dug into his knees and elbows.

The cacophony from the helicopters poured over him as more metal beasts rose over the mountain. With each new rocket explosion the ground vibrated, and the air swirled with dust and gunpowder residue. Tension rippled through the earth, gripping him to his bones.

He looked over his shoulder. Marina shook her head at him and gestured for him to move. Beyond her, helicopters hovered at the edge of the mountain, their split windshields like the hungry eyes of giant, prehistoric insects. Machine gun muzzles protruded from under the eyes, and smoke from the expended rocket tubes swirled away in the downwash. Stretched out on the rocky ground, he froze, staring at the half dozen, black, armored war machines, their hurricane winds and thundering voices intimidating every lowly creature who hugged the earth.

One of the helicopters yawed to its left and lowered its dark nose toward several small huts by an overgrown mound along the northern slope of *Puuc Witz*. Bursts of machine gun fire flashed from the twin muzzles, cutting a jagged swath through the huts and surrounding jungle. For seconds after the last burst, saplings and small tress slowly fell, littering the ground with bits of blown leaf and shattered twig.

The shock of hearing and seeing the savage effects of these weapons stunned Griffith. Was it possible for anyone to become inured to such violence? In the abrupt, apparent silence following the last burst, he just stared at the newly-exposed patch of jungle.

When a small hand grabbed his wrist, he screamed into the din. His bladder loosened, and he squeezed to avoid wetting himself. Under his *xikul*, a single, warm drop of urine spurted onto his thigh. From her knees, Sara tugged on his arm and yelled for him to hurry up.

He recaptured his breath and nodded at her. Crawling on his knees and good right hand, he followed her around the rocks. When he saw her scrambling toward the small, shadowed opening into the earth at the center of *Xibalba*'s ruins, he stopped short.

Primordial fear clutched him. Specters of sacrificial death rushed by him. He ached for a reason to avoid entering this tiny, black hole into the earth. He knew it was irrational, but still he recoiled from the mythological tug of his dream cave. With the incessant pounding on the earth around him, he couldn't think.

Sara slithered into the cave entrance not much bigger than a man-hole cover. Through the noise, her voice, echoic and faint, called to him from inside. Before steeling himself to crawl into that black void, he turned, expecting to find Marina behind him. She was hidden, gone somewhere among the rocks.

To his left, the helicopters continued their attack on the small village. Turbo-powered engines wound up, and the plosive release of rockets hissing from their tubes urged Griffith forward. Rapid-fire machine guns tore through the brush, pulverizing the ground and blasting the ruins into powder.

He scrambled toward the tiny hole in the earth. At the entrance of the cave, he saw Sara reaching out to him. He swallowed a breath. Hugging his wounded arm to his chest, he dove onto his right side into the darkness.

CHAPTER TWENTY-TWO
XIBALBA'S CAVE

Puuc Witz
Tuesday evening

> The way in which the world is imagined determines at any particular moment what men will do.
>
> *Public Opinion*
> Walter Lippman
> 1889—1974

Inside, he scrambled deeper into the darkness, crawling toward the faint, white ghosts of the children's tunics. He kept his watery eyes down, trying to adjust to the darkness. With each concussion, the knot in his stomach wrenched tighter. He crawled over small rocks until his aches and cuts commanded him to stop.

"We're safe here," he heard Tito's voice from below him.

Rocket blasts pounded the earth, and the tiny light from the entrance limned the billowing curtains of dust outside. Griffith knelt along the wall. Below him, shapes took form as the meager light slowly peeled back the darkness. He saw the white of the children's *xikuls*. Touching the wall behind him, its cool, damp, flat surface surprised him. It was stone, worn but obviously cut.

Sara and Tito sat down on either side of Griffith. One of the rockets exploded within yards of the entrance, blasting loose rock and dirt from the ceiling and walls. The children huddled against Griffith, and he wrapped his arms around their shoulders. The ache in his left shoulder was bearable, and the comfort he found with the children in his arms gradually overcame his panicky anxiety.

They huddled together as each explosion rocked the earth. For ten minutes the assault continued. But then, abruptly, the attack stopped. Minutes later, the roar of the engines faded away.

"What now?" asked Sara.

"Should we wait?" asked Tito. "Perhaps Papá hasn't had time to come get us yet."

"*Sí*, Griffith *ahau*," agreed Sara. "The army doesn't understand."

"Yeah," said Griffith, "I'll agree with that. Unfortunately, your father may have heard and decided an attack was the best way to save you two."

"He wouldn't ignore what we said," said Tito.

"I wish you'd spoken to me first," said Griffith quietly.

"We're sorry," said Sara, "but we didn't want to worry you."

"Then why didn't you tell me?"

"Marina said we should," added Tito.

"And...?" Griffith asked again.

"The truth?" asked Sara.

"Sure, why not?"

"You wouldn't have let us," she said.

"Was this Marina's idea?"

"No," replied Tito quickly. "She didn't like it."

"I don't understand," said Griffith, confused but relieved that Marina had opposed their ideas.

"We convinced her," explained Sara. "It was a chance to help the people who saved us. And we believe in you."

"Believe in me? What were you thinking?"

"But you're so smart," pleaded Tito, "and all these people believe in you."

"Okay, I don't want to argue about it." In reality, he didn't want to confront his own anger. "You did it, and we'll just have to make it work."

"It will," assured Sara. "You don't know our father."

"It's possible, you know," countered Griffith, "since you refused to go home, your father might think you're still hostages."

"Then we need to tell him again," said Sara.

"Let's try," said Tito.

"I'm afraid it's not going to work in here," replied Griffith. "We're underground."

From above them, outside the entrance, they heard someone coming. They froze. Griffith's heart throbbed in his chest, and more adrenaline heated his blood.

"You need to be quiet down there," said Marina in a whisper that carried to them with distinct clarity. "The soldiers have landed."

She handed in a burlap bag.

"Some food and water. We'll talk later. You'll be safe here."

"But Marina…" started Griffith.

"I'll be back," she said and disappeared from the entrance.

"Oh, Christ on a crutch," mumbled Griffith. What an awful way to live, he thought ruefully. "Either of you afraid of the dark?"

"Not with you here," answered Sara softly.

"Shhh," admonished Tito. "Soldiers might be close."

"Yes," whispered Griffith into the shadows, "you're right."

After several minutes sitting silently in the dark, Tito began to investigate the sack Marina had handed them.

"Look!" he whispered.

Out of the darkness, a narrow beam of light blinked on. Tito waved it at Griffith's eyes, blinding him.

"A flashlight."

"Shhh," responded Griffith. "Let's move farther down where they can't hear us."

Carrying the burlap sack, Tito lit the way down for Sara and Griffith who hauled the rest of the equipment. The rough, high stairs were steep and worn, and the walls narrowed as they descended. Each carved step was surprisingly tall, some eighteen inches high. The odd heights weren't attributable to careless workmanship, Griffith decided, since this ancient stonework had just withstood a barrage of modern warfare without collapsing. Eighteen steps to the bottom and the staircase turned ninety degrees to the right. It continued eighteen more steps down to the next landing, and revealed yet another staircase still narrower and deeper into the earth.

"This ought to be far enough," suggested Griffith at the second landing.

He stopped and watched Tito and Sara make their way down the third flight, the tiny light dancing over the dank walls. The narrow beam flittered over worn depressions and channels revealing some ancient stone carver's work. Small rusty splotches, fading drabs, and pale azure flecks hinted at the dimmed artistry of history.

A scrape across loose rock drifted down to Griffith. He turned his head, and the faint tread of feet reached his ear. People were above them. More than one, he knew.

"Sh-h-h," he whispered and reaching out for the near wall, he cautiously moved down the third flight.

"Someone's up there, children. We need to be quiet."

"What if they find us," asked Tito.

Griffith thought for moment. If any soldiers decided to search the tiny hole in the ground, they were effectively trapped.

Unless...

A dream memory surfaced. If a cave *were* at the bottom of this staircase, it might be a hiding place. He wasn't sure he wanted to know. Enough coincidences had already convinced too many people of the impossible. What would they think if he did find a cave?

"Tito," he whispered, "hand me the flashlight, please."

Without a sound, he flicked the light around. They were in a small, corbelled vault, its ceiling just inches above his head. In the center, filling the room nearly to the side walls, was a large stone slab resting over a wide base. The slab was carved and worn.

Despite the cool air of the stone chamber, Griffith began to sweat profusely. This was a burial chamber similar to the one in his dream. He wiped the sweat from his forehead and listened for a moment. Hearing nothing, he stretched over the sarcophagus and shone the flashlight on the back wall. More carved stone. He climbed part way onto the slab and looked at the back floor. Nothing there, either.

He breathed a sigh of relief. Sitting back on the cool, stone slab, he turned his ear upward.

"I don't hear anything?" Tito whispered.

"Me either, but perhaps we should stay down here a while longer," suggested Griffith.

"*Sí*," agreed Sara softly.

So they waited. Griffith shone their light over the walls and ceiling. Above their heads, two sweeping lines resembling long, feathered tails stretched from one corner across the angled ceiling and connected to a carved figure of a very stylized bird. He thought of Karen and how excited she'd been over visiting this ancient world. Everything had started so beautifully. *Na-Bolom*, the *Lagunas*, the first horseback ride through the jungle—it was all so romantic. Even the touching gift of the quetzal feather from Esmeralda. He wondered if it was still in her hair. Of course not, he realized. Feathers would hardly be standard prison issue.

"What a place," he whispered sadly.

"*Sí*," agreed Sara, echoing his bitterness. "I've learned much about my country."

"What? Oh, yes, me too. I'm sorry, I was thinking of Karen and a quetzal feather she was given at *Na-Bolom*."

"A good sign," suggested Tito.

"Of what?" asked Griffith.

"For us. Chan K'in said a bird dream was good."

"But it wasn't a dream, Tito. I was just reminiscing."

"It came from the same place you dream," answered Tito.

The irony of the President's son getting caught up in the mysticism of the *hach winik*'s belief system bothered Griffith's rational, skeptical biases.

"Tito," whispered Griffith, "it's important to know the difference between what's real and what's created inside our heads. Maybe you and your sister *can* help the *hach winik* get their land back. But if they're going to make it to the next century, they need more than dreams and superstitions."

"But this is what they believe, Griffith *ahau*," answered Sara.

"Sara," he replied, "if... when we get out of here, and if you succeed in your goals for them, they're going to have to find a way to live with the modern world because it is not going to leave them alone. If Chan K'in and Marina and the others don't learn how to deal with it, they'll just get exploited in a different way."

"Are you going to make them change their beliefs, Griffith *ahau*?" asked Tito.

"No, of course not, Tito. I'm not saying that. I can't make them do anything—I wouldn't anyway—but they'll have to learn about the modern world. Because their belief system is still based on a hunter/gatherer viewpoint, it's too easy for someone with a different world view, a different agenda, to take advantage of the wealth of these people—both the material and spiritual wealth."

"Sometimes I don't understand you, Griffith *ahau*," giggled Tito. "You sound like a professor."

"Because that's what I am, Tito. And I'm not their *ahau*, even if they say so."

"But isn't that their choice, Griffith *ahau*?" asked Sara. "And ours?"

"Well, yes, it is, Sara. But I have a choice, too. And my choice is to help you get out of this war zone so I can go home with my wife—who's probably in a Mexican jail right now. The idea of leading a group of people I know nothing about somewhere I'm completely ignorant of is way too arrogant for me."

"I see," replied Sara.

"But they need someone to help them," protested Tito. "Chan K'in said so. And they trust you. They don't trust anyone else."

"They have Marina and Chan Nuk, and all of them can learn. Look what Marina's done. And they have you two to help them. You're both very important."

"So you won't help?" asked Tito, unwilling to hide his disillusionment.

"Oh, Tito," conceded Griffith, "of course I'll do what I can. But I have to go back to the States with Karen when this is over."

"But Griffith *ahau*," replied Sara, "when this is over, won't the *hach winik* still need our help?"

"With me in Virginia and you in school, what do you suggest?"

"You and Karen could stay here and teach." said Tito.

"Tito," interrupted Sara, "that's not the answer."

"How do you know, Sara?"

"Because Griffith *ahau* has already shown us an answer." Sara patted the laptop. "He can teach us with computers."

"That's just technology, Sara," explained Griffith.

"*Sí*," countered Tito, "but Father can get lots of them."

"Tito, by themselves, computers are just a tool."

"So can't you teach everybody how to use the tools."

"Not as easily as you two can. You're in the same country."

"But you're a professor, and Karen's a teacher, too."

"Yes, Tito, but I teach physics. I don't know how much help that will be."

"Griffith *ahau*," said Sara, her voice low and confident. "You can teach us how to learn. Isn't that what's important?"

Teach us *how* to learn. Yes. Griffith had heard that same philosophy from Karen. He knew how rare it was for any school to rise above recitation and memory as basic education. Karen, however, had always insisted that once critical thinking skills were established, a slow but precise process at the elementary level, her students could do more than recite information—they'd be able to find a way to utilize that knowledge.

"After getting us all safely home, yes, Sara," he agreed, "you're right, of course. Learning how to apply their knowledge to this uncompromising new world is going to be most important for them."

"Then you'll help?" asked Tito.

"How about if we all do what we can?"

"Okay, Griffith *ahau*," answered Tito.

"Tito, Sara, do you suppose you could drop the *ahau* from my name? It makes me feel awkward."

"But Griffith *ahau*," said Sara, "it's very good politics."

"It's also perpetuating a myth."

"What's that mean?" asked Tito.

"It means I'm not really a lord from some mythical past."

"Of course not," agreed Sara, "but it will make more people listen with more interest."

"Wisdom from children of the millennium," said Griffith with some awe. "Another area I really don't understand very much. But then, my father was just a druggist in Culpeper, Virginia."

"Griffith *ahau*," reassured Sara, "your title tells others you are important. Nobody ever listened to the *hach winik* before. Perhaps now they will."

"Shouldn't people be listening to the truth rather than some fictionalized mysticism? You know, both of you are absolutely right about the *hach winik*. They need everything you've asked for, and a great deal more, but not because they believe some legend has come to life. Why does everything have to be wrapped and sold as some New Age, occult message when the reality is damning enough?"

"Because it's easy," answered Sara without hesitating. "And it will help, Griffith *ahau*. Trust us."

"Yes, well," sighed Griffith, "I've never had young people trust me like you two have—like you've had to—and since you've quite dramatically cast the die…"

"What's that mean, Griffith *ahau?*" asked Tito.

"We've already made our choice, Tito. We're in this together, to the end."

"See, Sara, I told you."

"But Tito," protested Sara, "he did object."

"Sara, not true. He agreed."

"Children," interrupted Griffith, "please?"

"See, Sara."

Griffith hoped this wouldn't continue until morning. It tired him to keep abreast of their wild swings between thoughtful young people and sniping adolescents.

Then, as if he heard Karen's voice, he realized they needed something to do. And he had it in his pocket—the lists of numbers Marina copied for him.

"Ah, look what I have," he said. "Turn on the light, Tito, please."

He took the two lists from his small side pouch and held them under Tito's light.

"What do you see on this list?" he asked

"Numbers," said Sara.

"What's on the other paper," asked Tito.

"More numbers. Here, Tito, Would you read them to me, please?"

He handed him the first list from the ransom note.

"Three-one-three, two-nine, seven-six..."

"Yes, that's kind of how I saw them."

"Griffith," said Sara, "Sometimes, like my brother, I don't understand you, either."

"He grouped the numbers by sets, not individually."

"Does that mean anything?" she asked. "They still look like numbers."

"Numbers, yes," he said, "but perhaps not just a list of

numbers. We naturally group things visually, just as Tito did when he read them—a three digit integer, then two pairs. This list may be more than randomly-generated numbers."

"What?" asked Tito.

"They could be prime numbers. At least the small groups look like it to me."

"What's a prime number?" Tito asked.

"They're very important numbers," he answered. "They're used for mathematical research and all kinds of equations and formulae. But there's something else they're used for that's very interesting."

"What?" asked Sara.

"But what's a prime number?" demanded Tito

"Good question, Tito," said Griffith. "Sara, do you know?"

"*Sí*, of course. I've studied mathematics. It's a number which can only be divided by one and itself."

"Look here, Tito," Griffith said. "Three's a prime, but so is thirty-one, and thirteen, and three hundred thirteen. All four can only be divided by one and the number itself."

"But what else are they used for?" asked Sara.

"They're used for cryptography."

"Cryptography?"

"Secret codes. For messages. Prime numbers make some of the best codes in the world. And the simple beauty of it starts with those first three numbers. A perfect example. Four primes in the first three numbers."

"Secret code for what?" asked Sara.

"Huh? Oh, right. These numbers came from your ransom note."

"When did you see the ransom note?"

"While you guys were filming. From your father's files."

"And you can figure this out?" asked Tito.

"No, I don't think so," he answered. "Only if it were the most simple prime code. These can get very complex very quickly. I studied it a little in a probabilities course once. A long time ago. Someone's even discovered the equivalent of prime words."

"Let's try," he said.

"It's probably going to be impossible without a program."

"Not if it were written in this country," replied Sara. "Even Tito understands computers better than Father, and he's the First Technocrat. It won't be that difficult."

He shook his head at her cynicism. Or maybe it was just optimism—a trait he admired in Karen.

"All right, then," he said, "let's take a look. Here's the first list."

"Look, there's three," Tito pointed out.

"And thirty-one and thirteen. Now, in the simplest code, numbers are substituted for letters. Running them together makes it more difficult to identify repeated letters and common short words like 'the' or 'and'."

"'Y' in Spanish," added Sara. "Only one letter."

"That's the idea, Sara. Now, since the number one isn't used for several reasons, let's make the letter 'a' a two, 'b' a three, and so on. Tito, if you write the alphabet above these prime numbers, we'll have our first key."

While Tito was writing, Sara held the light between Griffith and him.

"The first three could be 'b', or as thirty-one, it could be what, Tito?"

"'J'," said Tito.

"And 313 is prime, but it's too high for us to be able to use."

"Thirteen could be an 'e'," said Sara.

"Okay, let's try that. 'B' and 'E'. Now 'two' or 'twenty-nine' could be what?"

"'A' or 'I'," said Tito, finishing his writing.

He handed Griffith the short pencil, and Griffith began to write.

3 1 3 2 9 7 6 1 3 2 5 3 5 6 1 1 1...
B E A

He paused.

"Nine's not prime, but ninety-seven is. What letter, Tito?"

"Ninety-seven is 'V'."

"'V', then six, no, sixty-one, Tito?..."

"'O'. This is easy," exclaimed Tito.

3 1 3 2 9 7 6 1 3 2 5 3 5 6 1 1 1...
B E A V O

"Perhaps," muttered Griffith, "but next, we're limited to three and two again, 'B' or 'A', because 325 isn't prime and anything above that is too large for our code."

"And 'BEAVO' doesn't look like a word, anyway" added Sara.

"Not in English, either. How about this? Twenty-nine was 'I'?"

"*Sí.*"

"Then the seven would be 'd', so it could be..."

"Griffith," interrupted Tito. "Seven is 'ch'."

"No, Tito," he corrected. "'Ch' is a diphthong. 'D' would be the fourth letter."

"But in Spanish, 'ch' is," he insisted.

"The fourth letter?"

"Tito's right, Griffith," said Sara. "He sometimes is."

"Okay. So it might look like this."

3 1 3 2 9 7 6 1 3 2 5 3 5 6 1 1 1...
B E I CH O

"Very good. Then it's followed by three, two, five, three, which has to be 'BACB', or maybe 'BA'... what's fifty-three, Tito?"

"Griffith," interrupted Sara, "I don't think we have any words that begin 'beich', or 'bei', or even 'ich'."

"In English, either. Could be German, maybe. Well, this is typical. Lots of dead ends. Let's start over with thirty-one, then."

"'J'," said Tito.

"So it could start this way," said Griffith scratching out the first attempt.

3 1 3 2 9 7 6 1 3 2 5 3 5 6 1 1 1...
J B I CH O B A

"Any words there?" asked Griffith.

"'J—B?'" replied Tito.

"'*Bicho*' means bug," said Sara.

"Probably coincidental," said Griffith. "Anyway, the next five could only work as, let's see, it must be 'N'."

"Fifty-three" confirmed Tito. "This is fun."

"Another five," said Griffith. "Let's make this one a 'C'."

"And another 'O'," added Sara, "would spell something."

3 1 3 2 9 7 6 1 3 2 5 3 5 6 1 1 1 1 3...

J B I CH O B A N C O

"'Banco' means bank, doesn't it?"

"*Sí*," she replied, "but bug bank?"

"What about the 'J'?" asked Tito. "That doesn't make sense."

"Let's skip that for a moment. I like what Sara's found here."

Eleven and thirteen became 'DE', and when Griffith wrote down a 'P' for the next sixty-seven, Sara immediately spoke up.

"That's 'Panama'," she announced.

"Wow," said Griffith, "that was fast."

"It was easy," she replied. "We know 'N' is fifty-three, and 'O' is sixty-one. Then forty-seven and sixty-seven must be 'M' and 'P'. After the insect, it spells *'Banco de Panama.'*"

"My God, you're right," said Griffith.

6 7 2 5 3 2 4 7 2
P A N A M A

It took another minute to work through most of the rest.

JBICHO BANCO DE PANAMA BALBOA ACCT...

But they were stuck again.

1 3 7 1 2 7 1 5 7 1 3 7 3 1 3

As he mumbled some possible letter combinations, he recognized a pattern—"one—*x*—seven"—four times before it fell apart. At the end, three-one-three stood out from the rest. Then it came to him.

"Look here. The same three numbers open and close the list. Maybe we've got numbers for numbers before the last 'JB'. Let me see your list of primes again, Tito. Yes, look, the nine prime numbers following 109 could represent zero and the first nine integers. So the account number in the Balboa Branch of the Bank of Panama could be... let's see... yes, that works. It would be 3, 1, 7, and 3, and then 313 again at the end."

"Maybe," added Sara, "the 'JB' is part of the account number rather than a word. One of my accounts has my initials as part of it."

One of her accounts, he thought wryly. He didn't get his first bank account until he received the insurance from his parents' deaths and went away to college.

"So what does it mean?" asked Tito. "Besides the name of some guy's bank. Is that where Father got the money. How much was it?"

"A very large sum, Tito. About two and a half billion pesos. But it might also be where the ransom was supposed to go."

Before Griffith could explore the possibilities implied by their discovery, however, they were interrupted by a slip of loose stones and gravel echoing down to them. Muffled voices filtered down through the darkness.

"Absolutely quiet, children," whispered Griffith, placing his hand over Tito's flashlight.

"Griffith *ahau*?"

Marina's voice.

"Yes, *sí*," he replied, releasing his breath in a rush.

"It's safe for you and the children. The soldiers have left."

Stiff and cool from sitting for hours, they picked up their belongings and climbed the steep steps toward the surface. Turning the corner of the last flight, Griffith looked up. Through the tiny opening, a single star twinkled in an ink blue sky. They climbed the last eighteen steps.

The night was warmer than their underground sanctuary. The moon shone high and full, and the single star Griffith had seen from inside the cave faded in the bright, lunar night. The stench of ash and cordite clung to the ground. A few thin, wispy columns of smoke hung vaporous in the spectral moonlight, unmoved by the vagrant night breeze. Around them, the mountain top had been blasted clean of the *hach winik*'s efforts.

"Was anyone hurt?" Griffith asked Marina.

Even in the lunar light, Griffith saw the tight creases outlining her eyes.

"They killed three. All *Haawo*. The *hach winik* found refuge in the jungle. They will wait until you tell them to return."

"Chan K'in and Chan Nuk?"

"They're both safe."

"Will they be all right in the jungle?"

"Even without shelter, it's still their home."

"Then they should stay away until this is resolved."

"*Sí*, I agree."

"Marina," he asked, "why did the soldiers leave?"

"It became too dangerous for them in the jungle." She reported this with some pride in her voice. "Especially once it got dark. We allowed them to leave with their wounded. As your Word, none of them was killed."

"You drove them away?" he asked unnecessarily.

"They'll use a different strategy next time."

"And I'm sure you'll be ready for them," replied Griffith, hoping he sounded sincere rather than amazed. "Should we stay here the rest of the night?"

"Let's try the computer again," suggested Tito.

"Okay, Tito," said Griffith. "You two set it up."

"I think," said Marina as the children got out the equipment, "we should stay near your cave."

"I don't think it's a cave," interjected Griffith. "The walls and steps are carved."

"*Sí*, you're correct. But traditionally, they lead to a true cave. *Lo siento*, Griffith *ahau*," she apologized, "you already know about *Xibalba*'s cave." Then she smiled. "But the door to the Underworld is a good place to hide from death, don't you think?"

Griffith appreciated the irony, but her deference to his supposed knowledge of their culture didn't seem to be helping them off the mountain. He knew the only way he could have dreamed about a cave at the bottom of a temple was if he had read or heard about such a tradition. Pointing that out, however, wasn't going to alter what people had chosen to believe.

"Also," continued Marina, "we have a new perimeter set up, and our runners are in place across the savannah. I don't think they'll surprise us."

"Will anything happen tonight?" asked Sara.

"Probably not, Sara," she answered. "Their young soldiers aren't very comfortable in the jungle, and the night can frighten anyone."

"We're ready, Griffith *ahau*," announced Tito.

Griffith typed in his number, and they waited. After several minutes of random noises, he punched it off and shut the antenna.

"Still cut off, aren't we?" asked Sara.

"Yes," he replied. "We just have to hope your father got your first transmission."

"I'm sure he did, Griffith *ahau*," said Tito. "It was a very good idea."

"Well, it hasn't seemed to work so far."

"I'm glad," said Tito.

"Glad?" asked Griffith. "You're glad it hasn't work?"

"No, I'm glad we're still together."

Griffith was touched.

"For another night anyway, huh? And look here." Griffith pointed to the bedrolls laid out for them on the ground. "A bed under the stars."

Still hours until dawn, the three of them curled up together, mostly for the added sense of security. Within minutes their breathing was relaxed and somnolent. During the night Marina walked her perimeter twice, watching the distant *Laguna* for activity. Across the valley, an occasional helicopter flew into the army's camp beyond the savannah. Other than that, she saw nothing.

The night remained warm and quiet. After midnight, a small thunderstorm passed west of them, over *Laguna Miramar*. The rest of the night, the full moon bathed the mountain in its false, pale light.

CHAPTER TWENTY-THREE
THE THREAT

Puuc Witz
Wednesday dawn

> Fear tastes like a rusty knife
> and do not let her into your house.
> Courage tastes of blood.
>
> *The Wapshot Chronicle*
> John Cheever
> 1912—1982

The dawn broke pink with streaks of orange and red reflecting under high cirrus clouds. On the mountain, the smell of burned-out fires, chemical and natural, lingered in the mist. Billows of misty blankets hugged the mountainside and stretched across the savannah hiding *Laguna Miramar*. The shadow of *Puuc Witz* still covered the valley.

Griffith rose with thoughts of his reunion with Karen. He couldn't recall any dreams, but he'd awakened aroused and anxious to end this walking nightmare. He wanted this to be the day.

Auroral light crept across the savannah, stirring the morning fog and chasing the shadows of *Puuc Witz* from the valley. A young *bach winik* woman brought him and the children a breakfast of scrambled eggs, *chiles*, and tomatoes wrapped in warm *tortillas*. They ate without talking.

After they finished, Griffith decided to attempt another link up, thinking the early hour might catch someone asleep. It may have, since they did connect to a server, but before they completed the links, the signal was lost. Tito dialed again but made no connection. He folded him arms in adolescent disgust.

"Patience, *niño*," encouraged Marina. "You've sent your message, and your father needs time to react."

"Yeah," added Griffith, "like the twenty-four hours they *didn't* give us."

"That was odd, wasn't it," she replied.

"Odd?" said Griffith. "It didn't seem that way to me. Isn't that what they do—attack with helicopters and blow up everything?"

"So it seems, but why at that moment?" she wondered. "Why in the middle of your broadcast? And last night more helicopters flew in."

"They intend to take us with force," concluded Griffith. "I suppose I knew it would come to this."

"If Father received our message," said Sara, "I don't think they would attack us. He'd be afraid for our lives."

"Yours, certainly," replied Griffith. "I'm not so sure Marina and the *bach winik* will get the same protection."

"And I," said Marina, "will not trust their intentions regarding your life, either, Griffith *ahau*."

"And neither will we," added Tito.

"Thank you," said Griffith. "I, uh, I...thanks."

He lowered his eyes and scratched the ground with the toe of his sneaker. He wanted to tell them how grateful he felt, how their concern touched him, but their uncertain future silenced his anxious heart.

One of the *Haawo* appeared among them and spoke quickly

with Marina. Even with most of the plateau's brush now burnt off, the hunter had crossed to them completely unnoticed by Griffith. He was awed by these people who movements blended so easily with their environment.

But their attitude toward him still baffled him. Why would such generous, confident people turn to someone from the very culture responsible for their diaspora four centuries ago? And for their existence on the edge of extinction today?

"Griffith *ahau?*"

"Yes, *sí*, Marina. Go ahead. You don't have to wait for permission. You're the one keeping us alive."

"Although more troops have arrived at their camp," she said, "an attack doesn't appear imminent. The runners say they're digging in."

"What does that mean?" he asked.

"Certainly a change in tactics. Perhaps they've received new orders."

Tito was looking to west, listening to their conversation, when two more *Haawo* appeared at the western staircase.

"I think something is happening," the boy said quietly.

From across the plateau, the *Haawo* faced them. One of them pointed across the valley and gestured in a way Griffith assumed was word specific. First thrusting her left arm out parallel to the ground, palm down, the *Haawo* then swung it across her waist and back. From the elbow, she raised her fist twice. The gestures were quick, and she repeated them once.

"Two helicopters have taken off from the *Laguna*," Marina said. "They're heading this way."

"Only two helicopters?" he said. "Try the Net, again, kids, by the Temple."

"I'll be close by," said Marina.

Griffith glanced around as she disappeared and saw only

the quivering grass of her passing. In that tiny moment, the dark eroticism of this powerful woman of the rain forest hit him. Like the great cats, both sensuous and dangerous, she swept invisibly through her verdant world. He was drawn to confident women, like Karen and Marina. Even the physical and cultural differences between these two women couldn't mask their similarities. Griffith understood how people, himself included, gained strength from them.

Sara tapped him on the shoulder and, holding up the phone, shook her head. To conserve the batteries, everything was turned off, and the three of them returned to the Temple where Marina was waiting for them.

At the small temple entrance, more rocks and scrub brush had been built up. *Xibalba*'s mouth appeared as nothing more than deep shadows. The whole area was now little more than ruined limestone, short grasses, and burnt patches.

With an ear to the west, Griffith paced. His pulse throbbed at his temples, and sweat ran down his ribcage. In the moments before the subsonic throb of the metal blades touched their ears, his thoughts swung wildly between their certain innocence and his quantifiable experiences with the authorities. His flight instincts grew more convincing as he heard the helicopters approach. Even the innocent needed to hide at times.

"I'm ready to become invisible," he told everyone, trying to keep the conditioned fear out of his voice. "Will you join us, Marina?"

"I think this time I will, *gracias*."

Within minutes they'd settled themselves several yards inside the entrance, ready to move deeper into *Xibalba*'s temple when the attack began. The numbing vibration of the helicopters rose over *Puuc Witz*. Griffith listened for the onset of explosives pounding the earth.

"Be ready to head downstairs," he whispered into the dark.

Caught between burrowing into the earth or raising his arms in surrender, he shivered in his own fears. But the helicopters only hovered. As each minute stretched interminably under the roaring voices in the air, Griffith's anxiety ate at him.

"*Señor* **Grant!**"

His name came booming, metallic and wind-swept, from powerful speakers in the sky.

They know my name!

"*Señor* **Grant.** *Cerro San Felipe* **is completely surrounded. There is no escape. Come out of the jungle with your hands above your head, and bring your hostages with you. You have one minute.**"

Hostages! So his plan had failed. All he'd done was pinpoint their location. His shoulders and arms trembled so violently he intertwined his fingers into a single, tight fist against his chest, trying to control his palsied fear. Now he and all the *hach winik* were about to become innocent prisoners in a foreign government's war. And that was the best he could hope for.

He peered into the shadows below for the children. They had folded their hands to their chests and lowered their heads. He shook his head. What kind of an education, he wondered, relied on miracle-working gods and religious mythology to deal with the practical problem of guns aimed at you? Not that he knew what to do, he admitted, but he didn't believe supplication would get them safely topside.

But surrender might. Just tell them what happened. They could do that. He took one long breath, emptied his lungs, and... decided to remain hidden. Too much weaponry and too many terrifying experiences for him to trust heavily armed, single-minded soldiers. Underground seemed the best place right now.

He shook his head and released the white knuckle grip on his hands. The children relaxed with him and lifted their heads. He was about to suggest they head down the stairs when the voice boomed out of the sky again.

"*Señor* **Grant. It is time to surrender the hostages. There will be no negotiations. We have your wife's confession."**

Griffith's head jerked toward the entrance. He crawled near the entrance, cocking an ear upward. A gentle hand on the back of his shoulder kept him from exposing himself.

"Marcos has confessed. It is time to give up the hostages and return the ransom. If you surrender immediately, we will hold our fire. If you do not, you will never see your wife alive."

Griffith scrunched back inside. He faced Marina. With the light to his back, his terrified eyes and quivering lips were hidden from her.

"What do they mean?" he asked weakly. "They don't mean they'd just kill her, do they?"

"*Señor* Grant. You have one last chance. Surrender the children and the ransom now, and you will receive a fair trial in our courts. If you do not, you will force us to execute Karen Grant immediately for abetting terrorism against the state and murder."

"What?" gasped Griffith. "How can they do that? They can't do that, can they?"

"In one minute, we will return your dead wife to you."

"Oh my God, she's here! They've got her in the helicopter!"

Griffith swung his head, first toward the entrance, then to the others, and back again. His sucked in gulps of air. Small, mewling noises scratched over his dry tongue.

"She's here. I've got to go out there," he rasped.

"Griffith *ahau*," protested Marina, "you can't do that."

"I have to," he said. "Can't you see that? I can't let them kill her."

"But Griffith *ahau*, it might be a bluff," suggested Marina. "If she were a prisoner, wouldn't they have her in jail, not here."

"How can I take that chance?" he asked.

"Then let me find out."

She crawled past Griffith to the entrance.

"We don't have time," he said to her.

But she was already at the entrance.

"Be careful," he pleaded.

She looked at him and placed her fingertips on his sternum.

"I will, Griffith *ahau*."

Holding his breath, Griffith watched her crawl part way out of the shadowy entrance. A few seconds later, she slid back into the temple and looked at Griffith, locking eyes with his for a moment before she spoke.

"Karen is in the helicopter farthest from us, toward the east. I'm sorry. If you need to go out, we'll try to protect you."

Her voice was low, barely audible over the noise, but Griffith heard her sadness.

"Griffith," said Tito, "don't give up. Didn't Marina say it's kill or be killed?"

"Oh, Tito," he said, "I don't even have that choice."

"But you said we were together," he protested, "and you'd help save the *hach winik*'s land. If we're right, won't God protect Karen?"

"Tito, I've got to save Karen, not God. Maybe after this is over, we can help the *hach winik*."

"But you said!" cried Tito. "I don't understand. Everybody said you could save us... save everything. You can't leave. You're their Lord, Griffith *ahau*. Don't you believe in us?"

"Marina? Sara? Do either of you understand?"

"*Sí*, Griffith *ahau*," said Marina, making sure her voice was clear and could be heard by all of them. "I have come to trust you for more reasons than even Chan K'in. Since I believe your choice must be correct, I and the *Haawo* will do what we can to help you fulfill your Word as *ahau*."

Pushed to the edge of his temper by their insane idea he was some kind of avatar, his anger slid like a dagger from its sheath.

"Marina!" His voice shook. "Children. Listen to me! I am not your *ahau*. I can't save you. I'm not a god. Nobody is. Not anyone. There are no gods to save us!"

Honed and pointed, the keen blade of his fury aimed at the ceaseless fears and expectations sucking his passion from every cell and organ. Each bleeding, festering indignation burst into blistering rage, eager to pierce someone, anyone, with his righteous ire.

"Don't you see? We're trapped. No one's going to rescue us. No one's going to miraculously right all the wrongs. Karen and I tried, and here we are. This is what's real. We're responsible for what's happening to us. We tried everything we could, and we failed. I failed!

"Nobody's going to help. No gods! No legends! Nobody! Damn, I should have known."

"Nevertheless," said Marina softly, "I will go outside with you."

"And I don't want Karen to die, either," said Sara. "They won't shoot if I'm with you."

"Me, too," added Tito. "I'm sorry, Griffith *ahau*. I didn't understand."

"Oh, Tito," replied Griffith, "thank you, all of you, but your lives would be in even more danger."

"But we have to save Karen now," he answered. "And you need me, too."

Griffith sighed deeply and in a voice filled with resignation and gratitude said, "Yes, I guess I do."

He lowered his head and considered how best to show themselves without getting everyone shot. The children watched him intently, their heads cocked sideways.

"I should go out first," he decided. "I don't want to upset their expectations and have them start shooting at everything that moves. I'll need something to wave, a white flag or something before I stick my head out."

Before anyone could respond, Marina unsheathed her hunting knife and proceeded to cut nearly a foot off the hem of her *xikul*. The shredding of the tough material tugged at his ear. He had to shake himself loose from a much too poignant memory of Karen.

"*Señor* **Grant. Your time is up. Do you come from hiding in the jungle, or do I execute your wife now and hunt you down like a rat?**"

"Quick," said Griffith, taking the white cloth and turning toward the children. "Tito and Sara, stay close behind me, and be ready to dive back in if anyone starts shooting."

Marina slipped out the entrance before Griffith could stop her and disappeared into the shadows of the ruins. With a deep exhalation of breath, he climbed through the entrance, holding the white flag firmly before him. The children crawled into place behind him.

Outside, he stood, nearly blind in the bright sunlight and its reflection off the white limestone ruins. The wash from the nearest helicopter, almost directly above them, whirled dust and ashes into the air, stinging his eyes and burning his nostrils. Blinking away the tears, he waved Marina's flag over his head. The children crowded behind him, holding onto the back of his *xikul*. Griffith couldn't see Marina hidden among the rocks, but he wasn't going to draw any unnecessary attention by looking for her. He kept waving the cloth.

Through the dust, the farther helicopter pivoted toward the eastern rim of *Puuc Witz*. Its wash bent the branches of the nest tree of the quetzals, one of the few unscorched trees remaining. Turned sideways, the helicopter's open hatch was on the far side, facing the forest. Griffith strained to pick out Karen's blonde hair through the ports, but grit blew into his eyes and coated his lashes. He waved the white flag more broadly.

A dark-visored helmet looked down and pointed toward them. The pilot slowly swung the helicopter around until the sun glinted off the ventilated barrel of a machine gun mounted in the open hatch. The gunner lowered the muzzle directly at him.

Griffith was about to shout at the children to flee when he saw her blonde hair. She was lying on the deck of the helicopter. Another soldier appeared out of the dark interior and roughly lifted her to her knees. He grabbed a handful of her hair and yanked her head up. She jerked her head free from his grip and screamed soundlessly through the roar of the engines.

Griffith's heart tightened.

CHAPTER TWENTY-FOUR
THE SACRIFICE

Puuc Witz
Wednesday dawn

> I acknowledge the Furies, I believe in them,
> I have heard the disastrous beating of their wings.
> *To Grant Richards*
> Theodore Dreiser
> 1871—1945

Her heart was racing, pumping heat throughout her body, warming even her cheek as it lay on the cold, ribbed metal deck. Each time Griffith's name blasted through the loudspeaker, her spirit lifted. It had been a week of such terror and pain for her, she rejoiced in knowing Griffith was still alive. With every bloodied bruise, with each scab scraped open by her clumsy captors, the pain told her she was alive and her lover was free of these monsters.

During this past week, she'd learned how to feign unconsciousness because virtually every time she had awakened, one of her captors had taken it upon himself to see how quickly he could beat her back into oblivion. But here, when one of them grabbed her by her bound wrists and waistband and lifted her completely off the cabin deck, banging her head against one of the ceiling mounts, she opened her swollen eyes. Fresh blood ran through her filthy scalp. The soldier was strong enough to turn her, still dangling in the air, toward the open hatch and force her onto her knees. He yanked her head up by her hair.

She blinked several times, trying to regain her focus in the sunlight. They were hovering over a clearing on top of a single, flattened mountain peak. Burnt scars stood out from the green of the surrounding jungle, and areas of gray and bleached white rubble dotted the plateau. On a small hill in the center stood Griffith waving a long piece of white cloth over his head. He was dressed in a *xikul*, but even at this distance, she knew immediately it was Griffith. And standing with him were Tito and Sara, clad like all the Lacandon children, holding onto his *xikul* and staring up at this black, metal beast.

She had feared she'd never see any of them again. From the moment she'd broken the surface of the stormy lake, her overriding concern and her source of strength had been the lives of her husband and the children. She was worried for Rafael, but had learned nothing of his situation. For seven days, she'd been captive—not even a prisoner since she'd gotten to see no one except her inquisitors. She'd not been given any kind of procedural rights and not been charged with any crime. For this past week, despite her protestations and willingness to tell them everything, they had chosen to believe that leaving *don* Pedro's with the children was exactly how a *gringa* terrorist would act.

Since they wouldn't accept her story of the rancher's apparent collusion with the real kidnappers or the coincidental availability of a government plane, they had felt obligated to utilize less sophisticated methods of extracting information. To their frustration, the physical abuse, first with its open-handed beatings on her face and breasts and then the blind side punches intended to knock her out, never resulted in any changes to her story.

Most days she was given only *tortillas* and water. For two

days, however, she had endured almost total sensory deprivation. Left naked in a stone cell, her only stimuli were the screams of the other immured souls. Each moment of shared horror only exacerbated her own utter helplessness.

Inadvertently, her captors' unabashed barbarity had taught her how to survive. Despite the onslaught of their physical, sexual, and psychological abuse—perhaps because of it—Karen had learned to separate her psyche from the body forced to endure their depravity. The screams from the blows and burns were all hers, but during those moments between each vicious invasion of her body, she had found enough strength to survive by telling herself Griffith and the children needed her alive.

She had endured. Even the blood between her thighs from the hard rubber baton they had used for more than raising welts had eventually stopped and dried.

Now, finally, she could see Griffith and the children. The man whose unquestioning love made her ache with passion and the children whose lives had come to depend on him were in sight. She had survived to find them, and there they stood, waving for attention and completely exposed to this unconscionable version of justice.

Inured to the pain, she tore her hair free from her captor's hand and screamed. The wash from the rotors blew her voice away. She threw her head and shoulders back and forth so violently she almost lost her balance. The soldier yanked her upright by her bound wrists, grabbed her hair again, and jerked her head back.

In the distance, above the valley, more aircraft were flying toward them. All her life she'd been taught never to give up, and throughout her imprisonment, even when her body longed for release into oblivion, she'd honestly believed they would all survive. In this moment, however, when she saw the fleet of helicopters, a dozen or more, all shapes and sizes, converging on them, her heart knew people were going to die

From behind her, the commanding officer shouted to the soldier at the machine gun.

"Gunner! Take him out."

Those words, the ultimate threat, the final challenge to Karen, ignited the fuse to the rage they'd pounded into her. She watched the gunner closely, every sense sparked into predatory focus.

"*Comandante*," he shouted, "I'll hit the children."

"What? Then use your rifle, *Cabo*! Take him out now!"

"*Comandante*, I'm a machine gunner."

"What about you?" he demanded of the *judicial* who held Karen.

"*Sí, Comandante*," he shouted.

"Can you take him out?"

"*Sí, Comandante*," he answered. "I have my weapon."

All that Karen had endured as their prisoner, all the human degradation and bestial misogyny, congealed in intense concentration. Nothing intruded. No pain or doubt interfered with her focus. Conscious thought was silenced as she absorbed everything with feline attention. Scents of machines and men were strong, even in the buffeting wind of the open hatch. In a single flowing image, she held each soldier's position and his relation to Griffith, the angle of the sun on the black deck below her, the scream of the engine, and the vibrations through her knees.

The other air traffic had arrived. None of the helicopters were like the black military Hueys which had haunted their entire honeymoon. Among the small fleet, the insect shape of a few open-framed ultra-lights hung behind the turbulence of the others.

"*Comandante*," the pilot said, "with all due respect, sir, weren't our orders updated?"

"Men were shot only yesterday, *Teniente*. Or have you forgotten already?" He stared at the lieutenant. "So if you will just hold the aircraft steady, we can end this terrorist threat. And, *sí*, we will rescue *el Presidente*'s precious children, as well. But I will not have any more of *our* precious men ambushed by these ignorant savages."

He turned to the corporal holding Karen in the open hatch.

"Put the *gringa* down, *Cabo*, and take the terrorist out immediately."

"*Sí, Comandante*."

The corporal dragged Karen away from the hatch and dumped her against the far side bulkhead. He picked up his rifle and checked the action and clip. He released his harness and reached forward to reclip it. The *Comandante* yelled.

"Now, *Cabo*! They're fleeing!"

"*Sí, Comandante*."

The corporal dropped the end of his harness and stepped to the hatch. Before releasing his grip on the ceiling bar, he asked the gunner to grab the back of his belt.

Karen's focus narrowed to the corporal. Away from their immediate attention, she rolled over onto her haunches. Balancing on her fervent, one-pointed intent to save her husband, she leaned back with her bound wrists behind her pressing against the cool metal bulkhead.

She would make this predator prey.

"Now, *Cabo*!"

Bracing his left elbow on his knee, the marksman raised his rifle to his right shoulder. He pressed his cheek against the stock and located his target.

The adrenaline rushed into Karen's legs. Without any hesitation, void of all doubts, her own fears obliterated by irrational passion, she launched herself at the man who threatened her love. With the full force of her back and legs, she drove the point of her shoulder into his exposed ribs. She felt one of his ribs crack with the explosion of air she crushed from his lung.

He never fired a shot. The rifle jumped out of his hands and clanged against the skids as it fell out the open hatch. The force of her attack tore the gunner's hold on the marksman's belt loose, ripping off two of his fingernails. Together, she and the assassin became airborne.

The downward blast of the blades hit her. Bathed in the brilliance of morning light, she plummeted toward the green embrace of *Puuc Witz*. Unable to control her fall, her body tumbled wildly to the earth. Just as the last of her consciousness was spun from her head, she flushed with contentment.

Griffith was alive.

CHAPTER TWENTY-FIVE
CONFRONTATION

Puuc Witz
Wednesday dawn

> This is death and the sole death,
> When a man's loss comes to him from his gain,
> Darkness from light, from knowledge ignorance,
> And lack of love from love made manifest.
> *Death in the Desert*
> Robert Browning
> 1812—1889

The irresistible imminence of danger froze Griffith's arm in mid-air. As he watched the black-clad *judicial* struggle with Karen in the open hatch of the helicopter, Griffith stared in dumb catatonia. Karen wanted him to flee with the children, and he was rigid with fear. When he saw her head jerked back, however, his paralysis shattered in a stunning realization of their intent.

"Back to the cave!" he shouted at the children, pushing them toward the entrance.

They ran, stumbling over the rocks and darting around bushes and boulders. Unable to see through the dust the other helicopter was churning, Tito tripped over a gnarled root and tumbled crying to the ground. Before he could shake his head clear from the fall, Griffith hauled him up with his right arm and kept running.

Sara reached the pile of cut blocks surrounding the Temple site and turned to see Griffith carrying her brother close behind. She looked up through the swirling dust at the farther helicopter. Her hands flew to her mouth, and her eyes widened. A scream burst from her, so piercing and uncontrolled that Griffith shuddered to a stop. He dropped Tito on his feet and spun around.

Seized by the unutterable reality of the instant, his terrified heart cried out, trying to freeze time with its agonized denial. Long, swirling blonde hair spiraled downward from the sky, searing the ghastly image into his scarred heart. Deaf to the roar of the helicopters above him, blind to the sniper slamming into the ground, all he knew was the mangled horror of crushed bones as Karen's body bounced off the earth, twisted once, and landed again.

He broke. Oblivious of the danger from above, unconscious of the dozen other helicopters looming over the western staircase, he pushed the children toward the temple and ran. His thoughts ceased to exist as he sprinted, disregarding any fragment of reality which might prevent him from getting to her. Down the hill and across the plateau, kicking up the ashes of burnt grass, he raced to her.

He stumbled to a skidding halt and landed on his knees beside her body. His heart bloated into an aching knot. His lungs heaved in sucking drafts. Reaching to lift her twisted body from the dirt, he hesitated, searching for the incandescent spark of life which had been his wife. He lifted a lock of bloodied hair from her face.

Nothing. Within the mangled corpse, Karen wasn't there.

Opening his mouth, the uncontrolled feral agony of his tormented soul ripped from his chest. His scream spun anguished in the wild air, and he collapsed in desperate sobs over her.

Behind him, the helicopter landed. An officer stepped out. In his black uniform, he stood spider-like in the middle of the bloody web he'd woven. He held his sidearm at ready. He twisted his head toward the stunned and frightened children. Sara pulled Tito's arm, and they ran toward their hidden shelter among the Temple rocks.

"Halt!" he shouted at them.

Muscles rippled across his narrow jaw, and his head jerked from side to side scanning his surroundings. He raised his pistol to fire over their heads. The instant he squeezed off the round, the *Haawo* emerged as if rising from the earth and surrounded him, their arrows nocked and aimed.

The crack of the pistol shot brought Griffith's head up. Gasping for air, his heart filled with a frightening guilt. He'd left the children alone, not even knowing if they'd gotten into *Xibalba*'s cave.

"Put down your weapons," shouted the officer, "or we'll open fire."

Griffith understood the *judicial*'s intent without understanding his Spanish. Squeezing Karen's body to his chest, he lifted her and turned. Six of the *Haawo*, including Marina, appeared between him and the helicopter. Other *Haawo* surrounded the children, and still more the helicopter, their arrows pointed at the pilot and machine gunner. The *judicial* glared, trying to mask his fear with the might of technological intimidation. His pistol quivered in his hand.

The needle of immediacy stabbed Griffith, engulfing him in its eternal, suffocating presence. He gagged in the deluge of blood and thunder flooding his world. Out of the sodden ashes of his anguish, Griffith forced himself to his feet, straining to lift Karen's body with his right arm. The thorny spike of unremitting fear deep within his spirit ripped free. He spit the bile from his tongue.

"No!" His words tore through the din. "Stop it!"

The officer spun to face him.

A shard of death-filled terror cut into Griffith's stomach. The strength drained from his legs. He sank to his knees, Karen still cradled in his arms. Mortally afraid and righteously defiant, he looked directly at the armed authority of the Mexican government. With one last effort, he shouted from the depths of his bloodied rage. His voice cut through the turbulent air, resonating deeply and directly at his adversary.

"Stop the killing!"

Griffith's simple words, his Word, hung between them, demanding and damning.

The *judicial* stared back. A moment later, he twisted his head to the right. His pilot and crew held their arms in the air. The *judicial* cocked his jaw to the sky. For the first time, he noticed the other helicopters—which weren't his at all—hovering and jostling for position as they circled the mountain.

In the hatch of the nearest one, the lens of a large camera reflected a spark of sunlight into his eyes. He blinked and recoiled at the large, blue letters painted on the side of the helicopter.

CNNI.

The officer snapped his focus back to Griffith.

"¡Qué tristeza, amigo!" he shouted with a grin.

With deliberate precision, he aimed his pistol at him. As the dark metal barrel swung toward Griffith, the *Haawo* archers of the *hach winik*, the last hunters of the rain forest, loosed their arrows.

CHAPTER TWENTY-SIX
XU'TAN

Puuc Witz
Wednesday dawn

> Contemporary man has rationalized the myths,
> but he has not been able to destroy them.
> Octavio Paz
> 1914—1998

Of all the live pictures flashing through cyberspace and into the broadcasting studios around the world that morning, one image dominated the world's attention—Griffith on his knees, barely able to hold his dead wife, his quetzal feather caught by the wind floating above his shoulder, his angry countenance and frightened eyes pleading to the sky. Among the hundreds of stories filling the television screens, a single picture captured the emotional conscience on every continent and in every city and village with access to world events. Frozen forever in time by the media, Griffith knelt in his bloodied *xikul*, embracing Karen's body, exhorting the heavens with his grief.

"Stop the Killing!" was about to become the sound byte to rally the Third World around the rights of the *hach winik*.

The children's message *had* been heard, generating a frantic clamor for more information throughout the Web and in every news agency branch office from Cancún to Tuxtla Gutiérrez.

Overnight, dozens of reporters, cameramen, and hackers already in country to cover the kidnapping converged on San Cristóbal to the west and Palenque to the north, scrambling to rent, buy, bribe, or steal a way into the rain forest. Since last night, taxis, rental cars, VW vans, and even open-framed ultra-lights had been pouring into *la Selva Lacandona*. Leading the way in their fleet of helicopters, the forward media guard lifted off at first light with their cameras and reached *Puuc Witz* in time to capture Karen's dramatic sacrifice and the quick disarming of the *Policía Judicial Federal* by primitive hunters.

Real-time pictures of the *hach winik* warriors awed the world with moving evidence of their skill and courage. One of their arrows had pierced the officer's forearm, and a second perfect shot had penetrated the back of his hand, driving the pistol from his grip. The cameras broadcast their live pictures from the air as he lay screaming through gritted teeth.

When the media helicopters began landing, the pilot and gunner aloft in the second black helicopter hesitated, uncertain of their orders. They had seen their CO go down, but the press of other eyes and cameras swooping in stalled their reaction. With the other pilot and gunners disarmed on the ground, the crew in the air decided to hold their position.

Griffith, too, had seen the officer fall. More blood. He slumped to his haunches and whispered choked apologies to the body of his wife. Over her battered corpse, he murmured his ache of incomprehension into the suffocating void.

The first reporter on the ground sprinted toward him, leaving his cameraman to struggle behind with the equipment. Others jumped from their helicopters before skids had settled. Two of them ran to the hunters surrounding the captured officer, others toward the children and Marina, and the rest converged on Griffith.

After days of terrified flight and isolation, Griffith no longer wanted to see anyone. Overcome with a ponderous inertia, he was empty of thought and emotion save his wrenching sorrow. As the first reporter ran up, the nearest *Haawo*, suspicious and protective, blocked the path to Griffith.

Out of breath and shaking with excitement, the reporter leaned around the *Haawo* and introduced himself. In Spanish, he told Griffith he was from CNN International. Griffith lifted his head and stared at him through puffy, red eyes. His beard glistened with drying blood and saliva. Tears washed muddy streaks across his cheeks.

The reporter introduced himself again, this time in English. Griffith, unable to form an articulate response, turned back to the body he cradled in his arms. The cameraman stumbled up behind the reporter, relieved not to have missed anything. The reporter then asked the *Haawo* if this man were the Griffith *ahau* who had spoken on the World Wide Web. The hunter remained expressionless.

As Tito, Sara, and Marina made their way to their grieving *ahau*, the cameraman set up quickly and started filming. Marina hand-gestured for the *Haawo* to hold their positions around their prisoner and his helicopter crew and to shield Griffith and the children more tightly.

By now a half dozen other journalists representing several Mexican newspapers, two television networks, and foreign magazines from France and Peru, crowded toward them with their cameramen and microphones. They shouted questions in different languages and transmitted their live pictures back to the relay stations. Uplink satellites connected their signals to computers and televisions around the world, including UVA's physics lab and the private office of *el Presidente*. The questions rolled over one another.

"Why are you here, Griffith *ahau*?"

"Are the children all right?"

"Do your soldiers control any other areas?"

"Why did you come back now, Lord *ahau*?"

Vulnerable, unable to deny the preeminence of this apocalyptic reality, Griffith kept his head down. Believing the nightmare had finally swallowed him into its yawning maw, he wept quietly, each tear spilling onto the pale flesh of Karen's cheek.

"Please," he whispered unheard, "go away."

"Will you release your captives in exchange for open negotiations?"

"Are the legends about you true?"

"How did you call your people to this place?"

Sara moved in front of Griffith and faced the reporters and the glass eyes of their cameras. Tito found his way next to her, and together they intercepted the flood of questions. Years of living with the crowds and reporters who routinely surrounded their father had accustomed them to the media's insistent behavior. Sara stood straight, her long, dark hair with its single quetzal feather prominent against her *xikul*. She placed her arm around Tito's shoulder and held up her other hand. She kept her voice low and steady, stifling the flow of questions.

"I want our father, *el Presidente*, to hear this." She paused until everyone was silent and focused on her. "Griffith Grant, *ahau* of the *hach winik*, has just lost his wife because of the *Policía Judicial Federal*."

More questions erupted from the small crowd. As she raised her hand to continue her impromptu statement, one last question flew out, catching her off guard.

"Did Griffith *ahau* order the capture of *Comandante* Bicho?"

"Who?" replied Sara, gripping Tito's shoulder to hide her surprise.

Even Griffith looked up when he heard Bicho's name.

"*Comandante* Juan Bicho of the *PJF*," one of them answered and pointed to the *judicial* surrounded by *Haawo* archers.

He was sitting up in pain, still bleeding, having refused the offer of aid from one of the hunters. Nevertheless, he was talking forcefully at the two reporters who were being escorted away by the *Haawo*.

The children turned to Griffith, away from the cameras. The expression on his face mirrored their own recognition of Bicho's name. He shook his head once in tacit answer to their questioning look.

Sara turned back to the cameras and ignored the continuing questions. She waited, clearly indicating her unwillingness to talk over the noise by the way she held her head. She made eye contact with each reporter until she silenced them.

"Nine days ago," she began, "Griffith and Karen Grant, who were here on their honeymoon, rescued my brother and me from our kidnappers. We were forced to keep running until the *hach winik* took us in and healed Griffith *ahau* who was dying. They recognized the special message he brought in his dreams and have come to these sacred ruins where Griffith *ahau* led us. Until today, we had no idea where Karen Grant was."

"Why did she fall from the helicopter?" interrupted the Peruvian journalist.

Not every one had seen what had happened although the CNNI cameraman had caught it on tape. Their real-time link hadn't been established until after they'd landed, but the tape of Karen's heroics was now looped and ready to feed a world hungry for heroism.

"I'm sure," continued Sara, "our father will want to know the answer to your question. It's time for him to come here and see what everyone, including the *PJF*, has done to these people, the original, rightful inhabitants of the rain forest.

"Tell our father and mother their children are still safe. *Comandante* Bicho will remain here until our father arrives. The military helicopters and their crews should leave the jungle."

The moment she finished, they fired more questions at her. This fourteen-year-old, who just a week ago was a frightened and abused child-hostage, now commanded the attention of a fascinated planet. She had grown from an aloof, pretty girl in white lace and linen to a handsome young woman who filled the monitors and television screens of the world with a sincerity that inspired belief.

"We would appreciate your cooperation in getting this message to our father. Until he arrives, we need to be with Griffith *ahau*."

Marina leaned close to Sara and whispered something to her.

"The *hach winik*," said Sara, turning back to the crowd, "will rebuild their village here. Everyone except the military is welcome to stay. You can see what has been done to their homes, and they could use a little help. *Muchas gracias.*"

She turned with Tito, but as the wall of *Haawo* encircling Griffith separated, one of the reporters called out in surprise.

"*Perdóneme, Señorita* Patrillo," he exclaimed. "*pero el Presidente esta aquí.*"

Sara spun around, bumping into Tito.

"Here?" they said in unison.

"I mean here." It was a nervous hacker, an assistant to one of the crews, who spoke. "On my monitor. I'm linked to his Website, and he's here. I mean he's linked from México, and he wants to speak with you and your brother. *Por favor.*"

Everyone turned, shouldering themselves into position to see the hacker. With Marina's assistance, Sara and Tito pushed their way to the his equipment. The monitor was a small laptop, and in the daylight, *el Presidente*'s image was difficult to discern. Sara stepped closer and heard her father's distorted voice.

"Sara, is that really you? You're alive. And Tito. *Dios*, your mother and I prayed for your deliverance. You're coming home, now. We'll meet you in San Cristóbal as soon as you can get there."

"Can he hear me?" she asked the hacker.

"*Sí*," he answered, and pointed at the camera on his tripod.

She looked directly at the camera lens.

"Father, did you get our message?"

"*Sí, sí*, my little Sarita. I saw a recording late last night. Your mother and I cried. But now you can come home. You're safe."

"Father, Tito and I have been safe. Except when the black helicopters blow up everything in sight. But now we're safe again. And we're not leaving here with anyone but you. We want you to come get us."

"Sara, it's okay, now. The *PJF* and army have been ordered to stand down. They'll bring you to San Cristóbal where your mother and I will meet you."

"Father, you're not listening to me. And I think you should because everyone else in the world is."

Presidente Patrillo wasn't prepared for Sara's new maturity, but the implication of her words registered. He paused just a moment and nodded.

"Of course," he said, "we'll come to get you and Tito. Or I will. You're right, that would be best. I'll ask the *PJF* to send you some protection until I arrive. Probably later this afternoon. Is that all right?"

"No, Father, do not let the *PJF* protect us."

"But Sara..."

"Father, tell them to leave the rain forest. Tito and I don't need them, and neither do the *hach winik*."

"But Sarita," he protested, "it's dangerous in the jungle."

"Father, please. We know how dangerous it can be, but we're completely safe with the *hach winik*."

"Where's Tito?" asked Patrillo, changing the subject. "Is he behind you?"

"*Sí*, Papá," answered Tito, stepping into view of the camera.

"Ready to come home, son?" asked his father.

Sara looked down at her brother with uncertain expectation. He ignored her, turned from the camera, and spoke directly to his father's image on the monitor.

"Father, we want you to come here to *Puuc Witz*. We have many things to show you. You have to come, okay? Today."

He leaned in close to the monitor, reached around the laptop, and unplugged the modem.

Sara stared at him for a moment, and then gave him a tight smile.

"Why did you do that?" asked the surprised hacker.

"An accident," replied Tito. "I think your connection is loose."

"But why?" he repeated.

Sara fixed her dark eyes on the hacker and spoke so only he and Tito could hear.

"*Señor*, our father will understand. We must be with Griffith *ahau*. I'm sure you understand, too."

She and Tito turned and followed Marina through the crowd. Without responding to the renewed onslaught of questions, they made their way to Griffith. Within his protective circle, Griffith was still hugging Karen's body, swaying gently with the rhythm of his breathing. Tito and Sara knelt and hugged him, clinging to the rough warmth they shared.

Wanting nothing to intrude on his self-absorbing grief,

Griffith resisted the love in their embrace. But the vibrancy of their bodies and breath, their clutching fingers and tiny arms, and even the texture of their emotions held him back from the hypnotic, icy void. The strength of their raw, youthful energy massaged and lifted him against his will. Within their arms, every emotional scar, each scabrous wound, and all the failures he'd suffered peeled slowly, painfully away until he loosened his terrified, lonely hold on Karen's body.

He slowly set his wife's body on the ground. With Sara and Tito's assistance, he got to his feet. Silently, he stared down at the broken, lifeless corpse. The children leaned close to him. With tremulous arms and gripping hands, they held on.

Marina stepped into Griffith's peripheral vision and waited without moving. Griffith bit his lower lip to stall its quivering and looked at her. He wanted to say something, but words and thoughts drifted beyond his reach. His eyes burned empty of their tears, his temples throbbed, and his sinuses ached. A long, cold sigh emptied from him.

"I don't know what to do now," he admitted and lowered his head.

"Until the President arrives," said Marina softly, "you need a camp."

Under her ordinary, pragmatic words, he heard the care in her voice and nodded.

"With your permission," she added, "your *Haawo* would like the honor of preparing Karen's body."

The deepest wound, pricked with the sharp dagger of necessity, held him in a world he no longer cared about. He lifted his head and faced Marina.

"Thank you, Marina," he said, "but I'm taking her back with me. I can't bury her here. I... I just can't. I hope you understand."

"Griffith *ahau*," she replied, "her place of rest is important. Only you should decide that. But it would be our honor to prepare her for her final trip with you?"

"Oh, yes, Marina, yes, that would be... yes, thank you."

***

Through the rest of the morning and the early afternoon, the *Haawo* kept people away from the ruins of *Xibalba*'s Temple where they set up a rough camp for Griffith and the children. Under the shade of a poled, thatched roof, the three of them talked softly among themselves.

The black *PJF* helicopters had left. News helicopters arrived frequently, but none carried *el Presidente*. All the reporters who landed got a quick briefing from Marina, and then despite what they were told, approached the *Haawo* surrounding Griffith and the children anyway, hoping to get an exclusive interview. The only time the *Haawo* deigned to react was when Sara expressed an interest in some new batteries for their cellular and laptop. The *Haawo* merely pointed to the equipment the reporters carried with them, and Sara ended up with a state-of-the-art laptop with a built-in DSL cellular/modem card.

With the aid of the *Haawo* and the quiet attention of the children, Griffith gradually found the strength to communicate. He was unwilling, unable to give up his grief, but the children and the genuine sorrow of the *hach winik* soothed him like a balm, drawing the enervating poison, drop by drop, from his cleft heart.

The children managed to keep his attention for several hours by convincing him to explore some computer ideas concerning the source and ultimate destination of the ransom money. They talked about presenting their evidence of Bicho's complicity in the kidnapping. They even got Griffith's input on an intriguing idea about the *hach winik*'s future.

In the middle of the afternoon, a curtain of silver mist descended on the valley. As its moist fingers crept up the sides the *Puuc Witz*, a light drizzle covered the ancient site. They closed the laptop, and Sara and Tito mulled over their ideas. Griffith, gazing into the gray, lost himself in the practical consequences of returning home. The ponderous emptiness of his future faced him like the rock of Sisyphus, draining him with its mundane needs.

When Chan K'in, who'd spent the night sheltered in the eastern jungle away from *Puuc Witz*, arrived out of the fog with Marina, they sat with Griffith and the children under their shelter. He'd been asked by the *Haawo* to take responsibility for ensuring Karen's body was given the most traditional rites. Through Marina, Chan K'in asked Griffith's permission to sing one final song for her farewell.

"Griffith *ahau*," he said softly, "there is no grief so great except for the living."

Griffith clenched his teeth, swallowing back the knot in his throat. He wanted to spit the bitterness out and grind it into the dust and ashes, but the aching knowledge that he and Karen had made the choice to come here held his tongue. Because it was his alone, he accepted the rancor, allowing it to gnaw silently within him.

"I don't know what any of this means, Chan K'in," he finally replied, "or why it happened, but I do hope you get your jungle back. If Karen knew you would succeed, I'm sure she would have said the sacrifice was worth it. I'm sorry, but it may take me a while to believe that."

"We must make our new world," said Chan K'in, "worth this sacrifice you and your wife have made."

"A victory Pyrrhus would appreciate, I'm sure," he said, but even his sarcasm tasted bad.

"Last night," continued Chan K'in, "I dreamed you left in a metal bird, and I never talked or drank or got sick with you again."

"Chan K'in," said Griffith, "you're right, I probably won't be coming back here. I have to take Karen home... take her body back."

"Perhaps," he said, "my dream meant you will return to *Puuc Witz* after I follow your wife into the Celestial World."

"Perhaps."

He wasn't going to argue. Whether they wanted him to stay or lead or even just advise them, he was going home, and he would not be their *ahau*. If the attention the *hach winik* received because Karen died on this mountain widens their support, he rationalized, and if the children actually have any power to help, then the future might have meaning.

For them.

When three of the *Haawo* brought the wrapped body of his wife and placed her on a rough bier of limestone below *Xibalba's* Temple, he ruefully realized how heavy their mantle of trust had become.

"Chan K'in," said Griffith, "Karen would be honored by your song. So would I. Thank you."

Earlier, the *Haawo* under Chan K'in's tutelage had prepared her body. First they had placed her on several wide pieces of rough, white cotton. Beside her, they then laid a crudely fashioned, palm-leaf dog effigy, a handful of dried corn, a small turkey bone, a bit of hair from each of them, one small candle, and the quetzal feather Griffith had unwoven from his hair.

Wrapping her body in the white cotton, they tied it tightly into a hammock and brought it to the ancient, eroded limestone platform at the base of the central hill hiding *Xibalba's* cave.

Under a newly-erected thatched roof, the *Haawo* stood a silent vigil.

With Sara, Tito, Marina, and Chan K'in near him, Griffith stood in the light rain while the *Haawo* kept the crowds and cameras at a distance. Below the bier, he looked up at the long, white wrapping. Drizzle beaded on his hair and beard. The air was heavy.

He ached for something solid to grasp. Fragments of memories, meaningless phrases, and the dark wisps of desire offered cold comfort. They'd been together less than two years and married not even two weeks. Once again, his life was rent with this monstrous, gaping hole, leaving him in the rain to fight the darkness pouring through.

He sobbed quietly.

He was oblivious to the dozens of cameras that zoomed in on the grieving hero, unaware they were sharing his most lonely and intimate tears with the world.

Chan K'in stepped over the crumbled rock at the foot of the ancient altar and placed a few kernels of dried corn next to Karen's wrapping. He began a chant that Marina memorized to translate later for Griffith and the children. Chan K'in's voice was old and worn, but his melodic tone and familiar rhythms gently cradled the ear and rocked the aching heart.

> Do not fear to leave this World.
> You have what you will need;
> your dog can guide you home,
> the corn may feed your soul,
> and a flame will light your way.
>
> Do not turn to see me weep.
> The sun can dry my tears,
> the moon will rise again,

CRAIG GOHEEN

and rain may taste as sweet.
Too soon I will follow you.

CHAPTER TWENTY-SEVEN
THE FIFTH WORLD

Puuc Witz
Wednesday

> I believe that unarmed truth and unconditional love will have the final word in reality.
> Nobel Peace Prize speech
> Martin Luther King, Jr.
> 1929—1968

Presidente Rodolfo Patrillo's arrival was delayed by the low cloud cover, but by late afternoon the sun had broken through. Although Patrillo used an unmarked helicopter to fly from San Cristóbal the hundred and fifty miles over the mountains into the jungle, his security insisted on having two fully armed, attack helicopters escort him. As the helicopters flew into the valley, cameras and computer links beamed this extraordinary event off the planet's satellites, the signals echoing into tens of thousands of servers, homes-users, news agencies, and televisions. When his helicopter landed, *el Presidente* remained inside while the cameras and reporters surrounded the aircraft.

"Should we go over to him?" asked Tito.

"It would look more official," replied his sister, "if he met us here at the Temple."

"Would you like the *Haawo* to greet him with an escort?" Marina asked.

The children looked up at Griffith.

"Griffith?" asked Sara. "What do you think?"

"Yes," he said quietly. "Whatever you decide."

Marina spoke quickly to one of her archers, and nine of them headed down the hill across the plateau. When Patrillo saw the *indígena* striding toward his helicopter, he understood his children's intention. He told his security to relax, but they flanked him inside the *Haawo*'s own protection in spite of his orders. The cameras caught everything, sending their pixels and bytes to the world's hungry eyes.

The welcome was emotional and demonstrative. When Patrillo first saw his children, standing on either side of Griffith, everyone dressed in *xikuls*, faces clean and hair brushed, he burst into tears. The children tried to hide their excitement and relief, but seeing their father's tears, they broke, as well. Hugs and thanks were offered repeatedly as the cameras rolled and the world watched.

"Papá," said Sara, "Tito and I want you to meet the man who saved our lives. Papá, this is Griffith Grant, *ahau* of the *hach winik*."

Sara flashed Griffith a tiny smile. Patrillo was gracious and warm in his thanks, expressing his regret over Karen's death. He shook Griffith's hand vigorously, thanking him, offering private flights, medical care under the best doctors in *la República*, and ample privacy at his own palatial home.

"Thank you, sir," was all Griffith could say.

Sara then introduced Chan K'in, *t'o'ohil* of the *hach winik*, and Marina, leader of the *Haawo*.

"Papá," she told her father, "this woman's knowledge, courage, and intelligence saved many lives. She is the kind of person you should listen to."

Patrillo nodded to both of them and shook their hands while the cameras embraced the historic and political contrasts.

"Papá," continued Sara, "Chan K'in and Marina believe Griffith and Karen came to the rain forest with a message for the *hach winik*. That's why all the *hach winik* have come to these sacred ruins. For many reasons, they and Tito and I believe he is a special man. This is why everyone calls him Griffith *ahau*, Lord of Light.

"Papá, you must understand the *PJF* did not rescue us—Griffith and Karen did, and Marina and her *Haawo*. The men in that helicopter, however, did kill Karen, and their attack last night killed several *hach winik*. A full investigation is necessary."

"Certainly," replied Patrillo, loudly enough for the cameras to hear. "We'll track down the kidnappers and bring them to swift justice."

"Father," she said firmly, "we know who our kidnapper was. We want you to arrest the *Comandante* of the *PJF*, the man we have in custody."

"Sara," said her father, stunned by her statement, "you don't mean arrest *Comandante* Bicho?"

"If you do not, Papá, the *hach winik* will try him for the murder of three of their people and the destruction of their villages."

"But of course we'll investigate and..."

Sara cocked her head as if to interrupt him, but paused when she caught his eye. She glanced over his shoulder at the humming cameras.

"And we'll arrest him," added Patrillo, "if you have evidence, of course."

"The ransom note can be traced to him."

"It wasn't the Zapatistas?"

"No, Papá. They had nothing to do with this. We never

saw any Zapatistas. Which means you must also release the man named Rafael who was falsely arrested with Karen."

"I can't release Marcos, Sara. Really."

"He's not Marcos, Papá. And he helped save our lives, too."

"Many people seemed to have helped you and Tito."

"That's right, Papá," said Tito. "You should be grateful."

"Oh, I am, my son," replied Patrillo. "I am. Is it necessary we talk about all this here? Now, I mean."

"*Sí*, Father, it is. You sent the army and *judiciales* away, didn't you?"

"*Sí*, Tito. They should gone by tomorrow."

"Is that okay, Griffith *ahau*?" he asked.

This was not what Griffith wanted. These were not his decisions. He was about to explain when Chan K'in stepped toward *el Presidente*. He glanced at Marina, who nodded she was ready to translate. The cameramen, anxious to feed this Third World-First World contact to their growing audiences, crowded more closely. Their technology sucked up these dramatic images. Sound bytes rolled off the journalists' tongues as they whispered their excitement into their mikes. "Arrows over armor" and the "cyber-jungle" were about to become the latest cliché's.

"Sir," said Chan K'in through Marina, "Griffith *ahau* understands the invisible world better than this one, and he speaks only of those matters with us. He is a physicist, a new word he taught us. That is why we call him Lord of Light. With your permission, I will answer.

"My father lived in this forest, and his father before him, back farther than I can remember. We saw the sun darkened from the ashes of your world. We heard the thunder of the machines and tasted the poisoned sweetness of your *pesos*. Griffith *ahau* came to us with dreams of the *hach winik*'s first contact with your world many centuries ago. I have lived through the second contact.

"This time, we have nowhere to hide. If the soldiers leave the forest, perhaps the game will come back. But the wild animals don't like the loggers or the oil men or the ranchers. And I don't like the *evangelistas* who tell us to wear pants and give up our *balche* and tobacco. We need your help, *Señor Presidente*, if we are going to survive."

"Father," continued Sara before he could respond to Chan K'in, "all the land north to Palenque, east to the *Río Usumacinta*, and south to Guatemala belongs to the *hach winik*. It has since before *la Revolución* and long before the *conquistadores* stole it. The *hach winik* want everyone to leave so they can care for it properly."

"But Sara," replied her father, "much of this land belongs to the *latifundistas*—some of it for several generations. There are many problems with your request. Trust me, we will ensure what they have is protected."

"They don't want protection, Father. They want everyone to leave."

"Sara, that would be impossible."

"But it's theirs," insisted Tito.

"Tito, you just can't take someone's land, at least without compensating them. Our economy can't afford that, and I'm sure these people can't buy all this land."

Sara glanced at Griffith, who nodded.

"Father, if the *hach winik* could pay for the land, would you support returning it to them?"

"But how could they do that, Sara?"

"Father," said Sara with a deliberate look to the cameras, "you have the power to do this. Right here, in front of the entire world, you could lead us in this new millennium."

It was obvious to Griffith that Sara and Tito grasped the nature of the media better than their father. He wondered if Patrillo recognized the political opportunity his own daughter was offering him.

"Is this what your people want, Chan K'in?" Patrillo asked.

"When the third world ended," answered Chan K'in, "the fires burned the great forest. Then the rains mixed the ashes with the blood of the animals and humans who had died. Our soil turned red, and nothing would grow. The *hach winik* who survived had to fight the vultures for the charred carrion rotting around them. Hachakyum, our Creator, pitied us and sent us his royal birds to lift our spirits. Within the droppings of that first quetzal pair were the seeds of the new forest.

"The World is now ending for the fourth time. Akyantho, your god of the West, now rules the sun. *Señor Presidente*, the *hach winik* have never been very good with the gifts of Akyantho. We don't know what to do with the radios and trucks you've given us for our trees and land. But Akyantho did return Marina, and he sent Griffith *ahau* and his wife, who paid the greatest sacrifice, and your brave children to show us the seeds hidden within all your shit."

The moment Marina finished, Patrillo blinked and paused. In awkward silence, *el Presidente* held out his hand. When Chan K'in simply nodded, the President stepped forward, took Chan K'in's hand, and shook it. Stepping back for the cameras, he flashed a wide smile and opened his arms.

"Chan K'in," he announced in his stage voice, "I, *Presidente* Patrillo, pledge my government will seek the return of the traditional lands of the *hach winik*. All government and all paramilitary troops are ordered to withdraw from these lands. I will initiate the process of negotiations over the disputed areas."

EPILOGUE

Charlottesville, Va.

> Good people... had, more or less successfully, solved the problem of existence, while I was quite sure I had not, and had a pretty strong conviction that the problem was insoluble.
> *Agnosticism*
> T. H. Huxley
> 1825—1895

Back in the States, the eighteenth day after his wedding, Griffith stood with Karen's family in a gray drizzle at the University Chapel for a small funeral service following the cremation. Unfortunately, the service was a portend of Griffith's life for the next several months. Not only did a throng of media descend on the Grounds of the University, hundreds of curiosity seekers, admirers, and marketing deal-makers arrived with them.

The media repeatedly urged him to recount the rescue of the children and the defeat of the *PJF* by primitive *bach winik* hunters. They claimed the public needed the details. Others wanted explanations of the connections between his fevered hallucinations, the quetzal pair, and the discovery of the ruins on *Puuc Witz*. The tabloid journalists expected him to show how he "psychically called the *bach winik* to *Puuc Witz*".

These questions were of no interest to Griffith.

Unfortunately, his monk-like silence simply added to the cloak of spiritual detachment Chan K'in had already given him.

The service brought little comfort to Griffith.

That August, with encouragement from those who mattered—Karen's parents, his colleagues in the lab, and Sara and Tito—he went back to work even though he'd been offered leave. Most of his time, however, was spent ignoring the repeated requests for interviews, the thousands of letters he received, and the dozens of other daily reminders of his loss. With the intrusive, resented attention came the continuing news and magazine features, the innumerable personality profiles of the grieving hero, the sensationalized stories of mystical intervention at *Puuc Witz*, and the ubiquitous psychic predictions for a world-wide Maya apocalypse.

He wanted time to grieve and rage, and none was given. A growing desire to isolate himself intensified.

In his undergraduate classes, his celebrity status made it difficult to keep the students focused on the syllabus. In the lab, he found little diversion, and the notoriety he brought interfered with everybody's research time. Whenever they went on-line, the normally easy connections with other labs and research institutes became crowded with irrelevancies and distractions. The positive attention the University received was welcomed in fund-raising and additional endowments, but the efforts required to conduct their research and teach their classes were often frustrated by unwanted, inappropriate attention.

Griffith apologized a great deal that semester. By October, fantasies about disappearing from the crowds and stress dominated his dreams.

In Mexico, the international pressure from environmental and human rights groups, as well as from diplomatic sources, continued throughout the summer and fall. Rafael was released, and that September, in a show of commitment to indigenous rights, a ski-masked Marcos led the Zapatista army, in front of the cameras, to the foot of *Puuc Witz* where they laid their weapons at the feet of Chan K'in and Marina. Marcos' slight limp went unnoticed by the media.

In late October, *Comandante* Bicho was tried. Because numerous witnesses failed to appear and no living connections to the computer sabotage or the kidnapping of the children were ever found, the decrypted ransom note failed to convict. Following his acquittal, Bicho disappeared.

Without a conviction, *Presidente* Patrillo felt obliged to negotiate a settlement with the *hach winik* or face political and familial exile. With the input of everyone from NAFTA officials to Chan K'in and Marina, the agreement required an independently reviewed, fair market offer be tendered for twelve months before any land owner was obligated to accept. Control of all other reservations and parks presently within the circumscribed area, including the natural resources on and below the surface, was transferred to the *hach winik*.

The *latifundistas* agreed to the deal with the tacit understanding from government insiders that any transfer of lands could take many decades. Nobody expected the *hach winik* to generate enough funds from their present natural resources to be able to buy any significant amount of privately-held land.

After the pact was publicly signed in early December, however, a half dozen banks in southern Mexico announced the surprise influx of nearly two and half billion *pesos* from anonymous sources "intended specifically and exclusively for long term, interest free loans to be guaranteed to any *hach winik* for the purchase of land, equipment, tools, materials or any other purpose related to their livelihood, health, arts, education, or archeology."

With the help of some hackers Griffith knew, the children had broken into Acct. #3173JB and secretly transferred the funds into specific escrow accounts they'd previously set up. The international media and the Internet were filled with stories of this financial windfall, and intense speculation focused on the imminent collapse of *latifundista* control in the jungle. The Mexican stock market, after an initially shaky start that day, rebounded, gaining over three percent.

On the morning after the bank announcements, the first light snow of the Charlottesville winter was already melting when Griffith checked his personal e-mail before leaving for the University. His e-mail icon blinked with its daily message from *"cinderella y caballero"*. They had kept him informed of their progress in "arming the *hach winik* with knowledge" as Marina called it. This included the recent installation of a server at *Na-Bolom* where Esmeralda had started a data base and information cyber-center to handle the tremendous attention *la Hacienda* was now receiving.

This particular e-mail, however, with the news of the bank announcements, turned out to be the stimulus for Griffith to act. Although he hadn't anticipated such an obvious catalyst, he'd known for weeks he could no longer permit others to lead his life. He needed to be done with that, but until now, he just hadn't known what to do. Teaching and research were impossible. Nothing attracted him, or distracted him. The emptiness remained. The questions still had no answers.

For months he'd been unable to escape a life too filled with constant reminders of his loneliness. But here, in a single e-mail out of the hundred or so the children had written since the summer, he saw a way out.

No, not an escape, he realized. It was not even an answer. But it was one final opportunity to act.

He gave the Net stories a perfunctory reading and then typed several messages. When Digger arrived at the lab later that morning, he found a message flagged for him on his computer. Griffith had asked him to process the leave papers he'd signed months ago and stuck in a drawer. Other than saying he'd write, that was the entire note. Rent and instructions to close the house for the winter were sent to his landlady. A stack of Christmas cards, signed, addressed, and stamped, was left on his kitchen table.

In late February, his mother-in-law, who came over to his house to clean once a month, noticed Karen's burial urn, painted in a recurring corn and quetzal motif, had gotten dusty. When she brushed it, the ceramic lid rattled. The seal was broken.

Lifting it from the shelf, she removed the top and saw the impression of fingers in the fine powder. A small handful of ashes had been scooped out.

THE END